EVERYMAN,

I WILL GO WITH THEE,

AND BE THY GUIDE,

IN THY MOST NEED

TO GO BY THY SIDE

WEDDING STORIES

EDITED BY DIANA SECKER TESDELL

EVERYMAN'S POCKET CLASSICS
Alfred A. Knopf New York London Toronto

THIS IS A BORZOI BOOK
PUBLISHED BY ALFRED A. KNOPF

This selection by Diana Secker Tesdell first published in
Everyman's Library, 2016
Copyright © 2016 by Everyman's Library
A list of acknowledgments to copyright owners appears at the back
of this volume.

www.randomhouse.com/everymans
www.everymanslibrary.co.uk

ISBN: 978-1-101-90786-3 (US)
978-1-84159-623-5 (UK)

A CIP catalogue reference for this book is available from the
British Library

Typography by Peter B. Willberg
Typeset in the UK by Input Data Services Ltd, Bridgwater, Somerset
Printed and bound in Germany by GGP Media GmbH, Pössneck

WEDDING STORIES

Contents

ENGAGEMENTS

CEREMONIES AND CELEBRATIONS

WEDDING GUESTS

WEDDING MISHAPS

BEYOND THE HONEYMOON

ENGAGEMENTS

A. A. MILNE

GETTING
MARRIED

I THE DAY

PROBABLY YOU THOUGHT that getting married was quite
a simple business. So did I. We were both wrong; it is the
very dickens. Of course, I am not going to draw back now.
As I keep telling Celia, her Ronald is a man of powerful fibre,
and when he says he will do a thing he does it – eventually.
She shall have her wedding all right; I have sworn it. But I do
wish that there weren't so many things to be arranged first.

The fact that we had to fix a day was broken to me one
afternoon when Celia was showing me to some relatives of
hers in the Addison Road. I got entangled with an elderly
cousin on the hearth-rug; and though I know nothing about
motor-bicycles I talked about them for several hours under
the impression that they were his subject. It turned out afterwards that he was equally ignorant of them, but thought they
were mine. Perhaps we shall get on better at a second meeting. However, just when we were both thoroughly sick of
each other, Celia broke off her gay chat with an aunt to say
to me:

'By the way, Ronald, we did settle on the eleventh,
didn't we?'

I looked at her blankly, my mind naturally full of motor-
bicycles.

'The wedding,' smiled Celia.

'Right-o,' I said with enthusiasm. I was glad to be assured
that I should not go on talking about motor-bicycles for ever,

15

and that on the eleventh, anyhow, there would be a short interruption for the ceremony. Feeling almost friendly to the cousin, I plunged into his favourite subject again.

On the way home Celia returned to the matter.

'Or you would rather it was the twelfth?' she asked.

'I've never heard a word about this before,' I said. 'It all comes as a surprise to me.'

'Why, I'm *always* asking you.'

'Well, it's very forward of you, and I don't know what young people are coming to nowadays. Celia, what's the *good* of my talking to your cousin for three hours about motor-bicycling? Surely one can get married just as well without that?'

'One can't get married without settling the day,' said Celia, coming cleverly back to the point.

Well, I suppose one can't. But somehow I had expected to be spared all this bother. I think my idea was that Celia would say to me suddenly one evening, 'By the way, Ronald, don't forget we're being married tomorrow,' and I should have said 'Where?' And on being told the time and place, I should have turned up pretty punctually; and after my best man had told me where to stand, and the clergyman had told me what to say, and my solicitor had told me where to sign my name, we should have driven from the church a happy married couple . . . and in the carriage Celia would have told me where we were spending the honeymoon.

However, it was not to be so.

'All right, the eleventh,' I said. 'Any particular month?'

'No,' smiled Celia, 'just any month. Or, if you like, every month.'

'The eleventh of June,' I surmised. 'It is probably the one day in the year on which my Uncle Thomas cannot come. But no matter. The eleventh let it be.'

'Then that's settled. And at St Miriam's?'

For some reason Celia has set her heart on St Miriam's. Personally I have no feeling about it. St Andrew's-by-the-Wardrobe or St Bartholomew's-Without would suit me equally well.

'All right,' I said, 'St Miriam's.'

There, you might suppose, the matter would have ended; but no.

'Then you will see about it tomorrow?' said Celia persuasively.

I was appalled at the idea.

'Surely,' I said, 'this is for you, or your father, or – or some-body to arrange.'

'Of *course* it's for the bridegroom,' protested Celia.

'In theory, perhaps. But anyhow not the bridegroom per-sonally. His best man ... or his solicitor ... or ... I mean, you're not suggesting that I myself— Oh, well, if you insist. Still, I must say I don't see what's the good of having a best man *and* a solicitor if— Oh, all right, Celia, I'll go tomorrow.'

So I went. For half an hour I padded round St Miriam's nervously, and then summoning up all my courage, I knocked my pipe out and entered.

'I want,' I said jauntily to a sexton or a sacristan or some-thing – 'I want – er – a wedding.' And I added, 'For two.'

He didn't seem as nervous as I was. He enquired quite calmly when I wanted it.

'The eleventh of June,' I said. 'It's probably the one day in the year on which my Uncle Thomas— However, that wouldn't interest you. The point is that it's the eleventh.'

The clerk consulted his wedding-book. Then he made the surprising announcement that the only day he could offer me in June was the seventeenth. I was amazed.

'I am a very old customer,' I said reproachfully. 'I mean, I have often been to your church in my time. Surely—'

'We've weddings fixed on all the other days.'

'Yes, yes, but you could persuade somebody to change his day, couldn't you? Or if he is very much set on being married on the eleventh you might recommend some other church to him. I daresay you know of some good ones. You see, Celia – my – that is, we're particularly keen, for some reason, on St Miriam's.'

The clerk didn't appreciate my suggestion. He insisted that the seventeenth was the only day.

'Then will you have the seventeenth?' he asked.

'My dear fellow, I can't possibly say off-hand,' I protested. 'I am not alone in this. I have a friend with me. I will go back and tell her what you say. She may decide to withdraw her offer altogether.'

I went back and told Celia.

'Bother,' she said. 'What shall we do?'

'There are other churches. There's your own, for example.'

'Yes, but you know I don't like that. Why *shouldn't* we be married on the seventeenth?'

'I don't know at all. It seems an excellent day; it lets in my Uncle Thomas. Of course, it may exclude my Uncle William, but one can't have everything.'

'Then will you go and fix it for the seventeenth tomorrow?'

'Can't I send my solicitor this time?' I asked. 'Of course, if you particularly want me to go myself, I will. But really, dear, I seem to be living at St Miriam's nowadays.'

And even that wasn't the end of the business. For, just as I was leaving her, Celia broke it to me that St Miriam's was neither in her parish nor in mine, and that, in order to qualify as a bridegroom, I should have to hire a room somewhere near.

'But I am very comfortable where I am,' I assured her.

'You needn't live there, Ronald. You only want to leave a hat there, you know.'

'Oh, very well,' I sighed.

She came to the hall with me; and, having said good-bye to her, I repeated my lesson.

'The seventeenth, fix it up tomorrow, take a room near St Miriam's, and leave a hat there. Good-bye.'

'Good-bye. . . . And oh, Ronald!' She looked at me critically as I stood in the doorway. 'You might leave *that* one,' she said.

II FURNISHING

'By the way,' said Celia suddenly, 'what have you done about the fixtures?'

'Nothing,' I replied truthfully.

'Well, we must do *something* about them.'

'Yes. My solicitor – he shall do something about them. Don't let's talk about them now. I've only got three hours more with you, and then I must dash back to my work.'

I must say that any mention of fixtures has always bored me intensely. When it was a matter of getting a house to live in I was all energy. As soon as Celia had found it, I put my solicitor on to it; and within a month I had signed my name in two places, and was the owner of a highly residential flat in the best part of the neighbourhood. But my effort so exhausted me that I have felt utterly unable since to cope with the question of the curtain-rod in the bathroom or whatever it is that Celia means by fixtures. These things will arrange themselves somehow, I feel confident.

Meanwhile the decorators are hard at work. A thrill of pride inflates me when I think of the decorators at work. I don't know how they got there; I suppose I must have ordered them. Celia says that *she* ordered them and chose all the papers herself, and that all I did was to say that the papers she had chosen were very pretty; but this doesn't sound like me in the least. I am convinced that I was the man of action when it came to ordering decorators.

'And now,' said Celia one day, 'we can go and choose the electric-light fittings.'

'Celia,' I said in admiration, 'you're a wonderful person. I should have forgotten all about them.'

'Why, they're about the most important thing in the flat.'

'Somehow I never regarded anybody as choosing them. I thought they just grew in the wall. From bulbs.'

When we got into the shop Celia became businesslike at once.

'We'd better start with the hall,' she told the man.

'Everybody else will have to,' I said, 'so we may as well.'

'What sort of a light did you want there?' he asked.

'A strong one,' I said; 'so as to be able to watch our guests carefully when they pass the umbrella-stand.'

Celia waved me away and explained that we wanted a hanging lantern. It appeared that this shop made a speciality not so much of the voltage as of the lamps enclosing it.

'How do you like that?' asked the man, pointing to a magnificent affair in brass. He wandered off to a switch, and turned it on.

'Dare you ask him the price?' I asked Celia. 'It looks to me about a thousand pounds. If it is, say that you don't like the style. Don't let him think we can't afford it.'

'Yes,' said Celia, in a careless sort of way. 'I'm not sure that I care about that. How much is it?'

'Two pounds.'

I was not going to show my relief. 'Without the light, of course?' I said disparagingly.

'How do you think it would look in the hall?' said Celia to me.

'I think our guests would be encouraged to proceed. They'd see that we were pretty good people.'

'I don't like it. It's too ornate.'

'Then show us something less ornate,' I told the man sternly.

He showed us things less ornate. At the end of an hour Celia said she thought we'd better get on to another room, and come back to the hall afterwards. We decided to proceed to the drawing-room.

'We must go all out over these,' said Celia; 'I want these to be really beautiful.'

At the end of another hour Celia said she thought we'd better get on to my workroom. My workroom, as the name implies, is the room to which I am to retire when I want complete quiet. Sometimes I shall go there after lunch ... and have it.

'We can come back to the drawing-room afterwards,' she said. 'It's really very important that we should get the right ones for that. Your room won't be so difficult, but, of course, you must have awfully nice ones.'

I looked at my watch.

'It's a quarter to one,' I said. 'At 2.15 on the seventeenth of June we are due at St Miriam's. If you think we shall have bought anything by then, let's go on. If, as seems to me, there is no hope at all, then let's have lunch today anyhow. After lunch we may be able to find some way out of the *impasse*.'

After lunch I had an idea.

'This afternoon,' I said, 'we will begin to get some furniture together.'

'But what about the electric fittings? We must finish off those.'

'This is an experiment. I want to see if we can buy a chest of drawers. It may just be our day for it.'

'And we settle the fittings tomorrow. Yes?'

'I don't know. We may not want them. It all depends on whether we can buy a chest of drawers this afternoon. If we can't, then I don't see how we can ever be married on the seventeenth of June. Somebody's got to be, because I've engaged the church. The question is whether it's going to be us. Let's go and buy a chest of drawers this afternoon, and see.'

The old gentleman in the little shop Celia knew of was delighted to see us.

'Chestesses? Ah, you 'ave come to the right place.' He led the way into the depths. 'There now. There's a chest – real old, that is.' He gave it a hearty smack. 'You don't see a chest like that nowadays. They can't *make* 'em. Three pound ten. You couldn't have got that tomorrer. I'd have sold it for four pound tomorrer.'

'I knew it was our day,' I said.

'Real old, that is. Spanish me'ogany, all oak lined. That's right, sir, pull the drawers out and see for yourself. Let the lady see. There's no imitation there, lady. A real old chest, that is. Come in 'ere in a week and you'd have to pay five pounds for it. Me'ogany's going up, you see, that's how.'

'Well?' I said to Celia.

'It's perfectly sweet. Hadn't we better see some more?'

We saw two more. Both of them Spanish me'ogany, oak lined, pull-the-drawers-out-and-see-for-yourself-lady. Half an hour passed rapidly.

'Well?' I said.

'I really don't know which I like best. Which do you?'

'The first; it's nearer the door.'

'There's another shop just over the way. We'd better just look there too, and then we can come back to decide tomorrow.'

We went out. I glanced at my watch. It was 3.30, and we were being married at 2.15 on the seventeenth of June.

'Wait a moment,' I said, 'I've forgotten my gloves.'

I may be a slow starter, but I am very firm when roused. I went into the shop, wrote a cheque for the three chests of drawers, and told the man where to send them. When I returned, Celia was at the shop opposite, pulling the drawers out of a real old mahogany chest which was standing on the pavement outside.

'This is even better,' she said. 'It's perfectly adorable. I wonder if it's more expensive.'

'I'll just ask,' I said.

I went in and, without an unnecessary word, bought that chest too. Then I came back to Celia. It was 3.45, and on the seventeenth of June at 2.15— Well, we had four chests of drawers towards it.

'Celia,' I said, 'we may just do it yet.'

III THE HONEYMOON

'I know I oughtn't to be dallying here,' I said; 'I ought to be doing something strenuous in preparation for the wedding. Counting the bells at St Miriam's, or varnishing the floors in the flat, or— Tell me what I ought to be doing, Celia, and I'll go on not doing it for a bit.'

'There's the honeymoon,' said Celia.

'I knew there was something.'

'Do tell me what you're doing about it?'

'Thinking about it.'

'You haven't written to anyone about rooms yet?'

'Celia,' I said reproachfully, 'you seem to have forgotten why I am marrying you.'

When Celia was browbeaten into her present engagement, she said frankly that she was only consenting to marry me because of my pianola, which she had always coveted. In return I pointed out that I was only asking her to marry me because I wanted somebody to write my letters. There opened before me, in that glad moment, a vista of invitations and accounts-rendered all answered promptly by Celia, instead of put off till next month by me. It was a wonderful vision to one who (very properly) detests letter-writing. And yet, here she was, even before the ceremony, expecting me to enter into a deliberate correspondence with all sorts of strange people who as yet had not come into my life at all. It was too much.

'We will get,' I said, 'your father to write some letters for us.'

'But what's he got to do with it?'

'I don't want to complain of your father, Celia, but it seems to me that he is not doing his fair share. There ought to be a certain give-and-take in the matter. *I* find you a nice church to be married in – good. *He* finds you a nice place to honeymoon in – excellent. After all, you are still his daughter.'

'All right,' said Celia, 'I'll ask Father to do it. "Dear Mrs Bunn, my little boy wants to spend his holidays with you in June. I am writing to ask you if you will take care of him and see that he doesn't do anything dangerous. He has a nice disposition, but wants watching."' She patted my head gently. 'Something like that.'

I got up and went to the writing-desk.

'I can see I shall have to do it myself,' I sighed. 'Give me the address and I'll begin.'

'But we haven't quite settled where we're going yet, have we?'

I put the pen down thankfully and went back to the sofa.

'Good! Then I needn't write today, anyhow. It is wonderful, dear, how difficulties roll away when you face them. Almost at once we arrive at the conclusion that I needn't write today. Splendid! Well, where shall we go? This will want a lot of thought. Perhaps,' I added, 'I needn't write tomorrow.'

'We had almost fixed on England, hadn't we?'

'Somebody was telling me that Lynton was very beautiful. I should like to go to Lynton.'

'But *everyone* goes to Lynton for their honeymoon.'

'Then let's be original and go to Birmingham. "The happy couple left for Birmingham, where the honeymoon will be spent." Sensation.'

' "The bride left the train at Ealing." More sensation.'

'I think the great thing,' I said, trying to be businesslike, 'is to fix the county first. If we fixed on Rutland, then the rest would probably be easy.'

'The great thing,' said Celia, 'is to decide what we want. Sea, or river, or mountains, or – or golf.'

At the word golf I coughed and looked out of the window.

Now I am very fond of Celia – I mean of golf, and – what I really mean, of course, is that I am very fond of both of them. But I do think that on a honeymoon Celia should come first. After all, I shall have plenty of other holidays for golf . . . although, of course, three weeks in the summer without any golf at all— Still, I think Celia should come first.

'Our trouble,' I said to her, 'is that neither of us has ever been on a honeymoon before, and so we've no idea what it will be like. After all, why should we get bored with each other? Surely we don't depend on golf to amuse us?'

'All the same, I think your golf *would* amuse me,' said Celia. 'Besides, I want you to be as happy as you possibly can be.'

'Yes, but supposing I was slicing my drives all the time, I should be miserable. I should be torn between the desire to go back to London and have a lesson with the professional and the desire to stay on honeymooning with you. One can't be happy in a quandary like that.'

'Very well then, no golf. Settled?'

'Quite. Now then, let's decide about the scenery. What sort of soil do you prefer?'

When I left Celia that day we had agreed on this much: that we wouldn't bother about golf, and that the mountains, rivers, valleys, and so on should be left entirely to nature. All we were to enquire for was (in the words of an advertisement Celia had seen) 'a perfect spot for a honeymoon'.

In the course of the next day I heard of seven spots; varying from a spot in Surrey 'dotted with firs', to a dot in the Pacific spotted with – I forget what, natives probably. Taken together they were the seven only possible spots for a honeymoon.

'We shall have to have seven honeymoons,' I said to Celia when I had told her my news. 'One honeymoon, one spot.'

'Wait,' she said. 'I have heard of an ideal spot.'

'Speaking as a spot expert, I don't think that's necessarily better than an only possible spot,' I objected. 'Still, tell me about it.'

'Well, to begin with, it's close to the sea.'

'So we can bathe when we're bored. Good.'

'And it's got a river, if you want to fish—'

'I don't. I should hate to catch a fish who was perhaps on his honeymoon too. Still, I like the idea of a river.'

'And quite a good mountain, and lovely walks, and, in fact, everything. Except a picture-palace, luckily.'

'It sounds all right,' I said doubtfully. 'We might just spend the next day or two thinking about my seven spots, and then I might . . . possibly . . . feel strong enough to write.'

'Oh, I nearly forgot. I *have* written, Ronald.'

'You have?' I cried. 'Then, my dear, what else matters? It's a perfect spot.' I lay back in relief. 'And there, thank 'evings, is another thing settled. Bless you.'

'Yes. And, by the way, there *is* golf quite close too. But that,' she smiled, 'needn't prevent us going there.'

'Of course not. We shall just ignore the course.'

'Perhaps, so as to be on the safe side, you'd better leave your clubs behind.'

'Perhaps I'd better,' I said carelessly.

All the same I don't think I will. One never knows what may happen . . . and at the outset of one's matrimonial career to have to go to the expense of an entirely new set of clubs would be a most regrettable business.

IV SEASONABLE PRESENTS

'I suppose,' I said, 'it's too late to cancel this wedding now?'

'Well,' said Celia, 'the invitations are out, and the presents are pouring in, and Mother's just ordered the most melting dress for herself that you ever saw. Besides, who's to live in the flat if we don't?'

'There's a good deal in what you say. Still, I am alarmed, seriously alarmed. Look here.' I drew out a printed slip and flourished it before her.

'Not a writ? My poor Ronald!'

'Worse than that. This is the St Miriam's bill of fare for weddings. Celia, I had no idea marriage was so expensive. I thought one rolled-gold ring would practically see it.'

It was a formidable document. Starting with 'full choir and organ' which came to a million pounds, and working down through 'boys' voices only', and 'red carpet' to 'policemen for controlling traffic – per policeman, 5s.', it included altogether some two dozen ways of disposing of my savings.

'If we have the whole *menu*,' I said, 'I shall be ruined. You wouldn't like to have a ruined husband.'

Celia took the list and went through it carefully.

'I might say "Season",' I suggested, 'or "Press".'

'Well, to begin with,' said Celia, 'we needn't have a full choir.'

'Need we have an organ or a choir at all? In thanking people for their kind presents you might add, "By the way, do you sing?" Then we could arrange to have all the warblers in the front. My best man or my solicitor could give the note.'

'Boys' voices only,' decided Celia. 'Then what about bells?'

'I should like some nice bells. If the price is "per bell" we might give an order for five good ones.'

'Let's do without bells. You see, they don't begin to ring till we've left the church, so they won't be any good to *us*.'

This seemed to me an extraordinary line to take.

'My dear child,' I remonstrated, 'the whole thing is being got up not for ourselves, but for our guests. We shall be much too preoccupied to appreciate any of the good things we provide – the texture of the red carpet or the quality of the singing. I dreamt last night that I quite forgot about the wedding-ring till 1.30 on the actual day, and the only cab

I could find to take me to a jeweller's was drawn by a camel. Of course, it may not turn out to be as bad as that, but it will certainly be an anxious afternoon for both of us. And so we must consider the entertainment entirely from the point of view of our guests. Whether their craving is for champagne or bells, it must be satisfied.'

'I'm sure they'll be better without bells. Because when the policemen call out "Mr Spifkins' carriage", Mr Spifkins mightn't hear if there were a lot of bells clashing about.'

'Very well, no bells. But, mind you,' I said sternly, 'I shall insist on a clergyman.'

We went through the rest of the *menu*, course by course.

'I know what I shall do,' I said at last. 'I shall call on my friend the Clerk again, and I shall speak to him quite frankly. I shall say, "Here is a cheque for a thousand pounds. It is all I can afford – and, by the way, you'd better pay it in quickly or it will be dishonoured. Can you do us up a nice wedding for a thousand inclusive?"'

'Like the Christmas hampers at the stores.'

'Exactly. A dozen boys' voices, a half-dozen of bells, ten yards of awning, and twenty-four oranges, or vergers, or whatever it is. We ought to get a nice parcel for a thousand pounds.'

'Or,' said Celia, 'we might send the list round to our friends as suggestions for wedding presents. I'm sure Jane would love to give us a couple of policemen.'

'We'd much better leave the whole thing to your father. I incline more and more to the opinion that it is *his* business to provide the wedding. I must ask my solicitor about it.'

'He's providing the bride.'

'Yes, but I think he might go further. I can't help feeling that the bells would come very well from him. "Bride's father to bridegroom – A peal of bells." People would think it was something in silver for the hall. It would do him a lot of good in business circles.'

'And that reminds me,' smiled Celia, 'there's been some talk about a present from Miss Popley.'

I have come to the conclusion that it is impossible to get married decently unless one's life is ordered on some sort of system. Mine never has been; and the result is that I make terrible mistakes – particularly in the case of Miss Popley. At the beginning of the business, when the news got round to Miss Popley, I received from her a sweet letter of congratulation. Knowing that she was rather particular in these matters I braced myself up and thanked her heartily by return of post. Three days later, when looking for a cheque I had lost, I accidentally came across her letter. 'Help, help!' I cried. 'This came days ago, and I haven't answered yet.' I sat down at once and thanked her enthusiastically. Another week passed and I began to feel that I must really make an effort to catch my correspondence up; so I got out all my letters of congratulation of the last ten days and devoted an afternoon to answering them. I used much the same form of thanks in all of them ... with the exception of Miss Popley's, which was phrased particularly warmly.

So much for that. But Miss Popley is Celia's dear friend also. When I made out my list of guests I included Miss Popley; so, in her list, did Celia. The result was that Miss Popley received two invitations to the wedding. ... Sometimes I fear she must think we are pursuing her.

'What does she say about a present?' I asked.

'She wants us to tell her what we want.'

'What *are* we to say? If we said an elephant—'

'With a small card tied on to his ear, and "Best wishes from Miss Popley" on it. It would look heavenly among the other presents.'

30

'You see what I mean, Celia. Are we to suggest something worth a thousand pounds, or something worth ninepence? It's awfully kind of her, but it makes it jolly difficult for us.'

'Something that might cost anything from ninepence to a thousand pounds,' suggested Celia.

'Then that washes out the elephant.'

'Can't you get the ninepenny ones now?'

'I suppose,' I said, reverting to the subject which most weighed on me, 'she wouldn't like to give the men's voices for the choir?'

'No, I think a clock,' said Celia. 'A clock can cost anything you like – or don't like.'

'Right-o. And perhaps we'd better settle now. When it comes, how many times shall we write and thank her for it?'

Celia considered. 'Four times, I think,' she said.

Well, as Celia says, it's too late to draw back now. But I shall be glad when it's all over. As I began by saying, there's too much 'arranging' and 'settling' and 'fixing' about the thing for me. In the necessary negotiations and preparations I fear I have not shone. And so I shall be truly glad when we have settled down in our flat ... and Celia can restore my confidence in myself once more by talking loudly to her domestic staff about 'The Master'.

SHIRLEY JACKSON

ABOUT TWO NICE PEOPLE

A PROBLEM OF some importance, certainly, these days, is that of anger. When one half of the world is angry at the other half, or one half of a nation is angry at the rest, or one side of town feuds with the other side, it is hardly surprising, when you stop to think about it, that so many people lose their tempers with so many other people. Even if, as in this case, they are two people not usually angry, two people whose lives are obscure and whose emotions are gentle, whose smiles are amiable and whose voices are more apt to be cheerful than raised in fury. Two people, in other words, who would much rather be friends than not and who yet, for some reason, perhaps chemical or sociological or environmental, enter upon a mutual feeling of dislike so intense that only a very drastic means can bring them out of it.

Take two such people:

Ellen Webster was what was referred to among her friends as a 'sweet' girl. She had pretty, soft hair and dark, soft eyes, and she dressed in soft colors and wore frequently a lovely old-fashioned brooch that had belonged to her grandmother. Ellen thought of herself as a very happy and very lucky person because she had a good job, and was able to buy herself a fair number of soft-colored dresses and skirts and sweaters and coats and hats; she had, by working hard at it evenings, transformed her one-room apartment from a bare, neat place into a charming little refuge with her sewing basket on the table and a canary at the window; she had a reasonable conviction that someday, perhaps soon, she would fall in love with a nice young man and they would be married and Ellen would devote herself wholeheartedly to children and baking cakes and mending socks. This not-very-unusual situation, with its perfectly ordinary state of mind, was a source of great happiness to Ellen. She was, in a word, not one of those who rail against their fate, who live in sullen hatred of the world. She was – her friends were right – a sweet girl.

On the other hand, even if you would not have called Walter Nesmith sweet, you would very readily have thought of him as a 'nice' fellow, or an 'agreeable' person, or even – if you happened to be a little old white-haired lady – a 'dear boy.' There was a subtle resemblance between Ellen Webster and Walter Nesmith. Both of them were the first resort of their friends in trouble, for instance. Walter's ambitions, which included the rest of his life, were refreshingly similar to Ellen's: Walter thought that someday he might meet some sweet girl, and would then devote himself wholeheartedly to coming home of an evening to read his paper, and perhaps work in the garden on Sundays.

Walter thought that he would like to have two children, a boy and a girl. Ellen thought that she would like to have three children, a boy and two girls. Walter was very fond of cherry pie, Ellen preferred Boston cream. Ellen enjoyed romantic movies. Walter preferred westerns. They read almost exactly the same books.

In the ordinary course of events, the friction between Ellen and Walter would have been very slight. But – and what could cause a thing like this? – the ordinary course of events was shattered by a trifle like a telephone call.

Ellen's telephone number was 3-4126. Walter's telephone number was 3-4216. Ellen lived in apartment 3-A and Walter lived in apartment 3-B; these apartments were across the hall from each other, and very often Ellen, opening her door at precisely quarter of nine in the morning and going toward the elevator, met Walter, who opened *his* door at precisely quarter of nine in the morning and went toward the elevator. On these occasions Ellen customarily said, 'Good morning,' and looked steadfastly the other way. Walter usually answered, 'Good morning,' and avoided looking in her direction. Ellen thought that a girl who allowed herself to be informal with strangers created a bad impression, and Walter thought that a man who took advantage of living in the same building to strike up an acquaintance with a girl was a man of little principle. One particularly fine morning he said to Ellen in the elevator, 'Lovely day,' and she replied, 'Yes, isn't it?' and both of them felt secretly that they had been bold. How this mutual respect for each other's dignity could have degenerated into fury is a mystery not easily understood.

It happened that one evening – and, to do her strict justice, Ellen had had a hard day: she was coming down with a cold, it had rained steadily for a week, her stockings were unwashed, and she had broken a fingernail – the phone which had the number 3-4126 rang. Ellen had been opening a can of chicken soup in the kitchenette, and she had her hands full; she said, 'Darn,' and managed to drop and break a cup in her hurry to answer the phone.

'Hello?' she said, thinking, *This is going to be something cheerful.*

'Hello, is Walter there?'

'Walter?'

'Walter Nesmith. I want to speak to Walter, please.'

'This is the wrong number,' Ellen said, thinking with the self-pity that comes with the first stages of a head cold, that *no* one ever called *her*.

'Is this three-four two one six?'

37

'This is three-four one two six,' Ellen said, and hung up.

At that time, although she knew that the person in the apartment across the hall was named Walter Nesmith, she could not have told the color of his hair or even of the outside of his apartment door. She went back to her soup and had a match in her hand to light the stove, when the phone rang again.

'Hello?' Ellen said without enthusiasm; this *could* be someone cheerful, she was thinking.

'Hello, is Walter there?'

'This is the wrong number again,' Ellen said; if she had not been such a very sweet girl she might have let more irritation show in her voice.

'I *want* to *speak* to Walter Nesmith, *please.*'

'This is three-four one two six again,' Ellen said patiently. 'You want three-four two one six.'

'What?' said the voice.

'This,' said Ellen, 'is number three-four one two six. The number you want is three-four two one six.' Like anyone who has tried to say a series of numbers several times, she found her anger growing. Surely anyone of *normal* intelligence, she was thinking, surely anyone *ought* to be able to dial a phone, anyone who can't dial a phone shouldn't be allowed to have a nickel.

She had got all the way back into the kitchenette and was reaching out for the can of soup before the phone rang again. This time when she answered she said, 'Hello?' rather sharply for Ellen, and with no illusions about who it was going to be.

'Hello, may I please speak to Walter?'

At that point it started. Ellen had a headache and it was raining and she was tired and she was apparently not going to get any chicken soup until this annoyance was stopped.

'Just a minute,' she said into the phone.

38

She put the phone down with an understandable bang on the table, and marched, without taking time to think, out of her apartment and up to the door across the hall. 'Walter Nesmith' said a small card at the doorbell. Ellen rang the doorbell with what was, for her, a vicious poke. When the door opened she said immediately, without looking at him:

'Are you Walter Nesmith?'

Now, Walter had had a hard day, too, and *he* was coming down with a cold, and *he* had been trying ineffectually to make himself a cup of hot tea in which he intended to put a spoonful of honey to ease his throat, that being a remedy his aunt had always recommended for the first onslaught of a cold. If there had been one fraction less irritation in Ellen's voice, or if Walter had not taken off his shoes when he came home that night, it might very probably have turned out to be a pleasant introduction, with Walter and Ellen dining together on chicken soup and hot tea, and perhaps even sharing a bottle of cough medicine. But when Walter opened the door and heard Ellen's voice, he was unable to answer her cordially, and so he said briefly:

'I am. Why?'

'Will you please come and answer my phone?' said Ellen, too annoyed to realize that this request might perhaps bewilder Walter.

'Answer your phone?' said Walter stupidly.

'Answer my phone,' said Ellen firmly. She turned and went back across the hall, and Walter stood in his doorway in his stocking feet and watched her numbly. 'Come *on*,' she said sharply as she went into her own apartment, and Walter, wondering briefly if they allowed harmless lunatics to live alone as though they were just like other people, hesitated for an instant and then followed her, on the theory that it would be wise to do what she said when she seemed so cross,

39

and reassuring himself that he could leave the door open and yell for help if necessary. Ellen stamped into her apartment and pointed at the phone where it lay on the table. 'There. Answer it.'

Eyeing her sideways, Walter edged over to the phone and picked it up. 'Hello,' he said nervously. Then, 'Hello? Hello?' Looking at her over the top of the phone, he said, 'What do you want me to do now?'

'Do you mean to say,' said Ellen ominously, 'that that terrible terrible person has hung up?'

'I guess so,' said Walter, and fled back to his own apartment.

The door had only just closed behind him, when the phone rang again, and Ellen, answering it, heard, 'May I speak to Walter, please?'

Not a very serious mischance, surely. But the next morning Walter pointedly avoided going down in the elevator with Ellen, and sometime during that day the deliveryman left a package addressed to Ellen at Walter's door.

When Walter found the package he took it manfully under his arm and went boldly across the hall and rang Ellen's doorbell. When Ellen opened her door she thought at first – and she may have been justified – that Walter had come to apologize for the phone call the evening before, and she even thought that the package under his arm might contain something delightfully unexpected, like a box of candy. They lost another chance then; if Walter had not held out the package and said, 'Here,' Ellen would not have gone on thinking that he was trying to apologize in his own shy way, and she would certainly not have smiled warmly, and said, 'You *shouldn't* have bothered.'

Walter, who regarded transporting a misdelivered parcel

across the hall as relatively little bother, said blankly, 'No bother at all,' and Ellen, still deceived, said, 'But it really wasn't *that* important.'

Walter went back into his own apartment convinced that this was a very odd girl indeed, and Ellen, finding that the package had been mailed to her and contained a wool scarf knitted by a cousin, was as much angry as embarrassed because, once having imagined that an apology is forthcoming, it is very annoying not to have one after all, and particularly to have a wool scarf instead of a box of candy.

How this situation disintegrated into the white-hot fury that rose between these two is a puzzle, except for the basic fact that when once a series of misadventures has begun between two people, everything tends to contribute further to a state of misunderstanding. Thus, Ellen opened a letter of Walter's by mistake, and Walter dropped a bottle of milk – he was still trying to cure his cold, and thought that perhaps milk toast was the thing – directly outside Ellen's door, so that even after his nervous attempts to clear it up, the floor was still littered with fragments of glass, and puddled with milk.

Then Ellen – who believed by now that Walter had thrown the bottle of milk against her door – allowed herself to become so far confused by this succession of small annoyances that she actually wrote and mailed a letter to Walter, asking politely that he try to turn down his radio a little in the late evenings. Walter replied with a frigid letter to the effect that certainly if he had known that she was bothered by his radio, he would surely never have dreamed—

That evening, perhaps by accident, his radio was so loud that Ellen's canary woke up and chirped hysterically, and Ellen, pacing her floor in incoherent fury, might have been heard – if there had been anyone to hear her, and if Walter's radio had not been so loud – to say, 'I'll get even with him!' A phrase, it must be said, which Ellen had never used before in her life.

Ellen made her preparations with a sort of loving care that might well have been lavished on some more worthy object. When the alarm went off she turned in her sleep and smiled before quite waking up, and, once awake and the alarm turned off, she almost laughed out loud. In her slippers and gown, the clock in her hand, she went across her small apartment to the phone; the number was one she was not soon apt to forget. The dial tone sounded amazingly loud, and for a minute she was almost frightened out of her resolution. Then, setting her teeth, she dialed the number, her hand steady. After a second's interminable wait, the ringing began. The phone at the other end rang three times, four times, with what seemed interminable waits between, as though even the mechanical phone system hesitated at this act. Then, at last, there was an irritable crash at the other end of the line, and a voice said, 'Wah?'

'*Good* morning,' said Ellen brightly. 'I'm so terribly sorry to disturb you at this hour.'

'Wah?'

'This is Ellen Webster,' said Ellen, still brightly. 'I called to tell you that my clock has stopped—'

'Wah?'

'—and I wonder if you could tell me what time it is?'

There was a short pause at the other end of the line. Then, after a minute, his voice came back: 'Tenny minna fah.'

'I beg your pardon?'

There was another short pause at the other end of the line, as of someone opening his eyes with a shock. 'Twenty minutes after four,' he said. '*Twenty minutes after four.*'

'The reason I thought of asking you,' Ellen said sweetly, 'was that you were so *very* obliging before. About the radio, I mean.'

'—calling a person at—'

'Thanks so much,' said Ellen. 'Goodbye.'

She felt fairly certain that he would not call her back, but she sat on her bed and giggled a little before she went back to sleep.

Walter's response to this was miserably weak: He contacted a neighboring delicatessen a day or so later, and had an assortment of evil-smelling cheeses left in Ellen's apartment while she was out. This, which required persuading the superintendent to open Ellen's apartment so that the package might be left inside, was a poor revenge but a monstrous exercise of imagination upon Walter's part, so that, in one sense, Ellen was already bringing out in him qualities he never knew he had. The cheese, it turned out, more than evened the score: The apartment was small, the day was warm, and Ellen did not get home until late, and long after most of the other tenants on the floor had gone to the superintendent with their complaints about something dead in the woodwork.

Since breaking and entering had thus become one of the rules of their game, Ellen felt privileged to retaliate in kind upon Walter. It was with great joy, some evenings later, that Ellen, sitting in her odorous apartment, heard Walter's scream of pure terror when he put his feet into his slippers and found a raw egg in each.

Walter had another weapon, however, which he had been so far reluctant to use; it was a howitzer of such proportions that Walter felt its use would end warfare utterly. After the raw eggs he felt no compunction whatever in bringing out his heavy artillery.

It seemed to Ellen, at first, as though peace had been declared. For almost a week things went along smoothly; Walter kept his radio turned down almost to inaudibility, so that Ellen got plenty of sleep. She was over her cold, the sun had come out, and on Saturday morning she spent three hours shopping, and found exactly the dress she wanted at less than she expected to pay.

About Saturday noon she stepped out of the elevator, her packages under her arm, and walked briskly down the hall to her apartment, making, as usual, a wide half circle to avoid coming into contact with the area around Walter's door.

Her apartment door, to her surprise, was open, but before she had time to phrase a question in her own mind, she had stepped inside and come face-to-face with a lady who – not to make any more mysteries – was Walter Nesmith's aunt, and a wicked old lady in her own way, possessing none of Walter's timidity and none of his tact.

'Who?' said Ellen weakly, standing in the doorway.

'Come in and close the door,' said the old lady darkly. 'I don't think you'll want your neighbors to hear what I have to say. I,' she continued as Ellen obeyed mechanically, 'am Mrs Harold Vongarten Nesmith. Walter Nesmith, young woman, is my nephew.'

'Then you are in the wrong apartment,' said Ellen quite politely, considering the reaction which Walter Nesmith's name was beginning by now to arouse in her. 'You want Apartment Three-B, across the hall.'

'I do *not*,' said the old lady firmly. 'I came here to see the designing young woman who has been shamelessly pursuing my nephew, and to warn her' – the old lady shook her gloves menacingly – 'to warn her that *not one cent* shall she have from me if she marries Walter Nesmith.'

'Marries?' said Ellen, thoughts too great for words in her heart.

'It has long been my opinion that some young woman would be after Walter Nesmith for his money,' said Walter's aunt with satisfaction.

'Believe me,' said Ellen wholeheartedly, 'there is not that much money in the world.'

'You deny it?' The old lady leaned back and smiled triumphantly. 'I expected something of the sort. Walter,' she called suddenly, and then, putting her head back and howling, 'Wallllter.'

'Shhh,' said Ellen fearfully. 'They'll hear you all over.'

'I expect them to,' said the old lady. 'Walllll— oh, there you are.'

Ellen turned, and saw Walter Nesmith, with triumph in his eyes, peering around the edge of the door. 'Did it work?' he asked.

'She denies everything,' said his aunt.

'About the eggs?' Walter said, confused. 'You mean, she denies about the eggs and the phone call and—'

'Look,' Ellen said to Walter, stamping across the floor to look at him straight in the eye, 'of all the insufferable, conceited, rude, self-satisfied—'

'What?' said Walter.

'I wouldn't want to marry you,' said Ellen, 'if – if—' She stopped for a word, helpless.

'If he were the last man on earth,' Walter's aunt supplied obligingly. 'I think she's really after your *money*, Walter.'

Walter stared at his aunt. 'I didn't tell you to tell her—' he began. He gasped, and tried again. 'I mean,' he said, 'I never thought—' He appealed to Ellen. 'I don't want to marry you, either,' he said, and then gasped again, and said, 'I mean, I told my aunt to come and tell you—'

45

'If this is a proposal,' Ellen said coldly, 'I decline.'

'All I wanted her to do was scare you,' Walter said finally.

'It's a good way,' his aunt said complacently. 'Turned out to be the only way with your uncle Charles and a Hungarian adventuress.'

'I mean,' Walter said desperately to Ellen, 'she owns this building. I mean, I wanted her to tell you that if you didn't stop – I mean, I wanted her to scare you—'

'Apartments are too hard to get these days,' his aunt said. 'That would have been *too* unkind.'

'That's how I got my apartment at all, you see,' Walter said to Ellen, still under the impression he was explaining something Ellen wanted to understand.

'Since you *have* got an apartment,' Ellen said with restraint, 'may I suggest that you take your aunt and the both of you—'

The phone rang.

'Excuse me,' said Ellen mechanically, moving to answer it. 'Hello?' she said.

'Hello, may I speak to Walter, please?'

Ellen smiled rather in the manner that Lady Macbeth might have smiled if she found a run in her stocking.

'It's for you,' she said, holding the phone out to Walter.

'For me?' he said, surprised. 'Who is it?'

'I really could not say,' said Ellen sweetly. 'Since you have so many friends that one phone is not adequate to answer all their calls—'

Since Walter made no move to take the phone, she put it gently back on the hook.

'They'll call again,' she assured him, still smiling in that terrible fashion.

'I ought to turn you both out,' said Walter's aunt. She turned to Ellen. 'Young woman,' she said, 'do you deny that all this nonsense with eggs and telephone calls is an attempt to entangle my nephew into matrimony?'

'Certainly not,' Ellen said. 'I mean, I *do* deny it.'

'Walter Nesmith,' said his aunt, 'do you admit that all your finagling with cheeses and radios is an attempt to strike up an acquaintance with this young woman?'

'Certainly,' said Walter. 'I mean, I do *not* admit it.'

'Good,' said Walter's aunt. 'You are precisely the pair of silly fools I would have picked out for each other.' She rose with great dignity, motioned Walter away from her, and started for the door. 'Remember,' she said, shaking her gloves again at Ellen, 'not one cent.'

She opened the door and started down the hall, her handkerchief over her eyes, and – a surprising thing in such an old lady – laughing until she had to stop and lean against the wall near the elevator.

'I'm sorry,' Walter was saying to Ellen, almost babbling. 'I'm *really* sorry this time – please believe me, I had *no* idea – I wouldn't for the world – nothing but the most profound respect – a joke, you know – hope you didn't really think—'

'I understand perfectly,' Ellen said icily. 'It is all perfectly clear. It only goes to show what I have always believed about young men who think that all they have to do is—'

The phone rang.

Ellen waited a minute before she spoke. Then she said, 'You might as well answer it.'

'I'm *terribly* sorry,' Walter said, not moving toward the phone. 'I mean, I'm *terribly* sorry.' He waved his hands in the air. 'About what she said about what she thought about what you wanted me to do—' His voice trailed off miserably.

Suddenly Ellen began to giggle.

Anger is certainly a problem that will bear much analysis. It is hardly surprising that one person may be angry at

47

another, particularly if these are two people who are gentle, usually, and rarely angry, whose emotions tend to be mild and who would rather be friends with everyone than be enemies with anyone. Such an anger argues a situation so acute that only the most drastic readjustment can remedy it.

Either Walter Nesmith or Ellen Webster could have moved, of course. But, as Walter's aunt had pointed out, apartments are not that easy to come by, and their motives and their telephone numbers were by now so inextricably mixed that on the whole it seemed more reasonable not to bother.

Moreover, Walter's aunt, who still snickers when her nephew's name is mentioned, did not keep them long in suspense, after all. She was not lavish, certainly, but she wrote them a letter that both of them found completely confusing, and enclosed a check adequate for a down payment on the extremely modest house in the country they decided upon without disagreement. They even compromised and had four children – two boys and two girls.

O. HENRY

THE MARRY MONTH OF MAY

PRITHEE, SMITE THE poet in the eye when he would sing to you praises of the month of May. It is a month presided over by the spirits of mischief and madness. Pixies and flibbertigibbets haunt the budding woods; Puck and his train of midgets are busy in town and country.

In May Nature holds up at us a chiding finger, bidding us remember that we are not gods, but overconceited members of her own great family. She reminds us that we are brothers to the chowder-doomed clam and the donkey; lineal scions of the pansy and the chimpanzee, and but cousins-german to the cooing doves, the quacking ducks, and the housemaids and policemen in the parks.

In May Cupid shoots blindfolded – millionaires marry stenographers; wise professors woo white-aproned gum-chewers behind quick-lunch counters; schoolma'ams make big bad boys remain after school; lads with ladders steal lightly over lawns where Juliet waits in her trellised window with her telescope packed; young couples out for a walk come home married; old chaps put on white spats and promenade near the Normal School; even married men, grown unwontedly tender and sentimental, whack their spouses on the back and growl: 'How goes it, old girl?'

This May, who is no goddess, but Circe, masquerading at the dance given in honor of the fair debutante, Summer, puts the kibosh on us all.

Old Mr Coulson groaned a little, and then sat up straight

in his invalid's chair. He had the gout very bad in one foot, a house near Gramercy Park, half a million dollars, and a daughter. And he had a housekeeper. Mrs Widdup. The fact and the name deserve a sentence each. They have it.

When May poked Mr Coulson he became elder brother to the turtledove. In the window near which he sat were boxes of jonquils, of hyacinths, geraniums, and pansies. The breeze brought their odor into the room. Immediately there was a well-contested round between the breath of the flowers and the able and active effluvium from gout liniment. The liniment won easily; but not before the flowers got an uppercut to old Mr Coulson's nose. The deadly work of the implacable, false enchantress May was done.

Across the park to the olfactories of Mr Coulson came other unmistakable, characteristic, copyrighted smells of spring that belong to the-big-city-above-the-Subway, alone. The smells of hot asphalt, underground caverns, gasoline, patchouli, orange peel, sewer gas, Albany grabs, Egyptian cigarettes, mortar and the undried ink on newspapers. The inblowing air was sweet and mild. Sparrows wrangled happily everywhere outdoors. Never trust May.

Mr Coulson twisted the ends of his white mustache, cursed his foot, and pounded a bell on the table by his side.

In came Mrs Widdup. She was comely to the eye, fair, flustered, forty, and foxy.

'Higgins is out, sir,' she said, with a smile suggestive of vibratory massage. 'He went to post a letter. Can I do anything for you, sir?'

'It's time for my aconite,' said old Mr Coulson. 'Drop it for me. The bottle's there. Three drops. In water. D— that is, confound Higgins! There's nobody in this house cares if I die here in this chair for want of attention.'

Mrs Widdup sighed deeply.

'Don't be saying that, sir,' she said. 'There's them that would care more than anyone knows. Thirteen drops you said, sir?'

'Three,' said old man Coulson.

He took his dose and then Mrs Widdup's hand. She blushed. Oh, yes, it can be done. Just hold your breath and compress the diaphragm.

'Mrs Widdup,' said Mr Coulson, 'the springtime's full upon us.'

'Ain't that right?' said Mrs Widdup. 'The air's real warm. And there's bock-beer signs on every corner. And the park's all yaller and pink and blue with flowers; and I have such shooting pains up my legs and body.'

'"In the spring,"' quoted Mr Coulson, curling his mustache, '"a y— that is, a man's – fancy lightly turns to thoughts of love."'

'Lawsy, now!' exclaimed Mrs Widdup; 'ain't that right? Seems like it's in the air.'

'"In the spring,"' continued old Mr Coulson, '"a livelier iris shines upon the burnished dove."'

'They do be lively, the Irish,' sighed Mrs Widdup, pensively.

'Mrs Widdup,' said Mr Coulson, making a face at a twinge of his gouty foot, 'this would be a lonesome house without you. I'm an – that is, I'm an elderly man – but I'm worth a comfortable lot of money. If half a million dollars' worth of Government bonds and the true affection of a heart that, though no longer beating with the first ardor of youth, can still throb with genuine—'

The loud noise of an overturned chair near the portières of the adjoining room interrupted the venerable and scarcely suspecting victim of May.

In stalked Miss Van Meeker Constantia Coulson, bony, durable, tall, high-nosed, frigid, well-bred, thirty-five, in-the-neighborhood-of-Gramercy-Parkish. She put up a lorgnette. Mrs Widdup hastily stooped and arranged the bandages on Mr Coulson's gouty foot.

'I thought Higgins was with you,' said Miss Van Meeker Constantia.

'Higgins went out,' explained her father, 'and Mrs Widdup answered the bell. That is better now, Mrs Widdup, thank you. No; there is nothing else I require.'

The housekeeper retired, pink under the cool, inquiring stare of Miss Coulson.

'This spring weather is lovely, isn't it, daughter?' said the old man, consciously conscious.

'That's just it,' replied Miss Van Meeker Constantia Coulson, somewhat obscurely. 'When does Mrs Widdup start on her vacation, Papa?'

'I believe she said a week from today,' said Mr Coulson.

Miss Van Meeker Constantia stood for a minute at the window gazing toward the little park, flooded with the mellow afternoon sunlight. With the eye of a botanist she viewed the flowers – most potent weapons of insidious May. With the cool pulses of a virgin of Cologne she withstood the attack of the ethereal mildness. The arrows of the pleasant sunshine fell back, frostbitten, from the cold panoply of her unthrilled bosom. The odor of the flowers waked no soft sentiments in the unexplored recesses of her dormant heart. The chirp of the sparrows gave her a pain. She mocked at May.

But although Miss Coulson was proof against the season, she was keen enough to estimate its power. She knew that elderly men and thick-waisted women jumped as educated fleas in the ridiculous train of May, the merry mocker of the months. She had heard of foolish old gentlemen marrying their housekeepers before. What a humiliating thing, after all, was this feeling called love!

The next morning at 8 o'clock, when the iceman called, the cook told him that Miss Coulson wanted to see him in the basement.

'Well, ain't I the Olcott and Depew; not mentioning the first name at all?' said the iceman, admiringly, of himself.

As a concession he rolled his sleeves down, dropped his icehooks on a syringe and went back. When Miss Van Meeker Constantia Coulson addressed him he took off his hat.

'There is a rear entrance to this basement,' said Miss Coulson, 'which can be reached by driving into the vacant lot next door, where they are excavating for a building. I want you to bring in that way within two hours 1,000 pounds of ice. You may have to bring another man or two to help you. I will show you where I want it placed. I also want 1,000 pounds a day delivered the same way for the next four days. Your company may charge the ice on our regular bill. This is for your extra trouble.'

Miss Coulson tendered a ten-dollar bill. The iceman bowed, and held his hat in his two hands behind him.

'Not if you'll excuse me, lady. It'll be a pleasure to fix things up for you any way you please.'

Alas for May!

About noon Mr Coulson knocked two glasses off his table, broke the spring of his bell, and yelled for Higgins at the same time.

'Bring an axe,' commanded Mr Coulson, sardonically, 'or send out for a quart of prussic acid, or have a policeman come in and shoot me. I'd rather that than be frozen to death.'

'It does seem to be getting cold, sir,' said Higgins. 'I hadn't noticed it before. I'll close the window, sir.'

'Do,' said Mr Coulson. 'They call this spring, do they? If it keeps up long I'll go back to Palm Beach. House feels like a morgue.'

Later Miss Coulson dutifully came in to inquire how the gout was progressing.

''Stantia,' said the old man, 'how is the weather outdoors?'

'Bright,' answered Miss Coulson, 'but chilly.'

'Feels like the dead of winter to me,' said Mr Coulson.

'An instance,' said Constantia, gazing abstractedly out of the window, 'of "winter lingering in the lap of spring," though the metaphor is not in the most refined taste.'

A little later she walked down by the side of the little park and on westward to Broadway to accomplish a little shopping.

A little later than that Mrs Widdup entered the invalid's room.

'Did you ring, sir?' she asked, dimpling in many places. 'I asked Higgins to go to the drug store, and I thought I heard your bell.'

'I did not,' said Mr Coulson.

'I'm afraid,' said Mrs Widdup, 'I interrupted you, sir, yesterday when you were about to say something.'

'How comes it, Mrs Widdup,' said old man Coulson, sternly, 'that I find it so cold in this house?'

'Cold, sir?' said the housekeeper, 'why, now, since you speak of it it do seem cold in this room. But outdoors it's as warm and fine as June, sir. And how this weather do seem to make one's heart jump out of one's shirt waist, sir. And the ivy all leaved out on the side of the house, and the hand-organs playing, and the children dancing on the sidewalk –

'tis a great time for speaking out what's in the heart. You were saying yesterday, sir—'

'Woman!' roared Mr Coulson; 'you are a fool. I pay you to take care of this house. I am freezing to death in my own room, and you come in and drivel to me about ivy and hand-organs. Get me an overcoat at once. See that all doors and windows are closed below. An old, fat, irresponsible, one-sided object like you prattling about springtime and flowers in the middle of winter! When Higgins comes back, tell him to bring me a hot rum punch. And now get out!'

But who shall shame the bright face of May? Rogue though she be and disturber of sane men's peace, no wise virgin's cunning nor cold storage shall make her bow her head in the bright galaxy of months.

Oh, yes, the story was not quite finished.

A night passed, and Higgins helped old man Coulson in the morning to his chair by the window. The cold of the room was gone. Heavenly odors and fragrant mildness entered.

In hurried Mrs Widdup, and stood by his chair. Mr Coulson reached his bony hand and grasped her plump one.

'Mrs Widdup,' he said, 'this house would be no home without you. I have half a million dollars. If that and the true affection of a heart no longer in its youthful prime, but still not cold could—'

'I found out what made it cold,' said Mrs Widdup, leaning against his chair. ''Twas ice – tons of it – in the basement and in the furnace room, everywhere. I shut off the registers that it was coming through into your room, Mr Coulson, poor soul! And now it's May-time again.'

'A true heart,' went on old man Coulson, a little

wanderingly, 'that the springtime has brought to life again, and – but what will my daughter say, Mrs Widdup?'

'Never fear, sir,' said Mrs Widdup, cheerfully, 'Miss Coulson, she ran away with the iceman last night, sir!'

ANNE TYLER

FROM
BREATHING
LESSONS

SERENA'S WEDDING REHEARSAL was a Friday evening. It wasn't a very formal rehearsal. Max's parents, for instance, didn't even bother attending, although Serena's mother showed up with her hair in a million pink rollers. And events happened out of order, with Maggie (standing in for the bride, for good luck) coming down the aisle ahead of all the musical selections because Max had a trainload of relatives to meet in half an hour. She walked alongside Anita, which was one of Serena's more peculiar innovations. 'Who else could give me away?' Serena asked. 'You surely don't imagine my father would do it.' Anita herself, however, didn't seem so happy with this arrangement. She teetered and staggered in her spike-heeled shoes and dug her long red nails into Maggie's wrist in order to keep her balance. At the altar Max slung an arm around Maggie and said, shoot, maybe he'd just settle for her instead; and Serena, sitting in a center pew, called, 'That'll be quite enough of that, Max Gill!' Max was the same freckled, friendly, overgrown boy he'd always been. It was hard for Maggie to picture him married.

After the vows Max left for Penn Station and the rest of them practiced the music. They all performed in a fairly amateurish style, Maggie thought, which was fine with her because she and Ira didn't sound their best that night. They started off raggedly, and Maggie forgot that they had planned to split up the middle verse. She sailed right into the first two lines along with Ira, then stopped in confusion, then missed her own cue and fell into a fit of giggles. At that moment, the laughter not yet faded from her face, she saw Boris Drumm in the foremost pew. He wore a baffled, rumpled frown, as if someone had just awakened him.

Well, she'd known he was due home for the summer, but he hadn't told her which day. She pretended not to recognize him. She and Ira finished their song, and then she reverted to Serena's role and marched back up the aisle, minus Max, so Sugar could practice the timing on 'Born to Be with You.' After that Serena clapped her hands and shouted, 'Okay, gang!' and they prepared to leave, all talking at once. They were thinking of going out for pizza. They swarmed toward Maggie, who waited at the rear of the church, but Boris stayed where he was, facing forward. He would be expecting Maggie to join him. She studied the back of his head, which was block-like and immobile. Serena handed her her purse and said, 'You've got company, I see.' Right behind Serena was Ira. He stopped in front of Maggie and looked down at her. He said, 'Will you be going for pizza?'

Maggie said, 'I guess not.'

He nodded, blank-faced, and left. But he walked in a different direction from the others, as if he didn't feel they would welcome him without Maggie. Which of course was nonsense.

Maggie went back up the aisle and sat next to Boris, and they kissed. She said, 'How was your trip?' and he said, 'Who was that you were singing with?' at exactly the same instant. She pretended she hadn't heard. 'How was your trip?' she asked again, and he said, 'Wasn't that Ira Moran?'

'Who, the one singing?' she asked.

'That was Ira Moran! You told me he was dead!'

'It was a misunderstanding,' she said.

'I heard you say it, Maggie.'

62

'I mean I misunderstood that he was dead. He was only, um, wounded.'

'Ah,' Boris said. He turned that over in his mind.

'It was only a flesh wound, was all,' Maggie told him. 'A scalp wound.' She wondered if the two terms contradicted each other. She riffled quickly through various movies she had seen.

'So then what? He just comes walking in one day?' Boris asked. 'I mean he just pops up, like some kind of ghost? How did it happen, exactly?'

'Boris,' Maggie said, 'I fail to comprehend why you keep dwelling on this in such a tiresome fashion.'

'Oh. Well. Sorry,' Boris said.

(Had she really sounded so authoritative? She found it hard to imagine, looking back.)

On the morning of the wedding, Maggie got up early and walked to Serena's apartment – the second floor of a form-stone row house – to help her dress. Serena seemed unruffled but her mother was all in a dither. Anita's habit when she was nervous was to speak very fast and with practically no punctuation, like someone in a hard-sell commercial. 'Why she won't roll her hair like everybody else when I told her way last week I said hon nobody wears long hair anymore you ought to go to the beauty shop and get you a nice little flip to peek out under your veil . . .' She was rushing around the shabby, sparsely equipped kitchen in a dirty pink satin bathrobe, with a cigarette dangling from her lips. She was making a great clatter but not much was getting accomplished. Serena, lazy and nonchalant in one of Max's big shirts, said, 'Take it easy, Mom, will you?' She told Maggie, 'Mom thinks we ought to change the whole ceremony.'

'Change it how?' Maggie asked.

'She doesn't have any bridesmaids!' Anita said. 'She doesn't have a maid of honor even and what's worse there's no kind of masculine person to walk her down the aisle!'

'She's upset she has to walk me down the aisle,' Serena told Maggie.

'Oh if only your uncle Maynard would come and do it instead!' Anita cried. 'Maybe we should move the wedding up a week and give him another chance because the way you have it now is all cockeyed it's too oddball I can just picture how those hoity-toity Gills will be scrupulizing me and smirking amongst themselves and besides that last perm I got scorched the tip-ends of my hair *I* can't walk down the aisle.'

'Let's go get me dressed,' Serena told Maggie, and she led her away.

In Serena's room, which was really just half of Anita's room curtained off with a draggled aqua bed sheet, Serena sat down at her vanity table. She said, 'I thought of giving her a belt of whiskey, but I worried it might backfire.'

Maggie said, 'Serena, are you sure you ought to be marrying Max?'

Serena squawked and wheeled to face her. She said, 'Maggie Daley, don't you start with me! I've already got my wedding cake frosted.'

'But I mean how do you know? How can you be certain you chose the right man?'

'I can be certain because I've come to the end of the line,' Serena said, turning back to the mirror. Her voice was at normal level now. She patted on liquid foundation, expertly dotting her chin and forehead and cheeks. 'It's just *time* to marry, that's all,' she said. 'I'm so tired of dating! I'm so tired of keeping up a good front! I want to sit on the couch with a regular, normal husband and watch TV for a thousand years. It's going to be like getting out of a girdle; that's exactly how I picture it.'

'What are you saying?' Maggie asked. She was almost afraid of the answer. 'Are you telling me you don't really love Max?'

'Of course I love him,' Serena said. She blended the dots into her skin. 'But I've loved other people as much. I loved Terry Simpson our sophomore year – remember him? But it wasn't time to get married then, so Terry is not the one I'm marrying.'

Maggie didn't know what to think. Did everybody feel that way? Had the grownups been spreading fairy tales? 'The minute I saw Eleanor,' her oldest brother had told her once, 'I said, "That girl is going to be my wife someday."' It hadn't occurred to Maggie that he might simply have been ready for a wife, and therefore had his eye out for the likeliest prospect.

So there again, Serena had managed to color Maggie's view of things. 'We're not in the hands of fate after all,' she seemed to be saying. 'Or if we are, we can wrest ourselves free any time we care to.'

Maggie sat down on the bed and watched Serena applying her rouge. In Max's shirt, Serena looked casual and sporty, like anybody's girl next door. 'When this is over,' she told Maggie, 'I'm going to dye my wedding dress purple. Might as well get some use out of it.'

Maggie gazed at her thoughtfully.

The wedding was due to start at eleven, but Anita wanted to get to the church much earlier, she said, in case of mishaps. Maggie rode with them in Anita's ancient Chevrolet. Serena drove because Anita said she was too nervous, and since Serena's skirt billowed over so much of the seat, Maggie and Anita sat in back. Anita was talking nonstop and sprinkling cigarette ashes across the lap of her shiny peach mother-of-the-bride dress. 'Now that I think of it Serena I can't imagine why you're holding your reception in the Angels of Charity building which is so damn far away and every time I've tried to find it I've gotten all turned around and had to ask directions from passing strangers . . .'

They came to the Alluring Lingerie Shop, and Serena double-parked and heaved her cascades of satin out of the car in order to go model her dress for Mrs Knowlton, her employer. While they waited for her, Anita said, 'Honestly you'd suppose if you can rent a man to come tend your bar or fix your toilet or check on why your door won't lock it wouldn't be any problem at all to engage one for the five eentsy minutes it takes to walk your daughter down the aisle don't you agree?'

'Yes, ma'am,' Maggie said, and she dug absently into a hole in the vinyl seat and pulled out a wad of cotton batting.

'Sometimes I think she's trying to show me up,' Anita said.

Maggie didn't know how to answer that.

Finally Serena returned to the car, bearing a wrapped gift. 'Mrs Knowlton told me not to open this till our wedding night,' she said. Maggie blushed and slid her eyes toward Anita. Anita merely gazed out the window, sending two long streamers of smoke from her nostrils.

In the church, Reverend Connors led Serena and her mother to a side room. Maggie went to wait for the other singers. Mary Jean was already there, and soon Sissy arrived with her husband and her mother-in-law. No Ira, though. Well, there was plenty of time. Maggie took her long white choir robe from its hanger and slipped it over her head, losing herself in its folds, and then of course she emerged all tousled and had to go off to comb her hair. But even when she returned, Ira was not to be seen.

The first of the guests had arrived. Boris sat in one of the pews, uncomfortably close. He was listening to a lady in a spotted veil and he was nodding intelligently, respectfully, but Maggie felt there was something tense about the set of his head. She looked toward the entrance. Other people were straggling in now, her parents and the Wrights next door and Serena's old baton teacher. No sign of the long, dark shape that was Ira Moran.

After she had let him walk off alone the night before, he must have decided to vanish altogether.

'Excuse me,' she said. She bumped down the row of folding chairs and hurried through the vestibule. One of her full sleeves caught on the knob of the open door and yanked her up short in a foolish way, but she shook herself loose before anybody noticed, she thought. She paused on the front steps. 'Well, hi!' an old classmate said. 'Um . . .' Maggie murmured, and she shaded her eyes and looked up and down the street. All she saw were more guests. She felt a moment's impatience with them; they seemed so frivolous. They were smiling and greeting each other in that gracious style they used only at church, and the women turned their toes out fastidiously as they walked, and their white gloves glinted in the sunlight.

In the doorway, Boris said, 'Maggie?'

She didn't turn around. She ran down the steps with her robe flowing behind her. The steps were the wide, exceptionally shallow sort unsuited for any normal human stride; she was forced to adopt a limping, uneven rhythm. 'Maggie!' Boris cried, so she had to run on after reaching the sidewalk. She shouldered her way between guests and then was past them, skimming down the street, ballooning white linen like a sailboat in a wind.

Sam's Frame Shop was only two blocks from the church, but they were long blocks and it was a warm June morning. She was damp and breathless when she arrived. She pulled open the plate-glass door and stepped into a close, cheerless interior with a worn linoleum floor. L-shaped samples of moldings hung from hooks on a yellowing pegboard wall, and the counter was painted a thick, cold gray. Behind this counter stood a bent old man in a visor, with shocks of white hair poking every which way. Ira's father.

She was surprised to find him there. The way she'd heard it, he never set foot in the shop anymore. She hesitated, and he said, 'Can I help you, miss?'

She had always thought Ira had the darkest eyes she'd ever seen, but this man's eyes were darker. She couldn't even tell where they were focused; she had the fleeting notion that he might be blind.

'I was looking for Ira,' she told him.

'Ira's not working today. He's got some kind of event.'

'Yes, a wedding; he's singing at a wedding,' she said. 'But he hasn't shown up yet, so I came to get him.'

'Oh?' Sam said. He moved his head closer to her, leading with his nose, not lessening in the least his impression of a blind man. 'You wouldn't be Margaret, would you?' he asked.

'Yes, sir,' she said.

He thought that over. He gave an abrupt, wheezy chuckle.

'Margaret M. Daley,' he said.

She stood her ground.

'So you assumed Ira was dead,' he said.

'Is he here?' she asked.

'He's upstairs, dressing.'

'Could you call him, please?'

'How did you suppose he'd died?' he asked her.

'I mistook him for someone else. Monty Rand,' she said, mumbling the words. 'Monty got killed in boot camp.'

'Boot camp!'

'Could you call Ira for me, please?'

'You'd never find Ira in boot camp,' Sam told her. 'Ira's got dependents, just as much as if he was married. Not that he

68

ever could be married in view of our situation. My heart has been acting up on me for years and one of his sisters is not quite right in the head. Why, I don't believe the army would have him even if he volunteered! Then me and the girls would have to go on welfare; we'd be a burden on the government. "Get along with you," those army folks would tell him. "Go on back to them that need you. We've got no use for you here."'

Maggie heard feet running down a set of stairs somewhere – a muffled, drumming sound. A door opened in the pegboard wall behind the counter and Ira said, 'Pop—'

He stopped and looked at her. He wore a dark, ill-fitting suit and a stiff white shirt, with a navy tie dangling unknotted from his collar.

'We'll be late for the wedding,' she told him.

He shot back a cuff and checked his watch.

'Come on!' she said. It wasn't only the wedding she was thinking of. She felt there was something dangerous about staying around Ira's father.

And sure enough, Sam said, 'Me and your little friend here was just discussing you going into the army.'

'Army?'

'*Ira* couldn't join the army, I told her. He's got us.'

Ira said, 'Well, anyhow, Pop, I ought to be back from this thing in a couple of hours.'

'You really have to take that long? That's most of the morning!' Sam turned to Maggie and said, 'Saturday's our busiest day at work.'

Maggie wondered why, in that case, the shop was empty. She said, 'Yes, well, we should be—'

'In fact, if Ira joined the army we'd just have to close this place up,' Sam said. 'Sell it off lock, stock, and barrel, when it's been in the family for forty-two years come October.'

'What are you talking about?' Ira asked him. 'Why would I want to join the army?'

'Your little friend here thought you'd gone into the army and got yourself killed,' Sam told him.

'Oh,' Ira said. Now the danger must have dawned on him too, for this time it was he who said, 'We should be going.'

'She thought you'd blown yourself up in boot camp,' Sam told him. He gave another of his wheezy chuckles. There was something mole-like and relentless about that way he led with his nose, Maggie felt. 'Ups and writes me a letter of condolence,' he said. 'Ha!' He told Maggie, 'Gave me quite a start. I had this half-second or so where I thought, Wait a minute. Has Ira *passed*? First I knew of it, if so. And first I'd heard of you. First I'd heard of any girl, matter of fact, in years. I mean it's not like he has any friends anymore. His chums at school were that brainy crowd that went away to college and by now they've all lost touch with him and he doesn't see a soul his own age. "Look here!" I told him. "A girl at last!" After I'd withstood the shock. "Better grab her while you got the chance," I told him.'

'Let's go,' Ira said to Maggie.

He lifted a hinged section of the counter and stepped through it, but Sam went on talking. 'Trouble is, now you know she can manage fine without you,' he said.

Ira paused, still holding up the hinged section.

'She writes a little note of condolence and then continues with her life, as merry as pie,' Sam told him.

'What did you expect her to do, throw herself in my grave?'

'Well, you got to admit she bore up under her grief mighty well. Writes me a nice little note, sticks a postage stamp in one corner, then carries on with her girlfriend's wedding arrangements.'

'Right,' Ira said, and he lowered the counter and came over to Maggie. Was he totally impenetrable? His eyes were flat, and his hand, when he took her arm, was perfectly steady.

'You're wrong,' Maggie told Sam.

'Huh?'

'I wasn't doing fine without him! I was barely existing.'

'No need to get all het up about it,' Sam said.

'And for your information, there's any number of girls who think he's perfectly wonderful and I am not the only one and also it's ridiculous to say he can't get married. You have no right; anyone can get married if they want to.'

'He wouldn't dare!' Sam told her. 'He's got me and his sisters to think of. You want us all in the poorhouse? Ira? Ira, you wouldn't dare to get married!'

'Why not?' Ira asked calmly.

'You've got to think of me and your sisters!'

'I'm marrying her anyhow,' Ira said.

Then he opened the door and stood back to let Maggie walk through it.

On the stoop outside, they stopped and he put his arms around her and drew her close. She could feel the narrow bones of his chest against her cheek and she heard his heart beating in her ear. His father must have been able to see everything through the plate-glass door, but even so Ira bent his head and kissed her on the lips, a long, warm, searching kiss that turned her knees weak.

Then they started off toward the church, although first there was a minor delay because the hem of her choir robe caught her up short. Ira had to open the door once again (not even glancing at his father) and set her loose.

CEREMONIES AND CELEBRATIONS

EDITH WHARTON

FROM
THE AGE OF
INNOCENCE

THE DAY WAS fresh, with a lively spring wind full of dust. All the old ladies in both families had got out their faded sables and yellowing ermines, and the smell of camphor from the front pews almost smothered the faint spring scent of the lilies banking the altar.

Newland Archer, at a signal from the sexton, had come out of the vestry and placed himself with his best man on the chancel step of Grace Church.

The signal meant that the brougham bearing the bride and her father was in sight; but there was sure to be a considerable interval of adjustment and consultation in the lobby, where the bridesmaids were already hovering like a cluster of Easter blossoms. During this unavoidable lapse of time the bridegroom, in proof of his eagerness, was expected to expose himself alone to the gaze of the assembled company; and Archer had gone through this formality as resignedly as through all the others which made of a nineteenth-century New York wedding a rite that seemed to belong to the dawn of history. Everything was equally easy – or equally painful, as one chose to put it – in the path he was committed to tread, and he had obeyed the flurried injunctions of his best man as piously as other bridegrooms had obeyed his own, in the days when he had guided them through the same labyrinth.

So far he was reasonably sure of having fulfilled all his obligations. The bridesmaids' eight bouquets of white lilac and lilies-of-the-valley had been sent in due time, as well as the gold and sapphire sleeve-links of the eight ushers and the best man's cat's-eye scarf-pin; Archer had sat up half the night trying to vary the wording of his thanks for the last batch of presents from men friends and ex-lady-loves; the fees for the Bishop and Rector were safely in the pocket of his best man; his own luggage was already at Mrs Manson Mingott's, where the wedding-breakfast was to take place, and so were the travelling-clothes into which he was to change; and a private compartment had been engaged in the train that was to carry the young couple to their unknown destination – concealment of the spot in which the bridal night was to be spent being one of the most sacred taboos of the prehistoric ritual.

'Got the ring all right?' whispered young van der Luyden Newland, who was inexperienced in the duties of a best man, and awed by the weight of his responsibility.

Archer made the gesture which he had seen so many bridegrooms make: with his ungloved right hand he felt in the pocket of his dark-grey waistcoat, and assured himself that the little gold circlet (engraved inside: *Newland to May, April –, 187 –*) was in its place; then, resuming his former attitude, his tall hat and pearl-grey gloves with black stitchings grasped in his left hand, he stood looking at the door of the church.

Overhead, Handel's March swelled pompously through the imitation stone vaulting, carrying on its waves the faded drift of the many weddings at which, with cheerful indifference, he had stood on the same chancel step watching other brides float up the nave towards other bridegrooms.

'How like a first night at the Opera!' he thought, recognizing all the same faces in the same boxes (no, pews), and wondering if, when the Last Trump sounded, Mrs Selfridge

Merry would be there with the same towering ostrich feathers in her bonnet, and Mrs Beaufort with the same diamond earrings and the same smile – and whether suitable proscenium seats were already prepared for them in another world.

After that there was still time to review, one by one, the familiar countenances in the first rows; the women's sharp with curiosity and excitement, the men's sulky with the obligation of having to put on their frock-coats before luncheon, and fight for food at the wedding-breakfast.

'Too bad the breakfast is at old Catherine's,' the bridegroom could fancy Reggie Chivers saying. 'But I'm told that Lovell Mingott insisted on its being cooked by his own *chef*, so it ought to be good if one can only get at it.' And he could imagine Sillerton Jackson adding with authority: 'My dear fellow, haven't you heard? It's to be served at small tables, in the new English fashion.'

Archer's eyes lingered a moment on the left-hand pew, where his mother, who had entered the church on Mr Henry van der Luyden's arm, sat weeping softly under her Chantilly veil, her hands in her grandmother's ermine muff.

'Poor Jancy!' he thought, looking at his sister, 'even by screwing her head around she can see only the people in the few front pews; and they're mostly dowdy Newlands and Dagonets.'

On the hither side of the white ribbon dividing off the seats reserved for the families he saw Beaufort, tall and red-faced, scrutinizing the women with his arrogant stare. Beside him sat his wife, all silvery chinchilla and violets; and on the far side of the ribbon, Lawrence Lefferts's sleekly brushed head seemed to mount guard over the invisible deity of 'Good Form' who presided at the ceremony.

Archer wondered how many flaws Lefferts's keen eyes

would discover in the ritual of his divinity; then he suddenly recalled that he too had once thought such questions important. The things that had filled his days seemed now like a nursery parody of life, or like the wrangles of medieval schoolmen over metaphysical terms that nobody had ever understood. A stormy discussion as to whether the wedding presents should be 'shown' had darkened the last hours before the wedding; and it seemed inconceivable to Archer that grown-up people should work themselves into a state of agitation over such trifles, and that the matter should have been decided (in the negative) by Mrs Welland's saying, with indignant tears: 'I should as soon turn the reporters loose in my house.' Yet there was a time when Archer had had definite and rather aggressive opinions on all such problems, and when everything concerning the manners and customs of his little tribe had seemed to him fraught with worldwide significance.

'And all the while, I suppose,' he thought, 'real people were living somewhere, and real things happening to them . . .'

'*There they come!*' breathed the best man excitedly; but the bridegroom knew better.

The cautious opening of the door of the church meant only that Mr Brown the livery-stable keeper (gowned in black in his intermittent character of sexton) was taking a preliminary survey of the scene before marshalling his forces. The door was softly shut again; then after another interval it swung majestically open and a murmur ran through the church: 'The family!'

Mrs Welland came first, on the arm of her eldest son. Her large pink face was appropriately solemn, and her plum-coloured satin with pale-blue side-panels, and blue ostrich plumes in a small satin bonnet, met with general approval;

but before she had settled herself with a stately rustle in the pew opposite Mrs Archer's the spectators were craning their necks to see who was coming after her. Wild rumours had been abroad the day before to the effect that Mrs Manson Mingott, in spite of her physical disabilities, had resolved on being present at the ceremony; and the idea was so much in keeping with her sporting character that bets ran high at the clubs as to her being able to walk up the nave and squeeze into a seat. It was known that she had insisted on sending her own carpenter to look into the possibility of taking down the end panel of the front pew, and to measure the space between the seat and the front; but the result had been discouraging and for one anxious day her family had watched her dallying with the plan of being wheeled up the nave in her enormous bath-chair and sitting enthroned in it at the foot of the chancel.

The idea of this monstrous exposure of her person was so painful to her relations that they could have covered with gold the ingenious person who suddenly discovered that the chair was too wide to pass between the iron uprights of the awning which extended from the church door to the kerb-stone. The idea of doing away with this awning, and revealing the bride to the mob of dressmakers and newspaper reporters who stood outside fighting to get near the joints of the canvas, exceeded even old Catherine's courage, though for a moment she had weighed the possibility. 'Why, they might take a photograph of my child *and put it in the papers!*' Mrs Welland exclaimed when her mother's last plan was hinted to her; and from this unthinkable indecency the clan recoiled with a collective shudder. The ancestress had had to give in; but her concession was bought only by the promise that the wedding-breakfast should take place under her roof, though (as the Washington Square connection said) with the

Wellands' house in easy reach it was hard to have to make a special price with Brown to drive one to the other end of nowhere.

Though all these transactions had been widely reported by the Jacksons a sporting minority still clung to the belief that old Catherine would appear in church, and there was a distinct lowering of the temperature when she was found to have been replaced by her daughter-in-law. Mrs Lovell Mingott had the high colour and glassy stare induced in ladies of her age and habit by the effort of getting into a new dress; but once the disappointment occasioned by her mother-in-law's non-appearance had subsided, it was agreed that her black Chantilly over lilac satin, with a bonnet of Parma violets, formed the happiest contrast to Mrs Welland's blue and plum-colour. Far different was the impression produced by the gaunt and mincing lady who followed on Mr Mingott's arm, in a wild dishevelment of stripes and fringes and floating scarves; and as this apparition glided into view Archer's heart contracted and stopped beating.

He had taken it for granted that the Marchioness Manson was still in Washington, where she had gone some four weeks previously with her niece, Madame Olenska. It was generally understood that their abrupt departure was due to Madame Olenska's desire to remove her aunt from the baleful eloquence of Dr Agathon Carver, who had nearly succeeded in enlisting her as a recruit for the Valley of Love; and in the circumstances no one had expected either of the ladies to return for the wedding. For a moment Archer stood with his eyes fixed on Medora's fantastic figure, straining to see who came behind her; but the little procession was at an end, for all the lesser members of the family had taken their seats, and the eight tall ushers, gathering themselves together like birds or insects preparing for some migratory manoeuvre, were already slipping through the side doors into the lobby.

'Newland – I say: *she's here!*' the best man whispered.

Archer roused himself with a start.

A long time had apparently passed since his heart had stopped beating, for the white and rosy procession was in fact half-way up the nave, the Bishop, the Rector and two white-winged assistants were hovering about the flower-banked altar, and the first chords of the Spohr symphony were strewing their flower-like notes before the bride.

Archer opened his eyes (but could they really have been shut, as he imagined?), and he felt his heart beginning to resume its usual task. The music, the scent of the lilies on the altar, the vision of the cloud of tulle and orange-blossoms floating nearer and nearer, the sight of Mrs Archer's face suddenly convulsed with happy sobs, the low benedictory murmur of the Rector's voice, the ordered evolutions of the eight pink bridesmaids and the eight black ushers: all these sights, sounds and sensations, so familiar in themselves, so unutterably strange and meaningless in his new relation to them, were confusedly mingled in his brain.

'My God,' he thought, '*have* I got the ring?' – and once more he went through the bridegroom's convulsive gesture.

Then, in a moment, May was beside him, such radiance streaming from her that it sent a faint warmth through his numbness, and he straightened himself and smiled into her eyes.

'Dearly beloved, we are gathered together here,' the Rector began ...

The ring was on her hand, the Bishop's benediction had been given, the bridesmaids were a-poise to resume their place in the procession, and the organ was showing preliminary symptoms of breaking out into the Mendelssohn March, without which no newly-wedded couple had ever emerged upon New York.

'Your arm – *I say, give her your arm!*' young Newland nervously hissed; and once more Archer became aware of having been adrift far off in the unknown. What was it that had sent him there? he wondered. Perhaps the glimpse, among the anonymous spectators in the transept, of a dark coil of hair under a hat which, a moment later, revealed itself as belonging to an unknown lady with a long nose, so laughably unlike the person whose image she had evoked that he asked himself if he were becoming subject to hallucinations.

And now he and his wife were pacing slowly down the nave, carried forward on the light Mendelssohn ripples, the spring day beckoning to them through widely opened doors, and Mrs Welland's chestnuts, with big white favours on their frontlets, curveting and showing off at the far end of the canvas tunnel.

The footman, who had a still bigger white favour on his lapel, wrapped May's white cloak about her, and Archer jumped into the brougham at her side. She turned to him with a triumphant smile and their hands clasped under her veil.

'Darling!' Archer said – and suddenly the same black abyss yawned before him and he felt himself sinking into it, deeper and deeper, while his voice rambled on smoothly and cheerfully: 'Yes, of course I thought I'd lost the ring; no wedding would be complete if the poor devil of a bridegroom didn't go through that. But you *did* keep me waiting, you know! I had time to think of every horror that might possibly happen.'

She surprised him by turning, in full Fifth Avenue, and

flinging her arms about his neck. 'But none ever *can* happen now, can it, Newland, as long as we two are together?'

Every detail of the day had been so carefully thought out that the young couple, after the wedding-breakfast, had ample time to put on their travelling-clothes, descend the wide Mingott stairs between laughing bridesmaids and weeping parents, and get into the brougham under the traditional shower of rice and satin slippers; and there was still half an hour left in which to drive to the station, buy the last weeklies at the bookstall with the air of seasoned travellers, and settle themselves in the reserved compartment in which May's maid had already placed her dove-coloured travelling-cloak and glaringly new dressing-bag from London.

The old du Lac aunts at Rhinebeck had put their house at the disposal of the bridal couple, with a readiness inspired by the prospect of spending a week in New York with Mrs Archer; and Archer, glad to escape the usual 'bridal suite' in a Philadelphia or Baltimore hotel, had accepted with an equal alacrity.

May was enchanted at the idea of going to the country, and childishly amused at the vain efforts of the eight bridesmaids to discover where their mysterious retreat was situated. It was thought 'very English' to have a country-house lent to one, and the fact gave a last touch of distinction to what was generally conceded to be the most brilliant wedding of the year; but where the house was no one was permitted to know, except the parents of bride and groom, who, when taxed with the knowledge, pursed their lips and said mysteriously: 'Ah, they didn't tell us—' which was manifestly true, since there was no need to.

Once they were settled in their compartment, and the train, shaking off the endless wooden suburbs, had pushed out into the pale landscape of spring, talk became easier than

Archer had expected. May was still, in look and tone, the simple girl of yesterday, eager to compare notes with him as to the incidents of the wedding, and discussing them as impartially as a bridesmaid talking it all over with an usher. At first Archer had fancied that this detachment was the disguise of an inward tremor; but her clear eyes revealed only the most tranquil unawareness. She was alone for the first time with her husband; but her husband was only the charming comrade of yesterday. There was no one whom she liked as much, no one whom she trusted as completely, and the culminating 'lark' of the whole delightful adventure of engagement and marriage was to be off with him alone on a journey, like a grown-up person, like a 'married woman', in fact.

It was wonderful that – as he had learned in the Mission garden at St Augustine – such depths of feeling could coexist with such absence of imagination. But he remembered how, even then, she had surprised him by dropping back to inexpressive girlishness as soon as her conscience had been eased of its burden; and he saw that she would probably go through life dealing to the best of her ability with each experience as it came, but never anticipating any by so much as a stolen glance.

Perhaps that faculty of unawareness was what gave her eyes their transparency, and her face the look of representing a type rather than a person; as if she might have been chosen to pose for a Civic Virtue or a Greek goddess. The blood that ran so close to her fair skin might have been a preserving fluid rather than a ravaging element; yet her look of indestructible youthfulness made her seem neither hard nor dull, but only primitive and pure. In the thick of this meditation Archer suddenly felt himself looking at her with the startled gaze of a stranger, and plunged into a reminiscence of the wedding-breakfast and of Granny Mingott's immense and triumphant pervasion of it.

May settled down to frank enjoyment of the subject. 'I was surprised, though – weren't you? – that aunt Medora came after all. Ellen wrote that they were neither of them well enough to take the journey; I do wish it had been she who had recovered! Did you see the exquisite old lace she sent me?'

He had known that the moment must come sooner or later, but he had somewhat imagined that by force of willing he might hold it at bay.

'Yes – I – no: it was beautiful,' he said, looking at her blindly, and wondering if, whenever he heard those two syllables, all his carefully built-up world would tumble about him like a house of cards.

'Aren't you tired? It will be good to have some tea when we arrive – I'm sure the aunts have got everything beautifully ready,' he rattled on, taking her hand in his; and her mind rushed away instantly to the magnificent tea and coffee service of Baltimore silver which the Beauforts had sent, and which 'went' so perfectly with uncle Lovell Mingott's trays and side-dishes.

In the spring twilight the train stopped at the Rhinebeck station, and they walked along the platform to the waiting carriage.

'Ah, how awfully kind of the van der Luydens – they've sent their man over from Skuytercliff to meet us,' Archer exclaimed, as a sedate person out of livery approached them and relieved the maid of her bags.

'I'm extremely sorry, sir,' said this emissary, 'that a little accident has occurred at the Miss du Lacs': a leak in the water-tank. It happened yesterday, and Mr van der Luyden, who heard of it this morning, sent a house-maid up by the early train to get the Patroon's house ready. It will be quite comfortable, I think you'll find, sir; and the Miss du Lacs have sent their cook over, so that it will be exactly the same as if you'd been at Rhinebeck.'

Archer stared at the speaker so blankly that he repeated in still more apologetic accents: 'It'll be exactly the same, sir, I do assure you—' and May's eager voice broke out, covering the embarrassed silence: 'The same as Rhinebeck? The Patroon's house? But it will be a hundred thousand times better – won't it, Newland? It's too dear and kind of Mr van der Luyden to have thought of it.'

And as they drove off, with the maid beside the coachman, and their shining bridal bags on the seat before them, she went on excitedly: 'Only fancy, I've never been inside it – have you? The van der Luydens show it to so few people. But they opened it for Ellen, it seems, and she told me what a darling little place it was: she says it's the only house she's seen in America that she could imagine being perfectly happy in.'

'Well – that's what we're going to be, isn't it?' cried her husband gaily; and she answered with her boyish smile: 'Ah, it's just our luck beginning – the wonderful luck we're always going to have together!'

TONI MORRISON

FROM
SULA

OLD PEOPLE WERE dancing with little children. Young boys with their sisters, and the church women who frowned on any bodily expression of joy (except when the hand of God commanded it) tapped their feet. Somebody (the groom's father, everybody said) had poured a whole pint jar of cane liquor into the punch, so even the men who did not sneak out the back door to have a shot, as well as the women who let nothing stronger than Black Draught enter their blood, were tipsy. A small boy stood at the Victrola turning its handle and smiling at the sound of Bert Williams' 'Save a Little Dram for Me.'

Even Helene Wright had mellowed with the cane, waving away apologies for drinks spilled on her rug and paying no attention whatever to the chocolate cake lying on the arm of her red-velvet sofa. The tea roses above her left breast had slipped from the brooch that fastened them and were hanging heads down. When her husband called her attention to the children wrapping themselves into her curtains, she merely smiled and said, 'Oh, let them be.' She was not only a little drunk, she was weary and had been for weeks. Her only child's wedding – the culmination of all she had been, thought or done in this world – had dragged from her energy and stamina even she did not know she possessed. Her house had to be thoroughly cleaned, chickens had to be plucked, cakes and pies made, and for weeks she, her friends and her daughter had been sewing. Now it was all happening and it took only a little cane juice to snap the cords of fatigue and damn the white curtains that she had pinned on the stretcher only the morning before. Once this day was over she would have a lifetime to rattle around in that house and repair the damage.

A real wedding, in a church, with a real reception afterward, was rare among the people of the Bottom. Expensive for one thing, and most newlyweds just went to the courthouse if they were not particular, or had the preacher come in and say a few words if they were. The rest just 'took up' with one another. No invitations were sent. There was no need for that formality. Folks just came, bringing a gift if they had one, none if they didn't. Except for those who worked in valley houses, most of them had never been to a big wedding; they simply assumed it was rather like a funeral except afterward you didn't have to walk all the way out to Beechnut Cemetery.

This wedding offered a special attraction, for the bridegroom was a handsome, well-liked man – the tenor of Mount Zion's Men's Quartet, who had an enviable reputation among the girls and a comfortable one among men. His name was Jude Greene, and with the pick of some eight or ten girls who came regularly to services to hear him sing, he had chosen Nel Wright.

He wasn't really aiming to get married. He was twenty then, and although his job as a waiter at the Hotel Medallion was a blessing to his parents and their seven other children, it wasn't nearly enough to support a wife. He had brought the subject up first on the day the word got out that the town was building a new road, tarmac, that would wind through Medallion on down to the river, where a great new bridge was to be built to connect Medallion to Porter's Landing, the town on the other side. The war over, a fake prosperity was still around. In a state of euphoria, with a hunger for more and more, the council of founders cast its eye toward a future that would certainly include trade from cross-river towns. Towns that needed more than a house raft to get to the merchants of Medallion. Work had already begun on the New River Road (the city had always meant to name it something else, something wonderful, but ten years later when the bridge idea was dropped for a tunnel it was still called the New River Road).

Along with a few other young black men, Jude had gone down to the shack where they were hiring. Three old colored men had already been hired, but not for the road work, just to do the picking up, food bringing and other small errands. These old men were close to feeble, not good for much else, and everybody was pleased they were taken on; still it was a shame to see those white men laughing with the grandfathers but shying away from the young black men who could tear that road up. The men like Jude who could do real work. Jude himself longed more than anybody else to be taken. Not just for the good money, more for the work itself. He wanted to swing the pick or kneel down with the string or shovel the gravel. His arms ached for something heavier than trays, for something dirtier than peelings; his feet wanted the heavy work shoes, not the thin-soled black shoes that the hotel required. More than anything he wanted the camaraderie of the road men: the lunch buckets, the hollering, the body movement that in the end produced something real, something he could point to. 'I built that road,' he could say. How much better sundown would be than the end of a day in the restaurant, where a good day's work was marked by the number of dirty plates and the weight of the garbage bin. 'I built that road.' People would walk over his sweat for years. Perhaps a sledge hammer would come crashing down on his foot, and when people asked him how come he limped, he could say, 'Got that building the New Road.'

It was while he was full of such dreams, his body already feeling the rough work clothes, his hands already curved to the pick handle, that he spoke to Nel about getting married. She seemed receptive but hardly anxious. It was after he stood in lines for six days running and saw the gang boss pick out thin-armed white boys from the Virginia hills and the bull-necked Greeks and Italians and heard over and over, 'Nothing else today. Come back tomorrow,' that he got the message. So it was rage, rage and a determination to take on a man's role anyhow that made him press Nel about settling down. He needed some of his appetites filled, some posture of adulthood recognized, but mostly he wanted someone to care about his hurt, to care very deeply. Deep enough to hold him, deep enough to rock him, deep enough to ask, 'How you feel? You all right? Want some coffee?' And if he were to be a man, that someone could no longer be his mother. He chose the girl who had always been kind, who had never seemed hell-bent to marry, who made the whole venture seem like his idea, his conquest.

The more he thought about marriage, the more attractive it became. Whatever his fortune, whatever the cut of his garment, there would always be the hem – the tuck and fold that hid his raveling edges; a someone sweet, industrious and loyal to shore him up. And in return he would shelter her, love her, grow old with her. Without that someone he was a waiter hanging around a kitchen like a woman. With her he was head of a household pinned to an unsatisfactory job out of necessity. The two of them together would make one Jude.

His fears lest his burst dream of road building discourage her were never realized. Nel's indifference to his hints about marriage disappeared altogether when she discovered his pain. Jude could see himself taking shape in her eyes. She actually wanted to help, to soothe, and was it true what Ajax said in the Time and a Half Pool Hall? That 'all they want, man, is they own misery. Ax em to die for you and they yours for life.'

Whether he was accurate in general, Ajax was right about Nel. Except for an occasional leadership role with Sula, she had no aggression. Her parents had succeeded in rubbing down to a dull glow any sparkle or splutter she had. Only with Sula did that quality have free reign, but their friendship was so close, they themselves had difficulty distinguishing one's thoughts from the other's. During all of her girlhood the only respite Nel had had from her stern and undemonstrative parents was Sula. When Jude began to hover around, she was flattered – all the girls liked him – and Sula made the enjoyment of his attentions keener simply because she seemed always to want Nel to shine. They never quarreled, those two, the way some girlfriends did over boys, or competed against each other for them. In those days a compliment to one was a compliment to the other, and cruelty to one was a challenge to the other.

Nel's response to Jude's shame and anger selected her away from Sula. And greater than her friendship was this new feeling of being needed by someone who saw her singly. She didn't even know she had a neck until Jude remarked on it, or that her smile was anything but the spreading of her lips until he saw it as a small miracle.

Sula was no less excited about the wedding. She thought it was the perfect thing to do following their graduation from general school. She wanted to be the bridesmaid. No others. And she encouraged Mrs Wright to go all out, even to borrowing Eva's punch bowl. In fact, she handled most of the details very efficiently, capitalizing on the fact that most people were anxious to please her since she had lost her mamma only a few years back and they still remembered the agony in Hannah's face and the blood on Eva's.

So they danced up in the Bottom on the second Saturday in June, danced at the wedding where everybody realized for the first time that except for their magnificent teeth, the deweys would never grow. They had been forty-eight inches tall for years now, and while their size was unusual it was not unheard of. The realization was based on the fact that they remained boys in mind. Mischievous, cunning, private and completely unhousebroken, their games and interests had not changed since Hannah had them all put into the first grade together.

Nel and Jude, who had been the stars all during the wedding, were forgotten finally as the reception melted into a dance, a feed, a gossip session, a playground and a love nest. For the first time that day they relaxed and looked at each other, and liked what they saw. They began to dance, pressed in among the others, and each one turned his thoughts to the night that was coming on fast. They had taken a housekeeping room with one of Jude's aunts (over the protest of Mrs Wright, who had rooms to spare, but Nel didn't want to make love to her husband in her mother's house) and were getting restless to go there.

As if reading her thoughts, Jude leaned down and whispered, 'Me too.' Nel smiled and rested her cheek on his shoulder. The veil she wore was too heavy to allow her to feel the core of the kiss he pressed on her head. When she raised her eyes to him for one more look of reassurance, she saw through the open door a slim figure in blue, gliding, with just a hint of a strut, down the path toward the road. One hand was pressed to the head to hold down the large hat against the warm June breeze. Even from the rear Nel could tell that it was Sula and that she was smiling; that something deep down in that litheness was amused.

JOY WILLIAMS

THE WEDDING

ELIZABETH ALWAYS WANTED to read fables to her little girl but the child only wanted to hear the story about the little bird who thought a steam shovel was its mother. They would often argue about this. Elizabeth was sick of the story. She particularly disliked the part where the baby bird said, 'You are not my mother, you are a *snort*, I want to get out of here!' At night, at the child's bedtime, Sam would often hear them complaining bitterly to each other. He would preheat the broiler for dinner and freshen his drink and go out and sit on the picnic table. In a little while, the screen door would slam and Elizabeth would come out, shaking her head. The child had frustrated her again. The child would not go to sleep. She was upstairs, wandering around, making 'cotton candy' in her bone-china bunny mug. 'Cotton candy' was Kleenex sogged in water. Sometimes Elizabeth would tell Sam the story that she had prepared for the child. The people in Elizabeth's fables were always looking for truth or happiness and they were always being given mirrors or lumps of coal. Elizabeth's stories were inhabited by wolves and cart horses and solipsists.

'Please relax,' Sam would say.

'Sam,' the child called, 'have some of my cotton candy. It's delicious.'

Elizabeth's child reminded Sam of Hester's little Pearl even though he knew that her father, far from being the 'Prince of the Air,' was a tax accountant. Elizabeth spoke about him occasionally. He had not shared the previous year's refund with her even though they had filed jointly and half of the year's income had been hers. The tax accountant told Elizabeth that she didn't know how to do anything right. Elizabeth, in turn, told her accountant that he was always ejaculating prematurely.

'Sam,' the child called, 'why do you have your hand over your heart?'

'That's my Scotch,' Sam said.

Elizabeth was a nervous young woman. She was nervous because she was not married to Sam. This desire to be married again embarrassed her, but she couldn't help it. Sam was married to someone else. Sam was always married to someone.

Sam and Elizabeth met as people usually meet. Suddenly, there was a deceptive light in the darkness. A light that blackly reminded the lonely of the darkness. They met at the wedding dinner of the daughter of a mutual friend. Delicious food was served and many peculiar toasts were given. Sam liked Elizabeth's aura and she liked his too. They danced. Sam had quite a bit to drink. At one point, he thought he saw a red rabbit in the floral centerpiece. It's true, it was Easter week, but he worried about this. They danced again. Sam danced Elizabeth out of the party and into the parking lot. Sam's car was nondescript and tidy except for a bag of melting groceries.

Elizabeth loved his kisses. On the other hand, when Sam saw Elizabeth's brightly flowered scanty panties, he thought he'd faint with happiness. He was a sentimentalist.

'I love you,' Elizabeth thought she heard him say.

Sam swore that he heard Elizabeth say, 'Life is an eccentric privilege.'

This worried him but not in time.

They began going out together. Elizabeth promised to always take the babysitter home. At first, Elizabeth and Sam attempted to do vile and imaginative things to each other. This culminated one afternoon when Sam spooned a mound of tiramisu between Elizabeth's legs. At first, of course, Elizabeth was nervous. Then she stopped being nervous and began watching Sam's sweating, good-looking shoulders with real apprehension. Simultaneously, they both gave up. This seemed a good sign. The battle is always between the pleasure principle and the reality principle, is it not? Imagination is not what it's cracked up to be. Sam decided to forget the petty, bourgeois rite of eating food out of another's orifices for a while. He decided to just love Elizabeth instead.

'Did you know that Charles Dickens wanted to marry Little Red Riding Hood?'

'What!' Sam exclaimed, appalled.

'Well, as a child he wanted to marry her,' Elizabeth said.

'Oh,' Sam said, relieved.

Elizabeth had a house and her little girl. Sam had a house and a car and a Noank sloop. The houses were thirteen hundred miles apart. They spent the winter in Elizabeth's house in the South and they drove up to Sam's house for the summer. The trip took two and a half days. They had done it twice now. It seemed about the same each time. They bought peaches and cigarettes and fireworks. The child would often sit on the floor in the front seat and talk into the air-conditioning vent.

'Emergency,' she'd say. 'Come in, please.'

*   *   *

On the most recent trip, Sam had called his lawyer from a Hot Shoppe on the New Jersey Turnpike. The lawyer told him that Sam's divorce had become final that morning. This had been Sam's third marriage. He and Annie had seemed very compatible. They tended to each other realistically, with affection and common sense. Then Annie decided to go back to school. She became interested in animal behaviorism. Books accumulated. She was never at home. She was always on field trips, in thickets or on beaches, or visiting some ornithologist in Barnstable.

'Annie, Annie,' Sam had pleaded. 'Let's have some people over for drinks. Let's prune the apple tree. Let's bake the orange cake you always made for my birthday.'

'I have never made an orange cake in my life,' Annie said.

'Annie,' Sam said, 'don't they have courses in seventeenth-century romantic verse or something?'

'You drink too much,' Annie said. 'You get quarrelsome every night at nine. Your behavior patterns are severely limited.'

Sam clutched his head with his hands.

'Plus you are reducing my ability to respond to meaningful occurrences, Sam.'

Sam poured himself another Scotch. He lit a cigarette. He applied a mustache with a piece of picnic charcoal.

'I am Captain Blood,' he said. 'I want to kiss you.'

'When Errol Flynn died, he had the body of a man of ninety,' Annie said. 'His brain was unrealistic from alcohol.'

She had already packed the toast rack and the pewter and rolled up the Oriental rug.

'I am just taking this one Wanda Landowska recording,' she said. 'That's all I'm taking in the way of records.'

Sam, with his charcoal mustache, sat very straight at his end of the table.

'The variations in our life have ceased to be significant,' Annie said.

Sam's house was on a hill overlooking a cove. The cove was turning into a saltwater marsh. Sam liked marshes but he thought he had bought property on a deepwater cove where he could take his boat in and out. He wished that he were not involved in witnessing his cove turning into a marsh. When he had first bought the place, he was so excited about everything that he had a big dinner party at which he served *soupe de poisson* using only the fish he had caught himself from the cove. He could not, it seems, keep himself from doing this each year. Each year, the *soupe de poisson* did not seem as nice as it had the year before. About a year before Annie left him, she suggested that they should probably stop having that particular dinner party.

When Sam returned to the table in the Hot Shoppe on the New Jersey Turnpike after learning about his divorce, Elizabeth didn't look at him.

'I have been practicing different expressions, none of which seem appropriate,' Elizabeth said.

'Well,' Sam said.

'I might as well be honest,' Elizabeth said.

Sam looked at his toast. He did not feel lean and young and unencumbered.

'In the following sentence, the same word is used in each of the missing spaces, but pronounced differently.' Elizabeth's head was bowed. She was reading off the place mat. 'Don't look at yours now, Sam,' she said, 'the answer's on it.' She slid his place mat off the table, accidentally spilling coffee on his cuff. '*A prominent and —— man came into a restaurant at the height of the rush hour. The waitress was —— to serve him immediately as she had ——.'*

Sam looked at her. She smiled. He looked at the child. The child's eyes were closed and she was hmming. Sam paid the bill. The child went to the bathroom. An hour later, just before the Tappan Zee Bridge, Sam said, *'Notable.'*

'What?' Elizabeth said.

'*Notable.* That's the word that belongs in all three spaces.'

'You looked,' Elizabeth said.

'Goddamn it,' Sam yelled. 'I did not look!'

'I knew this would happen,' Elizabeth said. 'I knew it was going to be like this.'

It is a very hot night. Elizabeth has poison ivy on her wrists. Her wrists are covered with calamine lotion. She has put Saran Wrap over the lotion and secured it with a rubber band. Sam is in love. He smells the wonderfully clean, sun-and-linen smell of Elizabeth and her calamine lotion.

Elizabeth is going to tell a fairy story to the child. Sam tries to convince her that fables are sanctimonious and dully realistic.

'Tell her any one except the "Frog King,"' Sam whispers.

'Why can't I tell her that one?' Elizabeth says. She is worried.

'The toad stands for male sexuality,' Sam whispers.

'Oh, Sam,' she says, 'that's so superficial. That's a very superficial analysis of the animal-bridegroom stories.'

Sam growls, biting her softly on the collarbone.

'Oh, Sam,' she says.

Sam's first wife was very pretty. She had the flattest stomach he had ever seen and very black, very straight hair. He adored her. He was faithful to her. He wrote both their names on the flyleaves of all his books. They went to Europe. They went to Mexico. In Mexico they lived in a grand room in a simple hotel opposite a square. The trees in the square were pruned in the shape of perfect boxes. Each night, hundreds of birds would come home to the trees. Beside the hotel was the shop of a man who made coffins. So many of the coffins seemed small, for children. Sam's wife grew depressed. She lay in bed for most of the day. She pretended she was dying. She wanted Sam to make love to her and pretend that she was dying. She wanted a baby. She was all mixed up.

Sam suggested that it was the ions in the Mexican air that made her depressed. He kept loving her but it became more and more difficult for them both. She continued to retreat into a landscape of chaos and warring feelings.

Her depression became general. They had been married for almost six years but they were still only twenty-four years old. Often they would go to amusement parks. They liked the bumper cars best. The last time they had gone to the amusement park, Sam had broken his wife's hand when he crashed head-on into her bumper car. They could probably have gotten over the incident had they not been so bitterly miserable at the time.

In the middle of the night, the child rushes down the hall and into Elizabeth and Sam's bedroom.

'Sam,' the child cries, 'the baseball game! I'm missing the baseball game.'

'There is no baseball game,' Sam says.

'What's the matter? What's happening!' Elizabeth cries.

'Yes, yes,' the child wails. 'I'm late, I'm missing it.'

'Oh, what is it!' Elizabeth cries.

'She's having an anxiety attack,' Sam says.

The child puts her thumb in her mouth and then takes it out again.

'She's too young for anxiety attacks,' Elizabeth says. 'It's only a dream.' She takes the child back to her room. When she comes back, Sam is sitting up against the pillows, drinking a glass of Scotch.

'Why do you have your hand over your heart?' Elizabeth asks.

'I think it's because it hurts,' Sam says.

Elizabeth is trying to stuff another fable into the child. She is determined this time. Sam has just returned from setting the mooring for his sailboat. He is sprawled in a hot bath, listening to the radio.

Elizabeth says, 'There were two men wrecked on a desert island and one of them pretended he was home while the other admitted—'

'Oh, Mummy,' the child says.

'I know that one,' Sam says from the tub. 'They both died.'

'This is not a primitive story,' Elizabeth says. 'Colorless, anticlimactic endings are typical only of primitive stories.'

Sam pulls his knees up and slides his head underneath the water. The water is really blue. Elizabeth had dyed curtains in the tub and stained the porcelain. Blue is Elizabeth's favorite color. Slowly, Sam's house is turning blue. Sam pulls the plug and gets out of the tub. He towels himself off. He puts on a shirt, a tie and a white summer suit. He laces up his sneakers. He slicks back his soaking hair. He goes into the child's room. The lights are out. Elizabeth and the child are looking at each other in the dark. There are fireflies in the room.

'They come in on her clothes,' Elizabeth says.

'Will you marry me?' Sam asks.

'I'd love to,' she says.

Sam calls his friends up, beginning with Peter, his oldest friend.

'I am getting married,' Sam says.

There is a pause, then Peter finally says, 'Once more the boat departs.'

It is harder to get married than one would think. Sam has forgotten this. For example, what is the tone that should be established for the party? Elizabeth's mother believes that a wedding cake is very necessary. Elizabeth is embarrassed about this.

'I can't think about that, Mother,' she says. She puts her mother and the child in charge of the wedding cake. At the child's suggestion, it has a jam center and a sailboat on it.

Elizabeth and Sam decide to get married at the home of a justice of the peace. Her name is Mrs Custer. Then they will come back to their own house for a party. They invite a lot of people to the party.

'I have taken out *obey*,' Mrs Custer says, 'but I have left in *love* and *cherish*. Some people object to the *obey*.'

'That's all right,' Sam says.

'I could start now,' Mrs Custer says. 'But my husband will be coming home soon. If we wait a few moments, he will be here and then he won't interrupt the ceremony.'

'That's all right,' Sam says.

They stand around. Sam whispers to Elizabeth, 'I should pay this woman a little something, but I left my wallet at home.'

'That's all right,' Elizabeth says.

'Everything's going to be fine,' Sam says.

They get married. They drive home. Everyone has arrived, and some of the guests have brought their children, who run around with Elizabeth's child. One little girl has long red hair and painted green nails.

'I remember you,' the child says. 'You had a kitty. Why didn't you bring your kitty with you?'

'That kitty bought the chops,' the little girl says.

Elizabeth overhears this. 'Oh, my goodness,' she says. She takes her daughter into the bathroom and closes the door.

'There is more than the seeming of things,' she says to the child.

'Oh, Mummy,' the child says, 'I just want my nails green like that girl's.'

'Elizabeth,' Sam calls. 'Please come out. The house is full of people. I'm getting drunk. We've been married for one hour and fifteen minutes.' He closes his eyes and leans his forehead against the door. Miraculously, he enters. The closed door is not locked. The child escapes by the same entrance, happy to be free. Sam kisses Elizabeth by the blue tub. He kisses her beside the sink and before the full-length mirror. He kisses her as they stand pressed against the windowsill. Together, in their animistic embrace, they float out the window and circle the house, gazing down at all those who have not found true love, below.

FRANCINE PROSE

DOG STORIES

SO OFTEN, AT weddings, one kisses and hugs the bride and groom and then stands there dumbstruck, grinning with dread. But today the guests congratulate Christine and John and immediately ask Christine, 'How's your leg?' If Christine's leg didn't hurt, she might almost feel thankful that a dog bit her a few days ago and gave her guests something to say.

Hardly anyone waits for an answer. They can see for themselves that Christine is wearing a bandage but limping only slightly. They rush on with the conversation, asking, 'What happened, exactly?' though nearly all of them live nearby, and nearly all of them know.

By now Christine can tell the story and at the same time scan the lawn to see who has come and who hasn't, to make sure someone is in charge of the champagne and the icy tubs of oysters, and to look for Stevie, her nine-year-old son. Stevie is where she knows he will be – watching the party from the edge, slouched, meditatively chewing his hand. The white tuxedo he picked out himself, at the antique store where Christine bought her thirties lawn dress, hangs on him like a zoot suit.

Many of the wedding guests wear elegant vintage clothes, or costly new ones designed to look vintage: péplums, organza, cabbage roses, white suits, and Panama hats; it is late afternoon, mid-July and unseasonably hot, so that quite a few of the guests look, like the garden, bleached of color and slightly blown. For a moment Christine wishes they'd held the wedding in June, when the irises and the peonies were in bloom; then she remembers it wasn't till May that they made up their minds to get married.

At first she tries to vary the dog-bite story from telling to telling – to keep herself interested, and for John's sake; John has had to listen to this thirty times. But finally she gives up. She says: 'I stopped at a barn sale near Lenox. I was crossing the road. A big black dog, some kind of shepherd-Labrador mix, came charging out of nowhere and sunk its teeth in my leg. I screamed – I think I screamed. A woman came out of a barn and called the dog. It backed off right away.'

Even as she tells it, Christine knows: despite its suddenness, its randomness, the actually getting bitten, it isn't much of a story. It lacks what a good dog story needs, that extra dimension of the undoglike and bizarre. She and John used to have a terrific dog story about their collie, Alexander – a story they told happily for a few years, then got bored with and told reluctantly when party talk turned to dog stories. At some point they had agreed that telling dog stories marked a real conversational low, and from then on they were self-conscious, embarrassed to tell theirs. That was even before Alexander died.

Yet today, as they greet their guests and the talk drifts from Christine's bite to dogs in general, Christine realizes that she now has another dog story. She tells it, she cannot avoid it, and the guests respond with escalating dog stories: dumb dogs, tricky dogs, lucky dogs with windfall inheritances, mean dogs that bite. From time to time John or Christine senses that the other is on the verge of telling the story about Alexander. Although they are both quite willing to hear it, both are relieved when the other holds back. Christine feels that this – thinking of the story and knowing the other is also thinking of it and not telling it – connects them more strongly than the ceremony about to take place.

Perhaps her dog-bite story would be livelier if she added some of the details that, for laziness and other private reasons, she has decided to leave out. She can't talk about the woman, the dog's owner, without hearing an edge of shrill complaint and nasty gossip about how awful strangers can be; your own wedding seems like a peculiar place to be sounding like that.

When the woman got hold of the dog, she had stayed a few feet away, not moving. The dog got quiet instantly.

The woman said, 'You scared of dogs?'

Christine's leg didn't really hurt yet, but her heart was pounding. 'We used to have a dog,' she said.

The woman cut her off. 'They always know when you're scared,' she said. Only then did she drag the dog away. 'Don't move,' she told Christine.

She came back with a bottle of alcohol. It could have been kerosene, yet Christine let her splash it on her leg. The pain made Christine's knees go rubbery. She turned and weaved toward the car. Probably the woman was right to yell after her, 'Hey, you shouldn't drive!'

Nearly all the wedding guests know that Christine is pregnant; it's part of the sympathy her dog-bite story evokes, and why everyone winces when she tells it. Men tend to ask about the dog: What's being done, has it bitten anyone before? The women ask about Stevie. Everyone is relieved to hear that Stevie was home with John. It isn't just his having been spared the sight of his mother being hurt, but that most of the guests have seen Stevie around dogs – any dog except Alexander. He simply turns to stone. It has taken Christine years not to smile apologetically as she pulls Stevie off to the car.

All week the house has been full of visiting friends, teen-agers hired to help out, carpenters converting part of the barn into a studio for Christine. It is her wedding present from John, for which she feels so grateful that she refrains from mentioning that the construction should have been finished weeks ago. And no wonder. All but one of the carpenters were on a perpetual coffee break at her kitchen table, smoking Camels and flirting with the catering girls, though the one the girls liked was the handsome one, Robert, who was never at the table but out working in the barn.

Christine began taking refuge in the studio, watching Robert work. A few days ago, she invited Robert to the wedding. Now she looks for him and sees him standing not far from Stevie.

Putting her weight on her good leg, Christine leans against John. 'Sit down,' he says. 'Take it easy.' He has been saying this since she got pregnant, more often since the bite. But if she greets the guests sitting, she will just have to talk about that. She tells herself that none of it – the adrenaline, the tetanus shot, the pain – has in fact been harmful. She wants desperately to protect the baby, though in the beginning she argued against having it. John said he understood, but she had to realize: Stevie was a baby for so long. It won't be like that again.

No one here has met Stevie's dad, who went back to Phila-delphia when Stevie was fifteen months old. One thing Christine likes about being settled is that she got tired of explaining. Describing how Stevie's dad left right after learn-ing that something was really wrong with Stevie, she was often uncertain how angry or self-righteous or sympathetic to sound.

When Stevie was two she had moved here to the country, found a rented house and a woman to watch him while she supported them, substitute-teaching art. Evenings, she would have long, loud conversations from across the house with Stevie, who couldn't yet sit up. That was when she met John. John has a small construction company; he built the house they live in. When Christine and Stevie moved in, she quit teaching, put Stevie in a special day program in Pittsfield, and was able to paint full time. Stevie loves John, and signs of Christine and John's success are everywhere: the house, the garden, the nail-polish-red Ferrari that Annette, Christine's art dealer, has just this moment driven up from New York.

Annette wears white pedal pushers and an enormous white man's shirt; her leopard high heels sink into the lawn so that pulling them out gives her walk a funny bounce. She plows through a circle surrounding Christine and John, first hugs, then briskly shakes hands with them both, then looks down at Christine's bandage and says, 'I hope they crucified Rin Tin Tin.' Christine wonders how literally Annette means this; she remembers a recent art piece, some sort of ecological statement involving a crucified stuffed coyote.

'The dog's under observation,' says Christine. 'The doctor called the town sheriff—'

'Observation!' Annette says. 'At the end of a loaded gun. Well, I don't know. Why would anyone want a dog? Remember when Wegman's dog got lost and he put up signs on the lampposts and of course the signs got recognized and taken down – they're worth fortunes now.'

'Did he ever find the dog?' John asks.

'Of course not,' says Annette.

'That's fabulous,' says John. Christine has often noticed how quickly Annette makes people sound like her, use her words – even John, who likes Annette, but not for the reasons Annette thinks. He isn't fooled by her asking him for business advice; he knows she has a perfectly good, high-powered accountant of her own.

Annette wedges herself between John and Christine, leans toward Christine, and says, 'Let's see the new studio.'

But John and Christine are watching a tall man with Donahue-platinum hair bounding toward them across the lawn. It's the minister, Hal Koch. 'Like in the cola,' he said when they went to see him in his study; Christine thought he must say that often, a good man guiding strangers in their choice between a soda and a dirty word. She'd wanted to go to a justice of the peace, elope without leaving town. But John wants something more formal, guests and God as witnesses that now she is really his. John has a religious streak, inherited no doubt from his mother, a wraith-like woman in an orange dress and wooden yoga beads, now edging timidly toward Stevie.

Without even registering Annette, Hal Koch shakes hands with John, then Christine. He says, 'Terrific place!' Within a few seconds he is questioning John about construction costs. John answers patiently, though Christine can tell it is driving him mad; it is a measure of his sweetness and patience that he will not even let himself catch her eye. In fact, she likes it that this sort of talk can take place, that people know John, respect him, know what to say. Christine had been grateful for this in Hal Koch's study, because John and the minister kept quietly talking about John's business while Stevie was switching the overhead light on and off as fast as he could.

When Stevie finally stopped, Hal had said, 'He's a beautiful kid.'

'I've learned a lot from him,' John said. 'I feel like I'm privileged to know him.'

This is how John stands up for Stevie, by telling the truth:

there is more to Stevie than anyone suspects. But there is also the way John says 'know him' and a funny thing he does with his eyes; she has seen him do it so many times and never has figured out how exactly he tells people without a word that Stevie isn't his. Everyone seems to catch on, even Hal Koch, who redirected his compliment to Christine. It isn't that John is disowning Stevie, distancing himself beyond ill luck or faulty genes. He just wants extra credit. And really, he deserves it. People who admire John for taking on Stevie can't imagine what it's meant. It's partly why this wedding – why John and Christine's life – makes the guests feel so good that a little dog bite can't touch it.

John and Christine and the minister walk over to the rose arbor. Everyone gathers round. The guests have nearly fallen silent when John holds up his hand and walks over and gets Stevie and pulls him under the arbor with them. He leans Stevie back against his stomach and joins his arms in a V down Stevie's chest. Stevie looks pleased. A wave of emotion rises up from the guests, a tide of pleasure and sympathy. And suddenly Christine hates them. It's not that she doesn't value their kindness but that she will scream if one more person, however genuinely, wishes her well.

Of course her nerves are raw: three months pregnant, the heat, the nonstop achy drumbeat of blood in her leg – and on top of that, getting married. She is glad that the service is short, the bare-bones civil ceremony, glad that it all goes by very fast and in a kind of fog. In his study, Hal Koch had asked if they wanted a prayer or a poem – he said lots of couples chose poems. He put this question to Christine, though the wedding was John's idea. Christine said, 'How about the Twenty-third Psalm?' and there had been a funny moment when the two men fell silent and looked at her until she laughed and said, 'Joke.'

With evening, the perfumy scent of the tall white lilies fills the entire garden. This is the worst time of year. It used to be taken for granted that people go crazy around midsummer night and stay up all night in the grip of unruly dreams and desires. All day the sun gives the world a hallucinatory buckle, and even in the evening, after a shower, heat seems to keep shimmering behind your eyes like the ocean's roll after a voyage. No one could look at the trees and the flowers and not know that this is their peak.

The air is humid and sweet, and the green of the grass is the brightest it has been all day. Christine feels suddenly dizzy. She's sure she can get away with a glass of white wine, but a few of the guests seem less certain, and before they move on to the lemon tarragon chicken and spinach salad, their glances stray accusingly toward her glass. John helps Stevie fill his plate. Christine sees Robert walking across the lawn toward the studio. There is something she wants to tell him: the reason she'd stopped at that barn sale was that they were selling a work sink she knew would be perfect for the studio. Maybe if the sink is still there, Robert could drive by and look at it.

Inside the studio, Robert leans against a sawhorse, slowly smoking a joint. He holds it out to Christine, and though she knows it is madness getting stoned at your wedding, with all its social obligations, and probably terrible for the baby, she takes it, takes a drag. Soon she feels uncomfortable standing, looks around for something to lean on, and nearly backs into the table saw before Robert points and yells, 'Yo!'

'That's all I need,' says Christine. 'A little something to match the dog tooth marks in my leg.'

'It's strange about weddings,' says Robert. 'I've noticed. People tend to get seriously accident-prone. One of my brothers got married with his arm in a sling, and a cousin got married in a neck brace.'

'At the same time?' asks Christine. 'What happened?'

'Different times.' Robert laughs. 'I don't know. My brother was hunting, fell out of a tree. The cousin I think was in a car wreck. How's your leg?'

'Fine,' Christine says, and then for some reason says, 'Really? Really, it hurts.'

Robert says, 'I'll take a look at it for you.' His voice has in it an unmistakable flirty edge, and Christine is pleasantly shocked, not so much by the sexual suggestion – which he can only make because he is younger and working for her and this is her wedding day and nothing can possibly come of it – as by the intimacy of his daring to joke about so serious a subject as her dog bite. In some ways it presumes more, makes some bolder claim than John's unfailing solici-tousness, and, by distracting her, works better to reassure her and dull the pain. She fears that Robert will ask what hap-pened exactly and that she'll get halfway through the story and stop. But what he says is, 'Was that the barn sale out on 7, a couple houses past the Carvel?'

'That's the one,' Christine says.

'I stopped there,' says Robert. 'Believe it or not. They were selling a work sink – big slabs of bluestone, copper fixtures, enormous, you could see it from the road. It will be great for this place. It was only a hundred and twenty-five bucks. If you guys don't want to pay for it, we can call it a wedding present from me. This must have been after you were there. There was no sign of a dog. I'm going back with some friends this week to help load it onto the pickup . . .'

Robert rattles on, clearly worried about spending John's money, and so doesn't see Christine's eyes fill with tears. One thing she'd thought as she stopped at the sale was how good the sink would look in the studio, and the other – she knew this and blamed herself at the moment the dog ran toward her and even thought this was *why* she was getting bitten – was the pleasure of telling Robert she'd found it; they had been talking a lot about sinks. This is another part of the story she's told no one. She feels as if she has been caught in some dreadful O. Henry plot, some 'Gift of the Magi' sort of thing except that couple were newlyweds and in it together and on their way up. The implications of this happening to her and Robert are in every way less simple.

All week, she has been saying that she fears the finishing of the studio because it means she must start working again. But that, she realizes now, isn't the reason at all. She feels as if just telling Robert that she, too, stopped for the sink would add up to more than it is, to some sort of declaration, an irrevocable act – though most likely he would just see it as your ordinary, everyday believe-it-or-not.

'Thank you,' she says. Even this comes out more heartfelt than she'd planned. She is so uncertain of what to say next that she's almost relieved when Annette walks in.

'What a space!' Annette says. 'God, I could fit my whole loft in that corner.'

'Robert built most of it,' Christine says and is instantly sorry. Annette wheels on Robert with that fleeting but intense curiosity – part affected, part sincere – that art-world people seem to have for anyone who actually does anything. As Annette looks at Robert, Christine wishes she'd given her the lightning studio tour, once around and out the door – she might not have even *seen* him. But isn't this what Christine wants, some version of the appreciation she desires when Annette comes to look at her work?

Robert looks directly at Annette and smiles. Annette gives

him her three-second downtown grin, but so good-humoredly and with such invitation that a wave of jealousy, loneliness, and embarrassment overcomes Christine. Why should she feel that way now? She, after all, is the bride. Her being the bride is probably why Robert sees no disloyalty in turning so easily from her to Annette.

'How *are* you?' Annette asks Christine, meaning – it's clear from her tone – the pregnancy, not the bite. She's trying hard to focus, to not let her sudden interest in Robert make her exclude Christine. But she is only making things worse, making Christine feel damaged, out of the running, like some guy with a war wound in a Hemingway novel.

'All right,' Christine says. 'The dog bite didn't help.'

'God,' Annette says. 'I just remembered. That's what happened to Jo-Jo the Dog Boy's mother. She got bitten by a dog when she was pregnant. Remember Jo-Jo the Dog Boy?'

'I sure do,' Robert says. 'Poor guy. The real-life Chewy-Chewbacca.' Both he and Annette seem pleased to have found this bit of trivia knowledge in common.

'Great,' says Christine. 'Thanks a lot. That's just what I need to hear.'

'Chris*tine*,' says Annette. 'No one believes that stuff anymore.'

'What are we talking about?' Robert says. The fact of Christine's pregnancy seems to have just dawned on him. 'Double congratulations!' he says. 'I wondered why you guys would bother getting married after all this time.'

He can't resist looking at Christine's belly. That he feels free to do this – and that he hadn't known, though she'd assumed that everyone knew – reminds Christine of what it's like to be pregnant: a secret for so long, and, even when it is obvious, still a secret – all those secret shifts and movements no one else can feel. When she was pregnant with

123

Stevie, that summer in New York, she used to walk down the street and feel herself skimming over the pavement, encased with Stevie in a bubble, one of those membraned, gelatinous eggs out of Hieronymus Bosch. That is how she feels now, that this bubble containing her and the child is hovering slightly above the studio floor, rising toward the window, then floating down again, near enough to see Robert and Annette moving closer by millimeters. Suddenly she is stung with envy, though not of Robert and Annette or their lives – which, she tells herself, lack everything she treasures most about her own life. She feels that her life is closing down; it has always been closed down.

It takes a while for the audio to come back. When it does, Annette is saying, 'People say dogs are smart. It's something people say. People who never had dogs. I say, compared to what? Cats? In my experience dogs are very, very dumb. When I was growing up in Anchorage, the family across from us had a dog team they'd let pull the kids down the hill in front of their house, and one day the dogs pulled the sled and three kids right in the path of a snowplow. Brilliant.'

'Jesus,' Robert says. And a moment later, 'You grew up in Anchorage?'

'Some dogs are smart,' says Christine. 'Alexander.'

'Well,' says Annette. 'Alexander. Christine's dog.'

'What kind of dog was he?' Robert asks.

'A romantic,' Annette says.

Robert looks quizzically at Christine. And now there is no way for Christine not to say it, not to tell the story she has been thinking about all day: 'Alexander fell in love. With a female collie down in Sheffield. He met her when we left him there with friends, one weekend we went away. The female lived up the road from our friends. She was in heat when we picked Alexander up, so we took her home with us, but she kept running away. So we brought her back to Sheffield, and the next day Alexander disappeared. He'd never run away before. We thought he was dead. And two days later our friends called to say he'd shown up at the collie family's house.'

'Sheffield's fifteen miles away,' Robert says.

'Fourteen point five,' Christine says. 'We clocked it.' She remembers watching the odometer on John's pickup, proud of their dog and jubilant that he was not only alive but in love. How eager they had been to fuse their lives then; for Stevie to be John's child, Alexander to be Christine's dog. But Alexander was never really – as Annette just called him – Christine's dog. She still misses him, but it is John who took him to the vet when she was down in the city, John who, without ever saying much, has grieved.

She remembers the night they went to get Alexander from the collie family: the family lived in a tiny house, a cabin, the dogs were inside, stuck together, everyone was laughing, jumping out of their way, it was impossible to talk, but even so it seemed wrong to separate them. They left Alexander there until the female went out of heat and he was ready to come home.

Robert and Annette are waiting for more, but Christine has nothing to say. She is sorry she told the story. She thinks she has told it at the wrong time, to the wrong people, for entirely the wrong reasons, and for a moment it seems likely that she will never tell it again. And what good can come from telling a story about a dog that was more capable of passion than its owners may ever be? She gives Annette and Robert a little wave. Then she goes outside.

The light is almost gone. The guests have finished their food and are sitting at the tables, talking quietly. On each table is a lighted candle inside a paper bag. The muted lights are at once festive and unbearably sad. Christine looks around for Stevie, whom – after a scary minute or two – she spots in the field behind the house. She had been searching for the white suit, but Stevie has changed his outfit. He has borrowed someone's black silk jacket with a map of Guam on the back; it comes nearly down to his knees. On his head is a set of stereo headphones, and instead of shoes he wears his winter moon-boots, silver Mylar that catches the light, thick soles that raise him inches off the ground. He is stalking fireflies in the high grass, lifting his legs very high, like a deer.

Christine is watching so intently that she jumps when John comes up beside her. They stand in easy silence for a few moments and then John says, 'It doesn't feel different, does it? Being married? It feels exactly the same.'

At first Christine doesn't answer, but keeps on watching Stevie, who is moving his head oddly, again like a deer, as if he is tracking fireflies, not by looking for light, but by listening. Several doctors told them that Stevie is partly deaf. Each time, Christine and John sat in the office, nodding, thinking about the fact that often, when they were home alone with Stevie, he would stand and go to the door, minutes before it was possible to hear John's truck or Christine's car in the driveway. John used to say it was something Stevie had picked up from Alexander.

John's face, in silhouette, strains forward. Staring across the dark lawn, he is trying very deliberately not to seem as if he is waiting for her to reply.

'It's fine,' Christine tells him. 'Nothing's changed. We've always been married,' she says.

ALICE McDERMOTT

FROM
AT WEDDINGS
AND WAKES

MAY'S WEDDING TOOK place on the last Saturday morning of July at 10 a.m., when the streets had not yet dried and the summer sunlight still seemed fresh and weightless in the thick green leaves of the trees. The wedding party arrived in two cars. May and Lucy and their brother John were in the first (May's arm in its pale white sleeve held to the window throughout the ride as she gripped the plush strap), Momma and Veronica and Agnes in the second, with the three children perched carefully on the jump seats. The girls wore their Easter dresses, the boy his navy-blue Confirmation suit that was already too short in the sleeves. On the floor of their bedrooms at home there were opened suitcases packed with summer clothes and in the front hallway two cardboard boxes filled with newly ironed sheets and towels that had hung in the sun all of yesterday afternoon, and the fresh sense of adventure and change, of meticulous preparedness, that the sight and the smell of these things had given them when they woke and dressed and followed their mother out the front door was with them still: glorious, miraculous, timeless day on the edge of the year's best journey – their first wedding.

The sunlight through the limousine windows fell at intervals upon the three women's clothes and hands and gave some new, clearer quality to each face as it was turned to the passing streets. Had May been here she would have been watching the children, gauging their delight in this elegant backwards ride, but Momma and Veronica and Agnes only smiled at them occasionally and then looked on ahead. There was a sense that they were anticipating, looking out for, not only the approach of the church but of the very hour that had for so long been expected. With their bottoms on the narrow seats, their fingers wrapped under the lip of each as if they feared it might at any minute spring closed on them, the children, too, were aware only of the hour they were headed toward; the streets they passed were indistinct shades of sunlight and shadow and sound, too distant from their own joy to be real.

When the car glided to a stop, Aunt Agnes held out a gloved hand and said, 'Wait. The bride first.' They waited and, looking over their shoulders, saw the chauffeur from the first car open the door and reach in to help Aunt May out. She wore a slim, off-white suit and a hat with a small veil and she stumbled a little as she stepped away from the car to look up at the church, the chauffeur turning just in time to catch her shoulder and her wrist and then, with astounding, bent-kneed alacrity, the small bridal bouquet that suddenly flew up out of her hand. He caught the bouquet against his heart and stood laughing with it, Aunt May laughing, too, and touching his arm, until their mother began to step out and he moved to help her. Once on the sidewalk their mother touched Aunt May's shoulder and both women looked down at the turned ankle and the uneven concrete and Aunt May's low white heels. Then Uncle John stepped out and their own chauffeur opened the limousine's door.

The church was the same one their mother had been married in and so they knew they had been to it any number of times before, but their having arrived at it in such a manner and on such a day made it seem utterly transformed. The girls placed their hands into the wide dry palm of the chauffeur and then stood on the sidewalk with Momma and Aunt Veronica as Agnes went forward to give some last-minute instructions to their mother and the bride. Uncle John held out his elbow and Aunt May slipped her hand beneath it, looked at the sky or at the church steeple and then began to go toward the steps. At the last minute she turned and smiled at the children and then waved with her bouquet that they should come along, as if the day was a gift from her to them, after all.

Their mother followed and then Aunt Agnes turned to move them all forward.

Inside the dark vestibule they noticed first that May and their mother had disappeared and then, with such a shock of recognition that the younger girl shouted a happy 'Hey!' that echoed into the sacristy (and drew a cautious look from both Uncle John and Agnes), their father grinning at them from the doorway. He held out both his arms and the two girls walked with him down the long aisle and through a garden of smiling, nodding faces. Their brother trailed behind them and at the last minute their father paused and indicated that he should step into the pew first so the girls could be on the end, 'to see better,' he whispered. And then he put his fingers to his lips and turned back down the aisle. Dutifully, and with the sound of his footsteps still echoing through the church, the children knelt and blessed themselves and said a quick and formless prayer before sliding back into their seats. Now, as if on a draught, the smell of the place came to them, the smell of snuffed candles and old incense, fresh roses and cold stone. The altar cloth was pure white trimmed with gold and on it was the same arrangement of baby's breath and white roses that had been placed on the coffee table at Momma's place this morning, although this morning the flowers were the last thing they noticed, given how the living room when they climbed the stairs (the key thrown out on this day by Momma herself) was filled with Agnes and Veronica in lovely clothes and Uncle John in his suit and a woman and a teenaged girl and boy whom, no one ever acknowledged, they had never met before.

Their father brought Aunt Veronica to the pew behind them and as she knelt to say her prayer at their back they were aware of the sweet, peppermint smell of her breath. 'You all look so lovely,' she whispered into their hair and then placed her gloved hand on the back of their bench and raised herself into her seat. Aunt Agnes came next. She wore a linen suit of deep rose and her dark, boldly graying hair was pulled back under a small rose hat. Coming down the aisle on their father's arm she nodded from side to side, acknowledging, it seemed to them, not only friends and acquaintances and relatives (Uncle John's wife, Aunt Arlene, and her two children among them) but all the time and effort and care she herself had given the day. She stepped into the pew with Veronica, briefly whispered something to their father, who nodded eagerly and said, 'All right,' told the staring children, 'Eyes front,' and then, with what seemed an imperceptible tilt of her head, brought the white-robed priest and his two altar boys and even, they suspected, the unseen organist to some kind of attention.

Momma came now on their father's arm in a dress of gray-blue lace, a large, pink, trembling orchid pinned to her shoulder. Her white hair had been curled and brushed out softly from her face and the lace cap she wore was set at what seemed a jaunty angle. She was smiling her thin smile and her eyes shone as deep and as black as ever. Her shoes were black, too, brand-new and shiny but still the same heavy lace-ups she wore at home. The children felt somewhat relieved by this, relieved that she had not, like May, appeared this morning in delicate heels. Theirs might have become another family altogether if amid this summer-morning sight of Uncle John and his smiling wife and near-grown children, of Aunt May wearing makeup and Veronica stepping into the sun, bending into a luxurious car, Momma had appeared in a young woman's shoes.

She did not kneel, only sat, broad and erect, on the seat in front of them. When he saw she was settled, their father went to the altar rail and, with an expertise that the two girls took as one more wonderful indication of the depth of his experience, began suddenly to unroll the white carpet down the length of the stone aisle. The priest and the altar boys stepped to the front of the altar. Fred and another man, who, in the same dark suit and with the same cautious, collar-tugging, elbow-lifting manner, seemed to the children to be his twin, stepped from a room just behind the pale white, life-sized Christ on the cross.

The organ struck a somber note and then, rising, a tempered but optimistic series of chords and all of them began to stand. And then the familiar march, the sound from cartoons and backyard games now played straight and seriously and at a volume that sent goosebumps down from each of the sisters' puffed sleeves. Their mother came first. She was smiling and yet it was easy enough to see that it was not her real smile and that the small bouquet she was carrying trembled.

The children had never seen their mother in such a role – all eyes on her with shoes dyed the same pale lavender color as her dress – and this momentary celebrity made them hope, as she approached on the thin white sheet of carpet, that when she passed them she would wave or wink or even reach out her hand to indicate to all the strangers gathered here that they were hers. The smaller girl stepped up on the soft cushion of the kneeling bench and leaned forward, but her mother with her trembling bouquet and her fixed smile only stared straight ahead, leaving them to recognize the familiar freckles on her bare forearms, the familiar curl of her dark hair as details of a treasure that had once been exclusively their own.

And then came the bride. Aunt May walked carefully beside her brother, her hand in his arm. She had brought the veil of her hat down over her eyes, so that the gold rims of her glasses sparkled behind it. She was smiling slightly, cautiously, it seemed, and the two older children were reminded especially of the way she had looked as a nun, of the delicate and uncertain way she would smile at them before, in some single moment when they were off by themselves, producing a gift from her robes. They saw in her careful smile, her veiled eyes, that same guarded delight: joy held in cupped hands against her heart.

But then as she approached them she looked fully into their faces, just as their mother had failed to do, and her smile became broad, open. She nearly laughed (her shoulders and her breath giving in to it, collapsing for a second as if she would laugh, although she made no sound), and then carried the vision of their young and astonished and much-loved faces across the last few feet she had to go, to the foot of the altar, where she turned to kiss her brother at the altar rail (his taut cheek smelling of alcohol, but bay rum or Bacardi she couldn't tell) and then passed through its gate, where Fred, looking wonderfully neat and dapper, stepped forward and took her arm, putting his bare hand over her gloved one just as she'd hoped he would do, while they climbed the last few steps toward the priest.

The two girls could not deny that they'd been disappointed this morning when Aunt May stepped out of Aunt

Agnes's bedroom and was not wearing a long, lace dress with a train and a thick veil, and were now disappointed again to learn that the priest would not merely get to the heart of the matter, the Do you's and the I do's, but put them all through an entire, interminable High Mass as well. They listened to their brother recite without hesitation the complex Latin of the Confiteor and knelt and stood with the bells. Creeping up the side of the church, their father had joined them from the other side of the pew and he sang each hymn in his familiar tenor. In front of them, Uncle John leaned a little to the right and knelt with a great deal of caution, but also turned to take his mother's arm each time they had to stand.

The Epistle was Saint Paul's, all the empty things he was without love. The Gospel was the Marriage Feast at Cana. When he had finished reading it, the priest kissed the Bible and intoned a solemn 'In the name of the Father ...' He was a stubby, white-haired man with only a trace of a brogue and he had met the groom at Mary Immaculate Hospital, where he had been chaplain in the last years of Fred's mother's life. On the day she died, the priest had just come into the room when Fred, his chair drawn up beside her bed and his hand on her arm, looked up and said, with more peace and resignation than the priest himself knew he could have managed, 'Father, I think she's slipped away.'

All week the priest had wondered if he should refer to this in his sermon today. He recalled it had been Good Friday. He recalled he had said, after the nurses had come in to confirm it, 'Not slipped away, Fred, but risen,' and been impressed once again how even for those with the barest shred of faith (and at the time he counted himself as one of them) Christ's story offered parallel and metaphor and a way for us to speak to one another.

All week long he wondered if he should speak of this now.

Both Fred and May had asked that their parents be named at the Memento and this he would do, but, he wondered, would it be appropriate to say in his sermon, too, that so much of what these two had lost in their parents' deaths had been returned to them in each other? The bride's aunt, the old lady in the front pew who, it occurred to him, was fingering her rosaries as if she were conversing with the Blessed Mother right over his head, not expecting to hear anything of value from him anyway, might take some offense if he were to hint that May had been bereft until now. And the children behind her – look at that moon-faced one in the flowered hat, off in dreamland by the look of it – might be confused by too much talk of death and dying on such a day.

'Our Lord,' he said, settling for some shortened version of the standard, what with the day's approaching heat and the Funeral Mass scheduled at noon, 'began his public ministry at a marriage feast, changing, at his beloved mother's request, plain water into the finest wine. Ahead of him were the three arduous years of his ministry and many more miracles, more spectacular, more breathtaking miracles: the healing of lepers, the casting out of devils, the raising of Lazarus from the dead. Ahead of him in three years' time was the last meal he would share with his disciples, when he would once again raise a cup of wine in love and commemoration, changing it this time into his own precious blood.' He turned to the couple now seated in two high-backed chairs behind him – 'Fred and May' – turned to the congregation again, 'Dear friends in Christ. Each of us has in our future our own last time when we will dine with friends, taste the fruits of the earth for a final time. Each of us has as we leave here today our own arduous way to follow toward death. But it is from such moments as these that we, following our Saviour's example, find the courage to go forward. Love sustains us. Our Lord understood this at Cana. He understood it at the Last Supper. He understands it now as he blesses our difficult way with the gift of love. Love that sustains us as we, each of us, make our inexorable journey toward those final moments. Love that will, through his most precious Blood, bring us life again. Everlasting life in the love of Christ. In the name of the Father . . .'

Uncle John took Momma's elbow as the congregation stood once more but she paid no attention to him, holding the hand with the rosaries tightly against her waist. His wife had proved to be plump and somewhat pretty, a blonde in a shiny pink dress that made a soft satiny pillow of her round belly. She had pale white skin dotted with rouge, bright red lipstick, and a happy, startled look about her big blue eyes. She'd said little this morning, smiling and nodding over her lipstick-stained teacup, adding a cheery 'Yeah, oh yeah' to what seemed to the children to be any conversation that would accept it. Whenever she'd looked at them she'd winked and smiled and wrinkled her eyes. Their father had driven her and her children to the church from Momma's place and tonight when they left Brooklyn the smell of her perfume would still be in his car.

Up on the altar, Aunt May and Uncle John raised their chins and closed their eyes, opening their mouths for Communion. Then the priest walked to their mother and the best man. Uncle John suddenly stood – for a moment the children thought he mistakenly believed it was time to go – stepped out of the pew and then stepped back to help Momma out. He followed her to the altar rail, where mother and son knelt side by side, their broad straight backs so similar that everyone in the congregation who knew it considered the fact that he alone of all of them was her full flesh and blood – as if the spinal cord itself were the vehicle of the entire genetic code.

Momma stood again, pushing off from the rail, and as she briefly faced the children as she walked back to her pew, her face seemed as beautiful and severe as they had ever seen it. 'From such moments as these,' the boy thought, turning the phrase over in his memory, imagining how it would serve him in the future. Uncle John followed his mother, his eyes on his clasped hands.

And then their father was standing in the pew and whispering, Go on, go on, raising the kneeling bench with his instep, and Aunt Agnes behind them was touching the younger girl's shoulder, Go on.

Other people, strangers, were filing out of the pew across from theirs and going to the altar, and as they joined them the children saw how Fred had risen from his kneeling bench and returned to his high-backed chair while Aunt May still knelt, her face in her hands, the clean soles of her new shoes pointing toward them.

They knelt themselves, just as the broad fragrant robes of the priest descended on them, pushing with what seemed a sudden haste the brittle Host onto their tongues. They rose again and, in the confusion of the other wedding guests now standing shoulder to shoulder behind them (Aunt Arlene with her satin-pillow tummy and her two tall children among them), turned this way and that, the two girls nearly walking into each other, before their father held out his arm and showed them the way to go.

It was this confusion and the new energy it inspired, as well as the pale, perfumed breeze set up by the wedding guests as they moved back and forth past their pew, that got the children giggling, poking each other with their elbows as they knelt to place their faces into their palms. Into the blackness of her cupped hands, the older girl let out a single, breathy laugh and received for it as she turned to slide back into her seat a look from Aunt Agnes, shot over her own folded hands as she knelt behind them, that would have melted lead.

Now the remaining wedding guests left the Communion rail and made their way back down the aisle, moving their sealed lips in the mute and unconscious way of Communicants, as if the Host in their mouths had left them struggling with something they could not say. (The boy nudged his sister and then moved his closed lips up and down in imitation of one of them but she felt her aunt's blue eyes on the back of her neck and so only turned away.)

With his hand on his breast and the golden chalice held delicately before him, an altar boy close to his heels, the priest moved swiftly up the bone-pale steps of the altar, where still, still, Aunt May knelt in her post-Communion prayer. Ascending the stair, the priest briefly touched her on the shoulder and she turned her face up to him as she had done to receive Communion. He paused, seemed to pull himself short, and then bent to whisper something to her, Fred all the while sitting alone behind her, his hands on his thighs and his face so sympathetic and confused that, watching him, the best man, unaccountably, felt his heart sink.

She nodded at what the priest said and then briefly bowed her head, blessed herself, and rose into her high-backed chair. In another chair just behind hers their mother quickly leaned forward, flourishing a white tissue. Aunt May took it from her, held it to her eyes and her nose, and then balled it in her hand.

On the altar, the priest was tidying up, finishing off the wine and wiping out the chalice with his sacred cloth. As he began his final prayers the congregation stood, Aunt May and her mailman once more side by side, her arm in its white sleeve brushing his as they all made the sign of the cross beneath the priest's blessing. She turned once more to accept her small bouquet from their mother and then the priest said, in English, 'Well, go ahead, man, give her a kiss,' and the two leaned toward each other. It was not the soft embrace a bride in a white gown would have received from her young husband but a brief, even hasty meeting of lips, his hands on her elbows, hers on his arms, that a long married couple might exchange on the verge of some unexpected parting.

The notes of the organ seemed to build a staircase in the bleached air above their heads and then to topple it over as Aunt May and Fred walked down the steps, through the altar rail, and out over the white carpet to the door. Their mother followed, looking a little more like herself now, except for the fact that she was on the arm of a stranger.

In the dark vestibule where racks of white pamphlets offered help in crisis and comfort in sorrow, rules of church order and brief, inspiring narratives of the lives of the saints, Aunt May stood beside her mailman, a married woman now, and greeted her guests. The doors of the church were open but no light reached her where she stood, smiling and nodding and lifting her cheek to be kissed. She touched the children's faces as they filed by but had no words for them, it seemed, although they heard Fred tell someone in the line behind them, 'Her sister's kids, she's wild about them,' and felt themselves some trepidation that their aunt's careful affection for them had been so boisterously revealed.

Outside, the July sun seemed to cancel even the recollection of the church's cool interior. The heat had descended in the last hour and was rising now in bars of quivering light from asphalt and stone and the roofs of parked cars. Now the brightly dressed wedding guests were milling about, the men squinting into the sun and the women pulling at the fronts of their dresses as if to settle themselves more comfortably into them. Their father passed around a bag of rice. A man beside them shook a handful of it in his fist as if he were about to throw a pair of dice.

Aunt May and her husband stood before the heavy door of the church for a moment as the photographer crouched before them in the sun. Then their mother and the best man were brought in, then the priest, now shed of his white vestments, then Momma and Veronica and Aunt Agnes, who would appear in the photographs to be solemnly preoccupied, looking, it would seem, toward some distant horizon.

Arm in arm, heads bent against the sudden white rain, the wedding party hurried down the steps and through the stone gates and out into the waiting limousine, all the guests trailing behind them, throwing rice, waving and laughing and calling good-bye with such enthusiasm that the younger girl thought for a moment that she had somehow misunderstood the protocol and this was, after all, the last of the bride and the groom that would be seen. As their car drove away she brushed the grains of rice that had stuck to her damp palm and then saw how all the others were doing the same, brushing at palms or suit skirts, shaking caught rice from their hair, quieted now and somehow desolate. There was a crumpled paper tissue in the gutter.

But then Aunt Agnes began giving orders – Johnny, help Momma into the car. Arlene, you'll come with us. Bob, Mr Doran here will follow you. Who else needs directions? – and the children found themselves rushing after their father over the gray, erupting sidewalk, their two new cousins in tow.

It was their father who started the horn-blowing, leaning playfully on his steering wheel as he maneuvered the car into the street and getting the man behind him to do the same. They pulled up in back of the limo that carried Uncle John and his wife as well as Momma and Veronica and Agnes, and even the limo driver, glancing into his rearview mirror, tapped his horn a few times. And then the other guests, pulling out of parking spaces on other streets, began to do the same and the children, excited by the wild cacophony, by the mad hunch of their father's shoulders as he pounded the horn, put their hands to their ears and shouted loud, nonsensical objections, amazed at the volume they and the cars had attained, at the sheer bravura, in this hot sun and after the wedding ceremony's cool solemnity, of the noise they were making, a noise that seemed to defy not only the heat and the lingering holiness but that encroaching sense of desolation as well. Laughing, their hands to their ears, they hoped that Aunt May could hear them from whatever street she was now on.

WEDDING GUESTS

F. SCOTT FITZGERALD

THE BRIDAL PARTY

THERE WAS THE usual insincere little note saying: 'I wanted you to be the first to know.' It was a double shock to Michael, announcing, as it did, both the engagement and the imminent marriage; which, moreover, was to be held, not in New York, decently and far away, but here in Paris under his very nose, if that could be said to extend over the Protestant Episcopal Church of the Holy Trinity, Avenue George-Cinq. The date was two weeks off, early in June.

At first Michael was afraid and his stomach felt hollow. When he left the hotel that morning, the *femme de chambre*, who was in love with his fine, sharp profile and his pleasant buoyancy, scented the hard abstraction that had settled over him. He walked in a daze to his bank, he bought a detective story at Smith's on the Rue de Rivoli, he sympathetically stared for a while at a faded panorama of the battlefields in a tourist-office window and cursed a Greek tout who followed him with a half-displayed packet of innocuous post cards warranted to be very dirty indeed.

But the fear stayed with him, and after a while he recognized it as the fear that now he would never be happy. He had met Caroline Dandy when she was seventeen, possessed her young heart all through her first season in New York, and then lost her, slowly, tragically, uselessly, because he had no money and could make no money; because, with all the energy and good will in the world, he could not find himself; because, loving him still, Caroline had lost faith and begun to see him as something pathetic, futile and shabby, outside the great, shining stream of life toward which she was inevitably drawn.

Since his only support was that she loved him, he leaned weakly on that; the support broke, but still he held on to it and was carried out to sea and washed up on the French coast with its broken pieces still in his hands. He carried them around with him in the form of photographs and packets of correspondence and a liking for a maudlin popular song called 'Among My Souvenirs.' He kept clear of other girls, as if Caroline would somehow know it and reciprocate with a faithful heart. Her note informed him that he had lost her forever.

It was a fine morning. In front of the shops in the Rue de Castiglione, proprietors and patrons were on the sidewalk gazing upward, for the Graf Zeppelin, shining and glorious, symbol of escape and destruction – of escape, if necessary, through destruction – glided in the Paris sky. He heard a woman say in French that it would not her astonish if that commenced to let fall the bombs. Then he heard another voice, full of husky laughter, and the void in his stomach froze. Jerking about, he was face to face with Caroline Dandy and her fiancé.

'Why, Michael! Why, we were wondering where you were. I asked at the Guaranty Trust, and Morgan and Company, and finally sent a note to the National City—'

Why didn't they back away? Why didn't they back right up, walking backward down the Rue de Castiglione, across the Rue de Rivoli, through the Tuileries Gardens, still walking backward as fast as they could till they grew vague and faded out across the river?

'This is Hamilton Rutherford, my fiancé.'

'We've met before.'

'At Pat's, wasn't it?'

'And last spring in the Ritz Bar.'

'Michael, where have you been keeping yourself?'

'Around here.' This agony. Previews of Hamilton Rutherford flashed before his eyes – a quick series of pictures, sentences. He remembered hearing that he had bought a seat in 1920 for a hundred and twenty-five thousand of borrowed money, and just before the break sold it for more than half a million. Not handsome like Michael, but vitally attractive, confident, authoritative, just the right height over Caroline there – Michael had always been too short for Caroline when they danced.

Rutherford was saying: 'No, I'd like it very much if you'd come to the bachelor dinner. I'm taking the Ritz Bar from nine o'clock on. Then right after the wedding there'll be a reception and breakfast at the Hotel George-Cinq.'

'And, Michael, George Packman is giving a party day after tomorrow at Chez Victor, and I want you to be sure and come. And also to tea Friday at Jebby West's; she'd want to have you if she knew where you were. What's your hotel, so we can send you an invitation? You see, the reason we decided to have it over here is because mother has been sick in a nursing home here and the whole clan is in Paris. Then Hamilton's mother's being here too—'

The entire clan; they had always hated him, except her mother; always discouraged his courtship. What a little counter he was in this game of families and money! Under his hat his brow sweated with the humiliation of the fact that for all his misery he was worth just exactly so many invitations. Frantically he began to mumble something about going away.

Then it happened – Caroline saw deep into him, and Michael knew that she saw. She saw through to his profound woundedness, and something quivered inside her, died out along the curve of her mouth and in her eyes. He had moved her. All the unforgettable impulses of first love had surged up once more; their hearts had in some way touched across two feet of Paris sunlight. She took her fiancé's arm suddenly, as if to steady herself with the feel of it.

They parted. Michael walked quickly for a minute; then he stopped, pretending to look in a window, and saw them farther up the street, walking fast into the Place Vendôme, people with much to do.

He had things to do also – he had to get his laundry.

'Nothing will ever be the same again,' he said to himself. 'She will never be happy in her marriage and I will never be happy at all any more.'

The two vivid years of his love for Caroline moved back around him like years in Einstein's physics. Intolerable memories arose – of rides in the Long Island moonlight; of a happy time at Lake Placid with her cheeks so cold there, but warm just underneath the surface; of a despairing afternoon in a little café on Forty-eighth Street in the last sad months when their marriage had come to seem impossible.

'Come in,' he said aloud.

The concierge with a telegram; brusque because Mr Curly's clothes were a little shabby. Mr Curly gave few tips; Mr Curly was obviously a *petit client*.

Michael read the telegram.

'An answer?' the concierge asked.

'No,' said Michael, and then, on an impulse: 'Look.'

'Too bad – too bad,' said the concierge. 'Your grandfather is dead.'

'Not too bad,' said Michael. 'It means that I come into a quarter of a million dollars.'

Too late by a single month; after the first flush of the news

150

his misery was deeper than ever. Lying awake in bed that night, he listened endlessly to the long caravan of a circus moving through the street from one Paris fair to another.

When the last van had rumbled out of hearing and the corners of the furniture were pastel blue with the dawn, he was still thinking of the look in Caroline's eyes that morning – the look that seemed to say: 'Oh, why couldn't you have done something about it? Why couldn't you have been stronger, made me marry you? Don't you see how sad I am?'

Michael's fists clenched.

'Well, I won't give up till the last moment,' he whispered. 'I've had all the bad luck so far, and maybe it's turned at last. One takes what one can get, up to the limit of one's strength, and if I can't have her, at least she'll go into this marriage with some of me in her heart.'

II

Accordingly he went to the party at Chez Victor two days later, upstairs and into the little salon off the bar where the party was to assemble for cocktails. He was early; the only other occupant was a tall lean man of fifty. They spoke.

'You waiting for George Packman's party?'

'Yes. My name's Michael Curly.'

'My name's—'

Michael failed to catch the name. They ordered a drink, and Michael supposed that the bride and groom were having a gay time.

'Too much so,' the other agreed, frowning. 'I don't see how they stand it. We all crossed on the boat together; five days of that crazy life and then two weeks of Paris. You' – he hesitated, smiling faintly – 'you'll excuse me for saying that your generation drinks too much.'

'Not Caroline.'

'No, not Caroline. She seems to take only a cocktail and a glass of champagne, and then she's had enough, thank God. But Hamilton drinks too much and all this crowd of young people drink too much. Do you live in Paris?'

'For the moment,' said Michael.

'I don't like Paris. My wife – that is to say, my ex-wife, Hamilton's mother – lives in Paris.'

'You're Hamilton Rutherford's father?'

'I have that honor. And I'm not denying that I'm proud of what he's done; it was just a general comment.'

'Of course.'

Michael glanced up nervously as four people came in. He felt suddenly that his dinner coat was old and shiny; he had ordered a new one that morning. The people who had come in were rich and at home in their richness with one another – a dark, lovely girl with a hysterical little laugh whom he had met before; two confident men whose jokes referred invariably to last night's scandal and tonight's potentialities, as if they had important rôles in a play that extended indefinitely into the past and the future. When Caroline arrived, Michael had scarcely a moment of her, but it was enough to note that, like all the others, she was strained and tired. She was pale beneath her rouge; there were shadows under her eyes. With a mixture of relief and wounded vanity, he found himself placed far from her and at another table; he needed a moment to adjust himself to his surroundings. This was not like the immature set in which he and Caroline had moved; the men were more than thirty and had an air of sharing the best of this world's good. Next to him was Jebby West, whom he knew; and, on the other side, a jovial man who immediately began to talk to Michael about a stunt for the bachelor dinner: They were going to hire a French girl to appear with an actual baby in her arms, crying: 'Hamilton, you can't desert me now!' The idea seemed stale and unamusing to Michael, but its originator shook with anticipatory laughter.

Farther up the table there was talk of the market – another drop today, the most appreciable since the crash; people were kidding Rutherford about it: 'Too bad, old man. You better not get married, after all.'

Michael asked the man on his left, 'Has he lost a lot?'

'Nobody knows. He's heavily involved, but he's one of the smartest young men in Wall Street. Anyhow, nobody ever tells you the truth.'

It was a champagne dinner from the start, and toward the end it reached a pleasant level of conviviality, but Michael saw that all these people were too weary to be exhilarated by any ordinary stimulant; for weeks they had drunk cocktails before meals like Americans, wines and brandies like Frenchmen, beer like Germans, whisky-and-soda like the English, and as they were no longer in the twenties, this preposterous *mélange*, that was like some gigantic cocktail in a nightmare, served only to make them temporarily less conscious of the mistakes of the night before. Which is to say that it was not really a gay party; what gayety existed was displayed in the few who drank nothing at all.

But Michael was not tired, and the champagne stimulated him and made his misery less acute. He had been away from New York for more than eight months and most of the dance music was unfamiliar to him, but at the first bars of the 'Painted Doll,' to which he and Caroline had moved through so much happiness and despair the previous summer, he crossed to Caroline's table and asked her to dance.

She was lovely in a dress of thin ethereal blue, and the proximity of her crackly yellow hair, of her cool and tender gray eyes, turned his body clumsy and rigid; he stumbled with their first step on the floor. For a moment it seemed that there was nothing to say; he wanted to tell her about his inheritance, but the idea seemed abrupt, unprepared for.

'Michael, it's so nice to be dancing with you again.'

He smiled grimly.

'I'm so happy you came,' she continued. 'I was afraid maybe you'd be silly and stay away. Now we can be just good friends and natural together. Michael, I want you and Hamilton to like each other.'

The engagement was making her stupid; he had never heard her make such a series of obvious remarks before.

'I could kill him without a qualm,' he said pleasantly, 'but he looks like a good man. He's fine. What I want to know is, what happens to people like me who aren't able to forget?'

As he said this he could not prevent his mouth from dropping suddenly, and glancing up, Caroline saw, and her heart quivered violently, as it had the other morning.

'Do you mind so much, Michael?'

'Yes.'

For a second as he said this, in a voice that seemed to have come up from his shoes, they were not dancing; they were simply clinging together. Then she leaned away from him and twisted her mouth into a lovely smile.

'I didn't know what to do at first, Michael. I told Hamilton about you – that I'd cared for you an awful lot – but it didn't worry him, and he was right. Because I'm over you now – yes, I am. And you'll wake up some sunny morning and be over me just like that.'

He shook his head stubbornly.

'Oh, yes. We weren't for each other. I'm pretty flighty, and I need somebody like Hamilton to decide things. It was that more than the question of – of—'

'Of money.' Again he was on the point of telling her what had happened, but again something told him it was not the time.

'Then how do you account for what happened when we met the other day,' he demanded helplessly – 'what happened just now? When we just pour toward each other like we used to – as if we were one person, as if the same blood was flowing through both of us?'

'Oh, don't,' she begged him. 'You mustn't talk like that; everything's decided now. I love Hamilton with all my heart. It's just that I remember certain things in the past and I feel sorry for you – for us – for the way we were.'

Over her shoulder, Michael saw a man come toward them to cut in. In a panic he danced her away, but inevitably the man came on.

'I've got to see you alone, if only for a minute,' Michael said quickly. 'When can I?'

'I'll be at Jebby West's tea tomorrow,' she whispered as a hand fell politely upon Michael's shoulder.

But he did not talk to her at Jebby West's tea. Rutherford stood next to her, and each brought the other into all conversations. They left early. The next morning the wedding cards arrived in the first mail.

Then Michael, grown desperate with pacing up and down his room, determined on a bold stroke; he wrote to Hamilton Rutherford, asking him for a rendezvous the following afternoon. In a short telephone communication Rutherford agreed, but for a day later than Michael had asked. And the wedding was only six days away.

They were to meet in the bar of the Hotel Jena. Michael knew what he would say: 'See here, Rutherford, do you realize the responsibility you're taking in going through with this marriage? Do you realize the harvest of trouble and regret you're sowing in persuading a girl into something contrary to the instincts of her heart?' He would explain that the barrier between Caroline and himself had been an artificial one and was now removed, and demand that the matter be put up to Caroline frankly before it was too late.

Rutherford would be angry, conceivably there would be a scene, but Michael felt that he was fighting for his life now.

He found Rutherford in conversation with an older man, whom Michael had met at several of the wedding parties.

'I saw what happened to most of my friends,' Rutherford was saying, 'and I decided it wasn't going to happen to me. It isn't so difficult; if you take a girl with common sense, and tell her what's what, and do your stuff damn well, and play decently square with her, it's a marriage. If you stand for any nonsense at the beginning, it's one of these arrangements – within five years the man gets out, or else the girl gobbles him up and you have the usual mess.'

'Right!' agreed his companion enthusiastically. 'Hamilton, boy, you're right.'

Michael's blood boiled slowly.

'Doesn't it strike you,' he inquired coldly, 'that your attitude went out of fashion about a hundred years ago?'

'No, it didn't,' said Rutherford pleasantly, but impatiently. 'I'm as modern as anybody. I'd get married in an aeroplane next Saturday if it'd please my girl.'

'I don't mean that way of being modern. You can't take a sensitive woman—'

'Sensitive? Women aren't so darn sensitive. It's fellows like you who are sensitive; it's fellows like you they exploit – all your devotion and kindness and all that. They read a couple of books and see a few pictures because they haven't got anything else to do, and then they say they're finer in grain than you are, and to prove it they take the bit in their teeth and tear off for a fare-you-well – just about as sensitive as a fire horse.'

'Caroline happens to be sensitive,' said Michael in a clipped voice.

At this point the other man got up to go; when the dispute about the check had been settled and they were alone, Rutherford leaned back to Michael as if a question had been asked him.

'Caroline's more than sensitive,' he said. 'She's got sense.'

His combative eyes, meeting Michael's, flickered with a gray light. 'This all sounds pretty crude to you, Mr Curly, but it seems to me that the average man nowadays just asks to be made a monkey of by some woman who doesn't even get any fun out of reducing him to that level. There are darn few men who possess their wives any more, but I am going to be one of them.'

To Michael it seemed time to bring the talk back to the actual situation: 'Do you realize the responsibility you're taking?'

'I certainly do,' interrupted Rutherford. 'I'm not afraid of responsibility. I'll make the decisions – fairly, I hope, but anyhow they'll be final.'

'What if you didn't start right?' said Michael impetuously. 'What if your marriage isn't founded on mutual love?'

'I think I see what you mean,' Rutherford said, still pleasant. 'And since you've brought it up, let me say that if you and Caroline had married, it wouldn't have lasted three years. Do you know what your affair was founded on? On sorrow. You got sorry for each other. Sorrow's a lot of fun for most women and for some men, but it seems to me that a marriage ought to be based on hope.' He looked at his watch and stood up.

'I've got to meet Caroline. Remember, you're coming to the bachelor dinner day after tomorrow.'

Michael felt the moment slipping away. 'Then Caroline's personal feelings don't count with you?' he demanded fiercely.

'Caroline's tired and upset. But she has what she wants, and that's the main thing.'

'Are you referring to yourself?' demanded Michael incredulously.

'Yes.'

'May I ask how long she's wanted you?'

'About two years.' Before Michael could answer, he was gone.

During the next two days Michael floated in an abyss of helplessness. The idea haunted him that he had left something undone that would sever this knot drawn tighter under his eyes. He phoned Caroline, but she insisted that it was physically impossible for her to see him until the day before the wedding, for which day she granted him a tentative rendezvous. Then he went to the bachelor dinner, partly in fear of an evening alone at his hotel, partly from a feeling that by his presence at that function he was somehow nearer to Caroline, keeping her in sight.

The Ritz Bar had been prepared for the occasion by French and American banners and by a great canvas covering one wall, against which the guests were invited to concentrate their proclivities in breaking glasses.

At the first cocktail, taken at the bar, there were many slight spillings from many trembling hands, but later, with the champagne, there was a rising tide of laughter and occasional bursts of song.

Michael was surprised to find what a difference his new dinner coat, his new silk hat, his new, proud linen made in his estimate of himself; he felt less resentment toward all these people for being so rich and assured. For the first time since he had left college he felt rich and assured himself; he felt that he was part of all this, and even entered into the scheme of Johnson, the practical joker, for the appearance of the woman betrayed, now waiting tranquilly in the room across the hall.

'We don't want to go too heavy,' Johnson said, 'because I imagine Ham's had a pretty anxious day already. Did you see Fullman Oil's sixteen points off this morning?'

'Will that matter to him?' Michael asked, trying to keep the interest out of his voice.

'Naturally. He's in heavily; he's always in everything heavily. So far he's had luck; anyhow, up to a month ago.'

The glasses were filled and emptied faster now, and men were shouting at one another across the narrow table. Against the bar a group of ushers was being photographed, and the flash light surged through the room in a stifling cloud.

'Now's the time,' Johnson said. 'You're to stand by the door, remember, and we're both to try and keep her from coming in — just till we get everybody's attention.'

He went on out into the corridor, and Michael waited obediently by the door. Several minutes passed. Then Johnson reappeared with a curious expression on his face.

'There's something funny about this.'

'Isn't the girl there?'

'She's there all right, but there's another woman there, too; and it's nobody we engaged either. She wants to see Hamilton Rutherford, and she looks as if she had something on her mind.'

They went out into the hall. Planted firmly in a chair near the door sat an American girl a little the worse for liquor, but

159

with a determined expression on her face. She looked up at them with a jerk of her head.

'Well, j'tell him?' she demanded. 'The name is Marjorie Collins, and he'll know it. I've come a long way, and I want to see him now and quick, or there's going to be more trouble than you ever saw.' She rose unsteadily to her feet.

'You go in and tell Ham,' whispered Johnson to Michael. 'Maybe he'd better get out. I'll keep her here.'

Back at the table, Michael leaned close to Rutherford's ear and, with a certain grimness, whispered:

'A girl outside named Marjorie Collins says she wants to see you. She looks as if she wanted to make trouble.'

Hamilton Rutherford blinked and his mouth fell ajar; then slowly the lips came together in a straight line and he said in a crisp voice:

'Please keep her there. And send the head barman to me right away.'

Michael spoke to the barman, and then, without returning to the table, asked quietly for his coat and hat. Out in the hall again, he passed Johnson and the girl without speaking and went out into the Rue Cambon. Calling a cab, he gave the address of Caroline's hotel.

His place was beside her now. Not to bring bad news, but simply to be with her when her house of cards came falling around her head.

Rutherford had implied that he was soft – well, he was hard enough not to give up the girl he loved without taking advantage of every chance within the pale of honor. Should she turn away from Rutherford, she would find him there.

She was in; she was surprised when he called, but she was still dressed and would be down immediately. Presently she appeared in a dinner gown, holding two blue telegrams in her hand. They sat down in armchairs in the deserted lobby.

'But, Michael, is the dinner over?'

'I wanted to see you, so I came away.'

'I'm glad.' Her voice was friendly, but matter-of-fact. 'Because I'd just phoned your hotel that I had fittings and rehearsals all day tomorrow. Now we can have our talk after all.'

'You're tired,' he guessed. 'Perhaps I shouldn't have come.'

'No. I was waiting up for Hamilton. Telegrams that may be important. He said he might go on somewhere, and that may mean any hour, so I'm glad I have someone to talk to.'

Michael winced at the impersonality in the last phrase.

'Don't you care when he gets home?'

'Naturally,' she said, laughing, 'but I haven't got much say about it, have I?'

'Why not?'

'I couldn't start by telling him what he could and couldn't do.'

'Why not?'

'He wouldn't stand for it.'

'He seems to want merely a housekeeper,' said Michael ironically.

'Tell me about your plans, Michael,' she asked quickly.

'My plans? I can't see any future after the day after tomorrow. The only real plan I ever had was to love you.'

Their eyes brushed past each other's, and the look he knew so well was staring out at him from hers. Words flowed quickly from his heart:

'Let me tell you just once more how well I've loved you, never wavering for a moment, never thinking of another girl. And now when I think of all the years ahead without you, without any hope, I don't want to live, Caroline darling. I used to dream about our home, our children, about holding you in my arms and touching your face and hands and hair that used to belong to me, and now I just can't wake up.'

Caroline was crying softly. 'Poor Michael – poor Michael.' Her hand reached out and her fingers brushed the lapel of his dinner coat. 'I was so sorry for you the other night. You looked so thin, and as if you needed a new suit and somebody to take care of you.' She sniffled and looked more closely at his coat. 'Why, you've got a new suit! And a new silk hat! Why, Michael, how swell!' She laughed, suddenly cheerful through her tears. 'You must have come into money, Michael; I never saw you so well turned out.'

For a moment, at her reaction, he hated his new clothes.

'I have come into money,' he said. 'My grandfather left me about a quarter of a million dollars.'

'Why, Michael,' she cried, 'how perfectly swell! I can't tell you how glad I am. I've always thought you were the sort of person who ought to have money.'

'Yes, just too late to make a difference.'

The revolving door from the street groaned around and Hamilton Rutherford came into the lobby. His face was flushed, his eyes were restless and impatient.

'Hello, darling; hello, Mr Curly.' He bent and kissed Caroline. 'I broke away for a minute to find out if I had any telegrams. I see you've got them there.' Taking them from her, he remarked to Curly, 'That was an odd business there in the bar, wasn't it? Especially as I understand some of you had a joke fixed up in the same line.' He opened one of the telegrams, closed it and turned to Caroline with the divided expression of a man carrying two things in his head at once.

'A girl I haven't seen for two years turned up,' he said. 'It seemed to be some clumsy form of blackmail, for I haven't and never have had any sort of obligation toward her whatever.'

'What happened?'

'The head barman had a Sûreté Générale man there in ten minutes and it was settled in the hall. The French blackmail laws make ours look like a sweet wish, and I gather they threw a scare into her that she'll remember. But it seems wiser to tell you.'

'Are you implying that I mentioned the matter?' said Michael stiffly.

'No,' Rutherford said slowly. 'No, you were just going to be on hand. And since you're here, I'll tell you some news that will interest you even more.'

He handed Michael one telegram and opened the other.

'This is in code,' Michael said.

'So is this. But I've got to know all the words pretty well this last week. The two of them together mean that I'm due to start life all over.'

Michael saw Caroline's face grow a shade paler, but she sat quiet as a mouse.

'It was a mistake and I stuck to it too long,' continued Rutherford. 'So you see I don't have all the luck, Mr Curly. By the way, they tell me you've come into money.'

'Yes,' said Michael.

'There we are, then.' Rutherford turned to Caroline. 'You understand, darling, that I'm not joking or exaggerating. I've lost almost every cent I had and I'm starting life over.'

Two pairs of eyes were regarding her – Rutherford's non-committal and unrequiring, Michael's hungry, tragic, pleading. In a minute she had raised herself from the chair and with a little cry thrown herself into Hamilton Rutherford's arms.

'Oh, darling,' she cried, 'what does it matter! It's better; I like it better, honestly I do! I want to start that way; I want to! Oh, please don't worry or be sad even for a minute!'

'All right, baby,' said Rutherford. His hand stroked her hair gently for a moment; then he took his arm from around her.

'I promised to join the party for an hour,' he said. 'So I'll say good night, and I want you to go to bed soon and get a good sleep. Good night, Mr Curly. I'm sorry to have let you in for all these financial matters.'

But Michael had already picked up his hat and cane. 'I'll go along with you,' he said.

III

It was such a fine morning. Michael's cutaway hadn't been delivered, so he felt rather uncomfortable passing before the cameras and moving-picture machines in front of the little church on the Avenue George-Cinq.

It was such a clean, new church that it seemed unforgivable not to be dressed properly, and Michael, white and shaky after a sleepless night, decided to stand in the rear. From there he looked at the back of Hamilton Rutherford, and the lacy, filmy back of Caroline, and the fat back of George Packman, which looked unsteady, as if it wanted to lean against the bride and groom.

The ceremony went on for a long time under the gay flags and pennons overhead, under the thick beams of June sunlight slanting down through the tall windows upon the well-dressed people.

As the procession, headed by the bride and groom, started down the aisle, Michael realized with alarm he was just where everyone would dispense with their parade stiffness, become informal and speak to him.

So it turned out. Rutherford and Caroline spoke first to him; Rutherford grim with the strain of being married, and Caroline lovelier than he had ever seen her, floating all softly down through the friends and relatives of her youth, down through the past and forward to the future by the sunlit door.

Michael managed to murmur, 'Beautiful, simply beautiful,' and then other people passed and spoke to him – old Mrs Dandy, straight from her sickbed and looking remarkably well, or carrying it off like the very fine old lady she was; and Rutherford's father and mother, ten years divorced, but walking side by side and looking made for each other and proud. Then all Caroline's sisters and their husbands and her little nephews in Eton suits, and then a long parade, all speaking to Michael because he was still standing paralyzed just at that point where the procession broke.

He wondered what would happen now. Cards had been issued for a reception at the George-Cinq; an expensive enough place, heaven knew. Would Rutherford try to go through with that on top of those disastrous telegrams? Evidently, for the procession outside was streaming up there through the June morning, three by three and four by four. On the corner the long dresses of girls, five abreast, fluttered many-colored in the wind. Girls had become gossamer again, perambulatory flora; such lovely fluttering dresses in the bright noon wind.

Michael needed a drink; he couldn't face that reception line without a drink. Diving into a side doorway of the hotel, he asked for the bar, whither a *chasseur* led him through half a kilometer of new American-looking passages.

But – how did it happen? – the bar was full. There were ten – fifteen men and two – four girls, all from the wedding, all needing a drink. There were cocktails and champagne in the bar; Rutherford's cocktails and champagne, as it turned out, for he had engaged the whole bar and the ballroom and the two great reception rooms and all the stairways leading up and down, and windows looking out over the whole square block of Paris. By and by Michael went and joined the long, slow drift of the receiving line. Through a flowery mist of 'Such a lovely wedding,' 'My dear, you were simply lovely,' 'You're a lucky man, Rutherford' he passed down the line. When Michael came to Caroline, she took a single step forward and kissed him on the lips, but he felt no contact in the kiss; it was unreal and he floated on away from it. Old Mrs Dandy, who had always liked him, held his hand for a minute and thanked him for the flowers he had sent when he heard she was ill.

'I'm so sorry not to have written; you know, we old ladies are grateful for—' The flowers, the fact that she had not written, the wedding – Michael saw that they all had the same relative importance to her now; she had married off five other children and seen two of the marriages go to pieces, and this scene, so poignant, so confusing to Michael, appeared to her simply a familiar charade in which she had played her part before.

A buffet luncheon with champagne was already being served at small tables and there was an orchestra playing in the empty ballroom. Michael sat down with Jebby West; he was still a little embarrassed at not wearing a morning coat, but he perceived now that he was not alone in the omission and felt better. 'Wasn't Caroline divine?' Jebby West said. 'So entirely self-possessed. I asked her this morning if she wasn't a little nervous at stepping off like this. And she said, "Why should I be? I've been after him for two years, and now I'm just happy, that's all."'

'It must be true,' said Michael gloomily.

'What?'

'What you just said.'

He had been stabbed, but, rather to his distress, he did not feel the wound.

He asked Jebby to dance. Out on the floor, Rutherford's father and mother were dancing together.

'It makes me a little sad, that,' she said. 'Those two hadn't met for years; both of them were married again and she divorced again. She went to the station to meet him when he came over for Caroline's wedding, and invited him to stay at her house in the Avenue du Bois with a whole lot of other people, perfectly proper, but he was afraid his wife would hear about it and not like it, so he went to a hotel. Don't you think that's sort of sad?'

An hour or so later Michael realized suddenly that it was afternoon. In one corner of the ballroom an arrangement of screens like a moving-picture stage had been set up and photographers were taking official pictures of the bridal party. The bridal party, still as death and pale as wax under the bright lights, appeared, to the dancers circling the modulated semidarkness of the ballroom, like those jovial or sinister groups that one comes upon in The Old Mill at an amusement park.

After the bridal party had been photographed, there was a group of the ushers; then the bridesmaids, the families, the children. Later, Caroline, active and excited, having long since abandoned the repose implicit in her flowing dress and great bouquet, came and plucked Michael off the floor.

'Now we'll have them take one of just old friends.' Her voice implied that this was best, most intimate of all. 'Come here, Jebby, George – not you, Hamilton; this is just my friends – Sally—'

A little after that, what remained of formality disappeared and the hours flowed easily down the profuse stream of champagne. In the modern fashion, Hamilton Rutherford sat at the table with his arm about an old girl of his and assured his guests, which included not a few bewildered but enthusiastic Europeans, that the party was not nearly at an end; it was to reassemble at Zelli's after midnight. Michael saw Mrs Dandy, not quite over her illness, rise to go and become caught in polite group after group, and he spoke of it to one of her daughters, who thereupon forcibly abducted her mother and called her car. Michael felt very considerate and proud of himself after having done this, and drank much more champagne.

'It's amazing,' George Packman was telling him enthusiastically. 'This show will cost Ham about five thousand dollars, and I understand they'll be just about his last. But did he countermand a bottle of champagne or a flower? Not he! He happens to have it – that young man. Do you know that T. G. Vance offered him a salary of fifty thousand dollars a year ten minutes before the wedding this morning? In another year he'll be back with the millionaires.'

The conversation was interrupted by a plan to carry Rutherford out on communal shoulders – a plan which six of them put into effect, and then stood in the four-o'clock sunshine waving good-by to the bride and groom. But there must have been a mistake somewhere, for five minutes later Michael saw both bride and groom descending the stairway to the reception, each with a glass of champagne held defiantly on high.

'This is our way of doing things,' he thought. 'Generous and fresh and free; a sort of Virginia-plantation hospitality, but at a different pace now, nervous as a ticker tape.'

Standing unself-consciously in the middle of the room to see which was the American ambassador, he realized with a start that he hadn't really thought of Caroline for hours. He looked about him with a sort of alarm, and then he saw her across the room, very bright and young, and radiantly happy. He saw Rutherford near her, looking at her as if he could never look long enough, and as Michael watched them they seemed to recede as he had wished them to do that day in the Rue de Castiglione – recede and fade off into joys and griefs of their own, into the years that would take the toll of Rutherford's fine pride and Caroline's young, moving beauty; fade far away, so that now he could scarcely see them, as if they were shrouded in something as misty as her white, billowing dress.

Michael was cured. The ceremonial function, with its pomp and its revelry, had stood for a sort of initiation into a life where even his regret could not follow them. All the bitterness melted out of him suddenly and the world reconstituted itself out of the youth and happiness that was all around him, profligate as the spring sunshine. He was trying to remember which one of the bridesmaids he had made a date to dine with tonight as he walked forward to bid Hamilton and Caroline Rutherford good-by.

CARSON McCULLERS

FROM
THE MEMBER OF
THE WEDDING

THE WEDDING WAS all wrong, although she could not point out single faults. The house was a neat brick house out near the limits of the small, baked town, and when she first put foot inside, it was as though her eyeballs had been slightly stirred; there were mixed impressions of pink roses, the smell of floor wax, mints and nuts in silver trays. Everybody was lovely to her. Mrs Williams wore a lace dress, and she asked F. Jasmine two times what grade she was in at school. But she asked, also, if she would like to play out on the swing before the wedding, in the tone grown people use when speaking to a child. Mr Williams was nice to her, too. He was a sallow man with folds in his cheeks and the skin beneath his eyes was the grain and color of an old apple core. Mr Williams also asked her what grade she was in at school; in fact, that was the main question asked her at the wedding.

She wanted to speak to her brother and the bride, to talk to them and tell them of her plans, the three of them alone together. But they were never once alone; Jarvis was out checking the car someone was lending for the honeymoon, while Janice dressed in the front bedroom among a crowd of beautiful grown girls. She wandered from one to the other of them, unable to explain. And once Janice put her arms around her, and said she was so glad to have a little sister – and when Janice kissed her, F. Jasmine felt an aching in her throat and could not speak. Jarvis, when she went to find him in the yard, lifted her up in a rough-house way and said:

Frankie the lankie the alaga fankie, the tee-legged toe-legged bow-legged Frankie. And he gave her a dollar.

She stood in the corner of the bride's room, wanting to say: I love the two of you so much and you are the we of me. Please take me with you from the wedding, for we belong to be together. Or even if she could have said: May I trouble you to step into the next room, as I have something to reveal to you and Jarvis? And get the three of them in a room alone together and somehow manage to explain. If only she had written it down on the typewriter in advance, so that she could hand it to them and they would read! But this she had not thought to do, and her tongue was heavy in her mouth and dumb. She could only speak in a voice that shook a little – to ask where was the veil?

'I can feel in the atmosphere a storm is brewing,' said Berenice. 'These two crooked joints can always tell.'

There was no veil except a little veil that came down from the wedding hat, and nobody was wearing fancy clothes. The bride was wearing a daytime suit. The only mercy of it was that she had not worn her wedding dress on the bus, as she had first intended, and found it out in time. She stood in a corner of the bride's room until the piano played the first notes of the wedding march. They were all lovely to her at Winter Hill, except that they called her Frankie and treated her too young. It was so unlike what she had expected, and, as in those June card games, there was, from first to last, the sense of something terribly gone wrong.

'Perk up,' said Berenice. 'I'm planning a big surprise for you. I'm just sitting here planning. Don't you want to know what it is?'

Frances did not answer even by a glance. The wedding was like a dream outside her power, or like a show unmanaged by her in which she was supposed to have no part. The living room was crowded with Winter Hill company, and the bride and her brother stood before the mantelpiece at the end of the room. And seeing them again together was more like singing feeling than a picture that her dizzied eyes could truly see. She watched them with her heart, but all the time she was only thinking: I have not told them and they don't know. And knowing this was heavy as a swallowed stone. And afterward, during the kissing of the bride, refreshments served in the dining room, the stir and party bustle – she hovered close to the two of them, but words would not come. They are not going to take me, she was thinking, and this was the one thought she could not bear.

When Mr Williams brought their bags, she hastened after with her own suitcase. The rest was like some nightmare show in which a wild girl in the audience breaks onto the stage to take upon herself an unplanned part that was never written or meant to be. You are the we of me, her heart was saying, but she could only say aloud: 'Take me!' And they pleaded and begged with her, but she was already in the car. At the last she clung to the steering wheel until her father and somebody else had hauled and dragged her from the car, and even then she could only cry in the dust of the empty road: 'Take me! Take me!' But there was only the wedding company to hear, for the bride and her brother had driven away.

LORRIE MOORE

THANK YOU FOR
HAVING ME

THE DAY FOLLOWING Michael Jackson's death, I was constructing my own memorial for him. I played his videos on YouTube and sat in the kitchen at night, with the iPod light at the table's center the only source of illumination. I listened to 'Man in the Mirror' and 'Ben,' my favorite, even if it was about a killer rat. I tried not to think about its being about a rat, as it was also the name of an old beau, who had e-mailed me from Istanbul upon hearing of Jackson's death. Apparently there was no one in Turkey to talk about it with. 'When I heard the news of MJackson's death I thought of you,' the ex-beau had written, 'and that sweet, loose-limbed dance you used to do to one of his up-tempo numbers.'

I tried to think positively. 'Well, at least Whitney Houston didn't die,' I said to someone on the phone. Every minute that ticked by in life contained very little information, until suddenly it contained too much.

'Mom, what are you doing?' asked my fifteen-year-old daughter, Nickie. 'You look like a crazy lady sitting in the kitchen like this.'

'I'm just listening to some music.'

'But like this?'

'I didn't want to disturb you.'

'You are so totally disturbing me,' she said.

Nickie had lately announced a desire to have her own reality show so that the world could see what she had to put up with.

I pulled out the earbuds. 'What are you wearing tomorrow?'

'Whatever. I mean, does it matter?'

'Uh, no. Not really.' Nickie sauntered out of the room. Of course it did not matter what young people wore: they were already amazing looking, without really knowing it, which was also part of their beauty. I was going to be Nickie's date at the wedding of Maria, her former babysitter, and Nickie was going to be mine. The person who needed to be careful what she wore was me.

It was a wedding in the country, a half-hour drive, and we arrived on time, but somehow we seemed the last ones there. Guests milled about semipurposefully. Maria, an attractive, restless Brazilian, was marrying a local farm boy, for the second time – a second farm boy on a second farm. The previous farm boy she had married, Ian, was present as well. He had been hired to play music, and as the guests floated by with their plastic cups of wine, Ian sat there playing a slow melancholic version of 'I Want You Back.' Except he didn't seem to want her back. He was smiling and nodding at everyone and seemed happy to be part of this send-off. He was the entertainment. He wore a T-shirt that read, THANK YOU FOR HAVING ME. This seemed remarkably sanguine and useful as well as a little beautiful. I wondered how it was done. I myself had never done anything remotely similar. 'Marriage is one long conversation,' wrote Robert Louis Stevenson. Of course, he died when he was forty-four, so he had no idea how long the conversation could really get to be.

'I can't believe you wore that,' Nickie whispered to me in her mauve eyelet sundress.

'I know. It probably was a mistake.' I was wearing a synthetic leopard-print sheath: I admired camouflage. A leopard's markings I'd imagined existed because a leopard's habitat had once been alive with snakes, and blending in was required. Leopards were frightened of snakes and also of chimpanzees, who were in turn frightened of leopards – a standoff between predator and prey, since there was a confusion as to which was which: this was also a theme in the wilds of my closet. Perhaps I had watched too many nature documentaries.

'Maybe you could get Ian some lemonade,' I said to Nickie. I had already grabbed some wine from a passing black plastic tray.

'Yes, maybe I could,' she said and loped across the yard. I watched her broad tan back and her confident gait. She was a gorgeous giantess. I was in awe to have such a daughter. Also in fear as in fearful for my life.

'It's good you and Maria have stayed friends,' I said to Ian. Ian's father, who had one of those embarrassing father-in-law crushes on his son's departing wife, was not taking it so well. One could see him misty-eyed, treading the edge of the property with some iced gin, keeping his eye out for Maria, waiting for her to come out of the house, waiting for an opening, when she might be free of others, so he could rush up and embrace her.

'Yes.' Ian smiled. Ian sighed. And for a fleeting moment everything felt completely fucked up.

And then everything righted itself again. It felt important spiritually to go to weddings: to give balance to the wakes and memorial services. People shouldn't have been set in motion on this planet only to grieve losses. And without weddings there were only funerals. I had seen a soccer mom become a rhododendron with a plaque, next to the soccer field parking lot, as if it had been watching all those matches that had killed her. I had seen a brilliant young student become a creative writing contest, as if it were all that writing that had been the thing to do him in. And I had seen a public defender become a justice fund, as if one paid for fairness with one's very life. I had seen a dozen people become hunks of rock with their names engraved so shockingly perfectly upon the surface it looked as if they had indeed turned to stone, been given a new life the way the moon is given it, through some lighting tricks and a face-like font. I had turned a hundred Rolodex cards around to their blank sides. So let a babysitter become a bride again. Let her marry over and over. So much urgent and lifelike love went rumbling around underground and died there, never got expressed at all, so let some errant inconvenient attraction have its way. There was so little time.

Someone very swanky and tall and in muddy high heels in the grass was now standing in front of Ian, holding a microphone, and singing 'Waters of March' while Ian accompanied. My mind imitated the song by wandering: A stick. A stone. A wad of cow pie. A teary mom's eye.

'There are a bazillion Brazilians here,' said Nickie, arriving with two lemonades.

'What did you expect?' I took one of the lemonades for Ian and put my arm around her.

'I don't know. I only ever met her sister. Just once. The upside is at least I'm not the only one wearing a color.'

We gazed across the long yard of the farmhouse. Maria's sister and her mother were by the rosebushes, having their pictures taken without the bride.

'Maria and her sister both look like their mother.' Her mother and I had met once before, and I now nodded in her direction across the yard. I couldn't tell if she could see me.

Nickie nodded with a slight smirk. 'Their father died in a car crash. So yeah, they don't look like him.'

I swatted her arm. 'Nickie. Sheesh.'

She was silent for a while. 'Do you ever think of Dad?'

'Dad who?'

'Come on.'

'You mean, Dad-eeeeee?'

The weekend her father left – left the house, the town, the country, everything, packing so lightly I believed he would come back – he had said, 'You can raise Nickie by yourself. You'll be good at it.'

And I had said, 'Are you on crack?' And he had replied, continuing to fold a blue twill jacket, 'Yes, a little.'

'Dadder. As in *badder*,' Nickie said now. She sometimes claimed to friends that her father had died, and when she was asked how, she would gaze bereavedly off into the distance and say, 'A really, really serious game of Hangman.' Mothers and their only children of divorce were a skewed family dynamic, if they were families at all. Perhaps they were more like cruddy buddy movies, and the dialogue between them was unrecognizable as filial or parental. It was extraterrestrial. With a streak of dog-walkers-meeting-at-the-park. It contained more sibling banter than it should have. Still, I preferred the whole thing to being a lonely old spinster, the fate I once thought I was most genetically destined for, though I'd worked hard, too hard, to defy and avoid it, when perhaps there it lay ahead of me regardless. If you were alone when you were born, alone when you were dying, *really absolutely* alone when you were dead, why 'learn to be alone' in between? If you had forgotten, it would quickly come back to you. Aloneness was like riding a bike. At gunpoint. With the gun in your own hand. Aloneness was the air in your tires, the wind in your hair. You didn't have to go looking for it with open arms. With open arms, you fell off the bike: I was drinking my wine too quickly.

Maria came out of the house in her beautiful shoulderless wedding dress, which was white as could be.

'What a fantastic costume,' said Nickie archly.

Nickie was both keen observer and enthusiastic participant in the sartorial disguise department, and when she was little there had been much playing of Wedding, fake bridal bouquets made of ragged plastic-handled sponges tossed up into the air and often into the garage basketball hoop, catching there. She was also into Halloween. She would trick-or-treat for UNICEF dressed in a sniper outfit or a suicide bomber outfit replete with vest. Once when she was eight, she went as a dryad, a tree nymph, and when asked at doors what she was, she kept saying, 'A tree-nip.' She had been a haughty trick-or-treater, alert to the failed adult guessing game of it – *you're a what? a vampire?* – so when the neighbors looked confused, she scowled and said reproachfully, 'Have you *never* studied Greek mythology?' Nickie knew how to terrify. She had sometimes been more interested in answering our own door than in knocking on others, peering around the edge of it with a witch hat and a loud cackle. 'I think it's time to get back to the customers,' she announced to me one Halloween when she was five, grabbing my hand and racing back to our house. She was fearless: she had always chosen the peanut allergy table at school since a boy she liked sat there – the cafeteria version of *The Magic Mountain*. Nickie's childhood, like all dreams, sharpened artificially into stray vignettes when I tried to conjure it, then faded away entirely. Now tall and long-limbed and inscrutable, she seemed more than ever like a sniper. I felt paralyzed beside her, and the love I had for her was less for this new spiky Nickie than for the old spiky one, which was still inside her somewhere, though it was a matter of faith to think so. Surely that was why faith had been invented: to raise teenagers without dying. Although of course it was also why death was invented: to escape teenagers altogether. When, in the last few months, Nickie had 'stood her ground' in various rooms of the house, screaming at me abusively, I would begin mutely to disrobe, slowly lifting my shirt over my head so as not to see her, and only that would send her flying out of the room in disgust. Only nakedness was silencing, but at least something was.

'I can't believe Maria's wearing white,' said Nickie.

I shrugged. 'What color should she wear?'

'Gray!' Nickie said immediately. 'To acknowledge having a brain! A little gray matter!'

'Actually, I saw something on PBS recently that said only the outer bark of the brain — and it does look like bark — is gray. Apparently the other half of the brain has a lot of white matter. For connectivity.'

Nickie snorted, as she often did when I uttered the letters *PBS*. 'Then she should wear gray in acknowledgment of having half a brain.'

I nodded. 'I get your point,' I said.

Guests were eating canapés on paper plates and having their pictures taken with the bride. Not so much with Maria's new groom, a boy named Hank, which was short not for Henry but for Johannes, and who was not wearing sunglasses like everyone else but was sort of squinting at Maria in pride and disbelief. Hank was also a musician, though he mostly repaired banjos and guitars, restrung and varnished them, and that was how he, Maria, and Ian had all met.

Now the air was filled with the old-silver-jewelry smell of oncoming rain. I edged toward Ian, who was looking for the next song, idly strumming, trying not to watch his father eye Maria.

'Whatcha got? "I'll Be There"?' I asked cheerfully. I had

always liked Ian. He had chosen Maria like a character, met her on a semester abroad and then come home already married to her – much to the marveling of his dad. Ian loved Maria, and was always loyal to her, no matter what story she was in, but Maria was a narrative girl and the story had to be spellbinding or she lost interest in the main character, who was sometimes herself and sometimes not. She was destined to marry and marry and marry. Ian smiled and began to sing 'I Will Always Love You,' sounding oddly like Bob Dylan but without the sneer.

I swayed. I stayed. I did not get in the way.

'You are a saint,' I said when he finished. He was a sweet boy, and when Nickie was little he had often come over and played soccer in the yard with her and Maria.

'Oh no, I'm just a deposed king of corn. She bought the farm. I mean, I sold it to her, and then she flipped it and bought this one instead.' He motioned toward the endless field beyond the tent, where the corn was midget and standing in mud, June not having been hot enough to evaporate the puddles. The tomatoes and marijuana would not do well this year. 'Last night I had a dream that I was in *West Side Story* and had forgotten all the words to "I like to be in America." Doesn't take a genius to figure that one out.'

'No,' I said. 'I guess not.'

'Jesus, what is my dad *doing*?' Ian said, looking down and away.

Ian's father was still prowling the perimeter, a little drunkenly, not taking his eyes off the bride.

'The older generation,' I said, shaking my head, as if it didn't include me. 'They can't take any change. There's too much missingness that has already accumulated. They can't take any more.'

'Geez,' Ian said, glancing up and over again. 'I wish my dad would just get over her.'

I swallowed more wine while holding Ian's lemonade. Over by the apple tree there were three squirrels. A threesome of squirrels looked ominous, like a plague. 'What other songs ya got?' I asked him. Nickie was off talking to Johannes Hank.

'I have to save a couple for the actual ceremony.'

'There's going to be an actual ceremony?'

'Sort of. Maybe not *actual* actual. They have things they want to recite to each other.'

'Oh yes, that,' I said.

'They're going to walk up together from this canopy toward the house, say whatever, and then people get to eat.' Everyone had brought food, and it was spread out on a long table between the house and the barn. I had brought two large roaster chickens, cooked accidentally on Clean while I was listening to Michael Jackson on my iPod. But the chickens had looked OK, I thought: hanging off the bone a bit but otherwise fine, even if not as fine as when they had started and had been Amish and air-chilled and a fortune. When I had bought them the day before at Whole Foods and gasped at the total on my receipt, the cashier had said, 'Yes. Some people know how to shop here and some people don't.'

'Thirty-three thirty-three. Perhaps that's good luck.'

'Yup. It's about as lucky as two dead birds get to be,' said the cashier.

'Is there a priest or anything? Will the marriage be legal?' I now asked Ian.

Ian smiled and shrugged.

'They're going to say "You do" after the other one says "I do." Double indemnity.'

I put his lemonade down on a nearby table and gave him a soft chuck on the shoulder. We both looked across the yard at Hank, who was wearing a tie made of small yellow pop beads that formed themselves into the shape of an ear of corn. It had ingeniousness and tackiness both, like so much else created by people.

'That's a lot of *dos*.'

'I know. But I'm not making a beeline for the jokes.'

'The jokes?'

'The doozy one, the do-do one. I'm not going to make any of them.'

'Why would you make jokes? It's not like you're the best man.'

Ian looked down and twisted his mouth a little.

'Oh, dear. You *are*?' I said. I squinted at him. When young I had practiced doing the upside-down wink of a bird.

'Don't ask,' he said.

'Hey, look.' I put my arm around him. 'George Harrison did it. And no one thought twice. Or, well, no one thought more than twice.'

Nickie approached me quickly from across the grass. 'Mom. Your chickens look disgusting. It's like they were hit by a truck.'

The wedding party had started to line up – except Ian, who had to play. They were going to get this ceremony over with quickly, before the storm clouds to the west drifted near and made things worse. The bridesmaids began stepping first, a short trajectory from the canopy to the rosebushes, where the *I dos* would be said. Ian played 'Here Comes the Bride.' The bridesmaids were in pastels: one the light peach of baby aspirin; one the seafoam green of low-dose clonazepam; the other the pale daffodil of the next lowest dose of clonazepam. What a good idea to have the look of Big

Pharma at your wedding. Why hadn't I thought of that? Why hadn't I thought of that until now?

'I take thee, dear Maria ...' They were uttering these promises themselves just as Ian said they would. Hank said, 'I do,' and Maria said, 'You do.' Then vice versa. At least Maria had taken off her sunglasses. *Young people*, I tried not to say out loud with a sigh. Time went slowly, then stood still, then became undetectable, so who knew how long all this was taking?

A loud noise like mechanized thunder was coming from the highway. Strangely, it was not a storm. A group of motorcyclists boomed up the road and, instead of roaring by us, slowed, then turned right in at the driveway, a dozen of them – all on Harleys. I didn't really know motorcycles, but I knew that every biker from Platteville to Manitowoc owned a Harley. That was just a regional fact. They switched off their engines. None of the riders wore a helmet – they wore bandannas – except for the leader, who wore a football helmet with some plush puppy ears which had been snipped from some child's stuffed animal then glued on either side. He took out a handgun and fired it three times into the air.

Several guests screamed. I could make no sound at all.

The biker with the gun and the puppy ears began to shout. 'I have a firearms license and those were blanks and this is self-defense because our group here has an easement that extends just this far into this driveway. Also? We were abused as children and as adults and moreover we have been eating a hell of a lot of Twinkies. Also? We are actually very peaceful people. We just know that life can get quite startling in its switches of channels. That there is a river and sea figure of speech as well as a TV one. Which is why as life moves rudely past, you have to give it room. We understand that. An occasion like this means No More Forks in the Road. All mistakes are behind you, and that means it's no longer really possible to make one. Not a big one. You already done that. I need to speak first here to the bride.' He looked around, but no one moved. He cleared his throat a bit. 'The errors a person already made can step forward and announce themselves and then freeze themselves into a charming little sculpture garden that can no longer hurt you. Like a cemetery. And like a cemetery it is the kind of freedom that is the opposite of free.' He looked in a puzzled way across the property toward Maria. 'It's the flickering quantum zone of gun and none, got and not.' He shifted uncomfortably, as if the phrase 'flickering quantum zone' had taken a lot out of him. 'As I said, now I need to speak to the bride. Would that be you?'

Maria shouted at him in Portuguese. Her bridesmaids joined in.

'What are they saying?' I murmured to Nickie.

'I forgot all my Portuguese,' she said. 'My whole childhood I only remember Maria saying "good job" to everything I did, so I now think of that as Portuguese.'

'Yes,' I murmured. 'So do I.'

'Good job!' Nickie shouted belligerently at the biker. 'Good job being an asshole and interrupting a wedding!'

'Nickie, leave this to the grown-ups,' I whispered.

But the guests just stood there, paralyzed, except Ian, who, seemingly very far off on the horizon, slowly stood, placing his guitar on the ground. He then took his white collapsible chair in both hands and raised it over his head.

'Are you Caitlin?' The puppy-eared biker continued to address Maria, and she continued to curse, waving her sprigs of mint and spirea at him. '*Vá embora, babaca!*' She gave him the finger, and when Hank tried to calm her, she gave Hank the finger. '*Fodase!*'

The cyclist looked around with an expression that suggested he believed he might have the wrong country wedding. He took out his cell phone, took off his helmet, pressed someone on speed dial, then turned to speak into it. 'Yo! Joe. I don't think you gave me the right address . . . yeah . . . no, you don't get it. This ain't Caitlin's place. . . . What? No, listen! What I'm saying is: wrong addressee! This ain't it. No speaky zee English here—' He slammed his phone shut. He put his helmet back on. But Ian was trotting slowly toward him with the chair over his head, crying the yelping cry of anyone who was trying to be a hero at his ex-wife's wedding.

'Sorry, people,' the biker said. He gave the approaching Ian only a quick unfazed double-take. He flicked one of his puppy ears at him and hurried to straddle his bike. 'Wrong address, everybody!' Then his whole too-stoned-to-be-menacing gang started up their engines and rode away in a roar, kicking up dust from the driveway gravel. It was a relief to see them go. Ian continued to run down the road after them, howling, chair overhead, though the motorcycles were quickly out of sight.

'Should we follow Ian?' asked Nickie. Someone near us was phoning the police.

'Let Ian get it out of his system,' I said.

'Yeah,' she said and now made a beeline for Maria.

'Good job!' I could hear Nickie say to Maria. 'Good job getting married!' And then Nickie threw her arms around her former caretaker and began, hunched and heaving, to weep on her shoulder. I couldn't bear to watch. There was a big black zigzag across my heart. I could hear Maria say, 'Tank you for combing, Nickie. You and your muzzer are my hairos.'

Ian had not returned and no one had gone looking for him. He would be back in time for the rain. There was a rent-a-disc-jockey who started to put on some music, which blared from the speakers. Michael Jackson again. Every day there was something new to mourn and something old to celebrate: civilization had learned this long ago and continued to remind us. Was that what the biker had meant? I moved toward the buffet table.

'You know, when you're hungry, there's nothing better than food,' I said to a perfect stranger. I cut a small chunk of ham. I place a deviled egg in my mouth and resisted the temptation to position it in front of my teeth and smile scarily, the way we had as children. I chewed and swallowed and grabbed another one. Soon no doubt I would resemble a large vertical snake who had swallowed a rat. That rat Ben. Snakes would eat a sirloin steak only if it was disguised behind the head of a small rodent. There was a lesson somewhere in there and just a little more wine would reveal it.

'Oh, look at those sad chickens!' I said ambiguously and with my mouth full. There were rumors that the wedding cake was still being frosted and that it would take a while. A few people were starting to dance, before the dark clouds burst open and ruined everything. Next to the food table was a smaller one displaying a variety of insect repellents, aerosols and creams, as if it were the vanity corner of a posh ladies' room, except with discrete constellations of gnats. Guests were spraying themselves a little too close to the food, and the smells of citronella and imminent rain combined in the air.

The biker was right: you had to unfreeze your feet, take blind steps backward, risk a loss of balance, risk an endless fall, in order to give life room. Was that what he had said? Who knew? People were shaking their bodies to Michael Jackson's 'Shake Your Body.' I wanted this song played at my funeral. Also the Doobie Brothers' 'Takin' It to the Streets.'

Also 'Have Yourself a Merry Little Christmas' – just to fuck with people.

I put down my paper plate and plastic wineglass. I looked over at Ian's dad, who was once again brooding off by himself. 'Come dance with someone your own age!' I called to him, and because he did not say, 'That is so not going to happen,' I approached him from across the lawn. As I got closer I could see that since the days he would sometimes come to our house to pick up Maria and drive her home himself in the silver sports car of the recently single, he had had some eye work done: a lift to remove the puff and bloat; he would rather look startled and insane than look fifty-six. I grabbed both his hands and reeled him around. 'Whoa,' he said with something like a smile, and he let go with one hand to raise it over his head and flutter it in a jokey jazz razzamatazz. In sign language it was the sign for applause. I needed my breath for dancing, so I tried not to laugh. Instead I fixed my face into a grin, and, ah, for a second the sun came out to light up the side of the red and spinning barn.

KELLY LINK

THE LESSON

THE FIGHT STARTS two days before Thanh and Harper are due to fly out to the wedding. The wedding is on a small private island somewhere off the coast of South Carolina. Or Alabama. The bride is an old friend. The fight is about all sorts of things. Thanh's long-standing resentment of Harper's atrocious work schedule, the discovery by Harper that Thanh, in a fit of industriousness, has thrown away all of Harper's bits and ends of cheese while cleaning out the refrigerator.

The fight is about money. Harper works too much. Thanh is an assistant principal in the Brookline school system. He hasn't had a raise in three years. The fight is about Thanh's relationship with the woman who is, precariously, six months pregnant with Harper and Thanh's longed-for child. Thanh tries once again to explain to Harper. He doesn't even really like Naomi that much. Although he is of course grateful to her. Why be grateful to her? Harper says. We're paying her. She's doing this because we're paying her money. Not because she wants to be friends with us. With you. The thing Thanh doesn't say is that he might actually like Naomi under other circumstances. Let's say, if they were stuck next to each other on a long flight. If they never had to see each other again. If she weren't carrying Harper and Thanh's baby. If she were doing a better job of carrying the baby. They have chosen not to know the gender of the baby.

The point is that liking Naomi isn't the point. The point

is rather that she grow to like – love, even – Thanh and, by association, of course (of course!) Harper. That she sees that they are deserving of love. Surely they are deserving of love. Naomi's goodwill, her friendship, her *affection*, is an insurance policy. They are both afraid, Thanh and Harper, that Naomi will change her mind when the baby is born. Then they will have no baby and no legal recourse and no money to try again.

Anyway the cheese was old. Harper is getting fat. The beard, which Thanh loathes, isn't fooling anyone. Thanh has spent too much money on the wedding present. The plane tickets weren't cheap, either.

Naomi, the surrogate, is on bed rest. Two weeks ago a surgeon put a stitch in her cervix. A cerclage, which almost sounds pretty. How did we end up with a surrogate with an incompetent cervix? says Harper. She's only twenty-seven!

Naomi gets out of bed to use the toilet and every other day she can take a shower. Her fellow graduate students come over and what do you think they talk about when they're not talking about linguistics? Thanh and Harper, probably, and how much Naomi is suffering. Does she confide in her friends? Tell them she thinks about keeping the baby? It was her egg, after all. That was probably a dumb idea.

Thanh keeps a toothbrush at Naomi's apartment. Easier than running upstairs. Their building is full of old Russians with rent-stabilized leases. The women exercise on the treadmills in high heels. They gossip in Russian. Never smile at Thanh when he comes into the exercise room to lift weights or run. They see him go in and out of Naomi's apartment.

Must wonder. Sometimes Thanh works at Naomi's kitchen table. One night he falls asleep on the bed beside her, Naomi telling him something about her childhood, the TV on. Naomi watches episode after episode of *CSI*. All that blood. It can't be good for the baby. When Thanh wakes up, she is watching him. You farted in your sleep, she says. And laughs. What time is it? He checks his phone and sees he has no missed calls. Harper is probably still at work. He doesn't like me very much, Naomi says. He likes you! Thanh says. (He knows who she means.) I mean he doesn't really like people. But he likes you. *Mm,* Naomi says. He'll like the baby, Thanh says. You should hear him talk about preschools, art lessons, he's already thinking about pets. Maybe a gerbil to start with? Or a chameleon. He's already started a college fund. *Mm,* Naomi says again. He's good-looking, she says. I'll give him that. You should have seen him when he was twenty-five, Thanh says. It's all been downhill since then. Hungry? He heats up the pho ga he made upstairs. His mother's recipe. He does the dishes afterward.

He accidentally saw a text on Naomi's phone the other day. To one of her friends. The short one. I AM HORNY ALL THE TIME. They should have used a donor egg. But that would have cost more money, and how much more money is there in the world? Wherever it is, it isn't in Harper and Thanh's bank account. They went through catalogs. IQs, hobbies, genetic histories. It seemed impersonal. Like ordering take-out food from an online menu. Should we have the chicken or the shrimp? Naomi and Harper have thick, curly blond hair, similar chins, mouths, athletic builds. So they decided to use Thanh's sperm. Harper says once, late at night: he thinks it would be harder to love his own child.

Thanh wants to tell Harper about the text. Maybe it would make him laugh. He doesn't. It wouldn't.

Eventually the fight is about the wedding. Should they cancel? Thanh thinks if they leave town now, something terrible will happen ... The baby will come: He can't say this to Harper. That would also be bad for the baby.

At this stage of a pregnancy a fetus's lungs are insufficiently developed. Should Naomi go into labor now, the baby will live or the baby will die. It's fifty-fifty. If the baby lives, the chances are one in five it will be severely disabled. Harper wants to go to the wedding. He won't know anyone there except for Thanh and Fleur, but Harper likes meeting people, especially when he knows he never has to see them again. Harper likes new people. Harper and Thanh have been together now for sixteen years. Married for six. Anyway, when will there be another chance for adventure? The next stage of their life is slouching over the horizon.

Naomi says go. The tickets are nonrefundable. Everything will be fine. Thanh's mother, Han, agrees to fly in from Chicago and stay with Naomi. Han and Naomi have become friends on Facebook. Han doesn't understand anything about Thanh's life, he has understood this for a long time, but she loves him anyway. She loves Naomi, too; because Naomi is carrying her grandchild. Naomi's own mother is not in the picture. Harper's parents are both assholes.

They go to Fleur's wedding.

Fleur was always in charge of parties. Always threw the best parties, the ones that people who have long since moved out to the wealthier suburbs – Newton, Sudbury, Lincoln – still talk about, the parties that took days in darkened rooms to recover from. Fleur was, in her twenties, thrifty, ruthless, psychologically astute. Able to wring maximum fun, maximum exhausting whimsy, out of all gatherings. And now Fleur has not only filthy improvisatory cunning, but money. Who is paying for all of this? Fleur's fiancé David's family owns the island. He does something that Fleur is vague about. Travels. There is family money. His family is in snacks. A van picks up Harper and Thanh, two other couples, and two women from Chula Vista. Friends of Fleur. Fleur moved out to Point Loma a few years ago, which is where she met David doing whatever it is that he does. The women are Marianne and Laura. They say David is nice. Good with his hands. A little scary. They don't really know him. They know Fleur from Bikram yoga. The air-conditioning in the van isn't working. The wedding guests are taken in the van from the tiny regional airport where everyone flew in on tiny, toy-sized prop planes to an equally tiny pier. Everything snack-sized. The boat that goes over to Bad Claw Island has a glass bottom. How cute, Marianne says. The pilot, a black guy with the greenest eyes Thanh has ever seen, is gay. Indisputably gay. Down here the Atlantic is softer. It seems bigger. But maybe that's because everything else is so much smaller. There's a cooler on the boat; in it, individual see-through thermoses filled with something citrusy and alcoholic. In a basket, prepackaged snacks, crackers, and cookies. Fleur spent her twenties as a bartender in various Boston bars. She and Thanh met at ManRay. ManRay has been closed for a long time now. Thousands of years.

Han has sent Thanh a text. Everything is fine. Okay? Fine! Great! She and Naomi are watching Bollywood musicals. Eating Belgian fries. Naomi wants to know all about Thanh and Harper when they were young and dumb. (Not that this is how Han puts it. Nevertheless.) Don't tell her anything, Thanh texts back. I mean it.

Harper is in one of his golden moods. Rare these days. He looks a hundred years younger than this morning when they caught the cab. He solicits information from the two couples. Which side of the wedding party. Where they are coming from. What they do. Everyone here is a friend of Fleur's, but no one has as long and distinguished a claim as Harper and Thanh. Harper, saying he has a bad back, lies down on the glass bottom of the boat. Everyone has to rearrange their feet. No one minds. He tells a story about the time Fleur, inebriated and in a rage, who knows what brought it on, kicked in the front of a jukebox at an Allston bar. The Silhouette. All of those early nineties alt-rock boys in their dirty black jeans. Legs like toothpicks, jeans so tight they could hardly bend their knees when they sat down. Thanh used to marvel at their barely-there asses. Allston rock butt. A U2 song is playing on the jukebox when Fleur kicks it in. Harper, nimble spinner of the spectacular untruth, improvises a story. Bono once jerked off on her little sister when she fell asleep backstage after a concert. After that, Fleur gets free drinks whenever they go to The Silhouette. She even works there for a few months.

Is this the kind of story you are supposed to tell to strangers on your way to a wedding? Better, Thanh supposes, than the one about the albatross. The best part of Harper's story is that Harper wasn't even at The Silhouette that night. It was just Thanh and Fleur, on some night. Thanh was the one who made up the story about Bono. But there is no story that Harper does not further embellish, does not re-embroider. Thanh wonders if that story still circulates. Did anyone ever tell it back to Bono himself? Maybe Thanh should Google it. You can see the lumpy profile of what must be Bad Claw Island, maybe half a mile away. Tide's out, the pilot says over the intercom. You can wade over from here. Water's maybe three feet deep. You can swim! If you want. Harper jumps up. His back good as new. Absolutely, he says. Who's in? Harper takes off his shoes, jeans, shirt. There's that fat, hairy belly. Leaves his briefs on. He goes over the side and down the ladder. Two men and a woman named Natasha join him. All in their underwear.

Thanh stays put beneath the white canopy of the boat. Little waves slap pleasantly at the hull. There's the most pleasant little breeze. He likes the way the water looks through the glass bottom. Like a magic trick. Why spoil it? Besides, he forgot to collect the laundry out of the dryer before they caught the plane. He isn't wearing any underwear. The boat gets to shore first, but before Thanh steps off onto the dock, Harper swims up under the glass. Presses his lips up. Then, suggestively, his wriggling hips. Here I am, Thanh, having sex with a boat. See, Thanh? I told you we would have a good time.

Fleur is on the dock, kissing her friends. The boat pilot, too. Why not? He's very good-looking. Fleur's wearing a white bikini and a top hat. Her hair is longer than Thanh has ever seen it. She's let it go back to its natural color. I'm the wedding party, she says, still giving those loving kisses. Exuberant kisses! She smells like frangipani and bourbon. Representing both the bride, me, and my groom, David. Because he's not here yet. He's delayed. Look at you, Thanh! Both of you! Has it really been two years? My God. Come up to the lodge. Everyone else has to sleep in a yurt on the beach. Well, everyone except the old people, who are staying over on the mainland. But you and Harper get a bed. A bed in an actual room and there's even a door. Remember the apartment in Somerville? The girl who came over from

Ireland to visit her girlfriend and got dumped before she even landed? We put a mattress behind the sofa and she stayed all summer? Have you seen Barb? Is she still in Prague? Do you know if you're having a boy or a girl yet? What's this woman like, the surrogate?

She never stops talking. Kissing, talking, Fleur likes to do both. The other wedding guests are sent off to claim their yurts. Fleur's sister Lenny takes them away. Thanh has never liked Lenny. He hasn't seen her in over a decade, but he doesn't like her any better now. Harper puts his pants back on and they follow Fleur up the beach. Did you ever sleep with her? Harper said once to Thanh. Of course not, Thanh said.

Bad Claw Lodge is an ugly wooden box done up in white gingerbread trim. Two stories. A listing porch, a banging screen door. Little dormer windows tucked under the flaking, papery eaves. The island is probably worth three million, Fleur says. The lodge? Some day it will blow out to sea, and I will get down on my knees and thank God. How big is the island? Harper asks. Two miles. Something like that. You can walk around it in half an hour. It gets bigger after every storm. But then the mainland is getting smaller.

There are buckets and pans set out on the painted floor of the lodge. On counters. On the mildew-stained couch and in the fireplace. It rained all night, Fleur says. All morning, too. I thought it would rain all day. The roof is a sieve. She takes them upstairs and down a hall so low that Harper must duck to get under a beam. Here, she says. Bathroom's next door. The water is all runoff, so if you want a hot shower, take it in the afternoon. The catchtank is on the roof. There's space enough in the room they're sleeping in for one twin bed, shoved up against the window. There's a three-legged table. On the bed is a Pyrex mixing bowl with an inch of rainwater at the bottom. Fleur says, I'll take that. On the little table is a piece of taxidermy. Something catlike, but with a peculiarly flattened, leathery tail. It has an angry face. A wrinkled, whiskery snout of a nose. What's that? Harper says. A beaver? Fleur says, That thing? It's something native down here. They had poisonous claws, or laid eggs, or something like that. They're extinct. That's worth a fortune, too. They were such a nuisance everyone just eradicated them. Shot them, trapped them, cut them up for bait. That was a long time ago, before anyone cared about stuff like that. Anyway! They never bothered to come up with a name for whatever they were, but then after they were gone they named the island after them. I think. Bad Claw. That thing is definitely worth more than this house. Thanh checks his phone again. There's no signal here, Fleur says. You have to go back to the mainland for that. Harper and Thanh look at each other. Is there a phone in the house?

There isn't.

Thanh and Harper fight about whether or not Thanh should go back to check messages, to call Han and Naomi. Whether they should stay on the mainland. We could have a real bed, Thanh says. Fleur will understand. I want to stay here, Harper says. And we are not going to say one word about this to Fleur. It's her wedding! Do you think she wants to have to pretend to feel worried about something that probably isn't even going to be an issue? Fine. Then I'll go in the boat the next time it's bringing people over, Thanh says. Call and make sure everything is okay, and then come right back. No, Harper says. I'll go. We'll tell Fleur it's a work thing.

It turns out that Harper can swim/wade back to the Mainland. The tide will be in later on, though, so he'll get a ride back on the boat. He puts his cell phone, with a couple of twenties, inside two plastic baggies. Fleur takes Thanh aside as soon as Harper is in the water. What's up? she says. Everything okay? We're fine, Thanh says. Really. Fine. Okay, Fleur says. Come help me mix drinks and tell me stuff. I need a quick crash course in marriage. What's sex like? Well, to start with, Thanh says, you need good lube and a lot of preparation. I also recommend two or three trapeze artists. And a marching band. The marching band is essential. They make drinks. People gather on the porch. Someone plays Leonard Cohen songs on a guitar. There are oysters and hot dogs and cold tomato halves filled with spinach and cheese. More drinks. Thanh says to Fleur, Tell me about David. He's a good guy? How am I supposed to answer that, Fleur says. She's gotten some sun. There are lines on her face that Thanh doesn't remember. She's doing what she used to do, back in the old days. Picking up abandoned drinks, finishing them. David has a terrible job. Did you know they had me vetted when we moved in together? To see if I was a security risk. We're at different ends of the political spectrum. But he's good to me. And he's rich. That doesn't hurt. And I love him. Well, Thanh says. He takes the empty glass from her hand.

It's nine at night by the time Harper gets back. People are playing Truth or Dare. Or, as Fleur calls it, Security Risk or Do Something Stupid Because It's Fun. There are other people on the boat with Harper. Thank God, Fleur says. He's here. But it isn't David. It's three men and a woman, all in knife-pleated pants, white shirts. Are those the caterers? someone asks. Fleur shshes them. Friends of David, she says, and goes down to the dock to meet them. No kisses this time. Thanh, Harper says. Let's go somewhere and talk.

They're at the top of the stairs when Thanh sees a plastic

bowl, rainwater in it, on the landing. Hold on, he tells Harper, and pukes into it. Takes the bowl into the bathroom, dumps the vomit and rainwater into the toilet. Rinses it. Rinses his mouth. Okay. He's okay. Harper is in their room, sitting on the little bed. They're okay, he says. They're in the hospital. She was having contractions. They've given her something to stop the contractions. And something else, uh, Dexamethasone. I looked it up on the phone. It's a steroid. It increases surfactants in the lungs. Whatever those are. So if he's born, he'll have a better chance. He, Thanh says. Oh, Harper says. Yeah. Naomi spilled the beans. Sorry about that. We need to go back, Thanh says. Thanh, Harper says. We can't. There are no flights. No seats. Not tomorrow anyway. I called. Han's there. The contractions have stopped. Tomorrow morning, first thing, you can go over to the mainland and talk to them. Thanh lies down on the bed. He doesn't undress. There's sand between his toes. He's cold. Harper lies down beside him. Harper says, It'll be okay. They'll be okay. They're almost asleep when Thanh says, I don't know about this David guy. I rode over with some of his work friends, Harper says. Bad news, those guys. I asked what exactly David did, and they started talking about the lesson of 9/11. Thanh says, Someone asked if they were the caterers. Caterers, Harper says. Like you'd want to eat anything they served you.

There are noises in the night. Thanh, Harper says. Do you hear that? Hear what? Thanh says. But then, he hears it, too. Little rustling noises, dry leaves' noises. Little scratchings. Harper gets out of bed, turns on the light. The noises stop. Harper turns off the light. Almost immediately the noises start up again. Harper gets up, the light is turned on, the noises stop. When it happens a third time, Harper leaves the light on. The taxidermied Bad Claw watches them with its glassy eyes, lips forever lifted in a sneer. There is nothing in the room except for Harper and Thanh and the Bad Claw, the table and the bed and their suitcases. Thanh checks his phone. There are no messages, no signal. The bed is too small. Harper begins to snore. He didn't used to snore. There are no other noises. Thanh only falls back asleep as the sun is coming up.

In the morning, Fleur and a bunch of other people are making a lot of noise on the porch. There's yelling. Little cries of delight. Has David arrived? They make their way down. Go on, Fleur is saying. Try them on. Everyone gets one. Everyone's a bride today. She is taking wedding dresses out of a set of oversized luggage. Remember these? she says to Thanh and Harper. Remember when I won all that money at the poker game in Somerville? She tells everyone else, I didn't know what to do with it. The next week was the wedding dress sale, Filene's Basement. It's famous, she tells her California friends. Everyone used to go. Even if you never, ever planned to get married. You went to watch grown women fight over dresses, and then there you are, buying a dress, too. So I went and got kind of fascinated with the dresses that no one else wanted. All of the really horrible dresses. At the end of the day they're practically paying you to take them. I spent all my poker money on wedding dresses. I've been saving them ever since. For a party. Or a wedding. Something. Here, she says to Harper. This one will look good on you. I was saving it just for you.

So Harper takes off his shirt. He steps into the dress, yanks it up over his chest. There are cap sleeves. Fake seed pearls. Fake buttons up the back. Was there really a time when women wore dresses like this and no one thought it was strange and everyone pretended that they looked beautiful and cried? How much did Fleur pay? There's a tag still attached. $3,000. A line through that. More prices, all crossed out. Fleur sees Thanh looking. You *know* I didn't pay more than fifty bucks for any of them, she says. Harper and Thanh were married in a courthouse office. They wore good suits. Red boxers, because red is lucky. Luck is necessary. Here's marriage advice Thanh could give Fleur. Be lucky.

How are the yurts? Thanh asks the woman from the van. Marianne? Or Laura. Whatever. The yurts? Really nice, the woman says. I've always wanted to stay in a yurt. Me, too, Thanh says. He's never entertained a single thought about a yurt in his entire life. Here, the woman says, will you zip me up? He zips her up. You look nice, he says. Really, she says. Yes, he says. It suits you somehow. But she doesn't seem pleased by this, the way she was pleased about the yurt. Maybe because it's such an awful dress. The (un)caterers are playing Hearts on the steps. Harper says to Fleur, I need to go back over to the mainland again. Work. Fleur says, Tide's in. I don't know when the boat is back over. It's already come once this morning, with groceries. Maybe after lunch? First we're going to go on an expedition. Put on a dress. (This to Thanh.) You guys, too. (This to the caterers.) Think of it as information gathering in field settings. Everybody needs coffee, grab coffee.

Everyone is amenable. Wedding guests in wedding dresses grab coffee and fruit and premade breakfast sandwiches. They put on sunblock, or hats, and troop off after Fleur. Thanh and Harper go along. Everyone goes. Even the caterers.

The center of the island, at least Thanh assumes it's the center of the island, is uphill. Laurel and pine. Loamy soil flecked with sand. There's a sort of path, pocketed with roots, and Fleur tells them to stay on it. Poison oak, she says. Sink-holes. Pines crowd in until the procession must go single file. Thanh has to hold up the train of his awful borrowed dress. The path becomes slippery with old needles. There's no breeze, just the medicinal smell of pine and salt. No one talks. The caterers are just in front of Thanh, Harper behind. He bets the caterers have a working phone. If the boat doesn't come soon, he'll figure out how to get it. Why did they sleep so late? Han will be no use to Naomi if things go wrong. She will be no use to Thanh and Harper. But then, what use would Thanh and Harper be? Nevertheless, they shouldn't be here. Here is of no use to anyone. The wedding party emerges into a clearing. At the center is an indentation, a sunken pocket of what Thanh realizes is water. A pond? Hardly big enough to be a pond. There's an algae bloom, bright as an egg yolk. So, Fleur says. We're here! This is where David's family comes every year, so they can each make a wish. Right, Sheila, Robert? She is addressing an older couple. Thanh hasn't even noticed them until now although they are the only people in the clearing who aren't wearing wedding dresses. This should make them stand out, he thinks. They don't. They could set themselves on fire, and you still probably wouldn't notice them. There's a cairn of pebbles and shells and bits of broken pottery. Fleur picks up a pebble, says, You make a wish and you throw something in. Come on, everyone gets a wish. Come on, come on. She tosses her pebble. Wedding guests gather around the mucky hole. Is it very deep? someone asks Fleur. She shrugs. Maybe, she says. Probably not. I don't know. Someone picks up a shell and drops it in. People make wishes. Harper rolls his eyes at Thanh. Shrugs. Picks up a pebble. People are making all sorts of wishes. A man in a watered silk dress with a mandarin collar, really it's the best of the awful dresses, wishes for a new job. Fair enough. The caterers make wishes, secret wishes. Even caterers get to make wishes. Marianne thinks, Let my mother die. Let her die soon. And Fleur? What did she wish? Fleur wishes with all of her heart, Please let him get here soon. Let him get here safely. Please let him love me. Please let this work. Thanh doesn't want to make a wish. He is suspicious of wishes. Go on, Fleur says. She puts a piece of shell in Thanh's hand. And then she waits. Should he wish that the baby inside Naomi stays inside a little longer? What would be the cost of that wish? Should he wish that the baby will live? If he lives, let him be healthy and strong and happy? He could wish that Naomi will not wish to keep the baby. He could wish to be a good father. That Harper would be a good father. Would that be a good wish? A safe wish? It seems dangerous to Thanh to make demands of God, of the universe, of a muddy hole. How can he anticipate the thing that he ought to wish for? Fleur is waiting. So Thanh throws the bit of shell in, and tries with all his heart not to make any wish at all. Even as he tries, he feels something – that wish, what is it, what is it? – rising up from his stomach, his lungs, his heart, spilling out. Too late! Down goes Thanh's bit of shell with all the other pebbles and bits, the other wishes. Harper sees Thanh's face. He wants that look to go away. What can be done? He wants to get back and see if the boat has come in. He'll go over to the mainland again if Thanh will let him. Harper doesn't believe in wishes, but he drops his pebble anyway. He thinks, I wonder what was making the noise last night? He holds Thanh's hand all the way back down the trail. The dresses are ridiculous. The kind of fun that they used to have is no longer fun. Now it seems more like work. David's parents are just in front of Harper and Thanh. They didn't make any wishes, but perhaps they have everything they want already. Thanh wonders. What kinds of things did they wish for their son? Harper decides that if the boat isn't back, he'll swim over in the ridiculous dress. What a great story that will make. He isn't thinking about Naomi and the baby. He is making every effort not to think about them at all. What a waste it will all be, what a disaster it will be if things go wrong at this stage. Will Thanh want to try again? They won't be able to afford it. Somehow all of this will be Harper's fault. They shouldn't have come to the wedding.

A baby born at twenty-four weeks may weigh just over a pound. The boat is at the dock. David has not come in on it. Thanh says, I should go this time. No, Harper says. You stay. I'll go. You should stay. Have some lunch. Take a nap. Really, Thanh should go, but Harper goes instead. He doesn't wear the dress. Before you are allowed to enter the NICU you must wash your hands and forearms up to the elbows for no less than two minutes each time. There is a clock and you watch the minute hand. This is to keep the babies safe from infection. Fleur suggests various games. Frisbee, Capture the Flag, Marco Polo in the water. The caterers play all of these games as if they are not playing games at all. Your wedding ring will fit around the wrist of a twenty-four-week baby. All of the wedding dresses have been bundled up in a pile on the beach with some driftwood. There will be a bonfire tonight. Lunch has been delivered on the boat. Thanh doesn't want any lunch. In a male baby born at twenty-four weeks, the scrotum and the glans of the penis have not yet developed. The skin cannot hold heat or moisture in. They have no fat. No reserves. They are stuck with needles, tubes, wires, monitors. Astronauts in the smallest diapers you have ever seen. Their ears don't resemble ears yet. They are placed in nests of artificial lambswool. Pink like cotton candy. Thanh doesn't want to play Capture the Flag. Fleur has made pitchers and pitchers of Bad Claw Island Ice Tea, and Thanh downs drink after drink after drink. He sits on the sand and drinks. Fleur sits with him for a while, and they talk about things that don't matter to either one of them. Fleur drinks, but not as much as Thanh. She must wonder. Does she wonder why he is drinking like this? She doesn't ask. David's mother sits down beside them. She says, I always wanted to write a book about this place. A book for children. It was going to be about the Bad Claws, before people ever lived here. But I couldn't figure out what the lesson would be. Children's books should have a lesson, don't you think? You should always learn something when you read a story. That's important. Premature baby girls have better outcomes than premature baby boys. Caucasian boys fare worst of all. Nurses have a name for this: Wimpy White Boys. Fleur says, I'm getting married tomorrow. If David doesn't show up, I'll marry the Bad Claw. The one in your room. Put that ring right around that poisonous little dew-claw. That would be funny, wouldn't it? Just watch. I'll do it. Eventually Thanh is sitting by himself, and then, later, someone is standing over him. Harper. Hey there, Harper is saying. Hey there, buddy. Thanh? What? Thanh says. What. He thinks this is what he says. He is asking a question, but he isn't sure what he is asking. Harper is telling him some-thing about someone whose name is William. The eyes of a twenty-four-week baby will still be fused shut. He can be given around five grams of breast milk a day through a gastro-nasal tube. Every diaper must be weighed. Urine out-put is monitored. Heart rate. Weight gain. Growth of the blood vessels in the retina. Lungs will not fully develop until the thirty-seventh week. Oxygen saturation of the blood is monitored. Everything noted in a binder book. Parents may look at the book. May ask questions. A high-speed oscillating ventilator may be required. Sometimes a tracheotomy is required. Supplemental oxygen. Blood transfusions. There is a price for all of these interventions. There is a cost. Cerebral palsy is a risk. Brain bleeds. Scarring of the lungs. Loss of vision. Necrotizing enterocolitis. The business of staying alive is hard work. Nurses say, He's so feisty. He's a fighter. That's a good thing. Harper goes away. Eventually he comes back with Fleur. The bonfire has been lit. It's dark. You have to eat something, Fleur says. Thanh? Here. She opens a packet of crackers. Thanh obediently eats cracker after cracker. Sips water. The crackers are sweetish. Dry. Nurses don't necessarily call the premature babies by their names. Why not? Maybe it makes it easier. They call the babies Peanut. Muffin. What an adorable muffin. What a little peanut. Parents may visit the NICU at any hour, day or night. Some parents find it hard to visit. Their presence is not essential. There is no vital task. Their child may die. There is no privacy. Every morning and every evening the doctors make rounds. Parents may listen in. They may ask questions. Parents may ask questions. There will not always be answers. There are motivational posters. Social workers. Financial counselors. A baby born at twenty-four weeks is expensive! Who knew a baby could cost so much? Fleur and Harper help Thanh up the stairs and into bed. Harper is saying, In the morning. We have standby seats. Turn him on his side. In case he pukes. There. The first twenty-four hours are the most critical.

Harper is snoring in Thanh's ear. Is this what has woken him? There's another noise in the room. That rustling again. That cellophane noise. Do you hear that? Thanh says. His tongue is thick. Harper. Harper says, Ungh. The noise increases. Harper says, What the hell, Thanh. Thanh is sitting up in bed now. He's still drunk, but he is piecing together the things that Harper tried to tell him a few hours ago. Naomi has had the baby. Harper, he says. Harper gets up and puts on the light. There is movement in the room, a kind of black liquid rushing. Beetles are pouring – a cataract – out of the Bad Claw onto the table and down the wall, across the floor, and toward the bed and the window. Something urgent in their progress, some necessary, timely task that they are engaged in. The lively, massed shape of them is the shadow of an unseen thing, moving through the room. Scurrying night. There will be a night in the NICU, much later, when Thanh looks over at another isolette. Sees, in the violet light, a spider moving across the inside wall. Every year, the nurse says when he calls her over. Every spring we get a migration or something. Spiders everywhere. She reaches in, scoops the spider into a cup. 'Christ on a bicycle!' Harper says. 'What the fuck?' He and Thanh are out of the room as fast as they can go. Down the stairs, and out of the house. They stumble down the rough beach to the dock. The lumpy yurts silent and black. The sky full of so many stars. God has an inordinate fondness for stars and also for beetles. The small and the very far away. Harper has the suitcase. Thanh carries their shoes. No doubt they've left something behind.

They sit on the dock. Do you remember anything I told you last night? Harper asks. Thanh says, Tell me. We have a son, Harper says. His name is William. Your mother picked that. William. She wanted him to have a name. In case. We'll call when we get to the mainland. We'll get the first flight. If there are no flights, we'll rent a car. We could swim, Thanh says. That's a terrible idea, Harper says. He puts his arms around Thanh. Breathes into his hair. It will be okay, Harper says. It may not be okay, Thanh says. I don't know if I can do this. Why did we want to do this? Harper says, Look. He points. There, far away, are the lights of the mainland. Closer: light moving over the water. The light becomes a boat and then the boat comes close enough that the pilot can throw a rope to Harper. He pulls the boat in. A man steps off. He looks at Harper, at Thanh, a little puzzled. This is the bridegroom. He says, 'Were you waiting for me?' Thanh begins to laugh, but Harper throws his arms open wide and embraces David. Welcomes him. Then David goes up the beach to the house. His shadow trails behind him, catches on beach grass and little pebbles. What kind of person is he? Not a good one, but he is loved by Fleur and what does it matter to Thanh and Harper anyway? Even caterers get married. There's no law against it. They get on the boat and ride back to the mainland. Fish swim up under the glass bottom, toward the light. Harper pays the pilot of the boat, whose name is Richard, a hundred bucks to take them to the airport. By the time they are on the prop plane that will take them to Charlotte where they will catch another flight to Boston, Thanh is undergoing a hangover of supernatural proportions. The hangover renders him incapable of thought. This is a mercy. Waiting for flights, Harper talks to Han, and once to Naomi. Thanh and Harper hold hands in the cab all the way to Children's Hospital, and Han meets them in the main lobby. 'Come up,' she says. 'Come up and meet your son.'

On an island, Fleur and David marry each other. There is cake. The wedding gift, which cost too much money, is opened. Days go by. Months go by. Years. Sometimes Thanh remembers Bad Claw, the procession of wedding dresses, the caterers, the boat coming toward the island. The place where he picked up a pebble. Sometimes Thanh wonders. Was this it, the thing that he had wished for, even as he had tried to wish for nothing at all? Was it this moment? Or was it this? Or this. Brief joys. The shadow of the valley of the shadow. Even here, even here, he wondered. Perhaps it was.

There is a day when they are able to bring the boy, their son, home from the NICU. They have prepared his room. There has been time, after all, a surplus of time to outfit the room with the usual things. A crib. Soft animals. A rug. A chair. A light.

One day the crib is too small. The boy learns to walk. Naomi graduates. Sometimes she takes the boy to the zoo or to museums. One day she says to Thanh, Sometimes I forget that he didn't die. Things were so bad for so long. Sometimes I think that he did die, and this is another boy entirely. I love him with all my heart, but sometimes I can't stop crying about the other one. Do you ever feel that way? Harper still works too much. Sometimes he tells the boy the story about how he was born, and the island, and the wedding. How Harper's wedding ring fit over his wrist. How Harper, wearing a wedding dress, rode over in a glass-bottomed boat, and was told that their son was born. Han gets older. She says, Sometimes I think that when I am dead and a ghost I will go back to that hospital. I spent so long there. I will be a ghost who washes her hands and waits. I won't know where else to haunt. The boy grows up. He is the same boy, even if sometimes it is hard to believe this could be true. Thanh and Harper stay married. The boy is loved. The loved one suffers.

All loved ones suffer. Love is not enough to prevent this. Love is not enough. Love is enough. The thing that you wished for. Was this it?

Here endeth the lesson.

EDWIDGE DANTICAT

FROM
CAROLINE'S
WEDDING

CAROLINE'S WEDDING WAS only a month away. She was very matter-of-fact about it, but slowly we all began to prepare. She had bought a short white dress at a Goodwill thrift shop and paid twelve dollars to dry-clean it. Ma, too, had a special dress: a pink lace, ankle-sweeping evening gown that she was going to wear at high noon to a civil ceremony. I decided to wear a green suit, for hope, like the handkerchief that wrapped Ma's marriage proposal letter from Papa's family.

Ma would have liked to have sewn Caroline's wedding dress from ten different patterns in a bridal magazine, taking the sleeves from one dress, the collar from another, and the skirt from another. Though in her heart she did not want to attend, in spite of everything, she was planning to act like this was a real wedding.

'The daughter resents a mother forever who keeps her from her love,' Ma said as we dressed to go to Eric's house for dinner. 'She is my child. You don't cut off your own finger because it smells bad.'

Still, she was not going to cook a wedding-night dinner. She was not even going to buy Caroline a special sleeping gown for her 'first' sexual act with her husband.

'I want to give you a wedding shower,' I said to Caroline in the cab on the way to Eric's house.

There was no sense in trying to keep it a secret from her.

'I don't really like showers,' Caroline said, 'but I'll let you give me one because there are certain things that I need.'

She handed me her address book, filled mostly with the names of people at Jackie Robinson Intermediate School where we both taught English as a Second Language to Haitian students.

Eric and Caroline had met at the school, where he was a janitor. They had been friends for at least a year before he asked her out. Caroline couldn't believe that he wanted to go out with her. They dated for eighteen months before he asked her to marry him.

'A shower is like begging,' Ma said, staring out of the car window at the storefronts along Flatbush Avenue. 'It is even more like begging if your sister gives one for you.'

'The maid of honor is the one to do it,' I said. 'I am the maid of honor, Ma. Remember?'

'Of course I remember,' she said. 'I am the mother, but that gives me claim to nothing.'

'It will be fun,' I tried to assure her. 'We'll have it at the house.'

'Is there something that's like a shower in Haiti?' Caroline asked Ma.

'In Haiti we are poor,' Ma said, 'but we do not beg.'

'It's nice to see you, Mrs Azile,' Eric said when he came to the door.

Eric had eyes like Haitian lizards, bright copper with a tint of jade. He was just a little taller than Caroline, his rich mahogany skin slightly darker than hers.

Under my mother's glare, he gave Caroline a timid peck on the cheek, then wrapped his arms around me and gave me a bear hug.

'How have you been?' Ma asked him with her best, extreme English pronunciation.

'I can't complain,' he said.

Ma moved over to the living room couch and sat down in front of the television screen. There was a nature program playing without sound. Mute images of animals swallowing each other whole flickered across the screen.

'So, you are a citizen of America now?' Eric said to me. 'Now you can just get on a plane anytime you feel like it and go anywhere in the world. Nations go to war over women like you. You're an American.'

His speech was extremely slow on account of a learning disability. He was not quite retarded, but not like everybody else either.

Ma looked around the room at some carnival posters on Eric's living room wall. She pushed her head forward to get a better look at a woman in a glittering bikini with a crown of feathers on her head. Her eyes narrowed as they rested on a small picture of Caroline, propped in a silver frame on top of the television set.

Eric and Caroline disappeared in the kitchen, leaving me alone with Ma.

'I won't eat if it's bad,' she said.

'You know Eric's a great cook,' I said.

'Men cooking?' she said. 'There is always something wrong with what he makes, here or at our house.'

'Well, pretend to enjoy it, will you?'

She walked around the living room, picking up the small wooden sculptures that Eric had in many corners of the room, mostly brown Madonnas with caramel babies wrapped in their arms.

Eric served us chicken in a thick dark sauce. I thrust my fork through layers of gravy. Ma pushed the food around her plate but ate very little.

After dinner, Eric and Caroline did the dishes in the kitchen while Ma and I sat in front of the television.

'Did you have a nice time?' I asked her.

'Nice or not nice, I came,' she said.

'That's right, Ma. It counts a lot that you came, but it would have helped if you had eaten more.'

'I was not very hungry,' she said.

'That means you can't fix anything to eat when you get home,' I said. 'Nothing. You can't fix anything. Not even bone soup.'

'A woman my age in her own home following orders.'

Eric had failed miserably at the game of Wooing Haitian Mother-in-Law. Had he known – or rather had Caroline advised him well – he would have hired a Haitian cook to make Ma some Haitian food that would taste (God forbid!) even better than her own.

'We know people by their stories,' Ma said to Caroline in the cab on the way home that night. 'Gossip goes very far. Grace heard women gossip in the Mass behind us the other day; and you hear what they say about Haitian women who forget themselves when they come here. Value yourself.'

'Yes, Ma,' Caroline said, for once not putting up a fight.

I knew she wanted to stay and spend the night with Eric but she was sparing Ma.

'I can't accuse you of anything,' Ma said. 'You never call someone a thief unless you catch them stealing.'

'I hear you, Ma,' Caroline said, as though her mind were a thousand miles away.

When we got home, she waited for Ma to fall asleep, then called a car service and went back to Eric's. When I got up the next morning, Ma was standing over my bed.

'Did your sister leave for school early again?' she asked.

'Yes, Ma,' I said. 'Caroline is just like you. She sleeps a hair thread away from waking, and she rises with the roosters.'

I mailed out the invitations for Caroline's wedding shower. We kept the list down to a bare minimum, just a few friends and Mrs Ruiz. We invited none of Ma's friends from Saint Agnès because she told me that she would be ashamed to have them ask her the name of her daughter's fiancé and have her tongue trip, being unable to pronounce it.

'What's so hard about Eric Abrahams?' I asked her. 'It's practically a Haitian name.'

'But it isn't a Haitian name,' she said. 'The way I say it is not the way his parents intended for it to be said. I say it Haitian. It is not Haitian.'

'People here pronounce our names wrong all the time.'

'That is why I know the way I say his name is not how it is meant to be said.'

'You better learn his name. Soon it will be your daughter's.'

'That will never be my daughter's name,' she said, 'because it was not the way I intended her name to be said.'

In the corner behind her bed, Caroline's boxes were getting full.

'Do you think Ma knows where I am those nights when I'm not here?' she asked.

'If she caught you going out the door, what could she do? It would be like an ant trying to stop a flood.'

'It's not like I have no intention of getting married,' she said.

'Maybe she understands.'

That night, I dreamed of my father again. I was standing on top of a cliff, and he was leaning out of a helicopter trying to grab my hand. At times, the helicopter flew so low that it nearly knocked me off the cliff. My father began to climb down a plastic ladder hanging from the bottom of the helicopter. He was dangling precariously and I was terrified.

I couldn't see his face, but I was sure he was coming to rescue me from the top of that cliff. He was shouting loudly, calling out my name. He called me Gracina, my full Haitian name, not Grace, which is what I'm called here.

It was the first time in any of my dreams that my father had a voice. The same scratchy voice that he had when he was alive. I stretched my hands over my head to make it easier for him to reach me. Our fingers came closer with each swing of the helicopter. His fingertips nearly touched mine as I woke up.

When I was a little girl, there was a time that Caroline and I were sleeping in the same bed with our parents because we had eaten beans for dinner and then slept on our backs, a combination that gives bad dreams. Even though she was in our parents' bed, Caroline woke up in the middle of the night, terrified. As she sobbed, Papa rocked her in the dark, trying to console her. His face was the first one she saw when Ma turned on the light. Looking straight at Papa with dazed eyes, Caroline asked him, 'Who are you?'

He said, 'It's Papy.'

'Papy who?' she asked.

'Your papy,' he said.

'I don't have a papy,' she said.

Then she jumped into Papa's arms and went right back to sleep.

My mother and father stayed up trying to figure out what made her say those things

'Maybe she dreamt that you were gone and that she was sleeping with her husband, who was her only comfort,' Ma said to Papa.

'So young, she would dream this?' asked Papa.

'In dreams we travel the years,' Ma had said.

Papa eventually went back to sleep, but Ma stayed up all night thinking.

The next day she went all the way to New Jersey to get Caroline fresh bones for a soup.

'So young she would dream this,' Papa kept saying as he watched Caroline drink the soup. 'So young. Just look at her, our child of the promised land, our New York child, the child who has never known Haiti.'

I, on the other hand, was the first child, the one they called their 'misery baby,' the offspring of my parents' lean years. I was born to them at a time when they were living in a shantytown in Port-au-Prince and had nothing.

When I was a baby, my mother worried that I would die from colic and hunger. My father pulled heavy carts for pennies. My mother sold jugs of water from the public fountain, charcoal, and grilled peanuts to get us something to eat.

When I was born, they felt a sense of helplessness. What if the children kept coming like the millions of flies constantly buzzing around them? What would they do then? Papa would need to pull more carts. Ma would need to sell more water, more charcoal, more peanuts. They had to try to find a way to leave Haiti.

Papa got a visa by taking vows in a false marriage with a widow who was leaving Haiti to come to the United States. He gave her some money and she took our last name. A few years later, my father divorced the woman and sent for my mother and me. While my father was alive, this was something that Caroline and I were never supposed to know.

We decorated the living room for Caroline's shower. Pink streamers and balloons draped down from the ceiling with the words *Happy Shower* emblazoned on them.

Ma made some patties from ground beef and codfish. She called one of her friends from Saint Agnès to bake the shower cake cheap. We didn't tell her friend what the cake was for. Ma wrote Caroline's name and the date on it after it had been delivered. She scrubbed the whole house, just in case one of the strangers wanted to use our bathroom. There wasn't a trace of dirt left on the wallpaper, the tiles, even the bathroom cabinets. If cleanliness is next to godliness, then whenever we had company my mother became a goddess.

Aside from Ma and me, there were only a few other people at the shower: four women from the junior high school where we taught and Mrs Ruiz.

Ma acted like a waitress and served everyone as Caroline took center stage sitting on the loveseat that we designated the 'shower chair.' She was wearing one of her minidresses, a navy blue with a wide butterfly collar. We laid the presents in front of her to open, after she had guessed what was inside.

'Next a baby shower!' shouted Mrs Ruiz in her heavy Spanish accent.

'Let's take one thing at a time,' I said.

'Never too soon to start planning,' Mrs Ruiz said. 'I promise to deliver the little one myself. Caroline, tell me now, what would you like, a girl or a boy?'

'Let's get through one shower first,' Caroline said.

I followed Ma to the kitchen as she picked up yet another empty tray.

'Why don't you sit down for while and let me serve?' I asked Ma as she put another batch of patties in the oven. She looked like she was going to cry.

When it was time to open the presents, Ma stayed in the kitchen while we all sat in a circle watching Caroline open her gifts.

She got a juicer, a portable step exerciser, and some other

household appliances from the schoolteachers. I gave her a traveling bag to take on her honeymoon.

Ma peeked through the doorway as we cooed over the appliances, suggesting romantic uses for them: breakfasts in bed, candlelight dinners, and the like. Ma pulled her head back quickly and went into the kitchen.

She was in the living room to serve the cake when the time came for it. While we ate, she gathered all of the boxes and the torn wrapping paper and took them to the trash bin outside.

She was at the door telling our guests good-bye as they left.

'Believe me, Mrs Azile, I will deliver your first grandchild,' Mrs Ruiz told her as she was leaving.

'I am sorry about your son,' I said to Mrs Ruiz.

'Now why would you want to bring up a thing like that?' Mrs Ruiz asked.

'Carmen, next time you come I will give you some of my bone soup,' Ma said as Mrs Ruiz left.

Ma gave me a harsh look as though I had stepped out of line in offering my belated condolences to Mrs Ruiz.

'There are things that don't always need to be said,' Ma told me.

Caroline packed her gifts before going to bed that night. The boxes were nearly full now.

We heard a knock on the door of our room as we changed for bed. It was Ma in her nightgown holding a gift-wrapped package in her hand. She glanced at Caroline's boxes in the corner, quickly handing Caroline the present.

'It is very sweet of you to get me something,' Caroline said, kissing Ma on the cheek to say thank you.

'It's very nothing,' Ma said, 'very nothing at all.'

Ma turned her face away as Caroline lifted the present out

of the box. It was a black and gold silk teddy with a plunging neckline.

'At the store,' Ma said, 'I told them your age and how you would be having this type of a shower. A girl there said that this would make a good gift for such things. I hope it will be of use.'

'I like it very much,' Caroline said, replacing it in the box.

After Caroline went to bed, I went to Ma's room for one of our chats. I slipped under the covers next to her, the way Caroline and I had come to her and Papa when our dreams had frightened us.

'That was nice, the teddy you got for Caroline,' I said. 'But it doesn't seem much like your taste.'

'I can't live in this country twenty-five years and not have some of it rub off on me,' she said. 'When will I have to buy you one of those dishonorable things?'

'When you find me a man.'

'They can't be that hard to find,' she said. 'Look, your sister found one, and some people might think it would be harder for her. He is a retard, but that's okay.'

'He's not a retard, Ma. She found a man with a good heart.'

'Maybe.'

'You like him, Ma. I know deep inside you do.'

'After Caroline was born, your father and me, we were so afraid of this.'

'Of what?'

'Of what is happening.'

'And what is that?'

'Maybe she jumps at it because she thinks he is being noble. Maybe she thinks he is doing her a favor. Maybe she thinks he is the only man who will ever come along to marry her.'

'Maybe he loves her,' I said.

'Love cannot make horses fly,' she said. 'Caroline should not marry a man if that man wants to be noble by marrying Caroline.'

'We don't know that, Ma.'

'The heart is like a stone,' she said. 'We never know what it is in the middle.'

'Only some hearts are like that,' I said.

'That is where we make mistakes,' she said. 'All hearts are stone until we melt, and then they turn back to stone again.'

'Did you feel that way when Papa married that woman?' I asked.

'My heart has a store of painful marks,' she said, 'and that is one of them.'

Ma got up from the bed and walked over to the closet with all her suitcases. She pulled out an old brown leather bag filled with tiny holes where the closet mice had nibbled at it over the years.

She laid the bag on her bed, taking out many of the items that she had first put in it years ago when she left Haiti to come to the United States to be reunited with my father.

She had cassettes and letters written by my father, his words crunched between the lines of aging sheets of ruled loose-leaf paper. In the letters he wrote from America to her while she was still in Haiti, he never talked to her about love. He asked about practical things; he asked about me and told her how much money he was sending her and how much was designated for what.

My mother also had the letters that she wrote back to him, telling him how much she loved him and how she hoped that they would be together soon.

That night Ma and I sat in her room with all those things

231

around us. Things that we could neither throw away nor keep in plain sight.

Caroline seemed distant the night before her wedding. Ma made her a stew with spinach, yams, potatoes, and dumplings. Ma did not eat any of the stew, concentrating instead on a green salad, fishing beneath the lettuce leaves as though there was gold hidden on the plate.

After dinner, we sat around the kitchen radio listening to a music program on the Brooklyn Haitian station.

Ma's lips were moving almost unconsciously as she mouthed the words to an old sorrowful bolero. Ma was putting the final touches on her own gown for the wedding.

'Did you check your dress?' she asked Caroline.

'I know it fits,' Caroline said.

'When was the last time you tried it on?'

'Yesterday.'

'And you didn't let us see it on you? I could make some adjustments.'

'It fits, Ma. Believe me.'

'Go and put it on now,' Ma said.

'Maybe later.'

'Later will be tomorrow,' Ma said.

'I will try it on for you before I go to sleep,' Caroline promised.

Ma gave Caroline some ginger tea, adding two large spoonfuls of brown sugar to the cup.

'You can learn a few things from the sugarcane,' Ma said to Caroline. 'Remember that in your marriage.'

'I didn't think I would ever fall in love with anybody, much less have them marry me,' Caroline said, her fingernails tickling the back of Ma's neck.

'Tell me, how do these outside-of-church weddings work?' Ma asked.

'Ma, I told you my reasons for getting married this way,' Caroline said. 'Eric and I don't want to spend all the money we have on one silly night that everybody else will enjoy except us. We would rather do it this way. We have all our papers ready. Eric has a friend who is a judge. He will perform the ceremony for us in his office.'

'So much like America,' Ma said, shaking her head. 'Everything mechanical. When you were young, every time someone asked you what you wanted to do when you were all grown up, you said you wanted to marry Pélé. What's happened to that dream?'

'Pélé who?' Caroline grimaced.

'On the eve of your wedding day, you denounce him, but you wanted to marry him, the Brazilian soccer player, you always said when you were young that you wanted to marry him.'

I was the one who wanted to marry Pélé. When I was a little girl, my entire notion of love was to marry the soccer star. I would confess it to Papa every time we watched a game together on television.

In our living room, the music was dying down as the radio station announced two a.m. Ma kept her head down as she added a few last stitches to her dress for the wedding.

'When you are pregnant,' Ma said to Caroline, 'give your body whatever it wants. You don't want your child to have port-wine marks from your cravings.'

Caroline went to our room and came back wearing her wedding dress *and* a false arm.

Ma's eyes wandered between the bare knees poking beneath the dress and the device attached to Caroline's forearm.

233

'I went out today and got myself a wedding present,' Caroline said. It was a robotic arm with two shoulder straps that controlled the motion of the plastic fingers.

'Lately, I've been having this shooting pain in my stub and it feels like my arm is hurting,' Caroline said.

'It does not look very real,' Ma said.

'That's not the point, Ma!' Caroline snapped.

'I don't understand,' Ma said.

'I often feel a shooting pain at the end of my left arm, always as though it was cut from me yesterday. The doctor said I have phantom pain.'

'What? The pain of ghosts?'

'Phantom limb pain,' Caroline explained, 'a kind of pain that people feel after they've had their arms or legs amputated. The doctor thought this would make it go away.'

'But your arm was never cut from you,' Ma said. 'Did you tell him that it was God who made you this way?'

'With all the pressure lately, with the wedding, he says that it's only natural that I should feel amputated.'

'In that case, we all have phantom pain,' Ma said.

When she woke up on her wedding day, Caroline looked drowsy and frazzled, as if she had aged several years since the last time we saw her. She said nothing to us in the kitchen as she swallowed two aspirins with a gulp of water.

'Do you want me to make you some soup?' Ma asked.

Caroline said nothing, letting her body drift down into Ma's arms as though she were an invalid. I helped her into a chair at the kitchen table. Ma went into the hall closet and pulled out some old leaves that she had been saving. She stuffed the leaves into a pot of water until the water overflowed.

Caroline was sitting so still that Ma raised her index finger under her nose to make sure she was breathing.

'What do you feel?' Ma asked.

'I am tired,' Caroline said. 'I want to sleep. Can I go back to bed?'

'The bed won't be yours for much longer,' Ma said. 'As soon as you leave, we will take out your bed. From this day on, you will be sleeping with your husband, away from here.'

'What's the matter?' I asked Caroline.

'I don't know,' she said. 'I just woke up feeling like I don't want to get married. All this pain, all this pain in my arm makes it seem so impossible somehow.'

'You're just nervous,' I said.

'Don't worry,' Ma said. 'I was the same on the morning of my wedding. I fell into a stupor, frightened of all the possibilities. We will give you a bath and then you lay down for a bit and you will rise as promised and get married.'

The house smelled like a forest as the leaves boiled on the stove. Ma filled the bathtub with water and then dumped the boiled leaves inside.

We undressed Caroline and guided her to the tub, helping her raise her legs to get in.

'Just sink your whole body,' Ma said, when Caroline was in the tub.

Caroline pushed her head against the side of the tub and lay there as her legs paddled playfully towards the water's surface.

Ma's eyes were fierce with purpose as she tried to stir Caroline out of her stupor.

'At last a sign,' she joked. 'She is my daughter after all. This is just the way I was on the day of my wedding.'

Caroline groaned as Ma ran the leaves over her skin.

'Woman is angel,' Ma said to Caroline. 'You must confess, this is like pleasure.'

Caroline sank deeper into the tub as she listened to Ma's voice.

'Some angels climb to heaven backwards,' Caroline said. 'I want to stay with us, Ma.'

'You take your vows in sickness and in health,' Ma said. 'You decide to try sickness first? That is not very smart.'

'You said this happened to you too, Ma?' Caroline asked.

'It did,' Ma said. 'My limbs all went dead on my wedding day. I vomited all over my wedding dress on the way to the church.'

'I am glad I bought a cheap dress then,' Caroline said, laughing. 'How did you stop vomiting?'

'My honeymoon.'

'You weren't afraid of that?'

'Heavens no,' Ma said, scrubbing Caroline's back with a handful of leaves. 'For that I couldn't wait.'

Caroline leaned back in the water and closed her eyes.

'I am eager to be a guest in your house,' Ma said to Caroline.

'I will cook all your favorite things,' Caroline said.

'As long as your husband is not the cook, I will eat okay.'

'Do you think I'll make a good wife, Ma?'

'Even though you are an island girl with one kind of season in your blood, you will make a wife for all seasons: spring, summer, autumn, and winter.'

Caroline got up from the tub and walked alone to Ma's bedroom.

The phone rang and Ma picked it up. It was Eric.

'I don't understand it, honey,' Caroline said, already sounding more lucid. 'I just felt really blah! I know. I know, but for now, Ma's taking care of me.'

Ma made her hair into tiny braids, and over them she put on a wig with a shoulder-length bob. Ma and I checked ourselves in the mirror. She in her pink dress and me in my green suit, the two of us looking like a giant patchwork quilt.

'How long do I have now?' Caroline asked.

'An hour,' I said.

'Eric is meeting us there,' Caroline said, 'since it's bad luck for the groom to see the bride before the wedding.'

'If the groom is not supposed to see the bride, how do they get married?' Ma asked.

'They're not supposed to see each other until the ceremony,' Caroline said.

Caroline dressed quickly. Her hair was slicked back in a small bun, and after much persuasion, Ma got her to wear a pair of white stockings to cover her jutting knees.

The robotic arm was not as noticeable as the first time we had seen it. She had bought a pair of long white gloves to wear over the plastic arm and her other arm. Ma put some blush on the apple of Caroline's cheeks and then applied some rice powder to her face. Caroline sat stiffly on the edge of her bed as Ma glued fake eyelashes to her eyelids.

I took advantage of our last few minutes together to snap some instant Polaroid memories. Caroline wrapped her arms tightly around Ma as they posed for the pictures.

'Ma, you look so sweet,' Caroline said.

We took a cab to the courthouse. I made Ma and Caroline pose for more pictures on the steps. It was as though we were going to a graduation ceremony.

The judge's secretary took us to a conference room while her boss finished an important telephone call. Eric was already there, waiting. As soon as we walked in, Eric rushed over to give Caroline a hug. He began stroking her mechanical arm as though it were a fascinating new toy.

'Lovely,' he said.

'It's just for the day,' Caroline said.

'It suits you fine,' he said.

Caroline looked much better. The rouge and rice powder had given her face a silky brown-sugar finish.

Ma sat stiffly in one of the cushioned chairs with her purse in her lap, her body closed in on itself like a cage.

'Judge Perez will be right with you,' the secretary said.

Judge Perez bounced in cheerfully after her. He had a veil of thinning brown hair and a goatee framing his lips.

'I'm sorry the bride and groom had to wait,' he said, giving Eric a hug. 'I couldn't get off the phone.'

'Do you two know what you're getting into?' he said, playfully tapping Eric's arm.

Eric gave a coy smile. He wanted to move on with the ceremony. Caroline's lips were trembling with a mixture of fear and bashfulness.

'It's really a simple thing,' Judge Perez said. 'It's like a visit to get your vaccination. Believe me when I tell you it's very short and painless.'

He walked to a coat rack in the corner, took a black robe from it, and put it on.

'Come forward, you two,' he said, moving to the side of the room. 'The others can stand anywhere you like.'

Ma and I crowded behind the two of them. Eric had no family here. They were either in another state or in the Bahamas.

'No best man?' Ma whispered.

'I'm not traditional,' Eric said.

'That wasn't meant to be heard,' Ma said, almost as an apology.

'It's all right,' Eric said.

'Dearly beloved,' Judge Perez began. 'We are gathered here today to join this man and this woman in holy matrimony.'

Caroline's face, as I had known it, slowly began to fade, piece by piece, before my eyes. Another woman was setting in, a married woman, someone who was no longer my little sister.

'I, Caroline Azile, take this man to be my lawful wedded husband.'

I couldn't help but feel as though she was divorcing us, trading in her old allegiances for a new one.

It was over before we knew it. Eric grabbed Caroline and kissed her as soon as the judge said, 'Her lips are yours.'

'They were mine before, too,' Eric said, kissing Caroline another time.

After the kiss, they stood there, wondering what to do next. Caroline looked down at her finger, admiring her wedding band. Ma took a twenty-dollar bill out of her purse and handed it to the judge. He moved her hand away, but she kept insisting. I reached over and took the money from Ma's hand.

'I want to take the bride and groom out for a nice lunch,' I said.

'Our plane leaves for Nassau at five,' Eric said.

'We'd really like that, right, Ma?' I said. 'Lunch with the bride and groom.'

Ma didn't move. She understood the extent to which we were unimportant now.

'I feel much better,' Caroline said.

'Congratulations, Sister,' I said. 'We're going to take you out to eat.'

'I want to go to the Brooklyn Botanic Garden to take some pictures,' Caroline said.

'All set,' Eric said. 'I have a photographer meeting us there.'

Ma said, 'How come you never told me you were leaving tonight? How come you never tell me nothing.'

'You knew she wasn't going back to sleep at the house with us,' I said to Ma.

'I am not talking to you,' Ma said, taking her anger out on me.

'I am going to stop by the house to pick up my suitcase,' Caroline said.

We had lunch at Le Bistro, a Haitian Restaurant on Flatbush Avenue. It was the middle of the afternoon, so we had the whole place to ourselves. Ma sat next to me, not saying a word. Caroline didn't eat very much either. She drank nothing but sugared water while keeping her eyes on Ma.

'There's someone out there for everyone,' Eric said, standing up with a champagne glass in the middle of the empty restaurant. 'Even some destined bachelors get married. I am a very lucky person.'

Caroline clapped. Ma and I raised our glasses for his toast. He and Caroline laughed together with an ease that Ma and I couldn't feel.

'Say something for your sister,' Ma said in my ear.

I stood up and held my glass in her direction.

'A few years ago, our parents made this journey,' I said. 'This is a stop on the journey where my sister leaves us. We will miss her greatly, but she will never be gone from us.'

It was something that Ma might have said.

* * *

The photographer met us at the wedding grove at the Botanic Garden. Eric and Caroline posed stiffly for their photos, surrounded by well-cropped foliage.

'These are the kinds of pictures that they will later lay over the image of a champagne glass or something,' Ma said. 'They do so many tricks with photography now, for posterity.'

We went back to the house to get Caroline's luggage.

'We cannot take you to the airport,' Ma said.

'It's all right, Mother,' Eric said. 'We will take a cab. We will be fine.'

I didn't know how long I held Caroline in my arms on the sidewalk in front of our house. Her synthetic arm felt weighty on my shoulder, her hair stuck to the tears on my face.

'I'll visit you and Ma when I come back,' she said. 'Just don't go running off with any Brazilian soccer players.'

Caroline and I were both sobbing by the time she walked over to say good-bye to Ma. She kissed Ma on the cheek and then quickly hopped in the taxi without looking back. Ma ran her hand over the window, her finger sliding along the car door as it pulled away.

'I like how you stood up and spoke for your sister,' she said.

'The toast?'

'It was good.'

'I feel like I had some help,' I said.

That night, Ma got a delivery of roses so red that they didn't look real.

'Too expensive,' she said when the delivery man handed them to her.

The guy waited for her to sign a piece of paper and then a bit longer for a tip.

Ma took a dollar out of her bra and handed it to him.

She kept sniffing the roses as she walked back to the kitchen.

'Who are they from?' I asked.

'Caroline,' she said. 'Sweet, sweet Caroline.'

Distance had already made my sister Saint Sweet Caroline.

'Are you convinced of Caroline's happiness now?' I asked.

'You ask such difficult questions.'

That night she went to bed with the Polaroid wedding photos and the roses by her bed. Later, I saw her walking past my room cradling the vase. She woke up several times to sniff the roses and change the water.

That night, I also dreamt that I was with my father by a stream of rose-colored blood. We made a fire and grilled a breadfruit for dinner while waiting for the stream to turn white. My father and I were sitting on opposite sides of the fire. Suddenly the moon slipped through a cloud and dived into the bloody stream, filling it with a sheet of stars.

I turned to him and said, 'Look, Papy. There are so many stars.'

And my father in his throaty voice said, 'If you close your eyes really tight, wherever you are, you will see these stars.'

I said, 'Let's go for a swim.'

He said, 'No, we have a long way to travel and the trip will be harder if we get wet.'

Then I said, 'Papa, do you see all the blood? It's very beautiful.'

His face began to glow as though it had become like one of the stars.

Then he asked me, 'If we were painters, which landscapes would we paint?'

I said, 'I don't understand.'

He said, 'We are playing a game, you must answer me.'

I said, 'I don't know the answers.'

'When you become mothers, how will you name your sons?'

'We'll name them all after you,' I said.

'You have forgotten how to play this game,' he said.

'What kind of lullabies do we sing to our children at night? Where do you bury your dead?'

His face was fading into a dreamy glow.

'What kind of legends will your daughters be told? What kinds of charms will you give them to ward off evil?'

I woke up startled, for the first time afraid of the father that I saw in my dreams.

I rubbed the sleep out of my eyes and went down to the kitchen to get a glass of warm milk.

Ma was sitting at the kitchen table, rolling an egg between her palms. I slipped into the chair across from her. She pressed harder on both ends of the egg.

'What are you doing up so late?' she asked.

'I can't sleep,' I said.

'I think people should take shifts. Some of us would carry on at night and some during the day. The night would be like the day exactly. All stores would be open and people would go to the office, but only the night people. You see, then there would be no sleeplessness.'

I warmed some cold milk in a pan on the stove. Ma was still pressing hard, trying to crush the egg from top and bottom. I offered her some warm milk but she refused.

'What did you think of the wedding today?' I asked.

'When your father left me and you behind in Haiti to move to this country and marry that woman to get our papers,' she said, 'I prepared a charm for him. I wrote his name on a piece of paper and put the paper in a calabash.

I filled the calabash with honey and next to it lit a candle. At midnight every night, I laid the calabash next to me in the bed where your father used to sleep and shouted at it to love me. I don't know how or what I was looking for, but somehow in the words he was sending me, I knew he had stopped thinking of me the same way.'

'You can't believe that, Ma,' I said.

'I know what I know,' she said. 'I am an adult woman. I am not telling you this story for pity.'

The kitchen radio was playing an old classic on one of the Haitian stations.

Beloved Haiti, there is no place like you.
I had to leave you before I could understand you.

'Would you like to see my proposal letter?' Ma asked.

She slid an old jewelry box across the table towards me. I opened it and pulled out the envelope with the letter in it.

The envelope was so yellowed and frail that at first I was afraid to touch it.

'Go ahead,' she said, 'it will not turn to dust in your hands.'

The letter was cracked along the lines where it had been folded all of these years.

My son, Carl Romélus Azile, would be honored to make your daughter, Hermine Françoise Génie, his wife.

'It was so sweet then,' Ma said, 'so sweet. Promise me that when I die you will destroy all of this.'

'I can't promise you that,' I said. 'I will want to hold on to things when you die. I will want to hold on to you.'

'I do not want my grandchildren to feel sorry for me,' she said. 'The past, it fades a person. And yes. Today, it was a nice wedding.'

My passport came in the mail the next day, addressed to Gracina Azile, my real and permanent name.

I filled out all the necessary sections, my name and address, and listed my mother to be contacted in case I was in an accident. For the first time in my life, I felt truly secure living in America. It was like being in a war zone and finally receiving a weapon of my own, like standing on the firing line and finally getting a bullet-proof vest.

We had all paid dearly for this piece of paper, this final assurance that I belonged in the club. It had cost my parents' marriage, my mother's spirit, my sister's arm.

I felt like an indentured servant who had finally been allowed to join the family.

The next morning, I went to the cemetery in Rosedale, Queens, where my father had been buried. His was one of many gray tombstones in a line of foreign unpronounceable names. I brought my passport for him to see, laying it on the grass among the wild daisies surrounding the grave.

'Caroline had her wedding,' I said. 'We felt like you were there.'

My father had wanted to be buried in Haiti, but at the time of his death there was no way that we could have afforded it.

The day before Papa's funeral, Caroline and I had told Ma that we wanted to be among Papa's pallbearers.

Ma had thought that it was a bad idea. Who had ever heard of young women being pallbearers? Papa's funeral was no time for us to express our selfish childishness, our *American* rebelliousness.

When we were children, whenever we rejected symbols of

Haitian culture, Ma used to excuse us with great embarrassment and say, 'You know, they are American.'

Why didn't we like the thick fatty pig skin that she would deep-fry so long that it tasted like rubber? We were Americans and we had *no taste buds*. A double tragedy.

Why didn't we like the thick yellow pumpkin soup that she spent all New Year's Eve making so that we would have it on New Year's Day to celebrate Haitian Independence Day? Again, because we were American and the Fourth of July was *our* independence holiday.

'In Haiti, you own your children and they find it natural,' she would say. 'They know their duties to the family and they act accordingly. In America, no one owns anything, and certainly not another person.'

'Caroline called,' Ma said. She was standing over the stove making some bone soup when I got home from the cemetery. 'I told her that we would still keep her bed here for her, if she ever wants to use it. She will come and visit us soon. I knew she would miss us.'

'Can I drop one bone in your soup?' I asked Ma.

'It is your soup too,' she said.

She let me drop one bone into the boiling water. The water splashed my hand, leaving a red mark.

'Ma, if we were painters which landscapes would we paint?' I asked her.

'I see. You want to play the game of questions?'

'When I become a mother, how will I name my daughter?'

'If you want to play then I should ask the first question,' she said.

'What kinds of lullabies will I sing at night? What kinds of legends will my daughter be told? What kinds of charms will I give her to ward off evil?'

'I have come a few years further than you,' she insisted. 'I have tasted a lot more salt. I am to ask the first question, if we are to play the game.'

'Go ahead,' I said, giving in.

She thought about it for a long time while stirring the bones in our soup.

'Why is it that when you lose something, it is always in the last place that you look for it?' she asked finally.

Because of course, once you remember, you always stop looking.

WEDDING MISHAPS

CHARLOTTE BRONTË

FROM
JANE EYRE

SOPHIE CAME AT seven to dress me; she was very long indeed in accomplishing her task; so long that Mr Rochester, grown, I suppose, impatient of my delay, sent up to ask why I did not come. She was just fastening my veil (the plain square of blond after all) to my hair with a brooch; I hurried from under her hands as soon as I could.

'Stop!' she cried in French. 'Look at yourself in the mirror: you have not taken one peep.'

So I turned at the door: I saw a robed and veiled figure, so unlike my usual self that it seemed almost the image of a stranger. 'Jane!' called a voice, and I hastened down. I was received at the foot of the stairs by Mr Rochester.

'Lingerer,' he said, 'my brain is on fire with impatience; and you tarry so long!'

He took me into the dining-room, surveyed me keenly all over, pronounced me 'fair as a lily, and not only the pride of his life, but the desire of his eyes', and then telling me he would give me but ten minutes to eat some breakfast, he rang the bell. One of his lately hired servants, a footman, answered it.

'Is John getting the carriage ready?'

'Yes, sir.'

'Is the luggage brought down?'

'They are bringing it down, sir.'

'Go you to the church: see if Mr Wood (the clergyman) and the clerk are there: return and tell me.'

The church, as the reader knows, was but just beyond the gates; the footman soon returned.

'Mr Wood is in the vestry, sir, putting on his surplice.'

'And the carriage?'

'The horses are harnessing.'

'We shall not want it to go to church; but it must be ready the moment we return: all the boxes and luggage arranged and strapped on, and the coachman in his seat.'

'Yes, sir.'

'Jane, are you ready?'

I rose. There were no groomsmen, no bridesmaids, no relatives to wait for or marshal: none but Mr Rochester and I. Mrs Fairfax stood in the hall as we passed. I would fain have spoken to her, but my hand was held by a grasp of iron: I was hurried along by a stride I could hardly follow; and to look at Mr Rochester's face was to feel that not a second of delay would be tolerated for any purpose. I wonder what other bridegroom ever looked as he did – so bent up to a purpose, so grimly resolute: or who, under such stedfast brows, ever revealed such flaming and flashing eyes.

I know not whether the day was fair or foul; in descending the drive, I gazed neither on sky nor earth: my heart was with my eyes; and both seemed migrated into Mr Rochester's frame. I wanted to see the invisible thing on which, as we went along, he appeared to fasten a glance fierce and fell. I wanted to feel the thoughts whose force he seemed breasting and resisting.

At the churchyard wicket he stopped: he discovered I was quite out of breath. 'Am I cruel in my love?' he said. 'Delay an instant: lean on me, Jane.'

And now I can recall the picture of the gray old house of God rising calm before me, of a rook wheeling round the steeple, of a ruddy morning sky beyond. I remember something, too, of the green grave-mounds; and I have not forgotten, either, two figures of strangers, straying amongst the low hillocks, and reading the mementoes graven on the few mossy head-stones. I noticed them, because, as they saw us, they passed round to the back of the church; and I doubted not they were going to enter by the side-aisle door, and witness the ceremony. By Mr Rochester they were not observed; he was earnestly looking at my face, from which the blood had, I dare say, momentarily fled: for I felt my forehead dewy, and my cheeks and lips cold. When I rallied, which I soon did, he walked gently with me up the path to the porch.

We entered the quiet and humble temple; the priest waited in his white surplice at the lowly altar, the clerk beside him. All was still: two shadows only moved in a remote corner. My conjecture had been correct: the strangers had slipped in before us, and they now stood by the vault of the Rochesters, their backs towards us, viewing through the rails the old time-stained marble tomb, where a kneeling angel guarded the remains of Damer de Rochester, slain at Marston Moor in the time of the civil wars; and of Elizabeth, his wife.

Our place was taken at the communion-rails. Hearing a cautious step behind me, I glanced over my shoulder: one of the strangers – a gentleman, evidently – was advancing up the chancel. The service began. The explanation of the intent of matrimony was gone through; and then the clergyman came a step further forward, and bending slightly towards Mr Rochester, went on.

'I require and charge you both (as ye will answer at the dreadful day of judgment, when the secrets of all hearts shall be disclosed), that if either of you know any impediment why ye may not lawfully be joined together in matrimony, ye do now confess it; for be ye well assured that so many as are coupled together otherwise than God's Word doth allow, are not joined together by God, neither is their matrimony lawful.'

He paused, as the custom is. When is the pause after that sentence ever broken by reply? Not, perhaps, once in a hundred years. And the clergyman, who had not lifted his eyes from his book, and had held his breath but for a moment, was proceeding: his hand was already stretched towards Mr Rochester, as his lips unclosed to ask, 'Wilt thou have this woman for thy wedded wife?' – when a distinct and near voice said:—

'The marriage cannot go on: I declare the existence of an impediment.'

The clergyman looked up at the speaker, and stood mute; the clerk did the same; Mr Rochester moved slightly, as if an earthquake had rolled under his feet: taking a firmer footing, and not turning his head or eyes, he said, 'Proceed.'

Profound silence fell when he had uttered that word, with deep but low intonation. Presently Mr Wood said:—

'I cannot proceed without some investigation into what has been asserted, and evidence of its truth or falsehood.'

'The ceremony is quite broken off,' subjoined the voice behind us. 'I am in a condition to prove my allegation: an insuperable impediment to this marriage exists.'

Mr Rochester heard, but heeded not: he stood stubborn and rigid: making no movement, but to possess himself of my hand. What a hot and strong grasp he had! – and how like quarried marble was his pale, firm, massive front at this moment! How his eye shone, still, watchful, and yet wild beneath!

Mr Wood seemed at a loss. 'What is the nature of the

impediment?' he asked. 'Perhaps it may be got over – explained away?'

'Hardly,' was the answer: 'I have called it insuperable, and I speak advisedly.'

The speaker came forwards, and leaned on the rails. He continued, uttering each word distinctly, calmly, steadily, but not loudly.

'It simply consists in the existence of a previous marriage: Mr Rochester has a wife now living.'

My nerves vibrated to those low-spoken words as they had never vibrated to thunder – my blood felt their subtle violence as it had never felt frost or fire: but I was collected, and in no danger of swooning. I looked at Mr Rochester: I made him look at me. His whole face was colourless rock: his eye was both spark and flint. He disavowed nothing: he seemed as if he would defy all things. Without speaking; without smiling; without seeming to recognise in me a human being, he only twined my waist with his arm, and riveted me to his side.

'Who are you?' he asked of the intruder.

'My name is Briggs – a solicitor of — street, London.'

'And you would thrust on me a wife?'

'I would remind you of your lady's existence, sir; which the law recognises, if you do not.'

'Favour me with an account of her – with her name, her parentage, her place of abode.'

'Certainly.' Mr Briggs calmly took a paper from his pocket, and read out in a sort of official, nasal voice:—

'"I affirm and can prove that on the 20th of October, A.D., —, (a date of fifteen years back) Edward Fairfax Rochester of Thornfield-Hall, in the county of —, and of Ferndean Manor, in —shire, England, was married to my sister, Bertha

Antoinetta Mason, daughter of Jonas Mason, merchant, and of Antoinetta his wife, a Creole – at — church, Spanish-Town, Jamaica. The record of the marriage will be found in the register of that church – a copy of it is now in my possession. Signed, Richard Mason."'

'That – if a genuine document – may prove I have been married, but it does not prove that the woman mentioned therein as my wife is still living.'

'She was living three months ago,' returned the lawyer.

'How do you know?'

'I have a witness to the fact; whose testimony even you, sir, will scarcely controvert.'

'Produce him – or go to hell.'

'I will produce him first – he is on the spot: Mr Mason, have the goodness to step forward.'

Mr Rochester, on hearing the name, set his teeth; he experienced, too, a sort of strong convulsive quiver; near to him as I was, I felt the spasmodic movement of fury or despair run through his frame. The second stranger, who had hitherto lingered in the background, now drew near; a pale face looked over the solicitor's shoulder – yes, it was Mason himself. Mr Rochester turned and glared at him. His eye, as I have often said, was a black eye: it had now a tawny, nay a bloody light in its gloom; and his face flushed – olive cheek, and hueless forehead received a glow, as from spreading, ascending heart-fire: and he stirred, lifted his strong arm – he could have struck Mason – dashed him on the church-floor – shocked by ruthless blow the breath from his body – but Mason shrank away, and cried faintly, 'Good God!' Contempt fell cool on Mr Rochester – his passion died as if a blight had shrivelled it up: he only asked, 'What have *you* to say?'

An inaudible reply escaped Mason's white lips.

'The devil is in it if you cannot answer distinctly. I again demand, what have *you* to say?'

'Sir – sir—' interrupted the clergyman, 'do not forget you are in a sacred place.' Then addressing Mason, he inquired gently, 'Are you aware, sir, whether or not this gentleman's wife is still living?'

'Courage,' urged the lawyer, – 'speak out.'

'She is now living at Thornfield-Hall;' said Mason, in more articulate tones: 'I saw her there last April. I am her brother.'

'At Thornfield-Hall!' ejaculated the clergyman. 'Impossible! I am an old resident in this neighbourhood, sir, and I never heard of a Mrs Rochester at Thornfield-Hall.'

I saw a grim smile contort Mr Rochester's lip and he muttered:—

'No – by God! I took care that none should hear of it – or of her under that name.' He mused – for ten minutes he held counsel with himself: he formed his resolve, and announced it:—

'Enough – all shall bolt out at once, like the bullet from the barrel. – Wood, close your book and take off your surplice; John Green, (to the clerk) leave the church: there will be no wedding today:' the man obeyed.

Mr Rochester continued, hardily and recklessly: 'Bigamy is an ugly word! – I meant, however, to be a bigamist: but fate has out-manoeuvred me; or Providence has checked me, – perhaps the last. I am little better than a devil at this moment; and, as my pastor there would tell me, deserve no doubt the sternest judgments of God, – even to the quenchless fire and deathless worm. Gentlemen, my plan is broken up! – what this lawyer and his client say is true: I have been married; and the woman to whom I was married lives! You say you never heard of a Mrs Rochester at the house up yonder, Wood: but I daresay you have many a time inclined your ear to gossip about the mysterious lunatic kept there under watch and ward. Some have whispered to you that she is my bastard half-sister: some, my cast-off mistress; I now inform you that she is my wife, whom I married fifteen years ago, – Bertha Mason by name; sister of this resolute person-age, who is now, with his quivering limbs and white cheeks, showing you what a stout heart men may bear. Cheer up, Dick! – never fear me! – I'd almost as soon strike a woman as you. Bertha Mason is mad; and she came of a mad family; – idiots and maniacs through three generations! Her mother, the Creole, was both a mad woman and a drunkard! – as I found out after I had wed the daughter: for they were silent on family secrets before. Bertha, like a dutiful child, copied her parent in both points. I had a charming partner – pure, wise, modest: you can fancy I was a happy man. – I went through rich scenes! Oh! my experience has been heavenly, if you only knew it! But I owe you no further explanation. Briggs, Wood, Mason, – I invite you all to come up to the house and visit Mrs Poole's patient, and *my wife!* – You shall see what sort of a being I was cheated into espousing, and judge whether or not I had a right to break the compact, and seek sympathy with something at least human. This girl,' he continued, looking at me, 'knew no more than you, Wood, of the disgusting secret: she thought all was fair and legal; and never dreamt she was going to be entrapped into a feigned union with a defrauded wretch, already bound to a bad, mad, and embruted partner! Come, all of you, follow!'

Still holding me fast, he left the church: the three gentle-men came after. At the front door of the hall we found the carriage.

'Take it back to the coach-house, John,' said Mr Rochester, coolly; 'it will not be wanted today.'

At our entrance, Mrs Fairfax, Adele, Sophie, Leah, advanced to meet and greet us.

'To the right about – every soul!' cried the master: 'away with your congratulations! Who wants them? – Not I! – they are fifteen years too late!'

He passed on and ascended the stairs, still holding my hand, and still beckoning the gentlemen to follow him; which they did. We mounted the first staircase, passed up the gallery, proceeded to the third story: the low, black door, opened by Mr Rochester's master key, admitted us to the tapestried room, with its great bed, and its pictorial cabinet.

'You know this place, Mason,' said our guide; 'she bit and stabbed you here.'

He lifted the hangings from the wall, uncovering the second door: this, too, he opened. In a room without a window, there burnt a fire, guarded by a high and strong fender, and a lamp suspended from the ceiling by a chain. Grace Poole bent over the fire, apparently cooking something in a saucepan. In the deep shade, at the further end of the room, a figure ran backwards and forwards. What it was, whether beast or human being, one could not, at first sight, tell: it grovelled, seemingly, on all fours; it snatched and growled like some strange wild animal: but it was covered with clothing; and a quantity of dark, grizzled hair, wild as a mane, hid its head and face.

'Good-morrow, Mrs Poole!' said Mr Rochester. 'How are you? and how is your charge today?'

'We're tolerable, sir, I thank you,' replied Grace, lifting the boiling mess carefully on to the hob: 'rather snappish, but not 'rageous.'

A fierce cry seemed to give the lie to her favourable report: the clothed hyena rose up, and stood tall on its hind feet.

'Ah, sir, she sees you!' exclaimed Grace: 'you'd better not stay.'

'Only a few moments, Grace: you must allow me a few moments.'

'Take care then, sir! – for God's sake, take care!'

The maniac bellowed: she parted her shaggy locks from her visage, and gazed wildly at her visitors. I recognised well that purple face, – those bloated features. Mrs Poole advanced.

'Keep out of the way,' said Mr Rochester, thrusting her aside: 'she has no knife now, I suppose? and I'm on my guard.'

'One never knows what she has, sir: she is so cunning: it is not in mortal discretion to fathom her craft.'

'We had better leave her,' whispered Mason.

'Go to the devil!' was his brother-in-law's recommendation.

'Ware!' cried Grace. The three gentlemen retreated simultaneously. Mr Rochester flung me behind him: the lunatic sprang and grappled his throat viciously, and laid her teeth to his cheek: they struggled. She was a big woman, in stature almost equalling her husband, and corpulent besides: she showed virile force in the contest – more than once she almost throttled him, athletic as he was. He could have settled her with a well-planted blow; but he would not strike: he would only wrestle. At last he mastered her arms; Grace Poole gave him a cord, and he pinioned them behind her: with more rope, which was at hand, he bound her to a chair. The operation was performed amidst the fiercest yells, and the most convulsive plunges. Mr Rochester then turned to the spectators: he looked at them with a smile both acrid and desolate.

'That is *my wife*,' said he. 'Such is the sole conjugal

embrace I am ever to know – such are the endearments which are to solace my leisure hours! And *this* is what I wished to have' (laying his hand on my shoulder): 'this young girl, who stands so grave and quiet at the mouth of hell, looking collectedly at the gambols of a demon. I wanted her just as a change after that fierce ragout. Wood and Briggs, look at the difference! Compare these clear eyes with the red balls yonder – this face with that mask – this form with that bulk; then judge me, priest of the Gospel and man of the law, and remember, with what judgment ye judge ye shall be judged! Off with you now. I must shut up my prize.'

We all withdrew. Mr Rochester stayed a moment behind us, to give some further order to Grace Poole. The solicitor addressed me as he descended the stair.

'You, madam,' said he, 'are cleared from all blame: your uncle will be glad to hear it – if, indeed, he should be still living – when Mr Mason returns to Madeira.'

'My uncle! What of him? Do you know him?'

'Mr Mason does: Mr Eyre has been the Funchal correspondent of his house for some years. When your uncle received your letter intimating the contemplated union between yourself and Mr Rochester, Mr Mason, who was staying at Madeira to recruit his health, on his way back to Jamaica, happened to be with him. Mr Eyre mentioned the intelligence; for he knew that my client here was acquainted with a gentleman of the name of Rochester. Mr Mason, astonished and distressed as you may suppose, revealed the real state of matters. Your uncle, I am sorry to say, is now on a sickbed; from which, considering the nature of his disease – decline – and the stage it has reached, it is unlikely he will ever rise. He could not then hasten to England himself, to extricate you from the snare into which you had fallen, but he implored Mr Mason to lose no time in taking steps to prevent the false marriage. He referred him to me for assistance. I used all despatch, and am thankful I was not too late: as you, doubtless, must be also. Were I not morally certain that your uncle will be dead ere you reach Madeira, I would advise you to accompany Mr Mason back: but as it is, I think you had better remain in England till you can hear further, either from or of Mr Eyre. Have we anything else to stay for?' he inquired of Mr Mason.

'No, no – let us be gone,' was the anxious reply; and without waiting to take leave of Mr Rochester, they made their exit at the hall door. The clergyman stayed to exchange a few sentences, either of admonition or reproof, with his haughty parishioner; this duty done, he too departed.

I heard him go as I stood at the half open door of my own room, to which I had now withdrawn. The house cleared, I shut myself in, fastened the bolt that none might intrude, and proceeded – not to weep, not to mourn, I was yet too calm for that, but – mechanically to take off the wedding dress, and replace it by the stuff gown I had worn yesterday, as I thought, for the last time. I then sat down: I felt weak and tired. I leaned my arms on a table, and my head dropped on them. And now I thought: till now I had only heard, seen, moved – followed up and down where I was led or dragged – watched event rush on event, disclosure open beyond disclosure: but *now, I thought.*

The morning had been a quiet morning enough – all except the brief scene with the lunatic: the transaction in the church had not been noisy; there was no explosion of passion, no loud altercation, no dispute, no defiance or challenge, no tears, no sobs: a few words had been spoken, a calmly pronounced objection to the marriage made; some stern, short questions put by Mr Rochester; answers, explanations given, evidence adduced; an open admission of the truth had been uttered by my master; then the living proof had been seen; the intruders were gone, and all was over.

I was in my own room as usual – just myself, without obvious change: nothing had smitten me, or scathed me, or maimed me. And yet, where was the Jane Eyre of yesterday? – where was her life? – where were her prospects?

Jane Eyre, who had been an ardent, expectant woman – almost a bride – was a cold, solitary girl again: her life was pale; her prospects were desolate. A Christmas frost had come at midsummer; a white December storm had whirled over June; ice glazed the ripe apples, drifts crushed the blowing roses; on hay-field and corn-field lay a frozen shroud: lanes which last night blushed full of flowers, today were pathless with untrodden snow; and the woods, which twelve hours since waved leafy and fragrant as groves between the tropics, now spread, waste, wild, and white as pine-forests in wintry Norway. My hopes were all dead – struck with a subtle doom, such as, in one night, fell on all the first-born in the land of Egypt. I looked on my cherished wishes, yesterday so blooming and glowing; they lay stark, chill, livid corpses that could never revive. I looked at my love: that feeling which was my master's – which he had created; it shivered in my heart, like a suffering child in a cold cradle; sickness and anguish had seized it; it could not seek Mr Rochester's arms – it could not derive warmth from his breast. Oh, never more could it turn to him; for faith was blighted – confidence destroyed! Mr Rochester was not to me what he had been; for he was not what I had thought him. I would not ascribe vice to him; I would not say he had betrayed me: but the attribute of stainless truth was gone from his idea; and from his presence I must go: *that* I perceived well. When – how – whither, I could not yet discern: but he himself,

I doubted not, would hurry me from Thornfield. Real affection, it seemed, he could not have for me; it had been only fitful passion: that was balked; he would want me no more. I should fear even to cross his path now: my view must be hateful to him. Oh, how blind had been my eyes! How weak my conduct!

My eyes were covered and closed: eddying darkness seemed to swim round me, and reflection came in as black and confused a flow. Self-abandoned, relaxed, and effortless, I seemed to have laid me down in the dried-up bed of a great river; I heard a flood loosened in remote mountains, and felt the torrent come: to rise I had no will, to flee I had no strength. I lay faint; longing to be dead. One idea only still throbbed life-like within me – a remembrance of God: it begot an unuttered prayer: these words went wandering up and down in my rayless mind, as something that should be whispered; but no energy was found to express them:—

'Be not far from me, for trouble is near: there is none to help.'

It was near: and as I had lifted no petition to Heaven to avert it – as I had neither joined my hands, nor bent my knees, nor moved my lips – it came: in full, heavy swing the torrent poured over me. The whole consciousness of my life lorn, my love lost, my hope quenched, my faith death-struck, swayed full and mighty above me in one sullen mass. That bitter hour cannot be described: in truth, 'the waters came into my soul; I sank in deep mire: I felt no standing; I came into deep waters; the floods overflowed me.'

GUY DE MAUPASSANT

A WEDDING GIFT

FOR A LONG time Jacques Bourdillere had sworn that he would never marry, but he suddenly changed his mind. It happened suddenly, one summer, at the seashore.

One morning as he lay stretched out on the sand, watching the women coming out of the water, a little foot had struck him by its neatness and daintiness. He raised his eyes and was delighted with the whole person, although in fact he could see nothing but the ankles and the head emerging from a flannel bathrobe carefully held closed. He was supposed to be sensual and a fast liver. It was therefore by the mere grace of the form that he was at first captured. Then he was held by the charm of the young girl's sweet mind, so simple and good, as fresh as her cheeks and lips.

He was presented to the family and pleased them. He immediately fell madly in love. When he saw Berthe Lannis in the distance, on the long yellow stretch of sand, he would tingle to the roots of his hair. When he was near her he would become silent, unable to speak or even to think, with a kind of throbbing at his heart, and a buzzing in his ears, and a bewilderment in his mind. Was that love?

He did not know or understand, but he had fully decided to have this child for his wife.

Her parents hesitated for a long time, restrained by the young man's bad reputation. It was said that he had an old sweetheart, one of these binding attachments which one always believes to be broken off and yet which always hold.

Besides, for a shorter or longer period, he loved every woman who came within reach of his lips.

Then he settled down and refused, even once, to see the one with whom he had lived for so long. A friend took care of this woman's pension and assured her an income. Jacques paid, but he did not even wish to hear of her, pretending even to ignore her name. She wrote him letters which he never opened. Every week he would recognize the clumsy writing of the abandoned woman, and every week a greater anger surged within him against her, and he would quickly tear the envelope and the paper, without opening it, without reading one single line, knowing in advance the reproaches and complaints which it contained.

As no one had much faith in his constancy, the test was prolonged through the winter, and Berthe's hand was not granted him until the spring. The wedding took place in Paris at the beginning of May.

The young couple had decided not to take the conventional wedding trip, but after a little dance for the younger cousins, which would not be prolonged after eleven o'clock, in order that this day of lengthy ceremonies might not be too tiresome, the young pair were to spend the first night in the parental home and then, on the following morning, to leave for the beach so dear to their hearts, where they had first known and loved each other.

Night had come, and the dance was going on in the large parlor. The two had retired into a little Japanese boudoir hung with bright silks and dimly lighted by the soft rays of a large colored lantern hanging from the ceiling like a gigantic egg. Through the open window the fresh air from outside passed over their faces like a caress, for the night was warm and calm, full of the odor of spring.

They were silent, holding each other's hands and from

time to time squeezing them with all their might. She sat there with a dreamy look, feeling a little lost at this great change in her life, but smiling, moved, ready to cry, often also almost ready to faint from joy, believing the whole world to be changed by what had just happened to her, uneasy, she knew not why, and feeling her whole body and soul filled with an indefinable and delicious lassitude.

He was looking at her persistently with a fixed smile. He wished to speak, but found nothing to say, and so sat there, expressing all his ardor by pressures of the hand. From time to time he would murmur: 'Berthe!' And each time she would raise her eyes to him with a look of tenderness; they would look at each other for a second and then her look, pierced and fascinated by his, would fall.

They found no thoughts to exchange. They had been left alone, but occasionally some of the dancers would cast a rapid glance at them, as though they were the discreet and trusty witnesses of a mystery.

A door opened and a servant entered, holding on a tray a letter which a messenger had just brought. Jacques, trembling, took this paper, overwhelmed by a vague and sudden fear, the mysterious terror of swift misfortune.

He looked for a long time at the envelope, the writing on which he did not know, not daring to open it, not wishing to read it, with a wild desire to put it in his pocket and say to himself: 'I'll leave that till tomorrow, when I'm far away!' But on one corner two big words, underlined, 'Very urgent,' filled him with terror. Saying, 'Please excuse me, my dear,' he tore open the envelope. He read the paper, grew frightfully pale, looked over it again, and, slowly, he seemed to spell it out word for word.

When he raised his head his whole expression showed how upset he was. He stammered: 'My dear, it's – it's from my best friend, who has had a very great misfortune. He has need of me immediately – for a matter of life or death. Will you excuse me if I leave you for half an hour? I'll be right back.'

Trembling and dazed, she stammered: 'Go, my dear!' not having been his wife long enough to dare to question him, to demand to know. He disappeared. She remained alone, listening to the dancing in the neighboring parlor.

He had seized the first hat and coat he came to and rushed downstairs three steps at a time. As he was emerging into the street he stopped under the gas-jet of the vestibule and reread the letter. This is what it said:

Sir: A girl by the name of Ravet, an old sweetheart of yours, it seems, has just given birth to a child that she says is yours. The mother is about to die and is begging for you. I take the liberty to write and ask you if you can grant this last request to a woman who seems to be very unhappy and worthy of pity.

Yours truly,

Dr Bonnard.

When he reached the sick-room the woman was already on the point of death. He did not recognize her at first. The doctor and two nurses were taking care of her. And everywhere on the floor were pails full of ice and rags covered with blood. Water flooded the carpet; two candles were burning on a bureau; behind the bed, in a little wicker crib, the child was crying, and each time it would moan the mother, in torture, would try to move, shivering under her ice bandages.

She was mortally wounded, killed by this birth. Her life was flowing from her, and, notwithstanding the ice and the care, the merciless hemorrhage continued, hastening her last hour.

She recognized Jacques and wished to raise her arms. They were so weak that she could not do so, but tears coursed down her pallid cheeks. He dropped to his knees beside the bed, seized one of her hands and kissed it frantically. Then, little by little, he drew close to the thin face, which started at the contact. One of the nurses was lighting them with a candle, and the doctor was watching them from the back of the room.

Then she said in a voice which sounded as though it came from a distance: 'I am going to die, dear. Promise to stay to the end. Oh! don't leave me now. Don't leave me in my last moments!'

He kissed her face and her hair, and, weeping, he murmured: 'Do not be uneasy; I will stay.'

It was several minutes before she could speak again, she was so weak. She continued: 'The little one is yours. I swear it before God and on my soul. I swear it as I am dying! I have never loved another man but you – promise to take care of the child.'

He was trying to take this poor pain-racked body in his arms. Maddened by remorse and sorrow, he stammered: 'I swear to you that I will bring him up and love him. He shall never leave me.'

Then she tried to kiss Jacques. Powerless to lift her head, she held out her white lips in an appeal for a kiss. He approached his lips to respond to this piteous entreaty.

As soon as she felt a little calmer, she murmured: 'Bring him here and let me see if you love him.'

He went and got the child. He placed him gently on the bed between them, and the little one stopped crying. She murmured: 'Don't move any more!' And he was quiet. And he stayed there, holding in his burning hand this other hand shaking in the chill of death, just as, a while ago, he had been holding a hand trembling with love. From time to time he would cast a quick glance at the clock, which marked midnight, then one o'clock, then two.

The physician had returned. The two nurses, after noiselessly moving about the room for a while, were now sleeping on chairs. The child was asleep, and the mother, with eyes shut, appeared also to be resting.

Suddenly, just as pale daylight was creeping in behind the curtains, she stretched out her arms with such a quick and violent motion that she almost threw her baby on the floor. A kind of rattle was heard in her throat, then she lay on her back motionless, dead.

The nurses sprang forward and declared: 'All is over!'

He looked once more at this woman whom he had so loved, then at the clock, which pointed to four, and he ran away, forgetting his overcoat, in the evening dress, with the child in his arms.

After he had left her alone the young wife had waited, calmly enough at first, in the little Japanese boudoir. Then, as she did not see him return, she went back to the parlor with an indifferent and calm appearance, but terribly anxious. When her mother saw her alone she asked: 'Where is your husband?' She answered: 'In his room; he is coming right back.'

After an hour, when everybody had questioned her, she told about the letter, Jacques' upset appearance and her fears of an accident.

Still they waited. The guests left; only the nearest relatives remained. At midnight the bride was put to bed, sobbing bitterly. Her mother and two aunts, sitting around the bed, listened to her crying, silent and in despair. The father had gone to the commissary of police to see if he could obtain some news.

At five o'clock a slight noise was heard in the hall. A door was softly opened and closed. Then suddenly a little cry like the mewing of a cat was heard throughout the silent house.

All the women started forward and Berthe sprang ahead of them all, pushing her way past her aunts, wrapped in a bathrobe.

Jacques stood in the middle of the room, pale and out of breath, holding an infant in his arms. The four women looked at him, astonished; but Berthe, who had suddenly become courageous, rushed forward with anguish in her heart, exclaiming: 'What is it? What's the matter?'

He looked about him wildly and answered shortly:

'I – I have a child and the mother has just died.'

And with his clumsy hands he held out the screaming infant.

Without saying a word, Berthe seized the child, kissed it and hugged it to her. Then she raised her tear-filled eyes to him, asking: 'Did you say that the mother was dead?' He answered: 'Yes – just now – in my arms. I had broken with her since summer. I knew nothing. The physician sent for me.'

Then Berthe murmured: 'Well, we will bring up the little one.'

ELIZABETH TAYLOR

PERHAPS A FAMILY
FAILING

OF COURSE, MRS Cotterell cried. Watery-eyed, on the arm of the bridegroom's father, she smiled in a bewildered way to left and right, coming down the aisle. Outside, on the church steps, she quickly dashed the tears away as she faced the camera, still arm-in-arm with Mr Midwinter, a man she detested.

He turned towards her and gave a great meaningless laugh just as the camera clicked and Mrs Cotterell had his ginny breath blown full in her face. Even in church he had to smell like that, she thought, and the grim words, 'Like father, like son,' disturbed her mind once more.

Below them, at the kerb's edge, Geoff was already helping his bride into the car. The solemnity of the service had not touched him. In the vestry, he had been as jaunty as ever, made his wife blush and was hushed by his mother, a frail, pensive creature, who had much, Mrs Cotterell thought, to be frail and pensive about.

It was Saturday morning and the bridal car moved off slowly among the other traffic. Mrs Cotterell watched until the white-ribboned motor disappeared.

The bridesmaids, one pink, one apple-green, were getting into the next car. Lissport was a busy place on Saturdays and to many of the women it was part of the morning's shopping-outing to be able to stand for a minute or two to watch a bride coming out of the church. Feeling nervous and self-conscious, Mrs Cotterell, who had often herself stood and watched and criticised, crossed the pavement to the car.

She was anxious to be home and wondered if everything was all right there. She had come away in a flurry of confused directions, leaving two of her neighbours slicing beetroot and sticking blanched almonds into the trifles. She was relieved that the reception was her own affair, that she could be sure that there would be no drunkenness, no rowdy behaviour and suggestive speeches, as there had been at Geoff's sister's wedding last year. One glass of port to drink a toast to the bride and bridegroom she had agreed to. For the rest she hoped that by now her kindly neighbours had mixed the orange cordial.

Mrs Cotterell cried again, much harder, when Beryl came downstairs in her going-away suit, and kissed her and thanked her (as if her mother were a hostess, not her own flesh and blood, Mrs Cotterell thought sorrowfully) and with composure got into Geoff's little car, to which Mr Midwinter had tied an empty sardine-tin.

Then everyone else turned to Mrs Cotterell and thanked her and praised the food and Beryl's looks and dress. It had all gone off all right, they said, making a great hazard of it. 'You'll miss her,' the women told her. 'I know what it's like,' some added.

The bridesmaids took off their flower wreaths and put on their coats. Geoff's brothers, Les and Ron, were taking them out for the evening. 'Not long till opening-time,' they said.

Mrs Cotterell went back into the house, to survey the wedding presents, and the broken wedding cake, with the trellis work icing she had done so lovingly, crumbled all over the table. Beryl's bouquet was stuck in a vase, waiting to be taken tomorrow to poor Grandma in hospital.

In the kitchen, the faithful neighbours were still hard at

work, washing up the piles of plates stained with beetroot and mustard and tomato sauce.

'She's gone,' Mrs Cotterell whispered into her crumpled handkerchief as her husband came in and put his arm round her.

'Soon be opening-time,' Geoff said, driving along the busy road to Seaferry. He had long ago stopped the car, taken the sardine-tin off the back axle and thrown it over a hedge. 'Silly old fool, Dad,' he had said fondly. 'Won't ever act his age.'

Beryl thought so, too, but decided not to reopen that old discussion, at such a time. For weeks, she had thought and talked and dreamt of the wedding, studied the advice to brides in women's magazines, on make-up, etiquette and Geoff's marital rights – which he must, she learnt, not be allowed to anticipate. 'Stop it, Geoff!' she had often said firmly. 'I happen to want you to respect me, thank you very much.' Unfortunately for her, Geoff was not the respectful kind, although, in his easy-going way, he consented to the celibacy – one of her girlish whims – and had even allowed the gratifying of his desires to be postponed from Easter until early summer, because she had suddenly decided she wanted sweet-peas in the bridesmaids' bouquets.

To the women's magazines Beryl now felt she owed every-thing; she had had faith in their advice and seen it justified. I expect Geoff's getting excited, she thought. She was really quite excited herself.

'Now where are you going?' she asked, as he swerved sud-denly off the road. It was perfectly plain that he was going into a public house, whose front door he had seen flung open just as he was about to pass it by.

'Well, here it is,' he said. 'The White Horse. The very first pub to have the privilege of serving a drink to Mr and Mrs Geoffrey Midwinter.'

This pleased her, although she wanted to get to the hotel as quickly as she could, to unpack her trousseau, before it creased too badly.

It was a dull little bar, smelling frowsty. The landlord was glumly watchful, as if they might suddenly get out of hand, or steal one of his cracked ash-trays.

Geoff, however, was in high spirits, and raised his pint pot and winked at his wife. 'Well, here's in anticipation,' he said. She looked demurely at her gin and orange, but she smiled. She loved him dearly. She was quite convinced of this, for she had filled in a questionnaire on the subject of love in one of her magazines, and had scored eighteen out of twenty, with a rating of 'You and Cleopatra share the honours.' Only his obsession with public houses worried her but she was sure that – once she had him away from the influence of his father and brothers – she would be able to break the habit.

At six o'clock Mr Midwinter took his thirst and his derogatory opinions about the wedding down to the saloon bar of the Starter's Orders. His rueful face, as he described the jugs of orangeade, convulsed his friends. 'Poor Geoff, what's he thinking of, marrying into a lot like that?' asked the barmaid.

'Won't make no difference to Geoff,' said his father. 'Geoff's like his dad. Not given to asking anybody's by-your-leave when he feels like a pint.'

Mrs Midwinter had stayed at home alone. It had not occurred to her husband that she might be feeling flat after the day's excitement. She would not have remarked on it herself, knowing the problem was insoluble. He could not have taken her to a cinema, because Saturday evening was sacred to drinking, and although she would have liked to go with him for a glass of stout, she knew why she could not. He always drank in the Men Only bar at the Starter's Orders. 'Well, you don't want me drinking with a lot of prostitutes, do you?' he often asked, and left her no choice, as was his habit.

Beryl had never stayed in an hotel before, and she was full of admiration at the commanding tone Geoff adopted as they entered the hall of the Seaferry Arms.

'Just one before we go up?' he enquired, looking towards the bar.

'Later, dear,' she said firmly. 'Let's unpack and tidy ourselves first; then we can have a drink before dinner.' The word 'dinner' depressed him. It threatened to waste a great deal of Saturday evening drinking time.

From their bedroom window they could see a bleak stretch of promenade, grey and gritty. The few people down there either fought their way against the gale, with their heads bowed and coats clutched to their breasts, or seemed tumbled along with the wind at their heels. The sun, having shone on the bride, had long ago gone in and it seemed inconceivable that it would ever come out again.

'No strolling along the prom tonight,' said Geoff.

'Isn't it a shame? It's the only thing that's gone wrong.'

Beryl began to hang up and spread about the filmy, lacy, ribboned lingerie with which she had for long planned to tease and entice her husband.

'The time you take,' he said. He had soon tipped everything out of his own case into a drawer. 'What's this?' he asked, picking up something of mauve chiffon.

'My nightgown,' she said primly.

'What ever for?'

'Don't be common.' She always affected disapproval when he teased her.

'What about a little anticipation here and now?' he suggested.

'Oh, don't be so silly. It's broad daylight.'

'Right. Well, I'm just going to spy out the lie of the land. Back in a minute,' he said.

She was quite content to potter about the bedroom, laying traps for his seduction; but when she was ready at last, she realised that he had been away a long time. She stood by the window, wondering what to do, knowing that it was time for them to go in to dinner. After a while, she decided that she would have to find him and, feeling nervous and self-conscious, she went along the quiet landing and down the stairs. Her common sense took her towards the sound of voices and laughter and, as soon as she opened the door of the bar, she was given a wonderful welcome from all the new friends Geoff had suddenly made.

'It seems ever so flat, doesn't it?' Mrs Cotterell said. All of the washing-up was done, but she was too tired to make a start on packing up the presents.

'It's the reaction,' her husband said solemnly.

Voices from a play on the wireless mingled with their own, but were ignored. Mrs Cotterell had her feet in a bowl of hot water. New shoes had given her agony. Beryl, better informed, had practised wearing hers about the house for days before.

'Haven't done my corns any good,' Mrs Cotterell mourned. Her feet ached and throbbed, and so did her heart.

'It all went off well, though, didn't it?' she asked, as she had asked him a dozen times before.

'Thanks to you,' he said dutifully. He was clearing out the

284

budgerigar's cage and the bird was sitting on his bald head, blinking and chattering.

Mrs Cotterell stared at her husband. She suddenly saw him as a completely absurd figure, and she trembled with anger and self-pity. Something ought to have been done for her on such an evening, she thought, some effort should have been made to console and reward her. Instead, she was left to soak her feet and listen to a lot of North Country accents on the radio. She stretched out her hand and switched them off.

'What ever's wrong, Mother?'

'I can't stand any more of that "By goom" and "Nowt" and "Eee, lad." It reminds me of that nasty cousin Rose of yours.'

'But we always listen to the play on a Saturday.'

'This Saturday isn't like other Saturdays.' She snatched her handkerchief out of her cuff and dabbed her eyes.

Mr Cotterell leant forward and patted her knee and the budgerigar flew from his head and perched on her shoulder.

'That's right, Joey, you go to Mother. She wants a bit of cheering-up.'

'I'm not his mother, if you don't mind, and I don't want cheering-up from a bird.'

'One thing I know is you're overtired. I've seen it coming. You wouldn't care to put on your coat and stroll down to the Public for a glass of port, would you?'

'Don't be ridiculous,' she said.

After dinner, they drank their coffee, all alone in the dreary lounge of the Seaferry Arms, and then Beryl went to bed. She had secret things to do to her hair and her face. 'I'll just pour you out another cup,' she said. 'Then, when you've drunk it, you can come up.'

'Right,' he said solemnly, nodding his head.

'Don't be long, darling.'

When she had gone, he sat and stared at the cupful of black coffee and then got up and made his way back to the bar.

All of his before-dinner cronies had left and a completely different set of people stood round the bar. He ordered some beer and looked about him.

'Turned chilly,' said the man next to him.

'Yes. Disappointing,' he agreed. To make friends was the easiest thing in the world. In no time, he was at the heart of it all again.

At ten o'clock, Beryl, provocative in chiffon, as the magazines would have described her, burst into tears of rage. She could hear the laughter – so much louder now, towards closing-time – downstairs in the bar and knew that the sound of it had drawn Geoff back. She was powerless – so transparently tricked out to tempt him – to do anything but lie and wait until, at bar's emptying, he should remember her and stumble upstairs to bed.

It was not the first happy evening Geoff had spent in the bar of the Seaferry Arms. He had called there with the team, after cricket-matches in the nearby villages. Seaferry was only twenty miles from home. Those summer evenings had all merged into one another, as drinking evenings should – and this one was merging with them. 'I'm glad I came,' he thought, rocking slightly as he stood by the bar with two of his new friends. He couldn't remember having met nicer people. They were a very gay married couple. The wife had a miniature poodle who had already wetted three times on the carpet. 'She can't help it, can you, angel?' her mistress protested. 'She's quite neurotic; aren't you, precious thing?'

Doris – as Geoff had been told to call her – was a heavy jolly woman. The bones of her stays showed through her frock, her necklace of jet beads was powdered with cigarette ash. She clutched a large, shiny handbag and had snatched from it a pound note, which she began to wave in the air, trying to catch the barmaid's eye. 'I say, miss! What's her name, Ted? Oh, yes. I say, Maisie! Same again, there's a dear girl.'

It was nearly closing-time, and a frenzied reordering was going on. The street door was pushed open and a man and woman with a murderous-looking bull terrier came in. 'You stay there,' the man said to the woman and the dog, and he left them and began to force his way towards the bar.

'Miss! Maisie!' Doris called frantically. Her poodle, venturing between people's legs, made another puddle under a table and approached the bull terrier.

'I say, Doris, call Zoë back,' said her husband. 'And put that money away. I told you I'll get these.'

'I insist. They're on me.'

'Could you call your dog back?' the owner of the bull terrier asked them. 'We don't want any trouble.'

'Come, Zoë, pet!' Doris called. 'He wouldn't hurt her, though. She's a bitch. Maisie! Oh, there's a dear. Same again, love. Large ones.'

Suddenly, a dreadful commotion broke out. Doris was nearly knocked off her stool as Zoë came flying back to her for protection, with the bull terrier at her throat. She screamed and knocked over somebody's gin.

Geoff, who had been standing by the bar in a pleasurable haze, watching the barmaid, was, in spite of his feeling of unreality, the first to spring to life and pounce upon the bull terrier and grab his collar. The dog bit his hand, but he was too drunk to feel much pain. Before anyone could snatch

Zoë out of danger, the barmaid lifted the jug of water and meaning to pour it over the bull terrier, flung it instead over Geoff. The shock made him loosen his grip and the fight began again. A second time he grabbed at the collar and had his hand bitten once more; but now – belatedly, everyone else thought – the two dog-owners came to his help. Zoë, with every likelihood of being even more neurotic in the future, was put, shivering, in her mistress's arms, the bull terrier was secured to his lead in disgrace, and Maisie called Time.

After some recriminations between themselves, the dog-owners thanked and congratulated Geoff. 'Couldn't get near them,' they said. 'The bar was so crowded. Couldn't make head or tail of what was going on.'

'Sorry you got so wet,' said Doris.

The bull terrier's owner felt rather ashamed of himself when he saw how pale Geoff was. 'You all right?' he asked. 'You look a bit shaken up.'

Geoff examined his hand. There was very little blood, but he was beginning to be aware of the pain and felt giddy. He shook his head, but could not answer. Something dripped from his hair on to his forehead, and when he dabbed it with his handkerchief, he was astonished to see water and not blood.

'You got far to go?' the man asked him. 'Where's your home?'

'Lissport.'

'That's our way, too, if you want a lift.' Whether Geoff had a car or not, the man thought he was in no condition to drive it; although, whether from shock or alcohol or both, it was difficult to decide.

'I'd *like* a lift,' Geoff murmured drowsily. 'Many thanks.'

'No, any thanks are due to *you*.'

'Doesn't it seem strange without Geoff?' Mrs Midwinter asked her husband. He was back from the Starter's Orders, had taken off his collar and tie and was staring gloomily at the dying fire.

'Les and Ron home yet?' he asked.

'No, they won't be till half-past twelve. They've gone to the dance at the Town Hall.'

'Half-past twelve! It's scandalous the way they carry on. Drinking themselves silly, I've no doubt at all. Getting decent girls into trouble.'

'It's only a dance, Dad.'

'*And* their last one. I'm not having it. Coming home drunk on a Sunday morning and lying in bed till all hours to get over it. When was either of them last at Chapel? Will you tell me that?'

Mrs Midwinter sighed and folded up her knitting.

'I can't picture why Geoff turned from Chapel like that.' Mr Midwinter seemed utterly depressed about his sons, as he often was at this time on a Saturday night.

'Well, he was courting . . .'

'First time I've been in a church was today, and I was not impressed.'

'I thought it was lovely, and you looked your part just as if you did it every day.'

'I wasn't worried about *my* part. Sort of thing like that makes no demands on *me*. What I didn't like was the service, to which I took exception, and that namby-pamby parson's voice. To me, the whole thing was – insincere.'

Mrs Midwinter held up her hand to silence him. 'There's a car stopping outside. It can't be the boys yet.'

From the street, they both heard Geoff's voice shouting goodbye, then a car door was slammed, and the iron gate opened with a whining sound.

'Dad, it's Geoff!' Mrs Midwinter whispered. 'There must have been an accident. Something's happened to Beryl.'

'Well, he sounded cheerful enough about it.'

They could hear Geoff coming unsteadily up the garden path. When Mrs Midwinter threw open the door, he stood blinking at the sudden light, and swaying.

'Geoff! What ever's wrong?'

'I've got wet, Mum, and I've hurt my hand,' Geoff said.

WILLIAM TREVOR

THE WEDDING IN THE GARDEN

EVER SINCE DERVLA was nine the people of the hotel had fascinated her. Its proprietor, Mr Congreve, wore clothes that had a clerical sombreness about them, though they were of a lighter hue than Father Mahony's stern black. Mr Congreve was a smiling man with a quiet face, apparently not in the least put out by reports in the town that his wife, in allying herself with a hotel proprietor, had married beneath her. Ladylike and elegant, she appeared not to regret her choice. Mrs Congreve favoured in her dresses a distinctive blend of greens and blues, her stylishness combining with the hotel proprietor's tranquil presence to lend the couple a quality that was unique in the town. Their children, two girls and an older boy, were imbued with this through the accident of their birth, and so were different from the town's other children in ways that might be termed superficial. 'Breeding,' Dervla's father used to say. 'The Congreves have great breeding in them.'

She herself, when she was nine, was fair-haired and skinny, with a graze always healing on one knee or the other because she had a way of tripping on her shoelaces. 'Ah, will you tie up those things!' her mother used to shout at her: her mother, big-faced and red, blinking through the steam that rose from a bucket of water. Her brothers and sisters had all left the house in Thomas MacDonagh Street by the time Dervla was nine; they'd left the town and the district, two of them in America even, one in London. Dervla was more than just the baby of the family: she was an afterthought, catching everyone unawares, born when her mother was forty-two. 'Chance had a hand in that one,' her father liked to pronounce, regarding her affectionately, as if pleased by this intervention of fate. When his brother from Leitrim visited the house in Thomas MacDonagh Street the statement was made often, being of family interest. 'If her mother didn't possess the strength of an ox,' Dervla's father liked to add, 'God knows how the end of it would have been.' And Dervla's Leitrim uncle, refreshing himself with a bottle of stout, would yet again wag his head in admiration and wonder at his sister-in-law's robust constitution. He was employed on the roads up in Leitrim and only came to the town on a Sunday, drawn to it by a hurling match. Dervla's father was employed by O'Mara the builder.

Even after she went to work in the Royal Hotel and came to know the family, her first image of them remained: the Congreves in their motor-car, an old Renault as she afterwards established, its canvas hood folded back, slowly making the journey to the Protestant church on a sunny Sunday morning. St Peter's Church was at one end of the town, the Royal Hotel at the other. It had, before its days as an hotel, apparently been owned by Mrs Congreve's family, and then people in the grocery business had bought it and had not lived there, people who had nothing to do with the town, who were not well known. After that Mr Congreve had made an offer with, so it was said, his wife's money.

The motor-car in the sunlight crept down Draper's Street, the bell of St Peter's Church still monotonously chiming. The boy – no older than Dervla herself – sat between his sisters in the back; Mr Congreve turned his head and said something to his wife. Daddy Phelan, outside Mrs Ryan's bar, saluted them in his wild way; Mrs Congreve waved back at him. The boy wore a grey flannel suit, the girls had fawn-coloured coats and tiny bows in their pigtails. The motor-car passed from view, and a moment later the bell ceased to chime.

Christopher couldn't remember the first time he'd been aware of her. All he knew was that she worked in the kitchen of the hotel, walking out from the town every day. Playing with Molly and Margery-Jane in the shrubberies of the garden, he had noticed now and again a solitary figure in a black coat, with a headscarf. He didn't know her name or what her face was like. 'Count to ten, Chris,' Margery-Jane would shrilly insist. 'You're not counting to ten!' Some game, rules now forgotten, some private family game they had invented themselves, stalking one another among the bamboos and the mahonias, Molly creeping on her hands and knees, not making a sound, Margery-Jane unable to control her excited breathing. The girl passed through the yard near by, a child as they were, but they paid her no attention.

A year or so later Mary, the elderly maid whose particular realm was the dining-room, instructed her in the clearing of a table. 'Dervla,' his mother said when the older waitress had led her away with cutlery and plates piled on to her tray. 'Her name is Dervla.' After that she was always in the dining-room at mealtimes.

It was then, too, that she began to come to the hotel on a bicycle, her day longer now, arriving before breakfast, cycling home again in the late evening. Once there was talk about her living there, but nothing had come of that. Christopher didn't know where she did live, had never once noticed Thomas MacDonagh Street in his wanderings about the town. Returning from boarding-school in Dublin, he had taken to going for walks, along the quay of the river where the sawmills were, through the lanes behind Brabazon's Brewery. He preferred to be alone at that time of his growing up, finding the company of his sisters too chattery. The river wound away through fields and sometimes a dog from the lanes or the cottages near the electricity plant would follow him. There was one in particular, a short-tailed terrier, its smooth white coat soiled and uncared for, ears and head flashed with black. There was a mongrel sheepdog also, an animal that ceased its customary cringing as soon as it gained the freedom of the fields. When he returned to the town these animals no longer followed him, but were occasionally involved in fights with other dogs, as though their excursion into the country had turned them into aliens who were no longer to be trusted. He went on alone then, through darkening afternoons or spitting rain, lingering by the shops that sold fruit and confectionery. There'd been a time when he and Margery-Jane and Molly had come to these shops with their pocket-money, for Peggy's Leg or pink bon-bons. More affluent now, he bought *Our Boys* and *Film Fun* and saved up for the *Wide World*.

His sisters had been born in the Royal Hotel, but he – before his father owned the place – in Dublin, where his parents had then lived. He did not remember Dublin: the hotel had become his world. It was a white building, set back a little from the street, pillars and steps prefacing its entrance doors. Its plain façade was decorated with a yellow AA sign and a blue RIAC one; in spring tulips bloomed in window-boxes on the downstairs windowsills. The words *Royal Hotel* were painted in black on this white façade and repeated in smaller letters above the pillared porch. At the back, beyond the yard and the garden, there was a row of garages and an entrance to them from Old Lane. The hotel's four employees came and went this way, Mrs O'Connor the cook, whatever maids there were, and Artie the boots. There was a stone-flagged hallway with doors off it to the kitchen and the larders and the scullery, and one to the passage that led to the back staircase. It was a dim hallway, with moisture sometimes on its grey-distempered walls, a dimness that was repeated in the passage that led to the back staircase and on the staircase itself. Upstairs there was a particular smell, of polish and old soup, with a tang of porter drifting up from the bar. The first-floor landing – a sideboard stretching along one wall, leather armchairs by the windows, occasional tables piled with magazines, a gold-framed mirror above the fire place – was the heart of the hotel. Off it were the better bedrooms and a billiard-room where the YMCA held a competition every March; above it there was a less impressive landing, little more than a corridor. On the ground floor the dining-room had glass swing-doors, twelve tables with white tablecloths, always set for dinner. The family occupied a corner one between the fire and the dumb-waiter, with its array of silver-plated sugar castors and salt and pepper and mustard containers, bottles of Yorkshire Relish, thick and thin, mint sauce in cut-glass jugs, and Worcester sauce, and jam and marmalade.

When Christopher was younger, before he went away to school, he and Margery-Jane and Molly used to play hide-and-seek in the small, cold bedrooms at the top of the house, skulking in the shadows on the uncarpeted stairs that led to the attics. Occasionally, if a visitor was staying in the hotel, their father would call up to them to make less noise, but this didn't happen often because a visitor was usually only in the hotel at night. They were mainly senior commercial travellers who stayed at the Royal, representatives of Wills or Horton's or Drummond's Seeds, once a year the Urney man; younger representatives lodged more modestly. Insurance men stayed at the hotel, and bank inspectors had been known to spend a fortnight or three weeks. Bord na Móna men came and went, and once in a while there was an English couple or a couple from the North, touring or on their honeymoon. When Miss Gilligan, who taught leatherwork at the technical college, first came to the town she spent nearly a month in the Royal before being satisfied with the lodging she was offered. Artie the boots, grey-haired but still in his forties, worked in the garden and the yard, disposed of empty bottles from the bar and often served there. Old Mary served there too, and at a busy time, which only rarely occurred, Mrs O'Connor would come up from the kitchen to assist. Dr Molloy drank at the Royal, and Hogarty the surveyor, and the agent at the Bank of Ireland, Mr McKibbin, and a few of the other bank men in the town. The bar was a quiet place, though, compared with the town's public houses; voices were never raised.

The main hall of the hotel was quiet also, except for the ticking of the grandfather clock and its chiming. There was the same agreeable smell there, of soup and polish, and porter from the bar. A barometer hung beneath a salmon in a glass case, notices of point-to-point races and the Dublin Spring Show and the Horse Show hung from hooks among coloured prints of Punchestown. The wooden floor was covered almost completely with faded rugs, and the upper half of the door to the bar was composed of frosted glass with a border of shamrocks. There were plants in brass pots on either side of a wide staircase with a greenish carpet, thread-bare in parts.

'Your inheritance one day,' Christopher's father said.

It was very grand, Dervla considered, to have your initials on a green trunk, and on a wooden box with metal brackets fixed to its edges. These containers stood in the back hall, with a suitcase, at the beginning of each term, before they were taken to the railway station. They stood there again when Christopher returned, before Artie helped him to carry them upstairs. On his first day back from school there was always a great fuss. His sisters became very excited, a special meal was prepared, Mr Congreve would light cigarette after cigarette, standing in front of the fire on the first-floor landing, listening to Christopher's tale of the long journey from Dublin. He always arrived in the evening, sometimes as late as seven o'clock but usually about half past five. In the dining-room when the family had supper he would say he was famished and tell his sisters how disgraceful the food at the school was, the turnips only half mashed, the potatoes with bits of clay still clinging to their skins, and a custard pudding called Yellow Peril. His mother, laughing at him, would say he shouldn't exaggerate, and his father would ask him about the rugby he had played, or the cricket. 'Like the game of tennis it would be,' Artie told her when Dervla asked him what cricket was. 'The way they'd wear the same type of clothing for it.' Miss Gillespie, the matron, was a tartar and Willie the furnace man's assistant told stories that couldn't be repeated. Dervla imagined the big grey house with a curving avenue leading up to it, and bells always ringing, and morning assemblies, and the march through cloisters to the chapel, which so often she had heard described. She imagined the boys in their grey suits kneeling down to say their prayers, and the ice on the inside of the windows on cold days. The chemistry master had blown his hair off, it was reported once in the dining-room, and Dervla thought of Mr Jerety who made up the prescriptions in the Medical Hall. Mr Jerety had no hair either, except for a little at the sides of his head.

Dervla managed the dining-room on her own now. Mary had become too rheumaticky to make the journey at any speed from the kitchen and found it difficult to lift the heavier plates from the table. She helped Mrs O'Connor with the baking instead, kneading dough on the marble slab at the side table in the kitchen, making pastry and preparing vegetables. It took her half a day, Dervla had heard Mr Congreve say, to mount the stairs to her bedroom at the top of the hotel, and the other half to descend it. He was fond of her, and would try to make her rest by the fire on the first-floor landing but she never did. 'Sure, if I sat down there, sir, I'd maybe never get up again.' It was unseemly, Dervla had heard old Mary saying in the kitchen, for an employee to be occupying an armchair in the place where the visitors and the family sat. Mr Congreve was devil-may-care about matters like that, but what would a visitor say if he came out of his bedroom and found a uniformed maid in an armchair? What would Byrne from Horton's say, or Boylan the insurance man?

In the dining-room, when she'd learnt how everything should be, 'the formalities', as Mr Congreve put it, Dervla didn't find her duties difficult. She was swift on her feet, as it was necessary to be, in case the food got cold. She could stack a tray with dishes and plates so economically that two journeys to the kitchen became one. She was careful at listening to what the visitors ordered and without writing anything down was able to relay the message to the kitchen. The family were never given a choice.

Often Christopher found himself glancing up from the food Dervla placed in front of him, to follow with his eyes her progress across the dining-room, the movement of her hips beneath her black dress, her legs clad in stockings that were black also. Once he addressed her in the backyard. He spoke softly, just behind her in the yard. It was dark, after seven, an evening in early March when a bitter wind was blowing. 'I'll walk with you, Dervla,' he said.

She wheeled her bicycle in Old Lane and they walked in silence except that once he remarked upon the coldness of the weather and she said she disliked rain more. When they reached the end of the lane he went one way and she the other.

'Hullo, Dervla,' he said one afternoon in the garden. It was late in August. He was lying on a rug among the hydran geas, reading. She had passed without noticing that he was there; she returned some minutes later with a bunch of parsley. It was then that he addressed her. He smiled, trying to find a different intonation, trying to make his greeting softer, less ordinary than usual. He wanted her to sit down on the brown checked rug, to enjoy the sun for a while, but of course that was impossible. He had wanted to wheel her bicycle for her that evening, as he would have done had she been another girl, Hazel Warren or Annie Warren, the coal merchant's daughters, or a girl he'd never even spoken to, someone's cousin, who used to visit the town every Christmas. But it hadn't seemed natural in any way at all to wheel the bicycle of the dining-room maid, any more than it would have been to ask a kitchen maid at school where she came from or if she had brothers and sisters.

'Hullo,' she said, replying to his greeting in the garden. She passed on with her bunch of parsley, seeming not to be in a hurry, the crisp white strings of her apron bobbing as she walked.

In her bedroom in the house in Thomas MacDonagh Street she thought of him every night before she went to sleep. She saw him as he was when he returned from his boarding-school, in his grey long-trousered suit, a green-and-white-striped tie knotted into the grey collar of his shirt. When she awoke in the morning she thought of him also, the first person to share the day with. In winter she lay there in the darkness, but in summer the dawn light lit the picture of the Virgin above the door, and when Dervla felt the Virgin's liquid eyes upon her she prayed, asking the Holy Mother for all sorts of things she afterwards felt she shouldn't have because they were trivial. She pleaded that he might smile when he thanked her for the rashers and sausages she put in front of him, that his little finger might accidentally touch her hand as only once it had. She pleaded that Mr Congreve wouldn't engage her in conversation at lunchtime, asking how her father was these days, because somehow – in front of him – it embarrassed her.

There was a nightmare she had, possessing her in varied forms: that he was in the house in Thomas MacDonagh Street and that her mother was on her knees, scrubbing the stone floor of the scullery. Her mother didn't seem to know who he was and would not stand up. Her father and her uncle from Leitrim sat drinking stout by the fire, and when she introduced him they remarked upon his clothes. Sometimes in the nightmare her uncle nudged him with his elbow and asked him if he had a song in him.

'That young Carroll has an eye for you,' her father said once or twice, drawing her attention to Buzzy Carroll who worked in Catigan's hardware. But she didn't want to spend Sunday afternoons walking out on the Ballydrim road with Buzzy Carroll, or to sit with his arms around her in the Excel cinema. One of the Christian Brothers had first called him Buzzy, something to do with the way his hair fluffed about his head, and after that no one could remember what Buzzy

Carroll's real name was. There were others who would have liked to go out with her, on walks or to the pictures, or to the Tara Dance Hall on a Friday night. There was Flynn who worked in Maguire's timber yard, and Chappie Reagan, and Butty Delaney. There was the porter at the auction rooms who had something the matter with his feet, the toes joined together in such a peculiar way that he showed them to people. And there was Streak Dwyer. 'You're nothing only a streak of woe,' the same Christian Brother had years ago pronounced. Streak Dwyer had ever since retained the sobriquet, serving now in Rattray's grocery, sombrely weighing flour and sugar. Dervla had once or twice wondered what walking out on the Ballydrim road with this melancholy shopman would be like and if he would suggest turning into one of the lanes, as Butty Delancy or Buzzy Carroll would have. She wouldn't have cared for it in the Excel cinema with Streak Dwyer any more than she cared for the idea of being courted by a man who showed people his toes.

'Dervla.'

On a wet afternoon, a Tuesday in September, he whispered her name on the first-floor landing. He put his arm around her, and she was frightened in case someone would come.

'I'm fond of you, Dervla.'

He took her hand and led her upstairs to Room 14, a tiny bedroom that was only used when the hotel was full. Both of them were shy, and their shyness evaporated slowly. He kissed her, stroking her hair. He said again he was fond of her. 'I'm fond of you too,' she whispered.

After that first afternoon they met often to embrace in Room 14. They would marry, he said at the end of that holidays; they would live in the hotel, just like his parents.

Over and over again in Room 14 the afternoon shadows gathered as sunlight slipped away. They whispered, clinging to one another, the warmth of their bodies becoming a single warmth. She sat huddled on his knee, holding tightly on to him in case they both fell off the rickety bedroom chair. He loved the curve of her neck, he whispered, and her soft fair hair, her lips and her eyes. He loved kissing her eyes.

Often there was silence in the bedroom, broken only by the faraway cries of Molly and Margery-Jane playing in the garden. Sometimes it became quite dark in the room, and she would have to go then because Mrs O'Connor would be wanting her in the kitchen.

'Not a bad fella at all,' her father said in Thomas MacDonagh Street. 'Young Carroll.' She wanted to laugh when her father said that, wondering what on earth he'd say if he knew about Room 14. He would probably say nothing; in silence he would take his belt to her. But the thought of his doing so didn't make her afraid.

'Oh, Dervla, how I wish the time would hurry up and pass!'

Over the years he had come to see the town as little better than a higgledy-piggledy conglomeration of dwellings, an ugly place except for the small bridge at the end of Mill Street. But it was Dervla's town, and it was his own; together they belonged there. He saw himself in middle age walking through its narrow streets, as he had walked during his childhood. He saw himself returning to the hotel and going at once to embrace the wife he loved with a passion that had not changed.

'Oh, Dervla,' he whispered in Room 14. 'Dervla, I'm so fond of you.'

*   *   *

304

'Well, now, I think we must have a little talk,' Mrs Congreve said.

They were alone in the dining-room; Dervla had been laying the tables for dinner. When Mrs Congreve spoke she felt herself reddening; the knives and forks felt suddenly cold in her hands.

'Finish the table, Dervla, and then we'll talk about it.'

She did as she was bidden. Mrs Congreve stood by a window, looking out at people passing on the street. When Dervla had finished she caught a glimpse of herself in the mirror over the fireplace. Her thin, pretty face had a frightened look, and seemed fragile, perhaps because she had paled. She averted her gaze almost as soon as the mirror reflected it. Mrs Congreve said:

'Mr Congreve and I are disappointed that this has happened. It's most unfortunate.'

Turning from the window, Mrs Congreve smiled a lingering, gracious smile. She was wearing one of her green-and-blue dresses, a flimsy, delicate garment with tiny blue buttons and a stylishly stiff white collar. Her dark hair was coiled silkily about her head.

'It is perhaps difficult for you to understand, Dervla, and certainly it is unpleasant for me to say. But there are differences between you and Christopher that cannot be overlooked or ignored.' Mrs Congreve paused and again looked out of the window, slightly drawing the net curtain aside. 'Christopher is not of your class, Dervla. He is not of your religion. You are a maid in this hotel. You have betrayed the trust that Mr Congreve and I placed in you. I'm putting it harshly, Dervla, but there's no point in pretending.'

Dervla did not say anything. She felt desolate and alone. She wished he wasn't away at school. She wished she could run out of the dining-room and find him somewhere, that he would help her in this terrifying conversation.

'Oh, Christopher has done wrong also. I can assure you we are aware of that. We are disappointed in Christopher, but we think it better to close the matter in his absence. He will not be back for another three months almost; we think it best to have everything finished and forgotten by then. Mr Congreve will explain to Christopher.'

Again there was the gracious smile. No note of anger had entered Mrs Congreve's voice, no shadow of displeasure disrupted the beauty of her features. She might have been talking about the annual bloodstock dinner, giving instructions about how the tables should be set.

'We would ask you to write a note now, to Christopher at school. Mr Congreve and I would like to see it, Dervla, before it goes on its way. That, then, would be the end of the matter.'

As she spoke, Mrs Congreve nodded sympathetically, honouring Dervla's unspoken protest: she understood, she said. She did not explain how the facts had come to be discovered, but suggested that in the note she spoke of Dervla should write that she felt in danger of losing her position in the Royal Hotel, that she was upset by what had taken place and would not wish any of it to take place again.

'That is the important aspect of it, Dervla. Neither Mr Congreve nor I wish to dismiss you. If we did, you – and we – would have to explain to your parents, even to Father Mahony, I suppose. If it's possible, Dervla, we would much rather avoid all that.'

But Dervla, crimson-faced, mentioned love. Her voice was weak, without substance and seeming to be without conviction, although this was not so. Mrs Congreve replied that that was penny-fiction talk.

306

'We want to get married, ma'am.' Dervla closed her eyes beneath the effort of finding the courage to say that. The palms of her hands, chilled a moment ago, were warmly moist now. She could feel pinpricks on her forehead.

'That's very silly, Dervla,' Mrs Congreve said in the same calm manner. 'I'm surprised you should be so silly.'

'I love him,' Dervla cried, all convention abruptly shattered. Her voice was shrill in the dining-room, tears ran from her eyes and she felt herself seized by a wildness that made her want to shriek out in fury. 'I love him,' she cried again. 'It isn't just a little thing.'

'Don't you feel you belong in the Royal, Dervla? We have trained you, you know. We have done a lot, Dervla.'

There was a silence then, except for Dervla's sobbing. She found a handkerchief in the pocket of her apron and wiped her eyes and nose with it. In such silly circumstances, Mrs Congreve said, Christopher would not inherit the hotel. The hotel would be sold, and Christopher would inherit nothing. It wasn't right that a little thing like this should ruin Christopher's life. 'So you see, you must go, Dervla. You must take your wages up to the end of the month and go this afternoon.'

The tranquillity of Mrs Congreve's manner was intensified by the sadness in her voice. She was on Dervla's side, her manner insisted; her admonitions were painful for her. Again she offered the alternative:

'Or simply write a few lines to him, and we shall continue in the hotel as though nothing has happened. That is possible, you know. I assure you of that, my dear.'

Miserably, Dervla asked what she could say in a letter. She would have to tell lies. She wouldn't know how to explain.

'No, don't tell lies. Explain the truth: that you realize the friendship must not continue, now that you and he are growing up. You've always been a sensible girl, Dervla. You must realize that what happened between you was for children only.'

Dervla shook her head, but Mrs Congreve didn't acknowledge the gesture.

'I can assure you, Dervla – I can actually promise you – that when Christopher has grown up a little more he will see the impossibility of continuing such a friendship. The hotel, even now, is everything to Christopher. I can actually promise you, also, that you will not be asked to leave. I know you value coming here.'

At school, when he received the letter, Christopher was astonished. In Dervla's rounded handwriting it said that they must not continue to meet in Room 14 because it was a sin. It would be best to bring everything to an end now, before she was dismissed. They had done wrong, but at least they could avoid the worst if they were sensible now.

It was so chilly a letter, as from a stranger, that Christopher could hardly believe what it so very clearly said. Why did she feel this now, when a few weeks ago they had sworn to love one another for as long as they lived? Were all girls as fickle and as strange? Or had the priests, somehow, got at her, all this stuff about sin?

He could not write back. His handwriting on the envelope would be recognized in the hotel, and he did not know her address since she had not included it in her letter. He had no choice but to wait, and as days and then weeks went by his bewilderment turned to anger. It was stupid that she should suddenly develop these scruples after all they'd said to one another. The love he continued to feel for her became tinged with doubt and with resentment, as though they'd had a quarrel.

'Now, I don't want to say anything more about this,' his father said at the beginning of the next holidays. 'But it doesn't do, you know, to go messing about with the maids.'

That was the end of the unfortunateness as far as his father was concerned. It was not something that should be talked about, no good could come of that.

'It wasn't messing about.'

'That girl was very upset, Christopher.'

Three months ago Christopher would have said he wanted to marry Dervla, forced into that admission by what had been discovered. He would have spoken of love. But his father had managed to draw him aside to have this conversation before he'd had an opportunity even to see her, let alone speak to her. He felt confused, and uncertain about his feelings.

'It would be hard on her to dismiss her. We naturally didn't want to do that. We want the girl to remain here, Christopher, since really it's a bit of a storm in a teacup.'

His father lit a cigarette and seemed more at ease once he had made that pronouncement. There was a lazier look about his face than there had been a moment ago; a smile drifted over his lips. 'Good term?' he said, and Christopher nodded.

'Is it the priests, Dervla?' They stood together in a doorway in Old Lane, her bicycle propped against the kerb. 'Did the priests get at you?'

She shook her head.

'Did my mother speak to you?'

'Your mother only said a few things.'

She went away, wheeling her bicycle for a while before mounting it. He watched her, not feeling as miserable as when her letter had arrived, for during the months that had passed since then he had become reconciled to the loss of their relationship: between the lines of her letter there had been a finality.

He returned to the hotel and Artie helped him to carry his trunk upstairs. He wished that none of it had ever happened.

Dervla was glad he made no further effort to talk to her, but standing between courses by the dumb-waiter in the dining-room, she often wondered what he was thinking. While the others talked he was at first affected by embarrassment because at mealtimes in the past there had been the thrill of surreptitious glances and forbidden smiles. But after a week or so he became less quiet, joining in the family conversation, and she became the dining-room maid again.

Yet for Dervla the moment of placing his food in front of him was as poignant as ever it had been, and in her private moments she permitted herself the luxury of dwelling in the past. In her bedroom in Thomas MacDonagh Street she closed her eyes and willed into her consciousness the afternoon sunlight of Room 14. Once more she was familiar with the quickening of his heart and the cool touch of his hands. Once more she clung to him, her body huddled into his on the rickety chair in the corner, the faraway cries of Molly and Margery-Jane gently disturbing the silence.

Dervla did not experience bitterness. She was fortunate that the Congreves had been above the pettiness of dismissing her, and when she prayed she gave thanks for that. When more time had gone by she found herself able to confess the sinning that had been so pleasurable in Room 14, and was duly burdened with a penance for both the misdemeanours and her long delay in confessing them. She had feared to lose what there had been through expiation, but the fear had been groundless: only reality had been lost. 'Young Carroll was asking for you,' her father reported in a bewildered way, unable to understand her reluctance even to consider Buzzy Carroll's interest.

Everything was easier when the green trunk and the box with the metal brackets stood in the back hall at the beginning of another term, and when a few more terms had come and gone he greeted her in the hotel as if all she had confessed to was a fantasy. Like his parents, she sensed, he was glad her dismissal had not been necessary, for that would have been unfair. 'Did my mother speak to you?' The quiet vehemence there had been in his voice was sweet to remember, but he himself would naturally wish to forget it now: for him, Room 14 must have come to seem like an adventure in indiscretion, as naturally his parents had seen it.

Two summers after he left school Dervla noticed signs in him that painfully echoed the past. An archdeacon's daughter sometimes had lunch with the family: he couldn't take his eyes off her. Serving the food and in her position by the dumb-waiter, Dervla watched him listening while the archdeacon's daughter talked about how she and her parents had moved from one rectory to another and how the furniture hadn't fitted the new rooms, how there hadn't been enough stair-carpet. The archdeacon's daughter was very beautiful. Her dark hair was drawn back from a centre parting; when she smiled a dimple came and went in one cheek only; her skin was like the porcelain of a doll's skin. Often in the dining-room she talked about her childhood in the seaside backwater where she had once lived. Every morning in summer and autumn she and her father had gone together to the strand to bathe. They piled their clothes up by a breakwater, putting stones on them if there was a wind, and then they would run down the sand to the edge of the sea. A man sometimes passed by on a horse, a retired lighthouse keeper, a lonely, widowed man. Christopher was entranced.

Dervla cleared away the dishes, expertly disposing of chop bones or bits of left-behind fat. Mary had years ago shown her how to flick the table refuse on to a single plate, a different one from the plate you gathered the used knives and forks on to. Doing so now, she too listened to everything the archdeacon's daughter said. Once upon a time the Pierrots had performed on the strand in August, and Hewitt's Travelling Fun Fair had come; regularly, June to September, summer visitors filled the promenade boarding-houses, arriving on excursion trains. Garish pictures were painted with coloured powders on the sand, castles and saints and gardens. 'I loved that place,' the archdeacon's daughter said.

Afterwards Dervla watched from an upstairs window, the window in fact of Room 14. The archdeacon's daughter sat with him in the garden, each of them in a deck-chair, laughing and conversing. They were always laughing: the archdeacon's daughter would say something and he would throw his head back with appreciation and delight. Long before the engagement was announced Dervla knew that this was the girl who was going to take her place, in his life and in the hotel.

The Archdeacon conducted the service in St Peter's, and then the guests made their way to the garden of the hotel. That the wedding reception was to be at the hotel was a business arrangement between the Archdeacon and Mr Congreve, for the expenses were to be the former's, as convention demanded. It was a day in June, a Thursday, in the middle of a heatwave.

Dervla and a new maid with spectacles handed round glasses of champagne. Artie saw to it that people had chairs to sit on if they wished to sit. The archdeacon's daughter wore a wedding-dress that had a faint shade of blue in it, and a Limerick lace veil. She was kissed by people in the garden, she smiled while helping to cut the wedding cake. Her four bridesmaids, Molly and Margery-Jane among them, kept saying she looked marvellous.

Speeches were made in the sunshine. Dr Molloy made one and so did the best man, Tom Gouvernet, and Mr Congreve. Dr Molloy remembered the day Christopher was born, and Mr Congreve remembered the first time he'd set eyes on the beauty of the archdeacon's daughter, and Tom Gouvernet remembered Christopher at school. Other guests remembered other occasions; Christopher said he was the lucky man and kissed the archdeacon's daughter while people clapped their hands with delight. Tom Gouvernet fell backwards off the edge of a raised bed.

There was an excess of emotion in the garden, an excess of smiles and tears and happiness and love. The champagne glasses were held up endlessly, toast after toast. Christopher's mother moved among the guests with the plump wife of the archdeacon and the Archdeacon himself, who was as frail as a stalk of straw. In his easy-going way Christopher's father delighted in the champagne and the sunshine, and the excitement of a party. Mr McKibbin, the bank agent, was there, and Hogarty the surveyor, and an insurance man who happened to be staying at the hotel. There was nothing Mr Congreve liked better than standing about talking to these bar-room companions.

'Thanks, Dervla.' Taking a glass from her tray,

Christopher smiled at her because for ages that had been possible again.

'It's a lovely wedding, sir.'

'Yes, it is.'

He looked at her eyes, and was aware of the demanding steadiness of her gaze. He sensed what she was wondering and wondered it himself: what would have happened if she'd been asked to leave the hotel? He guessed, as she did: they would have shared the resentment and the anger that both of them had separately experienced; defiantly they would have continued to meet in the town; she would have accompanied him on his walks, out into the country and the fields. There would have been talk in the town and scenes in the hotel, their relationship would again have been proscribed. They would have drawn closer to one another, their outraged feelings becoming an element in the forbidden friendship. In the end, together, they would have left the hotel and the town and neither of them would be standing here now. Both their lives would be quite different.

'You'll be getting married yourself one of these days, Dervla.'

'Ah, no no.'

She was still quite pretty. There was a simplicity about her freckled features that was pleasing; her soft fair hair was neat beneath her maid's white cap. But she was not beautiful. Once, not knowing much about it, he had imagined she was. It was something less palpable that distinguished her.

'Oh, surely? Surely, Dervla?'

'I don't see myself giving up the hotel, sir. My future's here, sir.'

He smiled again and passed on. But his smile, which remained while he listened to a story of Tom Gouvernet's about the hazards to be encountered on a honeymoon, was uneasy. An echo of the eyes that had gazed so steadily remained with him, as did the reference she had made to her future. That she had not been turned out of the hotel had seemed something to be proud of at the time: a crudity had been avoided. But while Tom Gouvernet's lowered voice continued, he found himself wishing she had been. She would indeed not ever marry, her eyes had stated, she would not wish to.

A hand of his wife's slipped into one of his; the voice of Tom Gouvernet ceased. The hand was as delicate as the petal of a flower, the fingers so tiny that involuntarily he lifted them to his lips. Had Dervla seen? he wondered, and he looked through the crowd for a glimpse of her but could not see her. Hogarty the surveyor was doing a trick with a hand-kerchief, entertaining the coal merchant's daughters. Mr McKibbin was telling one of his stories.

'Ah, he's definitely the lucky man,' Tom Gouvernet said, playfully winking at the bride.

It had never occurred to Christopher before that while he and his parents could successfully bury a part of the past, Dervla could not. It had never occurred to him that because she was the girl she was she did not appreciate that some experiences were best forgotten. Ever since the Congreves had owned the Royal Hotel a way of life had obtained there, but its subtleties had naturally eluded the dining-room maid.

'When you get tired of him,' Tom Gouvernet went on in the same light manner, 'you know who to turn to.'

'Oh, indeed I do, Tom.'

He should have told her about Dervla. If he told her now she would want Dervla to go; any wife would, in perfect reasonableness. An excuse must be found, she would say, even though a promise had been made.

'But I won't become tired of him,' she was saying, smiling at Tom Gouvernet. 'He's actually quite nice, you know.'

In the far distance Dervla appeared, hurrying from the hotel with a freshly laden tray. Christopher watched her, while the banter continued between bride and best man.

'He had the shocking reputation at school,' Tom Gouvernet said.

'Oh? I didn't know that.' She was still smiling; she didn't believe it. It wasn't true.

'A right Lothario you've got yourself hitched to.'

He would not tell her. It was too late for that, it would bewilder her since he had not done so before. It wouldn't be fair to require her not to wish that Dervla, even now, should be asked to go; or to understand that a promise made to a dining-room maid must be honoured because that was the family way.

Across the garden the Archdeacon lifted a glass from Dervla's tray. He was still in the company of his plump wife and Christopher's mother. They, too, took more champagne and then Dervla walked towards where Christopher was standing with his bride and his best man. She moved quickly through the crowd, not offering her tray of glasses to the guests she passed, intent upon her destination.

'Thank you, Dervla,' his wife of an hour said.

'I think Mr Hogarty,' he said himself, 'could do with more champagne.'

He watched her walking away and was left again with the insistence in her eyes. As the dining-room maid, she would become part of another family growing up in the hotel. She would listen to a mother telling her children about the strand where once she'd bathed, where a retired lighthouse keeper had passed by on a horse. For all his life he would daily look upon hers, but no words would ever convey her undramatic revenge because the right to speak, once his gift to her, had been taken away. He had dealt in cruelty and so now did she: her gift to him, held over until his wedding day, was that afternoon shadows would gather for ever in Room 14, while she kept faith.

BEYOND THE
HONEYMOON

STEPHEN CRANE

THE BRIDE COMES
TO YELLOW SKY

THE GREAT PULLMAN was whirling onward with such dignity of motion that a glance from the window seemed simply to prove that the plains of Texas were pouring eastward. Vast flats of green grass, dull-hued spaces of mesquite and cactus, little groups of frame houses, woods of light and tender trees, all were sweeping into the east, sweeping over the horizon, a precipice.

A newly married pair had boarded this coach at San Antonio. The man's face was reddened from many days in the wind and sun, and a direct result of his new black clothes was that his brick-colored hands were constantly performing in a most conscious fashion. From time to time he looked down respectfully at his attire. He sat with a hand on each knee, like a man waiting in a barber's shop. The glances he devoted to other passengers were furtive and shy.

The bride was not pretty, nor was she very young. She wore a dress of blue cashmere, with small reservations of velvet here and there and with steel buttons abounding. She continually twisted her head to regard her puff sleeves, very stiff, straight, and high. They embarrassed her. It was quite apparent that she had cooked, and that she expected to cook, dutifully. The blushes caused by the careless scrutiny of some passengers as she had entered the car were strange to see upon this plain, under-class countenance, which was drawn in placid, almost emotionless lines.

They were evidently very happy. 'Ever been in a parlor-car before?' he asked, smiling with delight.

'No,' she answered, 'I never was. It's fine, ain't it?'

'Great! And then after a while we'll go forward to the diner and get a big layout. Finest meal in the world. Charge a dollar.'

'Oh, do they?' cried the bride. 'Charge a dollar? Why, that's too much – for us – ain't it, Jack?'

'Not this trip, anyhow,' he answered bravely. 'We're going to go the whole thing.'

Later, he explained to her about the trains. 'You see, it's a thousand miles from one end of Texas to the other, and this train runs right across it and never stops but four times.' He had the pride of an owner. He pointed out to her the dazzling fittings of the coach, and in truth her eyes opened wider as she contemplated the sea-green figured velvet, the shining brass, silver, and glass, the wood that gleamed as darkly brilliant as the surface of a pool of oil. At one end a bronze figure sturdily held a support for a separated chamber, and at convenient places on the ceiling were frescoes in olive and silver.

To the minds of the pair, their surroundings reflected the glory of their marriage that morning in San Antonio. This was the environment of their new estate, and the man's face in particular beamed with an elation that made him appear ridiculous to the negro porter. This individual at times surveyed them from afar with an amused and superior grin. On other occasions he bullied them with skill in ways that did not make it exactly plain to them that they were being bullied. He subtly used all the manners of the most unconquerable kind of snobbery. He oppressed them, but of this oppression they had small knowledge, and they speedily forgot that infrequently a number of travelers covered them

324

with stares of derisive enjoyment. Historically there was supposed to be something infinitely humorous in their situation.

'We are due in Yellow Sky at 3:42,' he said, looking tenderly into her eyes.

'Oh, are we?' she said, as if she had not been aware of it. To evince surprise at her husband's statement was part of her wifely amiability. She took from a pocket a little silver watch, and as she held it before her and stared at it with a frown of attention, the new husband's face shone.

'I bought it in San Anton' from a friend of mine,' he told her gleefully.

'It's seventeen minutes past twelve,' she said, looking up at him with a kind of shy and clumsy coquetry. A passenger, noting this play, grew excessively sardonic, and winked at himself in one of the numerous mirrors.

At last they went to the dining-car. Two rows of negro waiters, in glowing white suits, surveyed their entrance with the interest and also the equanimity of men who had been forewarned. The pair fell to the lot of a waiter who happened to feel pleasure in steering them through their meal. He viewed them with the manner of a fatherly pilot, his countenance radiant with benevolence. The patronage, entwined with the ordinary deference, was not plain to them. And yet, as they returned to their coach, they showed in their faces a sense of escape.

To the left, miles down a long purple slope, was a little ribbon of mist where moved the keening Rio Grande. The train was approaching it at an angle, and the apex was Yellow Sky. Presently it was apparent that, as the distance from Yellow Sky grew shorter, the husband became commensurately restless. His brick-red hands were more insistent in their prominence. Occasionally he was even rather absent-minded and far-away when the bride leaned forward and addressed him.

As a matter of truth, Jack Potter was beginning to find the shadow of a deed weigh upon him like a leaden slab. He, the town marshal of Yellow Sky, a man known, liked, and feared in his corner, a prominent person, had gone to San Antonio to meet a girl he believed he loved, and there, after the usual prayers, had actually induced her to marry him, without consulting Yellow Sky for any part of the transaction. He was now bringing his bride before an innocent and unsuspecting community.

Of course, people in Yellow Sky married as it pleased them, in accordance with a general custom; but such was Potter's thought of his duty to his friends, or of their idea of his duty, or of an unspoken form which does not control men in these matters, that he felt he was heinous. He had committed an extraordinary crime. Face to face with this girl in San Antonio, and spurred by his sharp impulse, he had gone headlong over all the social hedges. At San Antonio he was like a man hidden in the dark. A knife to sever any friendly duty, any form, was easy to his hand in that remote city. But the hour of Yellow Sky, the hour of daylight, was approaching.

He knew full well that his marriage was an important thing to his town. It could only be exceeded by the burning of the new hotel. His friends could not forgive him. Frequently he had reflected on the advisability of telling them by telegraph, but a new cowardice had been upon him. He feared to do it. And now the train was hurrying him toward a scene of amazement, glee, and reproach. He glanced out of the window at the line of haze swinging slowly in towards the train.

Yellow Sky had a kind of brass band, which played

painfully, to the delight of the populace. He laughed without heart as he thought of it. If the citizens could dream of his prospective arrival with his bride, they would parade the band at the station and escort them, amid cheers and laughing congratulations, to his adobe home.

He resolved that he would use all the devices of speed and plains-craft in making the journey from the station to his house. Once within that safe citadel he could issue some sort of a vocal bulletin, and then not go among the citizens until they had time to wear off a little of their enthusiasm.

The bride looked anxiously at him. 'What's worrying you, Jack?'

He laughed again. 'I'm not worrying, girl. I'm only thinking of Yellow Sky.'

She flushed in comprehension.

A sense of mutual guilt invaded their minds and developed a finer tenderness. They looked at each other with eyes softly aglow. But Potter often laughed the same nervous laugh. The flush upon the bride's face seemed quite permanent.

The traitor to the feelings of Yellow Sky narrowly watched the speeding landscape. 'We're nearly there,' he said.

Presently the porter came and announced the proximity of Potter's home. He held a brush in his hand and, with all his airy superiority gone, he brushed Potter's new clothes as the latter slowly turned this way and that way. Potter fumbled out a coin and gave it to the porter, as he had seen others do. It was a heavy and muscle-bound business, as that of a man shoeing his first horse.

The porter took their bag, and as the train began to slow they moved forward to the hooded platform of the car. Presently the two engines and their long string of coaches rushed into the station of Yellow Sky.

'They have to take water here,' said Potter, from a constricted throat and in mournful cadence, as one announcing death. Before the train stopped, his eye had swept the length of the platform, and he was glad and astonished to see there was none upon it but the station-agent, who, with a slightly hurried and anxious air, was walking toward the water-tanks. When the train had halted, the porter alighted first and placed in position a little temporary step.

'Come on, girl,' said Potter hoarsely. As he helped her down they each laughed on a false note. He took the bag from the negro, and bade his wife cling to his arm. As they slunk rapidly away, his hang-dog glance perceived that they were unloading the two trunks, and also that the station-agent far ahead near the baggage-car had turned and was running toward him, making gestures. He laughed, and groaned as he laughed, when he noted the first effect of his marital bliss upon Yellow Sky. He gripped his wife's arm firmly to his side, and they fled. Behind them the porter stood chuckling fatuously.

II

The California Express on the Southern Railway was due at Yellow Sky in twenty-one minutes. There were six men at the bar of the 'Weary Gentleman' saloon. One was a drummer who talked a great deal and rapidly; three were Texans who did not care to talk at that time; and two were Mexican sheep-herders who did not talk as a general practice in the 'Weary Gentleman' saloon. The barkeeper's dog lay on the board walk that crossed in front of the door. His head was on his paws, and he glanced drowsily here and there with the constant vigilance of a dog that is kicked on occasion. Across the sandy street were some vivid green grass plots, so wonderful in appearance amid the sands that burned near them in a blazing sun that they caused a doubt in the mind. They exactly resembled the grass mats used to represent lawns on the stage. At the cooler end of the railway station a man without a coat sat in a tilted chair and smoked his pipe. The fresh-cut bank of the Rio Grande circled near the town, and there could be seen beyond it a great, plum-colored plain of mesquite.

Save for the busy drummer and his companions in the saloon, Yellow Sky was dozing. The new-comer leaned gracefully upon the bar, and recited many tales with the confidence of a bard who has come upon a new field.

'—and at the moment that the old man fell down stairs with the bureau in his arms, the old woman was coming up with two scuttles of coal, and, of course—'

The drummer's tale was interrupted by a young man who suddenly appeared in the open door. He cried: 'Scratchy Wilson's drunk, and has turned loose with both hands.' The two Mexicans at once set down their glasses and faded out of the rear entrance of the saloon.

The drummer, innocent and jocular, answered: 'All right, old man. S'pose he has. Come in and have a drink, anyhow.'

But the information had made such an obvious cleft in every skull in the room that the drummer was obliged to see its importance. All had become instantly solemn. 'Say,' said he, mystified, 'what is this?' His three companions made the introductory gesture of eloquent speech, but the young man at the door forestalled them.

'It means, my friend,' he answered, as he came into the saloon, 'that for the next two hours this town won't be a health resort.'

The barkeeper went to the door and locked and barred it. Reaching out of the window, he pulled in heavy wooden shutters and barred them. Immediately a solemn, chapel-like gloom was upon the place. The drummer was looking from one to another.

'But, say,' he cried, 'what is this, anyhow? You don't mean there is going to be a gun-fight?'

'Don't know whether there'll be a fight or not,' answered one man grimly. 'But there'll be some shootin' – some good shootin'.'

The young man who had warned them waved his hand. 'Oh, there'll be a fight fast enough if anyone wants it. Anybody can get a fight out there in the street. There's a fight just waiting.'

The drummer seemed to be swayed between the interest of a foreigner and a perception of personal danger.

'What did you say his name was?' he asked.

'Scratchy Wilson,' they answered in chorus.

'And will he kill anybody? What are you going to do? Does this happen often? Does he rampage around like this once a week or so? Can he break in that door?'

'No, he can't break down that door,' replied the barkeeper. 'He's tried it three times. But when he comes you'd better lay down on the floor, stranger. He's dead sure to shoot at it, and a bullet may come through.'

Thereafter the drummer kept a strict eye upon the door. The time had not yet been called for him to hug the floor, but, as a minor precaution, he sidled near to the wall. 'Will he kill anybody?' he said again.

The men laughed low and scornfully at the question.

'He's out to shoot, and he's out for trouble. Don't see any good in experimentin' with him.'

'But what do you do in a case like this? What do you do?'

A man responded: 'Why, he and Jack Potter—'

'But,' in chorus, the other men interrupted, 'Jack Potter's in San Anton'.'

'Well, who is he? What's he got to do with it?'

'Oh, he's the town marshal. He goes out and fights Scratchy when he gets on one of these tears.'

'Wow,' said the drummer, mopping his brow. 'Nice job he's got.'

The voices had toned away to mere whisperings. The drummer wished to ask further questions which were born of an increasing anxiety and bewilderment; but when he attempted them, the men merely looked at him in irritation and motioned him to remain silent. A tense waiting hush was upon them. In the deep shadows of the room their eyes shone as they listened for sounds from the street. One man made three gestures at the barkeeper, and the latter, moving like a ghost, handed him a glass and a bottle. The man poured a full glass of whisky, and set down the bottle noiselessly. He gulped the whisky in a swallow, and turned again toward the door in immovable silence. The drummer saw that the barkeeper, without a sound, had taken a Winchester from beneath the bar. Later he saw this individual beckoning to him, so he tiptoed across the room.

'You better come with me back of the bar.'

'No, thanks,' said the drummer, perspiring. 'I'd rather be where I can make a break for the back door.'

Whereupon the man of bottles made a kindly but peremptory gesture. The drummer obeyed it, and finding himself seated on a box with his head below the level of the bar, balm was laid upon his soul at sight of various zinc and copper fittings that bore a resemblance to armor-plate. The barkeeper took a seat comfortably upon an adjacent box.

'You see,' he whispered, 'this here Scratchy Wilson is a

331

wonder with a gun – a perfect wonder – and when he goes on the war trail, we hunt our holes – naturally. He's about the last one of the old gang that used to hang out along the river here. He's a terror when he's drunk. When he's sober he's all right – kind of simple – wouldn't hurt a fly – nicest fellow in town. But when he's drunk – whoo!'

There were periods of stillness. 'I wish Jack Potter was back from San Anton',' said the barkeeper. 'He shot Wilson up once – in the leg – and he would sail in and pull out the kinks in this thing.'

Presently they heard from a distance the sound of a shot, followed by three wild yowls. It instantly removed a bond from the men in the darkened saloon. There was a shuffling of feet. They looked at each other. 'Here he comes,' they said.

III

A man in a maroon-colored flannel shirt, which had been purchased for purposes of decoration and made, principally, by some Jewish women on the east side of New York, rounded a corner and walked into the middle of the main street of Yellow Sky. In either hand the man held a long, heavy, blue-black revolver. Often he yelled, and these cries rang through a semblance of a deserted village, shrilly flying over the roofs in a volume that seemed to have no relation to the ordinary vocal strength of a man. It was as if the surrounding stillness formed the arch of a tomb over him. These cries of ferocious challenge rang against walls of silence. And his boots had red tops with gilded imprints, of the kind beloved in winter by little sledding boys on the hill-sides of New England.

The man's face flamed in a rage begot of whisky. His eyes,

rolling and yet keen for ambush, hunted the still doorways and windows. He walked with the creeping movement of the midnight cat. As it occurred to him, he roared menacing information. The long revolvers in his hands were as easy as straws; they were moved with an electric swiftness. The little fingers of each hand played sometimes in a musician's way. Plain from the low collar of the shirt, the cords of his neck straightened and sank, straightened and sank, as passion moved him. The only sounds were his terrible invitations. The calm adobes preserved their demeanor at the passing of this small thing in the middle of the street.

There was no offer of fight; no offer of fight. The man called to the sky. There were no attractions. He bellowed and fumed and swayed his revolvers here and everywhere.

The dog of the barkeeper of the 'Weary Gentleman' saloon had not appreciated the advance of events. He yet lay dozing in front of his master's door. At sight of the dog, the man paused and raised his revolver humorously. At sight of the man, the dog sprang up and walked diagonally away, with a sullen head, and growling. The man yelled, and the dog broke into a gallop. As it was about to enter an alley, there was a loud noise, a whistling, and something spat the ground directly before it. The dog screamed, and, wheeling in terror, galloped headlong in a new direction. Again there was a noise, a whistling, and sand was kicked viciously before it. Fear-stricken, the dog turned and flurried like an animal in a pen. The man stood laughing, his weapons at his hips.

Ultimately the man was attracted by the closed door of the 'Weary Gentleman' saloon. He went to it, and hammering with a revolver, demanded drink.

The door remaining imperturbable, he picked a bit of paper from the walk and nailed it to the framework with a knife. He then turned his back contemptuously upon this popular resort, and walking to the opposite side of the street, and spinning there on his heel quickly and lithely, fired at the bit of paper. He missed it by a half inch. He swore at himself, and went away. Later, he comfortably fusilladed the windows of his most intimate friend. The man was playing with this town. It was a toy for him.

But still there was no offer of fight. The name of Jack Potter, his ancient antagonist, entered his mind, and he concluded that it would be a glad thing if he should go to Potter's house and by bombardment induce him to come out and fight. He moved in the direction of his desire, chanting Apache scalp-music.

When he arrived at it, Potter's house presented the same still front as had the other adobes. Taking up a strategic position, the man howled a challenge. But this house regarded him as might a great stone god. It gave no sign. After a decent wait, the man howled further challenges, mingling with them wonderful epithets.

Presently there came the spectacle of a man churning himself into deepest rage over the immobility of a house. He fumed at it as the winter wind attacks a prairie cabin in the North. To the distance there should have gone the sound of a tumult like the fighting of 200 Mexicans. As necessity bade him, he paused for breath or to reload his revolvers.

IV

Potter and his bride walked sheepishly and with speed. Sometimes they laughed together shamefacedly and low.

'Next corner, dear,' he said finally.

They put forth the efforts of a pair walking bowed against a strong wind. Potter was about to raise a finger to point the first appearance of the new home when, as they circled the corner, they came face to face with a man in a maroon-colored shirt who was feverishly pushing cartridges into a large revolver. Upon the instant the man dropped his revolver to the ground, and, like lightning, whipped another from its holster. The second weapon was aimed at the bridegroom's chest.

There was silence. Potter's mouth seemed to be merely a grave for his tongue. He exhibited an instinct to at once loosen his arm from the woman's grip, and he dropped the bag to the sand. As for the bride, her face had gone as yellow as old cloth. She was a slave to hideous rites gazing at the apparitional snake.

The two men faced each other at a distance of three paces. He of the revolver smiled with a new and quiet ferocity.

'Tried to sneak up on me,' he said. 'Tried to sneak up on me!' His eyes grew more baleful. As Potter made a slight movement, the man thrust his revolver venomously forward. 'No, don't you do it, Jack Potter. Don't you move a finger toward a gun just yet. Don't you move an eyelash. The time has come for me to settle with you, and I'm goin' to do it my own way and loaf along with no interferin'. So if you don't want a gun bent on you, just mind what I tell you.'

Potter looked at his enemy. 'I ain't got a gun on me, Scratchy,' he said. 'Honest, I ain't.' He was stiffening and steadying, but yet somewhere at the back of his mind a vision of the Pullman floated, the sea-green figured velvet, the shining brass, silver, and glass, the wood that gleamed as darkly brilliant as the surface of a pool of oil – all the glory of the marriage, the environment of the new estate. 'You know I fight when it comes to fighting, Scratchy Wilson, but I ain't got a gun on me. You'll have to do all the shootin' yourself.'

His enemy's face went livid. He stepped forward and lashed his weapon to and fro before Potter's chest. 'Don't you tell me you ain't got no gun on you, you whelp. Don't tell me no lie like that. There ain't a man in Texas ever seen you without no gun. Don't take me for no kid.' His eyes blazed with light, and his throat worked like a pump.

'I ain't takin' you for no kid,' answered Potter. His heels had not moved an inch backward. 'I'm takin' you for a — fool. I tell you I ain't got a gun, and I ain't. If you're goin' to shoot me up, you better begin now. You'll never get a chance like this again.'

So much enforced reasoning had told on Wilson's rage. He was calmer. 'If you ain't got a gun, why ain't you got a gun?' he sneered. 'Been to Sunday-school?'

'I ain't got a gun because I've just come from San Anton' with my wife. I'm married,' said Potter. 'And if I'd thought there was going to be any galoots like you prowling around when I brought my wife home, I'd had a gun, and don't you forget it.'

'Married!' said Scratchy, not at all comprehending.

'Yes, married. I'm married,' said Potter distinctly.

'Married?' said Scratchy. Seemingly for the first time he saw the drooping, drowning woman at the other man's side. 'No!' he said. He was like a creature allowed a glimpse of another world. He moved a pace backward, and his arm with the revolver dropped to his side. 'Is this the lady?' he asked.

'Yes, this is the lady,' answered Potter.

There was another period of silence.

'Well,' said Wilson at last, slowly, 'I s'pose it's all off now.'

'It's all off if you say so, Scratchy. You know I didn't make the trouble.' Potter lifted his valise.

'Well, I 'low it's off, Jack,' said Wilson. He was looking at the ground. 'Married!' He was not a student of chivalry; it was merely that in the presence of this foreign condition he was a simple child of the earlier plains. He picked up his starboard revolver, and placing both weapons in their holsters, he went away. His feet made funnel-shaped tracks in the heavy sand.

ALICE MUNRO

A REAL LIFE

A MAN CAME along and fell in love with Dorrie Beck. At least, he wanted to marry her. It was true.

'If her brother was alive, she would never have needed to get married,' Millicent said. What did she mean? Not something shameful. And she didn't mean money either. She meant that love had existed, kindness had created comfort, and in the poor, somewhat feckless life Dorrie and Albert lived together, loneliness had not been a threat. Millicent, who was shrewd and practical in some ways, was stubbornly sentimental in others. She believed always in the sweetness of affection that had eliminated sex.

She thought it was the way that Dorrie used her knife and fork that had captivated the man. Indeed, it was the same way as he used his. Dorrie kept her fork in her left hand and used the right only for cutting. She did not shift her fork continually to the right hand to pick up her food. That was because she had been to Whitby Ladies College when she was young. A last spurt of the Becks' money. Another thing she had learned there was a beautiful handwriting, and that might have been a factor as well, because after the first meeting the entire courtship appeared to have been conducted by letter. Millicent loved the sound of Whitby Ladies *College*, and it was her plan – not shared with anybody – that her own daughter would go there someday.

Millicent was not an uneducated person herself. She had taught school. She had rejected two serious boyfriends – one

341

because she couldn't stand his mother, one because he tried putting his tongue in her mouth – before she agreed to marry Porter, who was nineteen years older than she was. He owned three farms, and he promised her a bathroom within a year, plus a dining-room suite and a chesterfield and chairs. On their wedding night he said, 'Now you've got to take what's coming to you,' but she knew it was not unkindly meant.

This was in 1933.

She had three children, fairly quickly, and after the third baby she developed some problems. Porter was decent – mostly, after that, he left her alone.

The Beck house was on Porter's land, but he wasn't the one who had bought the Becks out. He bought Albert and Dorrie's place from the man who had bought it from them. So, technically, they were renting their old house back from Porter. But money did not enter the picture. When Albert was alive, he would show up and work for a day when important jobs were undertaken – when they were pouring the cement floor in the barn or putting the hay in the mow. Dorrie had come along on those occasions, and also when Millicent had a new baby, or was housecleaning. She had remarkable strength for lugging furniture about and could do a man's job, like putting up the storm windows. At the start of a hard job – such as ripping the wallpaper off a whole room – she would settle back her shoulders and draw a deep, happy breath. She glowed with resolution. She was a big, firm woman with heavy legs, chestnut-brown hair, a broad bashful face, and dark freckles like dots of velvet. A man in the area had named a horse after her.

In spite of Dorrie's enjoyment of housecleaning, she did not do a lot of it at home. The house that she and Albert had lived in – that she lived in alone, after his death – was large and handsomely laid out but practically without furniture.

Furniture would come up in Dorrie's conversation – the oak sideboard, Mother's wardrobe, the spool bed – but tacked onto this mention was always the phrase 'that went at the Auction.' The Auction sounded like a natural disaster, something like a flood and windstorm together, about which it would be pointless to complain. No carpets remained, either, and no pictures. There was just the calendar from Nunn's Grocery, which Albert used to work for. Absences of such customary things – and the presence of others, such as Dorrie's traps and guns and the boards for stretching rabbit and muskrat skins – had made the rooms lose their designations, made the notion of cleaning them seem frivolous. Once, in the summer, Millicent saw a pile of dog dirt at the head of the stairs. She didn't see it while it was fresh, but it was fresh enough to seem an offense. Through the summer it changed, from brown to gray. It became stony, dignified, stable – and strangely, Millicent herself found less and less need to see it as anything but something that had a right to be there.

Delilah was the dog responsible. She was black, part Labrador. She chased cars, and eventually this was how she was going to get herself killed. After Albert's death, both she and Dorrie may have come a little unhinged. But this was not something anybody could spot right away. At first, it was just that there was no man coming home and so no set time to get supper. There were no men's clothes to wash – cutting out the ideas of regular washing. Nobody to talk to, so Dorrie talked more to Millicent or to both Millicent and Porter. She talked about Albert and his job, which had been driving Nunn's Grocery Wagon, later their truck, all over the countryside. He had gone to college, he was no dunce, but when he came home from the Great War he was not very well, and he thought it best to be out-of-doors, so he got the job driving for Nunn's and kept it until he died. He was a man of inexhaustible sociability and did more than simply deliver groceries. He gave people a lift to town. He brought patients home from the hospital. He had a crazy woman on his route, and once when he was getting her groceries out of the truck, he had a compulsion to turn around. There she stood with a hatchet, about to brain him. In fact her swing had already begun, and when he slipped out of range she had to continue, chopping neatly into the box of groceries and cleaving a pound of butter. He continued to deliver to her, not having the heart to turn her over to the authorities, who would take her to the asylum. She never took up the hatchet again but gave him cupcakes sprinkled with evil-looking seeds, which he threw into the grass at the end of the lane. Other women – more than one – had appeared to him naked. One of them arose out of a tub of bathwater in the middle of the kitchen floor, and Albert bowed low and set the groceries at her feet. 'Aren't some people amazing?' said Dorrie. And she told further about a bachelor whose house was overrun by rats, so that he had to keep his food slung in a sack from the kitchen beams. But the rats ran out along the beams and leaped upon the sack and clawed it apart, and eventually the fellow was obliged to take all his food into bed with him.

'Albert always said people living alone are to be pitied,' said Dorrie – as if she did not understand that she was now one of them. Albert's heart had given out – he had only had time to pull to the side of the road and stop the truck. He died in a lovely spot, where black oaks grew in a bottomland, and a sweet clear creek ran beside the road.

Dorrie mentioned other things Albert had told her concerning the Becks in the early days. How they came up the river in a raft, two brothers, and started a mill at the Big Bend, where there was nothing but the wildwoods. And nothing now, either, but the ruins of their mill and dam. The farm was never a livelihood but a hobby, when they built the big house and brought out the furniture from Edinburgh. The bedsteads, the chairs, the carved chests that went in the Auction. They brought it round the Horn, Dorrie said, and up Lake Huron and so up the river. Oh, Dorrie, said Millicent, that is not possible, and she brought a school geography book she had kept, to point out the error. It must have been a canal, then, said Dorrie. I recall a canal. The Panama Canal? More likely it was the Erie Canal, said Millicent.

'Yes,' said Dorrie. 'Round the Horn and into the Erie Canal.'

'Dorrie is a true lady, no matter what anybody says,' said Millicent to Porter, who did not argue. He was used to her absolute, personal judgments. 'She is a hundred times more a lady than Muriel Snow,' said Millicent, naming the person who might be called her best friend. 'I say that, and I love Muriel Snow dearly.'

Porter was used to hearing that too.

'I love Muriel Snow dearly and I would stick up for her no matter what,' Millicent would say. 'I love Muriel Snow, but that does not mean I approve of everything she *does*.'

The smoking. And saying hot damn, Chrissakes, *poop. I nearly pooped my pants.*

Muriel Snow had not been Millicent's first choice for best friend. In the early days of her marriage she had set her sights high. Mrs Lawyer Nesbitt. Mrs Dr Finnegan. Mrs Doud. They let her take on a donkey's load of work in the Women's Auxiliary at the church, but they never asked her to their tea parties. She was never inside their houses, unless it was to a meeting. Porter was a farmer. No matter how many farms he owned, a farmer. She should have known.

She met Muriel when she decided that her daughter Betty

Jean would take piano lessons. Muriel was the music teacher. She taught in the schools as well as privately. Times being what they were, she charged only twenty cents a lesson. She played the organ at the church, and directed various choirs, but some of that was for nothing. She and Millicent got on so well that soon she was in Millicent's house as often as Dorrie was, though on a rather different footing.

Muriel was over thirty and had never been married. Getting married was something she talked about openly, jokingly, and plaintively, particularly when Porter was around. 'Don't you know any men, Porter?' she would say. 'Can't you dig up just one decent man for me?' Porter would say maybe he could, but maybe she wouldn't think they were so decent. In the summers Muriel went to visit a sister in Montreal, and once she went to stay with some cousins she had never met, only written to, in Philadelphia. The first thing she reported on, when she got back, was the man situation.

'Terrible. They all get married young, they're Catholics, and the wives never die – they're too busy having babies.

'Oh, they had somebody lined up for me but I saw right away he would never pan out. He was one of those ones with the mothers.

'I did meet one, but he had an awful failing. He didn't cut his toenails. Big yellow toenails. Well? Aren't you going to ask me how I found out?'

Muriel was always dressed in some shade of blue. A woman should pick a color that really suits her and wear it all the time, she said. Like your perfume. It should be your signature. Blue was widely thought to be a color for blondes, but that was incorrect. Blue often made a blonde look more washed-out than she was to start with. It suited best a warm-looking skin, like Muriel's – skin that took a good tan and never entirely lost it. It suited brown hair and brown eyes, which were hers as well. She never skimped on clothes – it was a mistake to. Her fingernails were always painted – a rich and distracting color, apricot or blood-ruby or even gold. She was small and round, she did exercises to keep her tidy waistline. She had a dark mole on the front of her neck, like a jewel on an invisible chain, and another like a tear at the corner of one eye.

'The word for you is not pretty,' Millicent said one day, surprising herself. 'It's *bewitching*.' Then she flushed at her own tribute, knowing she sounded childish and excessive.

Muriel flushed a little too, but with pleasure. She drank in admiration, frankly courted it. Once, she dropped in on her way to a concert in Walley, which she hoped would yield rewards. She had an ice-blue dress on that shimmered.

'And that isn't all,' she said. 'Everything I have on is new, and everything is silk.'

It wasn't true that she never found a man. She found one fairly often but hardly ever one that she could bring to supper. She found them in other towns, where she took her choirs to massed concerts, in Toronto at piano recitals to which she might take a promising student. Sometimes she found them in the students' own homes. They were the uncles, the fathers, the grandfathers, and the reason that they would not come into Millicent's house, but only wave – sometimes curtly, sometimes with bravado – from a waiting car, was that they were married. A bedridden wife, a drinking wife, a vicious shrew of a wife? Perhaps. Sometimes no mention at all – a ghost of a wife. They escorted Muriel to musical events, an interest in music being the ready excuse. Sometimes there was even a performing child, to act as chaperon. They took her to dinners in restaurants in distant towns. They were referred to as friends. Millicent defended her. How could there be any harm when it was all so out in the open? But it wasn't, quite, and it would all end in misunderstandings, harsh words, unkindness. A warning from the school board. Miss Snow will have to mend her ways. A bad example. A wife on the phone. Miss Snow, I am sorry we are cancelling— Or simply silence. A date not kept, a note not answered, a name never to be mentioned again.

'I don't expect so much,' Muriel said. 'I expect a friend to be a friend. Then they hightail it off at the first whiff of trouble after saying they'd always stand up for me. Why is that?'

'Well, you know, Muriel,' Millicent said once, 'a wife is a wife. It's all well and good to have friends, but a marriage is a marriage.'

Muriel blew up at that, she said that Millicent thought the worst of her like everybody else, and was she never to be permitted to have a good time, an innocent good time? She banged the door and ran her car over the calla lilies, surely on purpose. For a day Millicent's face was blotchy from weeping. But enmity did not last and Muriel was back, tearful as well, and taking blame on herself.

'I was a fool from the start,' she said, and went into the front room to play the piano. Millicent got to know the pattern. When Muriel was happy and had a new friend, she played mournful tender songs, like 'Flowers of the Forest.' Or:

> *'She dressed herself in male attire,*
> *And gaily she was dressed—'*

Then when she was disappointed, she came down hard and fast on the keys, she sang scornfully.

Sometimes Millicent asked people to supper (though not the Finnegans or the Nesbitts or the Douds), and then she liked to ask Dorrie and Muriel as well. Dorrie was a help to wash up the pots and pans afterward, and Muriel could entertain on the piano.

She asked the Anglican minister to come on Sunday, after evensong, and bring the friend she had heard was staying with him. The Anglican minister was a bachelor, but Muriel had given up on him early. Neither fish nor fowl, she said. Too bad. Millicent liked him, chiefly for his voice. She had been brought up an Anglican, and though she'd switched to United, which was what Porter said he was (so was everybody else, so were all the important and substantial people in the town), she still favored Anglican customs. Evensong, the church bell, the choir coming up the aisle in as stately a way as they could manage, singing – instead of just all clumping in together and sitting down. Best of all the words. *But thou O God have mercy upon us miserable offenders. Spare thou them, O Lord, which confess their faults. Restore thou them that are penitent, according to the Promise.* . . .

Porter went with her once and hated it.

Preparations for this evening supper were considerable. The damask was brought out, the silver serving-spoon, the black dessert plates painted with pansies by hand. The cloth had to be pressed and all the silverware polished, and then there was the apprehension that a tiny smear of polish might remain, a gray gum on the tines of a fork or among the grapes round the rim of the wedding teapot. All day Sunday, Millicent was torn between pleasure and agony, hope and suspense. The things that could go wrong multiplied. The Bavarian cream might not set (they had no refrigerator yet and had to chill things in summer by setting them on the cellar floor). The angel food cake might not rise to its full glory. If it did rise, it might be dry. The biscuits might taste of tainted flour or a beetle might crawl out of the salad. By five o'clock she was in such a state of tension and misgiving that nobody could stay in the kitchen with her. Muriel had arrived early to help out, but she had not chopped the potatoes finely enough, and had managed to scrape her knuckles while grating carrots, so she was told off for being useless, and sent to play the piano.

Muriel was dressed up in turquoise crêpe and smelled of her Spanish perfume. She might have written off the minister but she had not seen his visitor yet. A bachelor, perhaps, or a widower, since he was travelling alone. Rich, or he would not be travelling at all, not so far. He came from England, people said. Someone had said no, Australia.

She was trying to get up the 'Polovtsian Dances.'

Dorrie was late. It threw a crimp in things. The jellied salad had to be taken down cellar again, lest it should soften. The biscuits put to warm in the oven had to be taken out, for fear of getting too hard. The three men sat on the veranda – the meal was to be eaten there, buffet style – and drank fizzy lemonade. Millicent had seen what drink did in her own family – her father had died of it when she was ten – and she had required a promise from Porter, before they married, that he would never touch it again. Of course he did – he kept a bottle in the granary – but when he drank he kept his distance and she truly believed the promise had been kept. This was a fairly common pattern at that time, at least among farmers – drinking in the barn, abstinence in the house. Most men would have felt there was something the matter with a woman who didn't lay down such a law.

But Muriel, when she came out on the veranda in her high

heels and slinky crêpe, cried out at once, 'Oh, my favorite drink! Gin and lemon!' She took a sip and pouted at Porter. 'You did it again. You forgot the gin again!' Then she teased the minister, asking if he didn't have a flask in his pocket. The minister was gallant, or perhaps made reckless by boredom. He said he wished he had.

The visitor who rose to be introduced was tall and thin and sallow, with a face that seemed to hang in pleats, precise and melancholy. Muriel did not give way to disappointment. She sat down beside him and tried in a spirited way to get him into conversation. She told him about her music teaching and was scathing about the local choirs and musicians. She did not spare the Anglicans. She twitted the minister and Porter, and told about the live chicken that walked onto the stage during a country school concert.

Porter had done the chores early, washed and changed into his suit, but he kept looking uneasily toward the barnyard, as if he recalled something that was left undone. One of the cows was bawling loudly in the field, and at last he excused himself to go and see what was wrong with her. He found that her calf had got caught in the wire fence and managed to strangle itself. He did not speak of this loss when he came back with newly washed hands. 'Calf caught up in the fence' was all he said. But he connected the mishap somehow with this entertainment, with dressing up and having to eat off your knees. He thought that was not natural.

'Those cows are as bad as children,' Millicent said. 'Always wanting your attention at the wrong time!' Her own children, fed earlier, peered from between the banisters to watch the food being carried to the veranda. 'I think we will have to commence without Dorrie. You men must be starving. This is just a simple little buffet. We sometimes enjoy eating outside on a Sunday evening.'

'Commence, commence!' cried Muriel, who had helped to carry out the various dishes – the potato salad, carrot salad, jellied salad, cabbage salad, the devilled eggs and cold roast chicken, the salmon loaf and warm biscuits, and relishes. Just when they had everything set out, Dorrie came around the side of the house, looking warm from her walk across the field, or from excitement. She was wearing her good summer dress, a navy-blue organdie with white dots and white collar, suitable for a little girl or an old lady. Threads showed where she had pulled the torn lace off the collar instead of mending it, and in spite of the hot day a rim of undershirt was hanging out of one sleeve. Her shoes had been so recently and sloppily cleaned that they left traces of whitener on the grass.

'I would have been on time,' Dorrie said, 'but I had to shoot a feral cat. She was prowling around my house and carrying on so. I was convinced she was rabid.'

She had wet her hair and crimped it into place with bobby pins. With that, and her pink shiny face, she looked like a doll with a china head and limbs attached to a cloth body, firmly stuffed with straw.

'I thought at first she might have been in heat, but she didn't really behave that way. She didn't do any of the rubbing along on her stomach such as I'm used to seeing. And I noticed some spitting. So I thought the only thing to do was to shoot her. Then I put her in a sack and called up Fred Nunn to see if he would run her over to Walley, to the vet. I want to know if she really was rabid, and Fred always likes the excuse to get out in his car. I told him to leave the sack on the step if the vet wasn't home on a Sunday night.'

'I wonder what he'll think it is?' said Muriel. 'A present?'

'No. I pinned on a note, in case. There was definite

352

spitting and dribbling.' She touched her own face to show where the dribbling had been. 'Are you enjoying your visit here?' she said to the minister, who had been in town for three years and had been the one to bury her brother.

'It is Mr Speirs who is the visitor, Dorrie,' said Millicent. Dorrie acknowledged the introduction and seemed unembarrassed by her mistake. She said that the reason she took it for a feral cat was that its coat was all matted and hideous, and she thought that a feral cat would never come near the house unless it was rabid.

'But I will put an explanation in the paper, just in case. I will be sorry if it is anybody's pet. I lost my own pet three months ago – my dog Delilah. She was struck down by a car.'

It was strange to hear that dog called a pet, that big black Delilah who used to lollop along with Dorrie all over the countryside, who tore across the fields in such savage glee to attack cars. Dorrie had not been distraught at the death; indeed she had said she had expected it someday. But now, to hear her say 'pet,' Millicent thought, there might have been grief she didn't show.

'Come and fill up your plate or we'll all have to starve,' Muriel said to Mr Speirs. 'You're the guest, you have to go first. If the egg yolks look dark it's just what the hens have been eating – they won't poison you. I grated the carrots for that salad myself, so if you notice some blood it's just where I got a little too enthusiastic and grated in some skin off my knuckles. I had better shut up now or Millicent will kill me.'

And Millicent was laughing angrily, saying, 'Oh, they are not! Oh, you did *not*!'

Mr Speirs had paid close attention to everything Dorrie said: Maybe that was what had made Muriel so saucy. Millicent thought that perhaps he saw Dorrie as a novelty, a Canadian wild woman who went around shooting things.

He might be studying her so that he could go home and describe her to his friends in England.

Dorrie kept quiet while eating and she ate quite a lot. Mr Speirs ate a lot too – Millicent was happy to see that – and he appeared to be a silent person at all times. The minister kept the conversation going describing a book he was reading. It was called *The Oregon Trail*.

'Terrible the hardships,' he said.

Millicent said she had heard of it. 'I have some cousins living out in Oregon but I cannot remember the name of the town,' she said. 'I wonder if they went on that trail.'

The minister said that if they went out a hundred years ago it was most probable.

'Oh, I wouldn't think it was that long,' she said. 'Their name was Rafferty.'

'Man the name of Rafferty used to race pigeons,' said Porter, with sudden energy. 'This was way back, when there was more of that kind of thing. There was money going on it, too. Well, he sees he's got a problem with the pigeons' house, they don't go in right away, and that means they don't trip the wire and don't get counted in. So he took an egg one of his pigeons was on, and he blew it clear, and he put a beetle inside. And the beetle inside made such a racket the pigeon naturally thought she had an egg getting ready to hatch. And she flew a beeline home and tripped the wire and all the ones that bet on her made a lot of money. Him, too, of course. In fact this was over in Ireland, and this man that told the story, that was how he got the money to come out to Canada.'

Millicent didn't believe that the man's name had been Rafferty at all. That had just been an excuse.

'So you keep a gun in the house?' said the minister to Dorrie. 'Does that mean you are worried about tramps and suchlike?'

Dorrie put down her knife and fork, chewed something up carefully, and swallowed. 'I keep it for shooting,' she said.

After a pause she said that she shot groundhogs and rabbits. She took the groundhogs over to the other side of town and sold them to the mink farm. She skinned the rabbits and stretched the skins, then sold them to a place in Walley which did a big trade with the tourists. She enjoyed fried or boiled rabbit meat but could not possibly eat it all herself, so she often took a rabbit carcass, cleaned and skinned, around to some family that was on Relief. Many times her offering was refused. People thought it was as bad as eating a dog or a cat. Though even that, she believed, was not considered out of the way in China.

'That is true,' said Mr Speirs. 'I have eaten them both.'

'Well, then, you know,' said Dorrie. 'People are pre-judiced.'

He asked about the skins, saying they must have to be re-moved very carefully, and Dorrie said that was true and you needed a knife you could trust. She described with pleasure the first clean slit down the belly. 'Even more difficult with the muskrats, because you have to be more careful with the fur, it is more valuable,' she said. 'It is a denser fur. Waterproof.'

'You do not shoot the muskrats?' said Mr Speirs.

No, no, said Dorrie. She trapped them. Trapped them, yes, said Mr Speirs, and Dorrie described her favorite trap, on which she had made little improvements of her own. She had thought of taking out a patent but had never gotten around to it. She spoke about the spring watercourses, the system of creeks she followed, tramping for miles day after day, after the snow was mostly melted but before the leaves came out, when the muskrats' fur was prime. Millicent knew that Dorrie did these things but she had thought she did them to get a little money. To hear her talk now, it would

355

seem that she was truly fond of that life. The blackflies out already, the cold water over her boot tops, the drowned rats. And Mr Speirs listened like an old dog, perhaps a hunting dog, that has been sitting with his eyes half shut, just prevented, by his own good opinion of himself, from falling into an unmannerly stupor. Now he has got a whiff of something nobody else can understand – his eyes open all the way and his nose quivers and his muscles answer, ripples pass over his hide as he remembers some day of recklessness and dedication. How far, he asked, and how high is the water, how much do they weigh and how many could you count on in a day and for muskrats is it still the same sort of knife?

Muriel asked the minister for a cigarette and got one, smoked for a few moments and stubbed it out in the middle of the Bavarian cream.

'So I won't eat it and get fat,' she said. She got up and started to help clear the dishes, but soon ended up at the piano, back at the 'Polovtsian Dances.'

Millicent was pleased that there was conversation with the guest, though its attraction mystified her. Also, she thought that the food had been good and there had not been any humiliation, no queer taste or sticky cup handle.

'I had thought the trappers were all up north,' said Mr Speirs. 'I thought that they were beyond the Arctic Circle or at least on the Pre-Cambrian shield.'

'I used to have an idea of going there,' Dorrie said. Her voice thickened for the first time, with embarrassment – or excitement. 'I thought I could live in a cabin and trap all winter. But I had my brother, I couldn't leave my brother. And I know it here.'

Late in the winter Dorrie arrived at Millicent's house with a large piece of white satin. She said that she intended to make a wedding dress. That was the first anybody had heard of a wedding – she said it would be in May – or learned the first name of Mr Speirs. It was Wilkinson. Wilkie.

When and where had Dorrie seen him, since that supper on the veranda?

Nowhere. He had gone off to Australia, where he had property. Letters had gone back and forth between them.

Sheets were laid down on the dining-room floor, with the dining table pushed against the wall. The satin was spread out over them. Its broad bright extent, its shining vulnerability cast a hush over the whole house. The children came to stare at it, and Millicent shouted to them to clear off. She was afraid to cut into it. And Dorrie, who could so easily slit the skin of an animal, laid the scissors down. She confessed to shaking hands.

A call was put in to Muriel to drop by after school. She clapped her hand to her heart when she heard the news, and called Dorrie a slyboots, a Cleopatra, who had fascinated a millionaire.

'I bet he's a millionaire,' she said. 'Property in Australia – what does that mean? I bet it's not a pig farm! All I can hope is maybe he'll have a brother. Oh, Dorrie, am I so mean I didn't even say congratulations!'

She gave Dorrie lavish loud kisses – Dorrie standing still for them as if she were five years old.

What Dorrie had said was that she and Mr Speirs planned to go through 'a form of marriage.' What do you mean, said Millicent, do you mean a marriage ceremony, is that what you mean, and Dorrie said yes.

Muriel made the first cut into the satin, saying that somebody had to do it, though maybe if she was doing it again it wouldn't be in quite that place.

Soon they got used to mistakes. Mistakes and rectifications.

357

Late every afternoon, when Muriel got there, they tackled a new stage – the cutting, the pinning, the basting, the sewing – with clenched teeth and grim rallying cries. They had to alter the pattern as they went along, to allow for problems unforeseen, such as the tight set of a sleeve, the bunching of the heavy satin at the waist, the eccentricities of Dorrie's figure. Dorrie was a menace at the job, so they set her to sweeping up scraps and filling the bobbin. Whenever she sat at the sewing machine, she clamped her tongue between her teeth. Sometimes she had nothing to do, and she walked from room to room in Millicent's house, stopping to stare out the windows at the snow and sleet, the long-drawn-out end of winter. Or she stood like a docile beast in her woolen underwear, which smelled quite frankly of her flesh, while they pulled and tugged the material around her.

Muriel had taken charge of clothes. She knew what there had to be. There had to be more than a wedding dress. There had to be a going-away outfit, and a wedding nightgown and a matching dressing gown, and of course an entire new supply of underwear. Silk stockings, and a brassière – the first that Dorrie had ever worn.

Dorrie had not known about any of that. 'I considered the wedding dress as the major hurdle,' she said. 'I could not think beyond it.'

The snow melted, the creeks filled up, the muskrats would be swimming in the cold water, sleek and sporty with their treasure on their backs. If Dorrie thought of her traps, she did not say so. The only walk she took these days was across the field from her house to Millicent's.

Made bold by experience, Muriel cut out a dressmaker suit of fine russet wool, and a lining. She was letting her choir rehearsals go all to pot.

Millicent had to think about the wedding luncheon. It was to be held in the Brunswick Hotel. But who was there to invite, except the minister? Lots of people knew Dorrie, but they knew her as the lady who left skinned rabbits on doorsteps, who went through the fields and the woods with her dog and gun and waded along the flooded creeks in her high rubber boots. Few people knew anything about the old Becks, though all remembered Albert and had liked him. Dorrie was not quite a joke – something protected her from that, either Albert's popularity or her own gruffness and dignity – but the news of her marriage had roused up a lot of interest, not exactly of a sympathetic nature. It was being spoken of as a freakish event, mildly scandalous, possibly a hoax. Porter said that bets were being laid on whether the man would show up.

Finally, Millicent recalled some cousins who had come to Albert's funeral. Ordinary respectable people. Dorrie had their addresses, invitations were sent. Then the Nunn brothers from the grocery, whom Albert had worked for, and their wives. A couple of Albert's lawn-bowling friends and their wives. The people who owned the mink farm where Dorrie sold her groundhogs? The woman from the bakeshop who was going to ice the cake?

The cake was being made at home, then taken to the shop to be iced by the woman who had got a diploma in cake decorating from a place in Chicago. It would be covered with white roses, lacy scallops, hearts and garlands and silver leaves and those tiny silver candies you can break your tooth on. Meanwhile it had to be mixed and baked, and this was where Dorrie's strong arms could come into play, stirring and stirring a mixture so stiff it appeared to be all candied fruit and raisins and currants, with a little gingery batter holding it together like glue. When Dorrie got the big bowl against her stomach and took up the beating spoon, Millicent heard the first satisfied sigh to come out of her in a long while.

Muriel decided that there had to be a maid of honor. Or a matron of honor. It could not be her, because she would be playing the organ. 'O Perfect Love.' And the Mendelssohn.

It would have to be Millicent. Muriel would not take no for an answer. She brought over an evening dress of her own, a long sky-blue dress, which she ripped open at the waist – how confident and cavalier she was by now about dressmaking! – and proposed a lace midriff, of darker blue, with a matching lace bolero. It will look like new and suit you to a T, she said.

Millicent laughed when she first tried it on and said, 'There's a sight to scare the pigeons!' But she was pleased. She and Porter had not had much of a wedding – they had just gone to the rectory, deciding to put the money saved into furniture. 'I suppose I'll need some kind of thingamajig,' she said. 'Something on my head.'

'Her veil!' cried Muriel. 'What about Dorrie's veil? We've been concentrating so much on wedding dresses, we've forgotten all about a veil!'

Dorrie spoke up unexpectedly and said that she would never wear a veil. She could not stand to have that draped over her, it would feel like cobwebs. Her use of the word 'cobwebs' gave Muriel and Millicent a start, because there were jokes being made about cobwebs in other places.

'She's right,' said Muriel. 'A veil would be too much.' She considered what else. A wreath of flowers? No, too much again. A picture hat? Yes, get an old summer hat and cover it with white satin. Then get another and cover it with the dark-blue lace.

'Here is the menu,' said Millicent dubiously. 'Creamed

chicken in pastry shells, little round biscuits, molded jellies, that salad with the apples and the walnuts, pink and white ice cream with the cake—'

Thinking of the cake, Muriel said, 'Does he by any chance have a sword, Dorrie?'

Dorrie said, 'Who?'

'Wilkie. Your Wilkie. Does he have a sword?'

'What would he have a sword for?' Millicent said.

'I just thought he might,' said Muriel.

'I cannot enlighten you,' said Dorrie.

Then there was a moment in which they all fell silent, because they had to think of the bridegroom. They had to admit him to the room and set him down in the midst of all this. Picture hats. Creamed chicken. Silver leaves. They were stricken with doubts. At least Millicent was, and Muriel. They hardly dared to look at each other.

'I just thought since he was English, or whatever he is,' said Muriel.

Millicent said, 'He is a fine man anyway.'

The wedding was set for the second Saturday in May. Mr Speirs was to arrive on the Wednesday and stay with the minister. The Sunday before this, Dorrie was supposed to come over to have supper with Millicent and Porter. Muriel was there, too. Dorrie didn't arrive, and they went ahead and started without her.

Millicent stood up in the middle of the meal. 'I'm going over there,' she said. 'She better be sharper than this getting to her wedding.'

'I can keep you company,' said Muriel.

Millicent said no thanks. Two might make it worse.

Make what worse?

She did not know.

She went across the field by herself. It was a warm day, and the back door of Dorrie's house was standing open. Between the house and where the barn used to be there was a grove of walnut trees whose branches were still bare, since walnut trees are among the very latest to get their leaves. The hot sunlight pouring through bare branches seemed unnatural. Her feet did not make any sound on the grass.

And there on the back platform was Albert's old armchair, never taken in all winter.

What was in her mind was that Dorrie might have had an accident. Something to do with a gun. Maybe while cleaning her gun. That happened to people. Or she might be lying out in a field somewhere, lying in the woods among the old dead leaves and the new leeks and bloodroot. Tripped while getting over a fence. Had to go out one last time. And then, after all the safe times, the gun had gone off. Millicent had never had any such fears for Dorrie before, and she knew that in some ways Dorrie was very careful and competent. It must be that what had happened this year made anything seem possible. The proposed marriage, such wild luck, could make you believe in calamity also.

But it was not an accident that was on her mind. Not really. Under this busy fearful imagining of accidents, she hid what she really feared.

She called Dorrie's name at the open door. And so prepared was she for an answering silence, the evil silence and indifference of a house lately vacated by somebody who had met with disaster (or not vacated yet by the body of the person who had met with, who had *brought about*, that disaster) – so prepared was she for the worst that she was shocked, she went watery in the knees, at the sight of Dorrie herself, in her old field pants and shirt.

362

'We were waiting for you,' she said. 'We were waiting for you to come to supper.'

Dorrie said, 'I must've lost track of the time.'

'Oh, have all your clocks stopped?' said Millicent, recovering her nerve as she was led through the back hall with its familiar mysterious debris. She could smell cooking.

The kitchen was dark because of the big, unruly lilac pressing against the window. Dorrie used the house's original wood cookstove, and she had one of those old kitchen tables with a drawer for the knives and forks. It was a relief to see that the calendar on the wall was for this year.

Dorrie was cooking some supper. She was in the middle of chopping up a purple onion to add to the bits of bacon and sliced potatoes she had frying up in the pan. So much for losing track of the time.

'You go ahead,' said Millicent. 'Go ahead and make your meal. I did get something to eat before I took it into my head to go and look for you.'

'I made tea,' said Dorrie. It was keeping warm on the back of the stove and, when she poured it out, was like ink.

'I can't leave,' she said, prying up some of the bacon that was sputtering in the pan. 'I can't leave here.'

Millicent decided to treat this as she would a child's announcement that she could not go to school.

'Well, that'll be a nice piece of news for Mr Speirs,' she said. 'When he has come all this way.'

Dorrie leaned back as the grease became fractious.

'Better move that off the heat a bit,' Millicent said.

'I can't leave.'

'I heard that before.'

Dorrie finished her cooking and scooped the results onto a plate. She added ketchup and a couple of thick slices of bread soaked in the grease that was left in the pan. She sat down to eat, and did not speak.

Millicent was sitting too, waiting her out. Finally she said, 'Give a reason.'

Dorrie shrugged and chewed.

'Maybe you know something I don't,' Millicent said. 'What have you found out? Is he poor?'

Dorrie shook her head. 'Rich,' she said.

So Muriel was right.

'A lot of women would give their eyeteeth.'

'I don't care about that,' Dorrie said. She chewed and swallowed and repeated, 'I don't care.'

Millicent had to take a chance, though it embarrassed her.

'If you are thinking about what I think you may be thinking about, then it could be that you are worried over nothing. A lot of time when they get older, they don't even want to bother.'

'Oh, it isn't that! I know all about that.'

Oh, do you, thought Millicent, and if so, how? Dorrie might imagine she knew, from animals. Millicent had sometimes thought that if she really knew, no woman would get married.

Nevertheless she said, 'Marriage takes you out of yourself and gives you a real life.'

'I have a life,' Dorrie said.

'All right then,' said Millicent, as if she had given up arguing. She sat and drank her poisonous tea. She was getting an inspiration. She let time pass and then she said, 'It's up to you, it certainly is. But there is a problem about where you will live. You can't live here. When Porter and I found out you were getting married, we put this place on the market, and we sold it.'

364

Dorrie said instantly, 'You are lying.'

'We didn't want it standing empty to make a haven for tramps. We went ahead and sold it.'

'You would never do such a trick on me.'

'What kind of a trick would it be when you were getting married?'

Millicent was already believing what she said. Soon it could come true. They could offer the place at a low enough price, and somebody would buy it. It could still be fixed up. Or it could be torn down, for the bricks and the woodwork. Porter would be glad to be rid of it.

Dorrie said, 'You would not put me out of my house.'

Millicent kept quiet.

'You are lying, aren't you?' said Dorrie.

'Give me your Bible,' Millicent said. 'I will swear on it.'

Dorrie actually looked around. She said, 'I don't know where it is.'

'Dorrie, listen. All of this is for your own good. It may seem like I am pushing you out, Dorrie, but all it is is making you do what you are not quite up to doing on your own.'

'Oh,' said Dorrie. 'Why?'

Because the wedding cake is made, thought Millicent, and the satin dress is made, and the luncheon has been ordered and the invitations have been sent. All this trouble that has been gone to. People might say that was a silly reason, but those who said that would not be the people who had gone to the trouble. It was not fair to have your best efforts squandered.

But it was more than that, for she believed what she had said, telling Dorrie that this was how she could have a life. And what did Dorrie mean by 'here'? If she meant that she would be homesick, let her be! Homesickness was never anything you couldn't get over. Millicent was not going to pay any attention to that 'here.' Nobody had any business living a life out 'here' if they had been offered what Dorrie had. It was a kind of sin to refuse such an offer. Out of mulishness, out of fearfulness, and idiocy.

She had begun to get the feeling that Dorrie was cornered. Dorrie might be giving up, or letting the idea of giving up seep through her. Perhaps. She sat as still as a stump, but there was a chance such a stump might be pulpy within.

But it was Millicent who began suddenly to weep. 'Oh, Dorrie,' she said. 'Don't be stupid!' They both got up, and grabbed hold of each other, and then Dorrie had to do the comforting, patting and soothing in a magisterial way, while Millicent wept and repeated some words that did not hang together. *Happy. Help. Ridiculous.*

'I will look after Albert,' she said, when she had calmed down somewhat. 'I'll put flowers. And I won't mention this to Muriel Snow. Or to Porter. Nobody needs to know.'

Dorrie said nothing. She seemed a little lost, absent-minded, as if she was busy turning something over and over, resigning herself to the weight and strangeness of it.

'That tea is awful,' said Millicent. 'Can't we make some that's fit to drink?' She went to throw the contents of her cup into the slop pail.

There stood Dorrie in the dim window light – mulish, obedient, childish, female – a most mysterious and maddening person whom Millicent seemed now to have conquered, to be sending away. At greater cost to herself, Millicent was thinking – greater cost than she had understood. She tried to engage Dorrie in a sombre but encouraging look, cancelling her fit of tears. She said, 'The die is cast.'

Dorrie walked to her wedding.

Nobody had known that she intended to do that. When

Porter and Millicent stopped the car in front of her house to pick her up, Millicent was still anxious.

'Honk the horn,' she said. 'She better be ready now.'

Porter said, 'Isn't that her down ahead?'

It was. She was wearing a light gray coat of Albert's over her satin dress, and was carrying her picture hat in one hand, a bunch of lilacs in the other. They stopped the car and she said, 'No, I want the exercise. It will clear out my head.'

They had no choice but to drive on and wait at the church and see her approaching down the street, people coming out of shops to look, a few cars honking sportively, people waving and calling out, 'Here comes the bride!' As she got closer to the church, she stopped and removed Albert's coat, and then she was gleaming, miraculous, like the Pillar of Salt in the Bible.

Muriel was inside the church playing the organ, so she did not have to realize, at this last moment, that they had forgotten all about gloves and that Dorrie clutched the woody stems of the lilac in her bare hands. Mr Speirs had been in the church, too, but he had come out, breaking all rules, leaving the minister to stand there on his own. He was as lean and yellow and wolfish as Millicent remembered, but when he saw Dorrie fling the old coat into the back of Porter's car, and settle the hat on her head – Millicent had to run up and fix it right – he appeared nobly satisfied. Millicent had a picture of him and Dorrie mounted high, mounted on elephants, panoplied, borne cumbrously forward, adventuring. A vision. She was filled with optimism and relief and she whispered to Dorrie, 'He'll take you everywhere! He'll make you a Queen!'

'I have grown as fat as the Queen of Tonga,' wrote Dorrie from Australia, some years on. A photograph showed that she was not exaggerating. Her hair was white, her skin brown, as if all her freckles had got loose and run together. She wore a vast garment, colored like tropical flowers. The war had come and put an end to any idea of travelling, and then when it was over, Wilkie was dying. Dorrie stayed on, in Queensland, on a great property where she grew sugarcane and pineapples, cotton, peanuts, tobacco. She rode horses, in spite of her size, and had learned to fly an airplane. She took up some travels of her own in that part of the world. She had shot crocodiles. She died in the fifties, in New Zealand, climbing up to look at a volcano.

Millicent told everybody what she had said she would not mention. She took credit, naturally. She recalled her inspiration; her stratagem, with no apologies. 'Somebody had to take the bull by the horns,' she said. She felt that she was the creator of a life – more effectively, in Dorrie's case, than in the case of her own children. She had created happiness, or something close. She forgot the way she had wept, not knowing why.

The wedding had its effect on Muriel. She handed in her resignation, she went off to Alberta. 'I'll give it a year,' she said. And within a year she had found a husband – not the sort of man she had ever had anything to do with in the past. A widower with two small children. A Christian minister. Millicent wondered at Muriel's describing him that way. Weren't all ministers Christian? When they came back for a visit – by this time there were two more children, their own – she saw the point of the description. Smoking and drinking and swearing were out, and so was wearing makeup, and the kind of music that Muriel used to play. She played hymns now, of the sort she had once made fun of. She wore any color at all and had a bad permanent – her hair, going gray, stood up from her forehead in frizzy bunches. 'A lot of my former life turns my stomach just to think about it,' she said, and Millicent got the impression that she and Porter were seen mostly as belonging to those stomach-turning times.

The house was not sold or rented. It was not torn down, either, and its construction was so sound that it did not readily give way. It was capable of standing for years and years and presenting a plausible appearance. A tree of cracks can branch out among the bricks, but the wall does not fall down. Window sashes settle at an angle, but the window does not fall out. The doors were locked, but it was probable that children got in, to write things on the walls and break up the crockery that Dorrie had left behind. Millicent never went in to see.

There was a thing that Dorrie and Albert used to do, and then Dorrie did alone. It must have started when they were children. Every year, in the fall, they – and then, she – collected up all the walnuts that had fallen off the trees. They kept going, collecting fewer and fewer walnuts, until they were reasonably sure that they had got the last, or the next-to-last, one. Then they counted them, and they wrote the final total on the cellar wall. The date, the year, the total. The walnuts were not used for anything once they were collected. They were just dumped along the edge of the field and allowed to rot.

Millicent did not continue this useless chore. She had plenty of other chores to do, and plenty for her children to do. But at the time of year when the walnuts would be lying in the long grass, she would think of that custom, and how Dorrie must have expected to keep it up until she died. A life of customs, of seasons. The walnuts drop, the muskrats swim in the creek. Dorrie must have believed that she was meant to live so, in her reasonable eccentricity, her manageable loneliness. Probably she would have got another dog.

But I would not allow that, thinks Millicent. She would not allow it, and surely she was right. She has lived to be an old lady, she is living yet, though Porter has been dead for decades. She doesn't often notice the house. It is just there. But once in a while she does see its cracked face and the blank, slanted windows. The walnut trees behind, losing again, again, their delicate canopy of leaves.

I ought to knock that down and sell the bricks, she says, and seems puzzled that she has not already done so.

GRAHAM SWIFT

REMEMBER THIS

THEY WERE MARRIED now and had been told they should make their wills, as if that was the next step in life, so one day they went together to see a solicitor, Mr Reeves. He was not as they'd expected. He was soft-spoken, silver-haired and kindly. He smiled at them as if he'd never before met such a sweet newly married young couple, so plainly in love yet so sensibly doing the right thing. He was more like a vicar than a solicitor, and later Nick and Lisa shared the thought that they'd wished Mr Reeves had actually married them. Going to see him was in fact not unlike getting married. It had the same mixture of solemnity and giggly disbelief – are we really doing this ? – the same feeling of being a child in adult's clothing

They'd thought it might be a rather grim process. You can't make a will without thinking about death, even when you're twenty-four and twenty-five. They'd thought Mr Reeves might be hard going. But he was so nice. He gently steered them through the delicate business of making provision for their dying together, or with the briefest of gaps in between. 'In a car accident say,' he said, with an apologetic smile. That was like contemplating death indeed, that was like saying they might die tomorrow.

But they got through it. And, all in all, the fact of having drafted your last will and testament and having left all your worldly possessions – pending children – to your spouse was every bit as significant and as enduring a commitment as a wedding. Perhaps even more so.

And then there was something . . . Something.

373

Though it was a twelve-noon appointment and wouldn't take long, they'd both taken the day off and, without discussing it but simultaneously, dressed quite smartly, as if for a job interview. Nick wore a suit and tie. Lisa wore a short black jacket, a dark red blouse and a black skirt which, though formal, was also eye-catchingly clingy. They both knew that if they'd turned up at Mr Reeves' office in jeans and T-shirts it wouldn't have particularly mattered – he was only a high street solicitor. On the other hand this was hardly an everyday event, for them at least. They both felt that certain occasions required an element of ceremony, even of celebration. Though could you celebrate making a will?

In any case, if just for themselves, they'd dressed up a bit, and perhaps Mr Reeves had simply been taken by the way they'd done this. Thus he'd smiled at them as if, so it seemed to them, he was going to consecrate their marriage all over again.

It was a bright and balmy May morning, so they walked across the common. There was no point in driving (and when Mr Reeves said that thing about a car accident they were glad they hadn't). There was no one else to think about, really, except themselves and their as yet unmet solicitor. As they walked they linked arms or held hands, or Nick's hand would wander to pat Lisa's bottom in her slim black skirt. The big trees on the common were in their first vivid green and full of singing birds.

They were newly married, but it had seemed to make no essential difference. It was a 'formality', as today was a formality. Formality was a lovely word, since it implied the existence of informality and even in some strange way gave its blessing to it. Nick let his palm travel and wondered if his glad freedom to let it do so was in any way altered, even enhanced, now that Lisa was his wife and not just Lisa.

374

Married or not, they were still at the stage of not being able to keep their hands off each other, even in public places. As they walked across the common to see Mr Reeves, Nick found himself considering that this might only be a stage – a stage that would fade or even cease one day. They'd grow older and just get used to each other. They wouldn't just grow older, they'd age, they'd *die*. It was why they were doing what they were doing today. And it was the deal with marriage.

It seemed necessary to go down this terminal path of thought even as they walked in the sunshine. Nonetheless, he let his palm travel.

And in Mr Reeves' office, though it was reassuring that Mr Reeves was so nice, one thing that helped Nick, while they were told about the various circumstances in which they might die, was thinking about Lisa's arse and hearing the tiny slithery noises her skirt made whenever she shifted in her seat.

It was a beautiful morning, but he'd heard a mixed forecast and he'd brought an umbrella. Having your will done seemed, generally, like remembering to bring an umbrella.

When they came out – it took less than half an hour – the clouds had thickened, though the bright patches of sky seemed all the brighter. 'Well, that's that,' Nick said to Lisa, as if the whole thing deserved only a relieved shrug, though they both felt an oddly exhilarating sense of accomplishment. Lisa said, 'Wasn't he *sweet*,' and Nick agreed immediately, and they both felt also, released back into the spring air, a great sense of animal vitality.

There was a bloom upon them and perhaps Mr Reeves couldn't be immune to it.

They retraced their steps, or rather took a longer route

via the White Lion on the edge of the common. It seemed appropriate, however illogical, after what they'd done, to have a drink. Yes, to celebrate. Lunch, a bottle of wine, why not? In fact, since they both knew that, above all, they were hungry and thirsty for each other, they settled for nothing more detaining than two prawn sandwiches and two glasses of Sauvignon. The sky, at the window, meanwhile turned distinctly threatening.

By the time they'd crossed back over the common the rain had begun, but Nick had the umbrella, under which it was necessary to huddle close together. As he put it up he had the fleeting thought that its stretched black folds were not unlike women's tight black skirts. He'd never before had this thought about umbrellas, only the usual thoughts – that they were like bats' wings or that they were vaguely funereal – and this was like other thoughts and words that came into his head on this day, almost as if newly invented. It was a bit like the word 'kindly' suddenly presenting itself as the exact word to describe Mr Reeves.

As they turned the corner of their street it began to pelt down and they broke into a run. Inside, in the hallway, they stood and panted a little. It was dark and clammy and with the rain beating outside a little like being inside a drum. They climbed the stairs to their flat, Lisa going first. Nick had an erection and the words 'stair rods' came into his mind.

It was barely two o'clock and the lower of the two flats was empty. Nick thought – though very quickly, since his thoughts were really elsewhere – of how incredibly lucky they were to be who they were and to have a flat of their own to go to on a rainy afternoon. It was supposed to be a 'starter home' and they owed it largely to Lisa's dad. It was supposed to be a first stage. He thought of stages again, if less bleakly this time. Everything in life could be viewed as a stage, leading to other stages and to having things you didn't yet have. But right now he felt they had everything, the best life could bring. What more could you want? And they'd even made their wills.

He'd hardly dropped the sopping umbrella into the kitchen sink than they were both, by inevitable progression, in the bedroom, and he'd hardly removed his jacket and pulled across the curtains than Lisa had unbuttoned her red blouse. She'd let him unzip her skirt, she knew how he liked to.

It rained all afternoon and kept raining, if not so hard, through the evening. They both slept a bit, then got up, picked up the clothes they'd hastily shed, and thought about going for a pizza. But it was still wet and they didn't want to break the strange spell of the day or fail to repeat, later, the manner of their return in the early afternoon. It seemed, too, that they might destroy the mood if they went out dressed in anything less special than what they'd worn earlier. But just for a pizza?

So – going to the other extreme – they took a shared bath, put on bathrobes, and settled for Welsh rarebit. They opened the only bottle of wine they had, a Rioja that someone had once brought them. They found a red twisty candle left over from Christmas. They put on a favourite CD. Outside, the rain persisted and darkness, though it was May, came early. The candle flame and their white-robed bodies loomed in the kitchen window.

Why this day had become so special, a day of celebration, of formality mixed with its flagrant opposite, neither of them could have said exactly. It happened. Having eaten and having drunk only half the bottle, it seemed natural to drift back to bed, less hurriedly this time, to make love again more lingeringly.

Then they lay awake a long time holding each other, talking and listening to the rain in the gutters and to the occasional slosh of a car outside. They talked about Mr Reeves. They wondered what it was precisely that had made him so sweet. They wondered if he was happily married and had a family, a grown-up family. Surely he would have all those things. They wondered how he'd met Mrs Reeves – they decided her name was Sylvia – and what she was like. They wondered if he'd been perhaps a little jealous of their own youth or just, in his gracious way, gladdened by it.

They wondered if he found wills merely routine or if he could be occasionally stopped short by the very idea of two absurdly young people making decisions about death. He must have made his own will. Surely – a good one. They wondered if a good aim in life might simply be to become like Mr Reeves, gentle, courteous and benign. Of course, that could only really apply to Nick, not to Lisa.

Then Lisa fell asleep and Nick lay awake still holding her and thinking. He thought: What is Mr Reeves doing now? Is he in bed with Mrs Reeves – with Sylvia? He wondered if when Mr Reeves had talked to them in his office he'd had any idea of how the two of them, his clients (and that was a strange word and a strange thing to be), would spend the rest of the day. He hoped Mr Reeves had had an inkling.

He wondered if he really might become like Mr Reeves when he was older. If he too would have (still plentiful and handsome) silver hair.

Then he forgot Mr Reeves altogether and the overwhelming thought came to him: Remember this, remember this. Remember this always. Whatever comes, remember this.

He was so smitten by the need to honour and consummate this thought that even as he held Lisa in his arms his chest felt full and he couldn't prevent his eyes suddenly welling. When Lisa slept she sometimes unknowingly nuzzled him, like some small creature pressing against its mother. She did this now, as if she might have quickly licked the skin at the base of his neck.

He was wide awake. Remember this. He couldn't sleep and he didn't want to sleep. The grotesque thought came to him that he'd just made his last will and testament, so he could die now, it was all right to die. This might be his death-bed and this, with Lisa in his arms, might be called dying happy – surely it could be called dying happy – the very thing that no will or testament, no matter how prudent its provisions, could guarantee.

But no, of course not! He clasped Lisa, almost wanting to wake her, afraid of his thought.

Of course not! He was alive and happy, intensely alive and happy. Then he had the thought that though he'd drafted his last testament it was not in any real sense a testament, it was not even *his* testament. It was only a testament about the minor matter of his possessions and what should become of them when he was no more. But it was not the real testament of his life, its stuff, its story. It was not a testament at all to how he was feeling *now*.

How strange that people solemnly drew up and signed these crucial documents that were really about their non-existence, and didn't draw up anything – there wasn't even a word for such a thing – that testified to their existence.

Then he realised that in all his time of knowing her he'd never written a love letter to this woman, Lisa, who was sleeping in his arms. Though he loved her completely, more than words could say – which was perhaps the simple reason why he'd never written such a thing. Love letters were classic-ally composed to woo and to win, they were a means of getting what you didn't have. What didn't he have? Perhaps

379

they were just silly wordy exercises anyway. He hardly wrote letters at all, let alone love letters, he hardly *wrote* anything. He wouldn't be any good at it.

And yet. And yet the need to write his wife a love letter assailed him. Not just a random letter that might, in theory, be one among many, but *the* letter, the letter that would declare to her once and for all how much he loved her and why. So it would be there always for her, as enduring as a will. The testament of his love, and thus of his life. The testament of how his heart had been full one rainy night in May when he was twenty-five. He would not need to write any other.

So overpowering was this thought that eventually he disengaged his arms gently from Lisa and got out of bed. He put on his bathrobe and went into the kitchen. There was the lingering smell of toasted cheese and there was the unfinished bottle of wine. They possessed no good-quality notepaper, unless Lisa had a private stash, but there was a box of A4 by the computer in the spare room and he went in and took a couple of sheets and found a blue roller-ball pen. He'd never had a fountain pen or used real ink, but he felt quite sure that this thing had to be handwritten, it would not be the thing it should be otherwise. He'd noticed that Mr Reeves had a very handsome fountain pen. Black and gold. No doubt a gift from Sylvia.

He returned to the kitchen, poured a little wine and very quickly wrote, so it seemed like a direct release of the thickness in his chest:

My darling Lisa,
One day you walked into my life and I never thought something so wonderful could ever happen to me. You are the love of my life . . .

The words came so quickly and readily that, not being a writer of any kind, he was surprised by his sudden ability. They were so right and complete and he didn't want to alter any of them. Though they were just the beginning.

But no more words came. Or it seemed that there were a number of directions he might take, in each of which certain words might follow, but he didn't know which one to choose, and didn't want, by choosing, to exclude the others. He wanted to go in all directions, he wanted a totality. He wanted to set down every single thing he loved about his wife, every moment he'd loved sharing with her – which was almost *every* moment – including of course every moment of this day that had passed: the walk across the common, the rain, her red blouse, her black skirt, the small slithery sounds she made sitting in a solicitor's office, which of course were the sounds any woman might make shifting position in a tight skirt, but the important thing was that *she* was making them. She was making them even as she made her will, or rather as they made *their* wills, which were really only wills to each other.

But he realised that if he went into such detail the letter would need many pages. Perhaps it would be better simply to say, 'I love everything about you. I love all of you. I love every moment spent with you.' But these phrases, on the other hand, though true, seemed bland. They might be said of anyone by anyone.

Then again, if he embarked on the route of detail, the letter could hardly all be written now. It would need to be a thing of stages – stages! – reflecting their continuing life together and incorporating all the new things he found to commemorate. That would mean that it would be all right if he wrote no more now, he could pick it up later. And he'd written the most important thing, the beginning. But then if he picked it up later, it might become an immense labour – if truly a labour of love – a labour of years. There'd be the question: When would he stop, when would he bring it to its conclusion and deliver it?

A love letter was useless unless it was delivered.

He'd hardly begun and already he saw these snags and complications, these reasons why this passionate undertaking might fail. And he couldn't even think of the next thing to say. Then the words that he'd said to himself silently in his head, even as he held Lisa in his arms, rushed to him, as the very words he should write to her now and the best way of continuing:

I never thought something so wonderful could happen to me. You are the love of my life. Remember this always. Whatever comes, remember this . . .

Adding those words, in this way, made his chest tighten again and his eyes go prickly. And he wondered if that in itself was enough. It was entirely true to his feelings and to this moment. He should just put the date on it and sign it in some way and give it to Lisa the next morning. Yes, that was all he needed to do.

But though emotion was almost choking him, it suddenly seemed out of place – so big, if brief, a statement looking back at him from a kitchen table, with the smell of toasted cheese all around him. Suppose the mood tomorrow morning was quite different, suppose he faltered. Then again, that 'whatever comes' seemed ominous, it seemed like tempting fate, it seemed when you followed it through even to be about catastrophe and death. It shouldn't be there at all perhaps. And yet it seemed the essence of the thing. 'Whatever comes, remember this.' That was the essence.

Then he reflected that the essence of love letters was that they were about separation. It was why they were needed in the first place. They were about yearning and longing and distance. But he wasn't separated from Lisa – unless being the other side of a wall counted as separation. He could be with her whenever he liked, as close to her as possible, he'd made love to her twice today. Though as he'd written those additional words, 'whatever comes', he'd had the strange sensation of being a long way away from her, like a man in exile or on the eve of battle. It was what had brought the tears to his eyes.

In any case there it was. It was written. And what was he supposed to do with it? Just keep it? Keep it, but slip it in with the copy of his will – the 'executed' copy – so that after his death Lisa would read it? Read what he'd written on the night after they'd made their wills. Is that what he intended?

And how did he know he would die *first*? He'd simply had that thought so it would enable Lisa to read the letter. But how did he know she wouldn't die first? And he didn't want to think about either of them dying, he didn't want to think of dying at all. And even supposing Lisa read these words – these very words on this bit of paper! – after his death, wouldn't they in one undeniable and inescapable sense be too late? Though wouldn't that moment, after his death, be in another sense precisely the right moment?

Love letters are written out of separation.

He didn't know what to do. He'd written a love letter and it had only brought on this paralysis. But he couldn't cancel what he'd written. He folded the sheet of A4 and, returning to the spare room, found an envelope, on which he wrote Lisa's name, simply her name: Lisa. Without sealing the envelope, he put the letter in a safe and fairly secret place.

There were no really secret places in the flat and he would have been glad to declare that he and Lisa had no secrets. Had the opportunity arisen, he might have done so to Mr Reeves. But now – it was almost like some misdeed – there was this secret.

But he couldn't cancel it. Some things you can't cancel, they stare back at you. There was nothing experimental or feeble or lacking about those words. His heart had spilled over in them.

He went back to bed. He fitted himself against Lisa's body. She'd turned now onto her other side, away from his side of the bed, but she was fast asleep. He kissed the nape of her neck. He wanted to cradle her and protect her. Thoughts came to him that he might add to the letter, if he added to it. But the letter was surely already complete.

His penis stiffened, contentedly and undemandingly, against his wife. She knew nothing about it, or about his midnight session with pen and paper. He thought again about Mr Reeves and about last wills and testaments. Pen. Penis. It was funny to think about the word penis and the word testament in the same breath, as it were. Words were strange things. He thought about the word 'testicle'.

The rain was still gurgling outside and whether it stopped before he fell asleep or he fell asleep first he didn't remember.

The truth is he did nothing with the letter the next morning. He might have propped it conspicuously, after sealing the envelope, on the kitchen table, but he didn't want to disturb the tender atmosphere that still lingered from yesterday, even though that same tenderness gave him his licence. Wouldn't the letter only endorse it? He felt a little cowardly, though why? For what he'd put in writing?

He looked adoringly, perhaps even rather pleadingly, at

Lisa, as if she might have helped him in his dilemma. She looked slightly puzzled, but she also looked happy. She was hardly going to say, 'Go on, give me the letter.'

His line of thought to himself was still that the letter wasn't finished. Yes, he'd add to it later. It would be premature, at this point, to hand it over. Though he also knew there was no better point. And the moment was passing.

It was a Saturday morning. Outside, the rain had stopped, but a misty breath hung in the air, and over them hung still the curiously palpable, anointing fact that they were people who'd made their wills.

The truth is he could neither keep nor deliver, nor destroy, nor even resume the letter. It was simply there. Though he did keep it, by default. His hesitation over delivering it, a thing at first of just minutes and hours, became a prolonged, perennial reality, a thing of years, like his excuse that he'd continue it.

And one day, one bad day, he did, nearly, destroy it. It was a long time later, but the letter was still there, still as it was on that wet night in May, still in the envelope with the single word 'Lisa' on it, but now like a piece of history.

And his will, now, would certainly need altering. But not yet. Not yet. He thought of destroying the letter. It had suddenly and almost accusingly come into his mind – that letter! But the thought of destroying a love letter seemed almost as melodramatic and sentimental as writing one.

How did you destroy a love letter? The only way was to burn it. The smell of Welsh rarebit reinvaded his nostrils. You found some ceremonial-looking dish and set light to the letter and watched it burn. Though the *real* way to burn a love letter was to fling it into a blazing fire and for good measure thrust a poker through it And to do this you should really be sitting at a hearth-side, rain at the window, in a long finely quilted silk dressing gown . . .

Then his chest filled and his eyes melted just as they'd done when he first penned the letter.

The truth is they separated. Then they needed lawyers, in duplicate, to decide on the settlement and on how the two children would be provided for. And, in due course, to draw up new wills. He didn't destroy the letter, and he didn't send it on finally to its intended recipient, as some last-ditch attempt to resolve matters and bring back the past, or even as some desperate act of guilt-inducement, of warped revenge. This would have betrayed its original impulse, and how hopeless anyway either gesture would have been. She might have thought it was all a fabrication, that he hadn't really written the letter on the 10th of May all those years ago – if so, why the hell hadn't he delivered it? – that he'd concocted it only yesterday. It was another, rather glaring, example of his general instability.

He didn't destroy it, he kept it. But not in the way he'd waveringly and wonderingly kept it for so many years. He kept it now only for himself. Who else was going to look at it?

Occasionally, he took it out and read it. He knew the words, of course, by heart, but it was important now and then, even on every 10th of May, to see them sitting on the paper. And when he looked at them it was like looking at his own face in the mirror, but not at a face that would obligingly and comfortingly replicate whatever he might do – wrinkle his nose, bare his teeth. It was a face that had found the separate power to smirk back at him when he wasn't smirking himself, and to have an expression in its eyes, which his own eyes could never have mustered, that said, 'You fool, you poor sad fool.'

EDITH PEARLMAN

ELDER JINKS

GRACE AND GUSTAVE were married in August, in Gustave's home – a squat, brown-shingled house whose deep front porch darkened the downstairs rooms. The house lot had ample space for a side garden. But there were only rhododendrons and azaleas, hugging the building, and a single apple tree stranded in the middle of the lawn. Every May, Gustave dragged lawn chairs from the garage to the apple tree and placed them side by side by side. When Grace had first seen this array, in July, she was reminded of a nursing home, though she wouldn't say anything so hurtful to Gustave – a man easily bruised, which you could tell from the way he flushed when he took a wrong turn, say, or forgot a proper name. So she simply crossed the grass and moved one of the chaises so that it angled against another, and then adjusted the angle. 'They're snuggling now.' The third chair she overturned. Gustave later righted it.

They had met in June in front of a pair of foxes who made their own reluctant home at Bosky's Wild Animal Preserve, on Cape Cod. Gustave was visiting his sister in her rented cottage. Grace had driven in from western Massachusetts with her pal Henrietta. The two women were camping in the state park.

'You're living in a tent?' Gustave inquired on that fateful afternoon. 'You look as fresh as a flower.'

'Which flower?' Grace was a passionate amateur gardener as well as a passionate amateur actress and cook and hostess.

Had she ever practiced a profession? Yes, long ago; she'd been a second-grade teacher until her own children came along to claim her attention.

'Which flower? A hydrangea,' Gustave answered, surprised at his own exhilaration. 'Your eyes,' he explained, further surprised, this time at his rising desire.

Her tilted eyes were indeed a violet blue. Her skin was only slightly lined. Her gray hair was clasped by a hinged comb that didn't completely contain its abundance. Her figure was not firm, but what could you expect.

'I'm Grace,' she said.

'I'm Gustave,' he said. He took an impulsive breath. 'I'd like to get to know you.'

She smiled. 'And I you.'

Grace was employing a rhetorical locution popular in her Northampton crowd – eclipsis: the omission of words easily supplied. Gustave, after a pause, silently supplied them. Then he bowed. (His late mother was Paris-born; he honored her Gallic manners even though – except for five years teaching in a Rouen lycée – he had lived his entire life in the wedge of Boston called Godolphin.)

Grace hoped that this small man bending like a head-waiter would now brush her fingers with his mustache – but no. Instead he informed her that he was a professor. His subject was the history of science. Her eyes widened – a practiced maneuver, though also sincere. Back in Northampton, her friends (there were scores of them) included weavers, therapists, advocates of holistic medicine, singers. And of course professors. But the history of science, the fact that science even had a history – somehow it had escaped her notice. Copernicus? Oh, Newton, and Einstein, yes, and

Watson and what's his name. 'Crick,' she triumphantly produced, cocking her head in the flirtatious way ...

'Is your neck bothering you?'

... that Hal Karsh had hinted was no longer becoming. She straightened her head and shook hands like a lady.

Gustave had written a biography of Michael Faraday, a famous scientist in the nineteenth century, though unknown to Grace. When he talked about this uneducated bookbinder inspired by his own intuition, Gustave's slight pomposity melted into affection. When he mentioned his dead wife he displayed a thinner affection, but he had apparently been a widower a long time.

In Northampton, Grace volunteered at a shelter, tending children who only irregularly went to school. 'Neglected kids, all but abandoned by their mothers,' she said, 'mothers themselves abandoned by the kids' fathers.' Gustave winced. When she went on to describe the necessity of getting onto the floor with these youngsters, instructor and pupils both cross-legged on scabby linoleum, Gustave watched her playfulness deepen into sympathy. She'd constructed an indoor window box high up in the makeshift basement schoolroom; she taught the life cycle of the daffodil, 'its biography, so to speak,' including some falsities that Gustave gently pointed out. Grace nodded in gratitude. 'I never actually studied botany in my university,' she confessed. The University of Wichita, she specified; later she would mention the University of Wyoming, but perhaps he had misheard one or the other – he'd always been vague about the West.

A lawyer friend of Gustave's performed the wedding ceremony in the dark living room. Afterward Grace sipped champagne under the apple tree with Gustave's sister. 'Oh, Grace, how peaceable you look. You'll glide above his little tantrums.'

'What?' Grace said, trying to turn toward her new sister-in-law but unable to move her head on her shoulders. A Godolphin hairdresser had advised the severe French twist that was pulling cruelly at her nape; Henrietta had urged the white tulle sombrero; Grace herself had selected the dress, hydrangea blue and only one size too small. Her grandchildren, who with their parents had taken the red-eye from San Francisco, marveled at the transformation of their tatterdemalion Gammy – but where had her hair gone to? 'What?' said the stiffened Grace again; but Gustave's sister forbore to elaborate, just as she had failed to mention that Gustave's first wife, who had died last January in Rouen, had divorced him decades ago, influenced by a French pharmacist she'd fallen in love with.

Gustave and Grace honeymooned in Paris, indulging themselves mightily – a hotel with a courtyard, starred restaurants, a day in Giverny, another in Versailles. They even attended a lecture on the new uses of benzene – Gustave interested in the subject; Grace, with little French and less science, interested in the somber crowd assembled at the Pasteur Institute. They both loved the new promenade and the new *musée*, and they sat in Sainte-Chapelle for two hours listening to a concert performed on old instruments – two recorders and a lute and a viola da gamba. That was the most blissful afternoon. Gustave put the disarray of their hotel room out of his mind, and also the sometimes fatiguing jubilation with which Grace greeted each new venture. Grace dismissed her own irritation at Gustave's habit of worrying about every dish on the menu – did it matter how much cream, how much butter, we all had to die of something.

Light streamed through the radiant window, turning into gold his trim mustache, her untidy chignon.

And now it was September, and classes had begun. Gustave taught Physics for Poets on Mondays, Wednesdays, and Fridays at nine, The Uses of Chemistry those same days at ten. He taught a graduate seminar in the philosophy of science on Thursday evenings. The first two weeks the seminar met in the usual drafty classroom. But then Grace suggested . . . Gustave demurred . . . she persisted . . . he surrendered. And so on the third week the seminar met in the brown-shingled house. Grace baked two apple tarts and served them with warm currant jelly. The students relived last Saturday's football game. Gustave – who, like Grace, professed a hatred of football – quietly allowed the conversation to continue until everyone had finished the treat, then turned the talk to Archimedes. Grace sat in a corner of the living room, knitting. The next day marked their first separation since the wedding. Gustave had a conference in Chicago. He'd take a cab to the airport right after The Uses of Chemistry. Early that morning he'd packed necessary clothing in one half of his briefcase. While he was reading the newspaper she slipped in a wedge of apple tart, wrapped in tinfoil. After they kissed at the doorway his eye wandered to the corner she had occupied on the previous evening. The chair was still strewn with knitting books and balls of yarn and the garment she was working on, no doubt a sweater for him. She'd already made him a gray one. This wool was rose. His gaze returned to his smiling wife. 'See you on Sunday,' he said.

'Oh, I'll miss you.'

She did miss him, immediately. She would have continued to miss him if she had not been invaded, half an hour later, by two old Northampton friends bearing Hal Karsh.

Hal was visiting from his current perch in Barcelona. He would return to Spain on Sunday. Hal – master of the broken villanelle, inventor of the thirteen-line sonnet; and oh, that poetic hair brushing his eyebrows, hair still mostly brown though he was only eight years younger than Grace. Those long fingers, adept at pen and piano but not at keyboard – the word processor was death to composition, he'd tell you, and tell you why, too, at length, anywhere, even in bed.

Gustave's upright piano could have used a tuning. Grace had meant to call someone, but she had been too busy putting in chrysanthemums and ordering bulbs and trying to revive her high school French. The foursome made music anyway. Lee and Lee, the couple who brought Hal, had brought their fiddles, too. Grace rummaged in a box of stuff not yet unpacked and found her recorder. Later she brewed chili. They raided Gustave's *cave*. They finally fell into bed – Lee and Lee in the spare room, Hal on the floor in Gustave's study, Grace, still dressed, on the marital bed. Then on Saturday they drove to Walden Pond and to the North Shore, and on Saturday night Cambridge friends came across the river. This time Grace made minestrone, in a different pan – the crock encrusted with chili still rested on the counter.

Hal wondered what Grace was doing in a gloomy house in a town that allowed no overnight parking. Such a regulation indicated a punitive atmosphere. And this husband so abruptly acquired – who was he, anyway? 'She picked him up in a zoo, in front of a lynx,' Lee and Lee told him. He hoped they were exercising their artistic habit of distortion. Hal loved Grace, with the love of an indulged younger brother, or a ragtag colleague – years ago he and she had taught at the same experimental grade school, the one that demanded dedication from its faculty but didn't care about degrees. (Hal did have a master's, but Grace had neglected to go to college.) Hal thought Grace was looking beautiful but unsettled. Did her new spouse share her taste for illicit substances, did he know of her occasional need to decamp without warning? She always came back ... When Hal had mentioned that the Cambridge folks would bring grass, Grace's eyes danced. Well, nowadays it was less easy to get here. In Barcelona you could pick it up at your tobacconist, though sometimes the stuff was filthy ...

This batch was fine. They all talked as they smoked; and recited poetry; and after a while played Charades. It was like the old times, he thought. He wished Henrietta had come along, too. 'I have no use for that fussbudget she married,' Henrietta had snapped. But the fussbudget was in Chicago.

It was like the old times, Grace, too, was thinking. And how clever they all were at the game; how particularly clever in this round, Lee and Lee standing naked back to back while she, fully clothed, traversed the living room floor on her belly. Odd that no one had yet guessed 'New Deal.' Odd, too, that no one was talking, though a few moments earlier there had been such merry laughter; and Hal, that man of parts, had put two of his fingers into his mouth and whistled. At Lee? Or at Lee? In silence Grace slithered toward the hall and saw, at eye level, a pair of polished shoes. Pressed trousers rose above the shoes. She raised her head, as an eel never could – perhaps she now resembled a worm, ruining the tableau. The belt around the trousers was Gustave's – yes, she had given it to him; it had a copper buckle resembling a sunburst within which bulged an oval turquoise. When it was hanging from his belt rack among lengths of black and brown leather with discreet matching buckles, the thing looked like a deity, Lord of the closet. Now, above dark pants, below striped shirt, it looked like a sartorial error, a *misalliance* ...

Scrambling to her feet, she found herself staring at Gustave's shirt. Where was his jacket? Oh, the night was warm, he must have taken it off before silently entering the house fifteen hours before he was expected. Her gaze slid sideways. Yes, he had placed – not thrown – his jacket on the hall chair; he had placed – not dropped – his briefcase next to that chair. She looked again at her husband. His exposed shirt bore a large stain in a rough triangular shape – the shape, she divined, of a wedge of tart. She touched it with a trembling forefinger.

'That tender little gift of yours – it leaked,' he said.

He surveyed his living room. That naked couple had attended his wedding, had drunk his champagne. A pair of know-it-alls. Their names rhymed. The other creatures he had never seen before. A skinny fellow with graying bangs advanced toward him.

'Gustave, I want you to meet—,' Grace began.

'Ask these people to leave,' he said in a growl she had never before heard.

They seeped away like spilled pudding ... Lee and Lee, first, dressed in each other's clothing, clutching their overnight cases and instruments, kissing Hal on the rush toward their car and its overnight parking tickets. They didn't kiss Grace. The Cambridge crowd didn't kiss anybody. But Hal – he stood his ground. He was a head taller than Gustave. He extended a hand. 'I'm—'

'Good-bye.'

'Listen here—'

'Get out!'

He got out, with his satchel in his left hand and, in the curve of his right arm, Grace. At the last minute she turned as if to look at Gustave, to plead with him, maybe – but it was only to snatch up her pocketbook from the hall table. Next to the pocketbook she saw a cone of flowers. Sweet peas, baby's breath, a single gerbera. An unimaginative bouquet; he must have picked it up ready-made at the airport stall.

Gustave climbed the stairs. The guests had apparently cavorted mostly on the first floor; except for the two unmade beds in the spare room, the only sign of their occupation were towels like puddles on the bathroom tiles. He went into his study and his eye flew to the bookcase where, in manuscript, between thick bindings, stood his biography of Faraday, still in search of a publisher. No one had stolen it. On the carpet lay a book – open, facedown. He leaned over and identified it as a Spanish grammar. He kicked it.

Downstairs again, he heated some minestrone – he had not eaten anything since his abrupt decision to abandon that boring conference and come home early. The soup was tasty. He looked for a joint – how sweet the house still smelled – but the crowd had apparently sucked their whole stash. He did find, in one corner, a recorder, but he couldn't smoke that. He put all the plates and glasses into the dishwasher. He tried to scrub the remains of chili from a pot, then left it to soak. He vacuumed. Then he went upstairs again and undressed, and, leaving his clothes on the floor – these gypsy ways were catching – slipped into Grace's side of the bed. With a sigh he recognized as an old man's, he flopped onto his back. His thoughts – which were uncharitable – did not keep him from falling asleep.

But a few hours later he found himself awake. He got up and went through the house again. He threw the Spanish grammar into the trash bag he had stuffed earlier and lugged the thing out to the garage, knowing that anyone who saw him in his striped pajamas under the floodlight at three o'clock in the morning would take him for a madman. So what. Their neighbors considered them a cute couple; he had overheard that demeaning epithet at the fish market. He'd rather be crazy than cute. He relocked the garage and returned to the house. And surely he had been deranged to marry a woman because of her alluring eyes. He'd mistaken a frolicsome manner for lasting charm. She was merely frivolous, and the minute she was left unsupervised ... He stomped into the living room. That rose-colored garment in progress now shared its chair with a wine bottle, good vineyard, good year ... empty. He'd like to rip the knitting out. The yarn would remain whorled; he'd wind it loosely into a one big whorl. When she came back she'd find a replica of Faraday's induction coil, pink. Come back? She could come back to collect her clothing and her paella pan and the bulbs she kept meaning to plant. He picked up the sweater. It would fit a ten-year-old. Insulting color, insulting size ... he went back to bed and lay there.

Grace, too, was awake. The hotel room was dark and malodorous. Hal slept at her side without stirring, without snoring. He had always been a devoted sleeper. He was devoted to whatever brought him pleasure. Under no circumstances would she accompany him to Barcelona, as he had idly suggested last night. (He had also suggested that she buy the drinks at the hotel bar downstairs; she supposed she'd have to pay for the room, too.) Anyway, she had left her passport next to Gustave's in his top drawer. She hoped he'd send it back to her in Northampton – she had not yet sold her house there, thank goodness, thank Providence, thank Whoever was in charge. She hoped he'd send all her things, without obsessive comment. She wanted no more of him. She wanted no more of Hal, either: it was enough that she had shared his toothbrush last night, and then his bed, and was now sleeping – well, failing to sleep – in one of his unlaundered shirts.

How hideous to have only yesterday's lingerie. Unshaved underarms were one thing: grotty underpants quite another. What time did stores open on Sundays? She'd slip out and shop, get a new sweater, maybe – that would pick up her spirits. She remembered the half-finished vest for her grand-daughter she'd left on the chair; she hoped Gustave would send that back, too . . .

'Amelie . . .,' muttered Hal.

'Grace,' she corrected.

If only she were back in Northampton already, where everyone was needy and she was needed. She wished she had never visited that wild-animal preserve at the Cape, had never paused to look at those foxes. She wished she had not married a man because he was learned and polite, espe-cially since he had turned out to be pedantic and sanctimonious.

From time to time that Sunday, Gustave thought of calling the lawyer who'd married them – she happened to specialize in divorce. Instead he read the papers, and watched the foot-ball game. What a sport: force directed by intelligence. He prepared for tomorrow's class, the one in which he and the students would reproduce one of Faraday's earliest experi-ments in electrification. They'd all come carrying foil-wrapped water-filled film canisters with a protruding nail. These were primitive Leyden jars in which to store elec-tricity. The electricity would be produced by a Styrofoam dinner plate nested in an aluminum pie pan – the kids would bring these friction makers, too. He went to bed early. He could see a low autumnal moon above the mansard across the street – well, only the upper half of the sphere was visible, but he could supply the rest.

Grace bought, among other things, a yellow sweater. She took her time getting back to the hotel. She found Hal showered and smiling. During a long walk by the river she listened to his opinions on magic realism and antonomasia – she'd forgotten what that was, she admitted. 'The use of an epithet instead of a proper name,' Hal said. '"The Fussbudget," say.' He told her of the Spanish medieval farsa, which was related to farce. And just when she thought her aching head would explode, it was time to put him into a cab to the airport. He seemed to have enough cash for the taxi. He thrust his head out of the open window as the vehicle left the curb. 'My apartment is near Las Ramblas, best location in Barcelona,' he called. She waved. The cab disappeared, and her headache with it.

She went back to their room, now hers, and read the papers and enjoyed a solitary supper in front of the TV, watching a replay of that afternoon's football game. Nice intercept! Such brave boys there on the screen. But Gustave had been brave, too, hadn't he, scorning savoir faire as he cleansed his house of unwelcome revelers. How red his face had become when Hal theatrically held out his hand . . . he'd felt wronged, hadn't he, or perhaps *in* the wrong; maybe he thought she'd summoned her friends, maybe he thought he'd failed her. If she ever saw him again she'd tell him about Hal's lonely rootlessness. She'd tell him about poor Lee and Lee's barn of unsalable paintings, if she ever saw him again . . . She put on her new nightgown and went to bed. She could see a curve of the dome of the Massachusetts statehouse, just enough to suggest the whole.

The lecture room was shaped like a triangle. The platform, holding lectern and lab bench, was at the apex, the lowest part of the room; concentric rows of slightly curved tables radiated upward toward the back. Three students sat at each table. The professor stood at the lectern when he talked, moved to his lab bench for demonstrating. He and the students employed their identical homemade equipment. As he talked and demonstrated – creating the electric charge, storing it – the students imitated. There was expectant laughter and an occasional excited remark and a general air of satisfaction. Only a few of these poets might change course and become physicists, but not one of them would hold science in contempt. 'Faraday made this experiment with equally crude apparatus,' he reminded them. 'And with faith that it would work. Faith – so unfashionable now – was his mainstay.'

The woman in the back row, alone at a table, without pie plate or film can, wished that she, too, had the implements, that she could obey the instructions of the measured, kindly voice; but mostly she marveled again at the story that voice was telling of the humble young Faraday setting himself upon his life's journey. 'He considered that God's presence was revealed in nature's design,' wound up the little man. He looked radiant.

When he at last noticed the figure in the yellow sweater, he was cast back to an afternoon in Paris when that same glowing color had been produced by sun refracted through stained glass, and the lips of his companion had parted as she listened to winds and strings send music aloft. She had thrilled, she had become elevated, she had generously carried him with her . . .

The lecture concluded to applause; the teenagers dispersed; the professor materialized in the chair next to the visitor's.

They looked at each other for a while.

'I'm Grace,' she said at last.

'I'm Gustave' – and how his heart leaped. 'I'd like to . . . get to know you.'

Another long pause while he belatedly considered the dangers in so ambitious an enterprise, for he too would have to be known, and his shabby secrets revealed, and his out-of-date convictions as well. They'd endure necessary disappointments, and they'd practice necessary forgivenesses, careful to note which subjects left the other fraught. Grace's mind moved along the same lines. Each elected to take the risk. Gustave showed his willingness by touching the lovely face, Grace hers by disdaining eclipsis. 'Me too,' was all she said.

ACKNOWLEDGMENTS

EDWIDGE DANTICAT: 'Caroline's Wedding' from *Krik? Krak!* copyright © 1991, 1995 by Edwidge Danticat, reprinted by permission of Soho Press, Inc. All rights reserved.

F. SCOTT FITZGERALD: Reprinted with the permission of Scribner, a division of Simon & Schuster, Inc. from *The Short Stories of F. Scott Fitzgerald* edited by Matthew J. Bruccoli. Copyright © 1931 by The Curtis Publishing Company. Copyright renewed 1959 by Frances Scott Fitzgerald Lanahan. All rights reserved.

SHIRLEY JACKSON: 'About Two Nice People' from *Just an Ordinary Day: Stories*, Bantam Books, an imprint of Random House, a division of Penguin Random House LLC, New York, 1997.

KELLY LINK: 'The Lesson' from *Get in Trouble*, Random House, an imprint and division of Penguin Random House LLC, New York, 2015.

CARSON McCULLERS: Excerpt from *The Member of the Wedding* by Carson McCullers. Copyright © 1946 by Carson McCullers, renewed by 1973 by Floria V. Lasky, Executor of the Estate of Carson McCullers. Used by permission of Houghton Mifflin Harcourt Publishing Company. All rights reserved.

ALICE McDERMOTT: From *At Weddings and Wakes*, Farrar, Straus & Giroux, New York, 1992; Bloomsbury, London, 1992.